PRAISE FOR

An Assassin's Guide to Love and Treason

A *Kirkus Reviews* Best Book of the Year

★ "**A scrumptious slice of history**. The conflicts
of religion, sexuality, class, and gender identity are
apropos to contemporary times. *Victor, Victoria* and
Shakespeare in Love: Meet your thrilling new sister.
Or brother." —*Kirkus Reviews* (starred review)

"Between its **harrowing** start and **nail-biting** conclusion,
Boecker creates **complex characters and a rich historical
setting** in a story that explores religious extremism, self-identity,
and the blindness of love." —*Publishers Weekly*

"A satisfying blend of early modern spycraft and
stagecraft… **suspense and romance**….[A] **breathless,
satisfying romp**." —*The Bulletin*

"A **fast-paced** historical mystery **rich in period detail**
that also explores gender and sexuality. **A great buy**." —*SLJ*

"**Shatters gender stereotypes**….Historical fiction
meets young adult literature in this **suspenseful** story
about two "star-crossed" lovers who face seemingly
insurmountable odds to be together." —*VOYA*

"*An Assassin's Guide to Love and Treason* is **a thrilling, immersive romp** through Shakespeare's London, and all the intrigue, alliances, and politics that shaped it.... With **snappy, energetic prose** that will appeal to both fans of historicals and contemporaries, there's something here for everyone. **I devoured this book with ravenous joy.** Bravo!" —Mackenzi Lee, *New York Times* bestselling author of *The Gentleman's Guide to Vice and Virtue*

"[Boecker] paints **a thrilling picture** of Tudor England with all the **intrigue, romance, and danger** a lover of historical fiction could want." —Sharon Biggs Waller, author of *The Forbidden Orchid* and *A Mad, Wicked Folly*

"An engrossing story of love and intrigue.... **I couldn't put it down!**" —Alexis Bass, author of *Love and Other Theories*

AN ASSASSIN'S GUIDE to LOVE & TREASON

an ASSASSIN'S GUIDE to LOVE & TREASON

✦ VIRGINIA BOECKER ✦

LITTLE, BROWN AND COMPANY
New York Boston

Copyright © 2018 by Virginia Boecker

Cover art copyright © 2018 by Howard Huang. Cover design by Marcie Lawrence. Cover copyright © 2018 by Hachette Book Group, Inc.

Little, Brown and Company
Hachette Book Group
1290 Avenue of the Americas, New York, NY 10104
Visit us at LBYR.com

Originally published in hardcover and ebook by Little, Brown and Company in September 2018
First Trade Paperback Edition: September 2019

Little, Brown and Company is a division of Hachette Book Group, Inc. The Little, Brown name and logo are trademarks of Hachette Book Group, Inc.

The publisher is not responsible for websites (or their content) that are not owned by the publisher.

The Library of Congress has cataloged the hardcover edition as follows:
Names: Boecker, Virginia, author.
Title: An assassin's guide to love and treason / Virginia Boecker.
Description: First edition. | New York ; Boston : Little, Brown and Company, 2018. | Summary: "Two star-crossed assassins in Elizabethan England must go undercover as actors in one of William Shakespeare's plays in a plot to kill the queen"— Provided by publisher. | Summary: In the early sixteen-hundreds, two star-crossed assassins, nineteen-year-old Toby and seventeen-year-old Kit, go undercover as actors in a Shakespeare play in a plot to kill Queen Elizabeth.
Identifiers: LCCN 2017051338 | ISBN 9780316327343 (hardcover) | ISBN 9780316327312 (library ebk.) | ISBN 9780316327282 (ebook)
Subjects: | CYAC: Assassins—Fiction. | Actors and actresses—Fiction. | Shakespeare, William, 1564–1616—Authorship—Fiction. | Great Britain—History—Elizabeth, 1558–1603—Fiction.
Classification: LCC PZ7.B6357175 As 2018 | DDC [Fic]—dc23
LC record available at https://lccn.loc.gov/2017051338

ISBNs: 978-0-316-32729-9 (pbk.), 978-0-316-32728-2 (ebook)

LSC-C

10 9 8 7 6 5 4 3 2 1

For my brother

December 20, 1972–March 26, 2017

Prologue

TOBY

ST. PAUL'S CATHEDRAL, LONDON
7 JANUARY 1602
12:02 AM

It is not the usual interrogation.

There are no manacles, no dark chambers, no threats, at least not those that involve chains or whips or whispers of bad things to come. There is, however, Richard Bancroft, bishop of London (BA, MA, DD, all from Cambridge—he would want you to know this), though it could be said he does nothing but whisper of bad things to come.

It takes place in the chapel in the crypt below St. Paul's, with its cold walls and grave lighting and it takes no great skill to reason why they've chosen this place. It's a reminder of the persecution of years past, heretics brought here to be toyed with words and tricked into confession before being marched into cells then strung up for treason. It's empty of guards and courtiers and people who come and go, empty of eyes and ears and mouths that would bear witness to what comes next.

There should not be witness to what comes next.

Sir Robert Cecil (secretary of state to Queen Elizabeth I is his official title, spymaster his unofficial. See also: Privy Councillor, former Chancellor of the Duchy of Lancaster, Member of Parliament, and Keeper of the Privy Seal—he would want you to know this, too) makes a big show of laying out his book before him, fat and leather-bound, treachery and lies spilling at the seams. This time, most of them mine.

What we've covered thus far: my name (Tobias Ellis to them; Duke Orsino to *him*); my occupation (watcher and cryptographer to them; player and playwright to *him*); my reputation (tarred and painted; this to everyone).

What remains uncovered: everything else.

"Who is he?"

"That depends," I reply, "on which *he* you're referring to."

Cecil's disdain is a shroud. "There is the one who was stabbed onstage, the one you named as the assassin, and then there is the one who got away. You tell me, Tobias. With which *he* would you like to begin?"

It doesn't matter; any one of them is enough to end me.

"Let's start with the one who got away." Cecil decides for me. "What did you say his name was?"

"I didn't." The ministers exchange glances. This balance I am walking, the line between ignorance and impudence, grows narrow. "He was called Christopher Alban. Went by Kit."

"Kit," Egerton repeats. (Thomas Egerton, Solicitor General. BA Oxford, QC Lincoln's Inn, Master of the Rolls, Lord Keeper of the Great Seal. His eye is sharp as his tongue and he is no fool.) "Interesting coincidence. What else?"

"He came from the country." I bypass the bait and continue the lie carefully, carefully. "Plymouth. He is young. Inexperienced." I want to swallow the words, keep them to myself. But I cannot give them nothing if I do not give them something.

"How did he get so far, then, if he is as young and inexperienced as you say? To the main stage, a principal role with the Lord Chamberlain's Men, to a place before the queen, holding a knife, a goddamned knife?" Such is Cecil's power that his blasphemy does not evoke the ire of the bishop, who has not taken his eyes from me since I walked into the room.

"Letting him get that far was the plan," I reply. "I can hardly ensnare a would-be assassin if the assassination is not attempted."

"Yet this would-be assassin is gone and here you are instead." His stare, a dark and heavy thing, weights me to my chair.

Above me, outside this room, and beyond this cathedral lies London: the whole of the city sprawling and reeling and still recovering from the Twelfth Night revelries. Mummers' plays and music, wassail and Twelfth Night cakes, sticky with butter and sugar and pressed into my hand with a gleam from saturnine eyes and a whisper from a voice sweeter than it all:

> If you get the clove you're a villain.
> If you get the twig you're a fool.
> If you get the rag you are a tarty lad.
> Which one are you?

Chapter I

KATHERINE

ST MAWGAN IN PYDAR, CORNWALL
25 OCTOBER 1601

A sound, sudden and echoing, wakes me from sleep.
At first I think it's a dream, as I am often woken by
nothing and for nothing: jolted awake believing someone is beside me or above me but no one ever is, their absence
never a relief so much as a reprieve. But no, there is the sound
again, someone hammering on the front door, insistent. A quick
glance out the window tells me it's sometime in the middle of the
night. I could be asking myself who is it, what do they want, can't
they come back in the morning, but I don't because I already
know the answer to all of it.

I know.

I am out of my bed at once, snatching up my dressing gown and then my coat, because the fire has died in my fireplace and it is so chilled in my chamber I can see my breath. I rush to the window, swipe the frost from the pane before sucking that cold breath right back in. Flickering flames bob across the night sky like fireflies, not the warm glow of candles but the aggressive heat of torches held high. They stretch past the gates that surround Lanherne, my home—belonging to my father and his father and his father before that, the seat of the Arundell family—into the marshy moors of Cornwall, as endless as the Celtic Sea.

We are surrounded.

Every sense I have tells me to run and hide. In this house, with its three floors and thirty-four rooms, there is no shortage of places I could tuck into and wait until this is all over. But that is not the plan. We have been over this, Father and I, what to do if this happened, if they finally discovered who we were and what we were doing. If and when they finally came for us.

My father—Sir Richard Arundell, receiver general of the Duchy of Cornwall—is to remain in his chamber, as if he is unaware of what is happening, as if it is wholly unexpected. Ryol—Father's manservant who is not really a servant at all but a priest—is to gather his vestments, vessels, altar furniture, and other incriminating items and slip into his hiding place, a small chamber accessed through a panel beside the chimney in the drawing room. Peran, Father's valet, is to answer the door, alongside at least one but not more than two maids in attendance. Enough to give ceremony but not enough to show fear.

I am to slip back between my sheets and wait. When the accusations come—and they will come—I am to appear at the top of the stairs, wide-eyed and tousle-headed, as if I could not be more surprised by their appearance, as if I have not been waiting for it nearly all my seventeen years. I am to inquire in a tiny, little-girl voice, *Is there something the matter, sirs?* This is to remind them that my father is a family man, that he has a daughter and once had a wife, that he is a nobleman and I am a lady. To make them forget what we really are:

Liars, criminals, heretics, and traitors.

I creep to my chamber door, finger the cold brass knob, and pull it open. From here I have a full view of the hallway and the staircase that winds below, all the way to the dark, empty entry and the front door that still groans under assault. I should turn from it, crawl back under my now-cold bedcovers and feign sleep, though it would be an impossibility. Instead, I close my eyes and begin to count backward from five in Cornish. It's a trick Father taught me as a way to manage my fear, a way for me to give in to it and let it have its way with me, but only for five seconds. After that, I have to let it go.

I've reached *dew*—two—when I hear the sharp tap of footsteps, hard soles on a lacquered floor. One servant's shaky light follows another as candles are lit and move down the hall toward the door, more rapidly than they should do, I think. A whisper of skirts, the clucking of worried tones in Cornish, then Father's reassuring voice replying, "*Ny da lowr*," which means "It will be all right." That is one—no, two—deviations from the plan I have known as long as I was old enough to know it, one I could recite as faithfully as if it were a catechism. From his place in the hall below, Father turns his head up to me, as if he somehow knew that's where I'd be.

"Back to bed, *Kerensa*," he says. His endearment—the word means "love"—was his childhood nickname for me and is meant to soothe, but it doesn't.

"Father—"

"*Ny da lowr*," he repeats. "I promise."

I nod but I don't obey, tucking myself into the shadows so as not to be seen. There's a hesitation, a deep indrawn breath, then Father turns back to the door, opening it to the sea of faces on the other side.

"John." He nods to the man in front of them all: Sir Jonathan Trelawney, the sheriff of Cornwall. I've seen him before; he is a friend of Father's and a regular visitor, though usually in daytime hours. "It's a bit late for a game of one and thirty, is it not?" He peers over Sir Jonathan's shoulder. "At any rate, you've brought too many men. It's a game for six, not sixty."

Father tries for levity, but his voice is as pinched as his face and for a moment, I see him. Not the quiet, devout man who raised me as gently as he could, despite my arrival heralding the death of my mother and the loss of another chance at the male heir he so desperately needed, but as others might. Black velvet breeches, black cloak trimmed with sable, flat black cap pulled resolutely over red hair, the same shade as mine. The most important man in the county. Only now he does not look hard, the way he does when he rides through the duchy collecting taxes or visiting tenants or doling out payment to the soldiers he maintains on behalf of the queen. He looks the way I do when I catch a reflection of myself unawares, when I forget to school my features otherwise.

He looks afraid.

"Would that I were here for games," Sir Jonathan replies. "But unfortunately it's for something far more disagreeable." He passes off his torch to one of many waiting pairs of hands and steps uninvited into the parlor. He does not remove his cape and the servants don't offer to take it. They have already scattered like mice, vanishing into the shadows—deviation number three.

"It's late, John." Father tries again. "Not even I do business at this hour. Not unless I'm in the cups and it is far past that hour as well. Perhaps tomorrow—" He attempts to usher Sir Jonathan back out the door, but the sheriff is unyielding.

"I am here to arrest you for countable crimes committed under the Act Against Recusants," he says. "Refusal to adhere to common prayers, sacraments, rites, and ceremonies of the Church of England. Refusal to swear allegiance to Her Majesty the Queen as the supreme governor of the Church of England. Possessing materials banned within the Commonwealth of England. Harboring a man known or suspected to be an agent of the bishop of Rome."

I don't move, but I am not still: Every part of me shakes. It is true, what he says, every last word. But to hear it out loud, the accusation, is to understand the severity of our crime all over again.

Father explained it to me like this: Our Protestant Queen Elizabeth feared the pope wanted to reclaim religious authority over England, the way he had before the queen's own father took it away. The queen was afraid that in order to get it back, the pope would unite Catholic Italy with England's Catholic enemies France and Spain, that they would form an alliance and, with help from England's prominent Catholic families, plot to overthrow her, put a Catholic on the throne, and restore Catholicism to England. She feared this so much she made all of us swear an oath stating our allegiance to her, her authority, her religion. Any family refusing to attend her Protestant services is suspect. Any family holding secret Catholic Mass is suspect. Any family harboring Catholic priests is suspect.

It is more than suspect: It is treason.

But Father does not admit guilt so easily. "You have no cause for this." He waves the sheriff's words away as if they were moths. "I do not wish to cause strife, John, but I answer to a higher power than yours, and that is Her Majesty's. And unless her word has ordered you to my doorstep, I'm afraid I'm going to have to bid you a good evening." Again, he tries to prod Trelawney out the door. But Trelawney reaches into his doublet to produce a scroll of parchment, rolled and sealed with a royal badge along the bottom that even from my place in the shadows I recognize.

ER.

Elizabeth Regina.

Elizabeth the queen.

This is my last chance to do something, to act; it is my last chance to play my part though everything else is uncertain. I throw off my coat, which I wouldn't be wearing if I just climbed out of bed, tighten the ties of my dressing gown. Then I step into a puddle of moonlight that falls through the windows and onto the dark floor of the hallway. I pretend I am standing in the choir stalls the way I do every Sunday, attending Protestant services to keep up appearances, readying myself to sing before the congregation. This helps to calm me.

"What's happening?" This line is new, and not part of any plan, but I can hardly ask if there's something the matter since clearly something is and it has already come to confrontation.

"Katherine." Father turns his head to look at me, as do Sir Jonathan and the row of red torchlit faces in the doorway. "Go back to your chamber. This doesn't concern you."

Sir Jonathan doesn't agree. He snaps his fingers and two men from the front line burst through the door and clamber up the stairs, making their way to me. I know that to run would be to admit guilt, so I allow them to take my arms and pull me down the stairs and up before the sheriff. He looks at me and I look right back.

"Katherine Arundell," he says. "How do you respond to the charges leveled at your father and his household? That of recusancy, and of unlawful adherence to the Catholic faith?"

"Catholic faith, sir?" I reply. "I'm not sure what you mean. I just saw you last week at St. Eval, if you recall. The Evensong service? My favorite hymn was 'Let God Arise in Majesty.' I especially liked how the chorister had us stretch *majesty* into five syllables. *Let God arise in ma-a-a-jes-ty…*"

Well, I am a fool now but it seems to work, at least a little. I have a beautiful voice and I know it, and it seems the men gripping my arms do, too, as they've let me go and are looking at me with soft little smiles. I stop singing and fold my hands together, as if I'm so overcome by the spirituality of it all I simply cannot continue. But Sir Jonathan's sympathy is as scant as his tithing envelope and with a scowl he says, "Your father has not been to Anglican services in over a year."

"Only because he is a very busy man," I say piously. "His duties for the queen cause him to be gone for so long—"

"You have not answered the question," he says. "So I'll ask you more plainly. Are you, or are you not, a Catholic?"

I know the answer to this question. It was written for me by Father, and easy enough to remember if impossible in elocution. It is to deny everything I know: my father, my upbringing, my whole life. But it seems my silence is reply enough.

Sir Jonathan turns to his men. "Search the house."

Before I can sound a single note of protest, the door is battered open on its hinges, the hall filled with the rain of boots and the voices of two dozen men thundering for justice. Father tries to stop them—tries—he pulls his sword to block them, but Sir Jonathan takes his out, too. They begin parrying as the rest of the men swarm through the house.

They tear down the hallway, up the stairs, into room after room. All of them armed: some with swords and knives, some with fire, others with sticks and rocks. Wall hangings ripped from their moors, the shred of knife after knife into chair after chair, tugging out feathers and jamming in hands. Floors are eviscerated, rugs torn aside, wood boards pried open. The servants, silent before, scream and wail and rush around in a frenzy of protest and fear and aborted escape.

I don't know what to do. Ryol is still in hiding, Father is still fighting, and everyone else is still running and shouting. The thought of being handled by more of Trelawney's men finally compels me to move and so I do, hiding behind a massive cabinet pressed into a corner beneath the staircase. I used to hide here as a child and the space was small even then. Now I barely fit.

I'm tucked into a ball, not moving and scarcely breathing, watching Father and Sir Jonathan. What started out as posturing has escalated into an ugly battle, blades rising and falling and clashing and coming far too close to hearts and guts and throats; an inch or two from becoming a fatal blow. I can't tell who is winning, if anyone is, but when I hear a shout and a laugh and the words *I've got him*, I know we have lost. Father turns to see them coming and in that brief moment of distraction, Trelawney has him: His blade pressed to Father's chest and there is no move left for Father to make.

Two men rush into the hall holding Ryol in an unforgiving grip; another holds his missal; still another holds a chalice and another a paten, all sacred items used during Mass, but they wave them over their heads as if they were a banner of victory. Trelawney scans them all with heartless eyes as Father stifles a groan and slumps against the wall, shoulders rising rapidly in time with his breathing. He looks as sick as I feel.

"Is he your man, Richard?" Sir Jonathan's treacherous gleam falters. Maybe he's thinking about the break on rent Father once gave him; maybe he's recalling the many nights they spent playing cards. Maybe he *is* thinking about how he saw me at Anglican services, dressed in my Sunday best. Whatever he is thinking, he has got the cat by its tail and he is considering, if only for a moment, whether to let it go. "If you were unaware he is a priest, bringing treason to your home, now is your chance to claim it."

Father says nothing.

"They'll hang you for it, Richard." Trelawney speaks the words I can barely think. "You'll lose your lands, your title. You'll be executed as a traitor."

Father looks to Trelawney. A moment, two; a lifetime passes before he says, "He is my man. He is my priest, and this is my belief. I have renounced them for long enough, and I will do so no longer."

Sir Jonathan snaps his fingers. One of his men steps forward, snatching Father's arm. Father stumbles forward with another muffled grunt, his sword clattering to the floor. There's a moment of confusion, a man shouts "Ho!" and Father's palm, pressed to his chest, now comes away red. Below him, puddled under his boots, a growing ring of blood.

Now I see why Father didn't renounce his faith, why he gave in so easily. Trelawney's sword had landed a blow, one Father didn't deflect and knew he couldn't recover from. I am on my knees behind the cabinet now, as if I could pray away what I know will come next.

Chapter 2

TOBY

LAMBETH HILL, QUEENHITHE WARD, LONDON
25 OCTOBER 1601

Tonight I am an Irish thug.

It's both close to and nowhere near what I really am, as all good disguises are: a rogue on one payroll disguised as another rogue on another payroll, doing a job no one else wants to. I have been hunched on this rain-soaked street for the better part of four hours, I'm wet, cold, hungry; I started shivering about an hour ago and that won't stop until I get what I came for.

Around me the streets are quiet. This part of London, the north bank of the Thames between Poles Wharf and Broken Wharf, is full of boats during the day, fishermen hauling their writhing wares from the quay, the air thick with curses and fish. After hours—from the time the sun sets until an hour before it rises—it falls silent, nothing but the slap of the tide against the dock and the toll of an occasional church bell. The perfect place for two contacts to meet, both of them up to no good.

It's well past eleven when the sound of footsteps finally does appear, slow across the slippery cobblestones. I look up but don't get up. The man I'm impersonating is taller than me, and stockier. The latter I can hide well enough under my cloak, but the former I have to work around.

My contact comes to stand before me. Black hair, black cape, black boots, indeterminate age, though I'll guess to be around mine—nineteen. Older men have better sense than to run jobs like this, nighttime meetings in dodgy spots throughout London in service of delivering a letter from one end of an illegal Catholic network to the other.

"I seem to have lost my way," the boy in black says, carefully reciting the coded greeting to ensure he's got the right man. "Can you point me in the direction of Knightrider Street?"

I jerk my thumb to my right. "A block a ways, left, then right."

The boy nods once. Waits. Then: "Arden Walsh?"

"*Dia dhuit.*" The person I'm meant to be also speaks half in Gaelic, which fortunately is one of my better accents. "Have something for me, do you?"

He pulls a letter from inside his cape, passing it to me quickly. I tuck it immediately beneath my own and into the folds of my shirt. If the ink gets wet it'll be impossible to read, more impossible to decipher. Then I hold out my hand, waiting for payment.

I've been tracking this network for six months and the arrangements are always this: The courier—in this case the boy in black—picks up a letter and gets paid. He drops the message to the carrier—in this case, me as Arden Walsh—and pays me, and I deliver it to yet another carrier. In complicated networks like this, multiple men are needed for one letter, partly to make it difficult to be followed but mainly to keep any one person from knowing both the origin and destination of the message.

But the boy in black doesn't give up the funds. This is unusual: Most messengers won't risk future jobs—or the ire of those who hired them—even for the possibility of extra payment. On top of that, it's stupid. Couriers are not hired for their kindness.

"*Téigh trasna ort féin*," I say. It's a seething curse, and though the boy in black doesn't understand, he knows the tone well enough. "Find some other *báltaí* to take your message. I don't work for free." I'm on my feet now, shorter than I should be, but there's no way around that. I know how this Irishman would react to this sudden withholding of payment. I met him once, in his cell at the Clink. He was put there as a precaution—can't have two messengers called Arden Walsh wandering around London—on charges of dice cogging and drunkenness and disturbing the peace, none of which were false.

The boy in black pulls his knife, but I pull mine faster. I've got him in a hold, his neck in the crook of my arm, my blade at his throat. Though he's bigger than me, I could drop him in a second, something he quickly concedes.

He fumbles in his cape pocket, pulls out a handful of coins. I make a quick count; he's holding about two shillings and a half dozen pence, and the way he didn't scrape around to retrieve them tells me there's still more.

"Four shillings," I say.

"The price was two," he grunts.

"That was before all this. You're lucky I don't leave you for dead and take it all."

He pulls out more coins. I take them and shove them in my pocket before releasing him. The boy in black pushes away from me, rattling off a string of slurs, *knave* and *cuckold* and *whore-master*. I lunge at him, taking offense the way I also know the real Arden Walsh would, and the boy scurries into the damp shadows, the tap of his boots now a fading echo.

The bells of St. Nicholas Olave ring midnight. Thanks to the boy in black's lateness and now this fucking kerfuffle, I've only got two hours to decipher this letter before delivering it to the next contact. If I had the four hours I was meant to, I would go back to my own lodgings with my own supplies and a guarantee of privacy.

Now I can't. If I'm late they'll know the network was compromised; they'll choose a different route and possibly add more men. It'll ruin half a year's worth of work and jeopardize my pay, and I can't have that.

Pluck up, Toby. Use your wits if you've got them. What would I do?

I can almost hear Marlowe's voice in my ear. Playwright, poet, sometime spy for the queen and my onetime mentor, now eight years dead and still giving me hell. It's not his fault I'm here, not really, but I blame him anyway. If he hadn't died, I'd still be his apprentice; I'd still be writing—I might even be good at it by now—not walking up Thames Street, affecting Arden

Walsh's Irish swagger and heading in the direction of my contingency plan: a brothel.

From here the stews are just across the river, ten minutes at most, in the same direction as my drop so I won't lose any more time. I'll have to part with a few of my shillings to get a room, and probably one or two more to ensure that room is empty—I'm already mourning the loss of the coal I was planning to buy with it—but at least I'll be alone. On the slim chance I'm being followed, there's not a watcher in all of London who would question what I was doing there.

Oh, is that where I'd go? You weren't paying very close attention, were you?

Shut it, Marlowe.

A sharp whistle at the wharf brings up a boat. I part with a penny—that's this week's laundry—and climb aboard. In ten minutes, almost to the second, I disembark at Southwark and duck into the nearest brothel, the quaintly named Castle upon Hope Inn, tucked between two taverns.

I enjoy the company of women from time to time, but I certainly don't pay for it, a principle I'm briefly tempted to overlook as a trio of girls in various stages of undress drape themselves over me, whispering outrageous promises. I disentangle myself and with a wave of my hand the woman who runs it all, the only one fully clothed, appears in a cloud of perfume. I tell her what I want: a quiet room with a desk, two bowls, one of water, the other empty. A stack of candles and a light, two clean pieces of parchment, a small towel and a butter knife—I can only imagine what she thinks I plan on doing with it all—and I hand over yet more coins.

Within minutes I'm seated at a table shoved beside an obscenely large bed, everything I asked for laid out before me. I take out the small, rounded butter knife and run it over the flame. It's got to be hot enough to soften the wax, but not hot enough to melt it or to scorch the paper. There's no other way to test this than by touching my finger to the blade. Just hot enough, but it won't be for long. I press the tip between the seal and the parchment, wiggling it slightly to get the lift I need.

To further prevent tampering, the note has been folded in careful squares, each of those folds filled with gunpowder. If it's opened too quickly, or without care, the powder will fall onto the parchment and stain it, not only obscuring what's written but tipping off the recipient that it's already been opened.

I make a quick note to myself as to how it was folded—a simple-enough pull-tab letter—then set about pouring the gunpowder into the empty bowl. I'll use the clean sheet of parchment to funnel it back in once I'm finished.

I pull the edges away, one after the other, until finally I see what's written inside:

φ2⊒ϑÒσΛ∇//sη|Δ∞ᵹ♯ↄ Òσ∆|∆ƐÒφΛᵹ
Ψf∇//ᵹ<Ψ□fÒφΛᵹ2Ɛηᴧ∇cφƐf|ᵹΔ mTSS
f□∇fᵹ|θφÒσ∆|∆ƐÒφΛᵹΨΔsÒ|φ

"*Cac*," I whisper: "Shit" in Gaelic. I knew the letter would be encrypted; they almost always are. It's never safe to send a letter via carrier written in plain text, even with all the anonymity of drops and messengers and double messengers and antitampering techniques. But it's usually alphabetic substitution, one letter swapped for another, easy enough to decipher. This is in a class of its own.

If someone had told me, back when I was twelve—all lanky limbs and shifting moods and lofty aspirations of being a famous playwright—that seven years later I'd be holed up in a cramped room in a perfumed brothel decoding traitorous letters, I wouldn't have believed it.

The only son of a butcher and not a very prosperous one—and without a mother since age five—I was apprenticed to the stationer William Barnard when my father could no longer care for me. Barnard educated me: taught me how to set print, how to bind; how to read and how to write, he taught me Latin and his native French. With no son of his own and his wife long dead, he cared for me as his own and I grew to consider him family. He died when I was ten, leaving both me and the shop in the custody of his younger brother, who cared nothing for words or for me, only the newly elevated status of merchant with a shop on prestigious Paternoster Row.

The younger Barnard liked that noblemen came to purchase

the plays and poems he (I) turned out. He liked the money it brought him, money he wasted on drink and dice, money that slowly dwindled to nothing despite the twelve hours a day I spent working. I sold books faster than I could make them but that hadn't mattered; within a year we lost the lease on the shop, and Barnard was too drunk and too absent to notice or to care. I was soon using my printer's skills to forge letters in Barnard's hand: to banks asking for loans, the landlord asking for extensions, his patron asking for mercy. The ruse ended when the latter, Sir George Carey, appeared at my doorstep alongside a playwright called Christopher Marlowe. They caught me red-handed— gold-leaf-handed, rather—hunched over a book, an agate burnisher in one hand, tip brush in the other.

"What did I tell you!" Marlowe bounded in, Carey on his heels. "I told you there was no chance that oaf turned out those books, and ha! I was right." He clapped me on the back, hard enough to dislodge the brush from my hand. "Who are you, then?" I looked up at him. Dark and disheveled, shirt half open and boots unlaced, hair curled and wild and half tucked behind his ears. He was in his twenties then, me just eleven. But it was infatuation at first sight, at least on my part.

"Tobias," I said. "You can call me Toby."

"Well, Toby," Sir Carey said. He was nothing but splendor, gilded and leathered and ribboned as any one of my books. "I've got a proposition for you."

Carey would retain his patronage of the shop, Barnard's debts would be forgiven, and I would be the sole printer of Marlowe's plays, an account worth over three pounds a year—all of which went directly into my pocket. But best of all was the patronage Marlowe offered me once my apprenticeship expired, helping me become the writer I wanted to be.

I shadowed him as he shadowed others, watching the world in that profound, incisive way of his. I watched him channel his skills not just into poems but also into occasional spy missions for Carey, who used Marlowe's penchant for street fighting, nefarious company, and sometimes blasphemous writing as leverage to get the information he needed. Marlowe ran messages and kept tabs on the queen's vast network of agents and couriers—none of whom could be trusted—in exchange for an arrangement with the Privy Council, one that kept Marlowe out of jail more than once. Marlowe was a blackguard of the deepest hue but even so, I watched everything he did because I wanted to do it, too, and because I loved him, a secret I kept from him as much as myself. But he was dead within the year and so was Barnard; I was alone and it was Carey who showed up at my door offering me a new proposition.

The desperation I once employed to keep Barnard's shop running despite his disinterest was now to be used for profit. Carey used my printing and forgery prowess to encode letters for the queen's ministers, my language skills and education to decode them. He even found a way to use my loneliness, turning me into a courier to ferry letters from Whitehall to all points across England, knowing that in my absence no one would miss me. In the end, I did everything Marlowe did, all except write. After he was gone, I had nothing left to say.

I turn from the past and back to the letter before me. And I get to work.

Chapter 3

KATHERINE

ST MAWGAN IN PYDAR, CORNWALL
25 OCTOBER 1601

The year I turned thirteen, I hated everything.

Father, with his constant complaints about the court and the queen. Cornwall, with its craggy cliffs and endless watery skyline. The families who lived nearby, most of whom I knew but would never really know, not with all the secrets we were keeping.

One evening, after an interminable day during Lent in which I did nothing but pray and repent and thought I couldn't take it any longer, I marched out to the stables. Bullied the groom—long since gone now and entirely my fault—into tacking up the biggest, fastest horse in the stable, a gray Andalusian named

Pallas after the mythological Greek giant. Pallas was hard to manage, moody and temperamental; he would only yield to my father but I was determined to make him bend to my will, even if nothing and no one else would.

There was a fence, hewn together with shale, one that marked the end of our property. I jammed a heel into Pallas's side, meaning for him to jump it. But he didn't. He reached the edge, legs bunched as if he were set to fly, then stopped. I was thrown off, my back hit the ground and my head one of those gray jagged stones, and the world went black. When the groom came to fetch me, Father by his side, they picked me up and carried me home. I don't remember hurting (that would come later), I just felt numb.

That is how I feel now. Numb. I can feel my breathing grow shallow as Trelawney's men first hover over Father's now prone and unmoving body, poking and prodding him to see if he will get up (*get up, please get up*), then Trelawney pulling a feather from his cap and holding it under Father's nose to see if it will flutter, to check if he is breathing. Both Father and feather are still. Trelawney has enough decency to press Father's eyelids closed and dispatch someone for a swath of bed linen, which he drapes over Father's body.

He is dead.

I sit hunched behind the cabinet, my body now racked with silent sobs. Watch as they shove Ryol toward the door, defiant in his black cassock, hands making the sign of the cross even as they're clamped in manacles, delivering to Father quick and muttered last rites ("*Gloria Patri, et Filio, et Spiritui Sancto...*"). They round up the servants, too, snatching their wrists as if they were criminals, ignoring the cries of fright and pleas of innocence. They're pushed down the hall and into the dark and the cold that blows in through the door, not one allowed a coat or even a hat.

"Where is the girl?" Trelawney turns to his men, the two who dragged me downstairs from my room. "You had her. Where did she go?" Neither of them reply and he snaps his fingers once more. "Search the house. Don't leave without her. I'll need to turn her over, too."

I stop crying at once. *Turn me over.* To who? I don't have to ask for what. I think of the torture Father said would be forthcoming if we were caught, what they would do to extract a confession from us. *No one stays righteous on the rack*, he told me, and I believed him.

Trelawney makes his exit, slamming the door behind him. His men look to one another.

"She can't have gone far," one of them says. "She's probably in the house somewhere. Unless she slipped outside..."

"You take the grounds," the other says. "I'll take the house. I don't want to be here all night, so let's make this quick."

The first man pulls his cloak tight and his hat low as he makes his way outdoors to somehow search all 360 acres of Lanherne alone, in the dead of night, as the other shuffles up the stairs, broken glass crunching under his feet like snails.

It's a short run from my hiding place to any number of doors and windows I can escape through. But from there—what? Not freedom. Just an endless moor of questions. Where will I go? How will I get there? How will I feed myself? Clothe myself?

How will I live? I have never once been out of Cornwall, never once had to fend for myself. I have never done anything but what was told to me, and now there's no one around to do even that. I am alone, the first time I have ever been alone in my life.

I am back to crying, and all I can do is look at Father's body, the blood from his wound now seeping through the white of the linen, fingers of his left hand splayed out from beneath it, curled as if beckoning. There is no amount of counting backward in Cornish that will help allay my grief but I make myself do it anyway, to give myself five seconds to feel what I need to before I have to move on. To sort out how to get out of this house and the thousand other things I'll need to sort after that.

There's an enormous thud from upstairs, a muffled grunt, and a litany of curses. Trelawney's man has dropped something, or something's fallen on him. Either way it's enough of a commotion that he won't hear me move, which I do, slipping silent and barefoot into Father's library, ducking low as to not be seen from any of the windows.

Like the rest of the house, the library has been torn lath from plaster: furniture upturned, books knocked from shelves, and drawers pulled open, contents dumped to the floor. But for all their destruction, Trelawney's men weren't very thorough. If they'd put aside their madness, their savage thrill at exposing Father and delighting in his fear, they would have found something even more incriminating than a hidden priest.

In the bookshelf beside the fireplace, third shelf from the top, there is a panel, behind which lies a niche no larger than a loaf of bread. It's where Father keeps his journal, along with important papers and the money he uses to pay the servants. It's meant to be a secret, which means I know all about it. Although I'm tall, I still have to stand on a footstool to reach it; the library ladder has been knocked to the floor and I can't risk the noise or the time to bring it back up.

I find what I'm looking for: a cache of letters tied together with black ribbon, a red velvet drawstring bag full of coins, and a dog-eared page in the journal, its contents rapidly memorized before it's tossed into the low, still-burning fire in the hearth. Then it's off the stool and back to the library door, listening for Trelawney's man. A scuffle tells me he's still rooting around upstairs, so I duck back into the hall, rounding the corner to the servants' wing. At first I mean to take some traveling dresses from the maids' chambers, then it occurs to me that Trelawney's men will be looking for a girl, not a boy, and so I snatch a pair of breeches from Father's valet's room instead, along with a shirt, cloak, and a pair of boots, gloves, and a hat. I put everything on except the shoes, then stuff my nightdress under the mattress. Secure the money bag to my belt and the letters inside my shirt and then, boots in hand as to not make any noise, slink back to where Father's body lies. It's a risk to be here, in full view of both the front door and the stairs where I could be seen. But I can't leave without saying goodbye. I clutch his cold hand, a whispered "I'm sorry" and "I love you" and "Goodbye" all spilling from my mouth.

There's more noise, footsteps, and crunching from upstairs; it's coming my way and it's time to go. I get to my feet and take one last look around. It's the last time I'll step foot in this hall, the last time I'll step foot inside Lanherne. The seat of the

Arundells, my father's and his father's before that, his death leaving it to me though no court in the world would recognize it. I am titleless, homeless, fatherless; I am so full of grief and rage I could scream. I might, if I didn't think it would be heard all the way to the sea.

I snatch up Father's sword and double back down the corridor until I reach the rear of the house and the door that leads outside. I lace on the boots, stuffing a glove in the toe of each for a better fit, then quietly, carefully, click the latch and slip through the door and into the night.

Clouds have covered the moon, so full and light before, and now it's so dark I can't see more than a foot in front of me. But I know the grounds of Lanherne as well as I know my own face so I am able to move quickly, dodging hedges and tree stumps and ground spots that are more bog than land. I need to reach the barn—and from there my horse—and though I can't see anything I know I'm getting close; I've walked this distance my entire life. Just a few hundred feet to go—

That's when I crash into someone.

The impact knocks me to the ground and judging by the surprised, muffled grunt, Trelawney's man is down, too. He scrambles to his feet but I'm up faster. I lift Father's sword high, muttering what I can remember from Psalm 51, a prayer for forgiveness which I'll need because I'm seconds away from becoming a murderer, before I recognize who I ran into. Dark hair, dark eyes, serious expression, one he wears even on days he's not being hunted by Catholic pursuivants. It's Jory, my father's horse groom.

Jory came to us last year from nearby Plymouth. He's the

only person in my household who is my age and not married, but like every other person in my household he is also a devout Catholic, and of course under my father's employ, which is to say unsuitable for a girl of my stature. Not to mention that his greatest desire in the world is to become a priest.

When Father hired him, I was desperate enough for male companionship that it didn't matter. When Jory would join us for Mass, I would make sure to sit near him so he could admire my singing voice. I wore virginal white, I carried my best rosary and my missal and my Bible; I was practically weighted to the floor with relics. I thought if I could be as pious as possible, he would forget this notion of becoming betrothed to God and betroth himself to me instead.

I have already mentioned I'm a fool, but it's probably worth mentioning again.

"Katherine?" Jory says. "Is that you?"

"It's me." I drop the sword, relieved I didn't take his head off. "What are you doing out here?"

"Hiding." He swipes his hair off his forehead. "I was in the barn before, but someone came in to search it so I came out here. I thought it might be safer out in the open like this."

"Is he still in there?"

"I don't know. It's so dark I can't tell."

"They didn't take the horses, did they?"

"No. But Katherine…why are you dressed that way? I didn't recognize you, not at first and not with the trousers and the hat…I thought you were one of them." A pause. "Did they take him? Your father? I saw them taking people away, but I couldn't see who."

I will not cry again, not tonight; I've already had my five seconds and so I say, "No. They didn't take him. They killed him."

Jory proceeds to cross himself and whisper a prayer, in Latin no less, and I let him do it even though it brings me no comfort at all. "What should we do?" he says when he's done. "We can't stay. If they find us they'll take us away, too."

"I know," I say. "I was on my way to take Father's horse so I could leave."

He nods, solemn as ever. "I'll get them. We should take Pallas and Samson, I think. They're the fastest and strongest."

I see now that I won't be alone in this escape, but I suppose I can't very well leave Jory behind. "Don't we want to wait for them to leave first?" I ask. "They might see or hear us leave, and they'll follow us."

"We could," Jory replies. "But the longer we stay, the more we risk them finding us. Or that others will come back." He pauses a moment to think. "I've got an idea. Stay here. I'll be back." He vanishes into the dark, and I'm alone again. It's starting to rain and the wind is picking up, the sea is restless and I can hear it from here, a dull roar whipping through waist-high meadow grass. Trelawney's men could be mere feet from me and I wouldn't be able to hear them. I'm crouched beside a hedge, still clutching Father's sword. I wait and wait, and when nothing happens, first I'm angry and then worried, because what if Jory was caught?

Just when I'm about to go after him I hear a stampede of hooves, then catch the shadow of a horse tearing across the moor at full tilt. From somewhere far off I hear a man shout, "Stop!" and I think for a moment that Jory has gone and taken off without me. Then I see Trelawney's man rush to the house, shout for the other, then the two of them race to the barn, and I start to see the shape of Jory's plan.

There's a whuffing noise and Jory appears before me, Samson and Pallas in hand.

"I let Cerus go," he says. "He's been trying to escape since the day your father bought him. Now he's got his chance. He'll make it all the way to Plymouth before stopping. He'll lead them on a good chase."

Jory hands me Samson's reins—I never did learn how to manage Pallas—and I climb onto his dusty, familiar back.

"Where to?" Jory says.

"London," I say. In the dark I can't see his expression but he doesn't object, not that it would stop me if he did. I pull my cloak tight around me, feeling first for the money and then for the letters, making sure they stay safe and dry. Father was an illegally practicing Catholic, a harborer of a priest smuggled into the country from Spain, a liar, and a traitor.

But those aren't the only secrets he was keeping.

Chapter 4

TOBY

St. Anne's Lane,
Aldersgate Ward, London
26 October 1601

The letter I intercepted and deciphered last night was akin to holding a bomb, the contents every bit as incendiary. I sat at the table in the brothel for longer than I should have, checking and rechecking each cipher to make sure I'd translated it correctly, that I didn't make a mistake, that it said what I eventually had to concede it did. After I delivered it to the next contact—ten minutes late, something I excused by way of smears on my cheeks left by red lips—I carried the translated copy all the way to Whitehall Palace, delivering it to the apartments of the queen's closest advisor.

When I received a summons early this morning, bidding me

to appear before the council in an hour, I was not at all surprised. In fact, I expected it and was already dressed and ready to go. I exit the door of my tiny garret room, down the narrow staircase and into the rainy alley of St. Anne's Lane, dodging puddles and detritus to reach the wide thoroughfare of Cheapside.

It should be a forty-five-minute walk to Somerset House, where the summons is to be held, but not in the rain and not today. It is all the furor of Friday here, merchants and carts and horses and men, a riot of noise and filth. By the time I reach Fleet Street and turn into Temple Bar and pass through the iron gates, I am mud-spattered and soaked and nearly late. The pale stone-columned facade of Somerset House greets me as kindly as a priest on Reformation Day, forbidding and foreboding, as do the royal-crested guards in red posted like andirons on either side of the main, arched doorway.

They consider me.

I am not recognized; I am not meant to be. I am meant to blend into the background, drab and unnoticeable as the brown trousers and loden cloak I wear, someone you see once and then forget. *But you will never be able to hide those eyes*, the queen told me once through rotting teeth. *Lovely as larkspurs in May, and every bit as blue.* It is these eyes that give the guards pause as they look me over from my hair made blacker by rain to my boots made blacker by mud and say, "Haven't we seen you before?"

"'Fraid not." I adopt a south-of-the-Thames accent and rock back on my heels. "Here to bring a message to Sir George Carey. He'll be expecting me." I tug a folded piece of parchment from my pocket by way of demonstration. It's blank, but they won't check it; from the look they give first the paper, then each other, my guess is neither of them can read.

The guards both nod then, easily sated, and allow me to pass. I'm halfway through the courtyard when Carey rounds into view, making his way to me with crisp and unhurried steps. Besides being the Baron Hunsdon, a Knight of the Garter, and a member of the Privy Council, he is also the Lord Chamberlain of the queen's household. He pays my salary, such that it is, which means I'm better acquainted with him than the other council members.

"Why didn't you come in through the side?" Carey jerks a thumb toward the east wing of Somerset. "The doors aren't watched there."

"I didn't think it wise for me to appear as if I knew that."

Carey throws me a look but this time really takes me in. He's got a youthful, unlined face that belies his fifty-odd years, bright blue eyes, and a head of bushy yellow hair with a matching beard and mustache, one that now twitches with affront.

"Why are you dressed that way?" He waves his hand along the length of me. "Those trousers. Aren't they a bit worn? Your boots appear as if you've been in combat and lost, and my God, man. Your cloak looks like it's just hatched." He peels off his own and gestures for me to do the same. I pause a beat longer than I normally would, careful to conceal the panic before it shows on my face. My cloak, though nothing special, is the dearest thing I own, and not only because it keeps me warm.

"I don't see what the problem is," I say eventually. "Didn't you once say that with a face like mine I could wear a grain sack and still charm? This is considerably better than a grain sack."

"Did you give your mother this much trouble?" Carey snaps his fingers for me to hurry. "The queen is here—didn't you read the summons? It said you were to see her."

There was no mention of the queen in this morning's message. I read it five times, committing every last word to memory before disposing of it by candle flame. I'm on alert now; there's been a change, and change almost always heralds trouble.

"Ever the skeptic," Carey says to my silence. "No matter. You're here and she's here, so we'll have to do the best we can."

I do what I'm told and take off my cloak, folding it carefully before handing it to Carey. In turn, he hands me his. It fits, if only in size; we're both of average height and slender build. As for the rest: absurd. It's plum brocade, trimmed in gold along the front, the collar high and stiff and uncomfortable.

I look down at myself. "This looks bad."

"Well, her eyesight is bad," Carey replies. "And she won't be looking past your eyes anyway." He throws me a wink. "Lovely as lavender in spring—"

I scowl. "It was larkspurs in May."

Carey laughs and takes my elbow, steering me into Somerset. "She's in a mood," he whispers, though there's no one around. "It's Essex, of course. She's just received his widow and denied her petition to restore the earldom to their son. That went well. *Christ*. Damned-to-hell Essex…"

The ghost of the Earl of Essex still haunts these halls. He was executed for treason only months ago after a five-hour interrogation by the very Privy Council I am about to stand before, after desperation led him to an ill-fated rebellion against the queen that lasted mere hours before he surrendered. Essex was one of her favorites, for all the good it did the both of them.

A set of closed double doors loom before me. Carey raps once, sharp, and they swing open. The room is bright and rich, the doublets of eleven Privy Council members glittering in muted light spilling through mullioned windows. The men stand in clustered obeisance before the queen, but I don't really see them: My eyes land on her first and foremost. She is something out of the theater, raised higher than all of us, a swan on a dais in white. She is old now, and doesn't like to be reminded of it. We trip over ourselves and our words to assure her she is still as lovely as she was in the Golden Age which is also no longer, both run to rot and ruin.

"Tobias."

I step forward to her chair, overwrought and overstuffed. She does not deign to rise. Up close she is even more theatrical: powdered face over pockmarked skin, cherry lips over browning teeth. But her eyes, touchstone black, are still as sharp as I'm told they always were, when she lived a life of secrets and lies and treasonous plots, when she wanted her sister's throne and her brother's before it, when she stopped her own cousin, the French Catholic Mary Queen of Scots, with the same ax that stopped Essex.

"Your Majesty." I sketch a well-practiced bow, then rise with a wink and a grin. It is not my first time before her and I know she likes a show of deference but also of cheek, especially from her male visitors.

"Saucy boy." She grins and slips a long-fingered hand into a gilded pouch at her waist and flips me a sovereign. I catch it high, then pinch it between my teeth as if checking its value. Her eyes gleam with amusement. "Now, tell me how you are, Tobias. How go your days?"

"They are spent in service of Your Majesty."

"And what of this service? Are you pleased with it?"

"I could not voice a complaint."

"Good, good." She snaps her fingers and a servant, just a boy, scurries from the shadows and presses a square of linen into her hand. She coughs into it, then thrusts the soiled cloth back into his hand. We all serve Her Majesty, one way or another.

"Tobias, you intercepted a letter last night. Run through the same network you've been monitoring the past several months, yet entirely different from the others you've intercepted."

"Yes, Your Majesty." The network I watch is used to run correspondence between Catholic families within England, with the sole purpose of gathering names of possible traitors. Most of the communication is relatively benign: who is holding Mass at what location, who plans to travel to which part of the country—Catholic families are forbidden to travel more than fifty miles from their home without permission. "The letter was in cipher, of course, nomenclature. Symbolic substitution code."

I describe the letter I picked up from the boy in black. It was encrypted using the same principle as alphabetic substitution code, only instead of letters replacing other letters, they are replaced by symbols. Symbolic substitution is a far more diffi-cult code to break, owing to the near-infinite number of glyphs that can be used, replacing in a written letter everything from words to numbers, spaces to punctuation, common words to phrases.

The queen, understanding this already, nods. "And you're not wrong about what it says."

"I'm not wrong."

The queen gives a dark smile. "Which is?"

I suppress a frown. Surely she knows what it says. Surely her ministers told her. I did not risk breaking my cover to get this letter in their hands last night for them not to inform her of it immediately. But a nod from Carey confirms I should tell her anyway and so I do.

"It speaks to a plot currently being devised by eight English noblemen—Catholic noblemen—and a priest from Spain, newly arrived to England."

"And what is the plot?"

I hesitate.

"I don't pay you to be fragile, Tobias." The queen waves an impatient hand. "What did the letter say?"

There is no dressing this down, so I simply say it. "To murder Your Majesty, to put the Archduchess Isabella from the Dutch Low Countries on the throne in your place, and to restore Catholicism to England, all with the financial backing of the king of Spain."

The sounds of ruffled parchment, cleared throats, and shuffling feet fall as swiftly as a curtain. The ministers exchange a glance and I know what they are thinking. Essex's execution was meant to put an end to domestic plots against the queen, to demonstrate that not even a wealthy nobleman, an earl and the queen's favorite, is immune from her wrath. But now I wonder if it's not done the opposite. If it's given more men the courage to rise up against her, to let them know that where there was one, there are others.

"First Essex and now this," the queen says. "It's enough to have Spain, the Low Countries, France, Ireland, and Scotland against me without adding my own men to the list. Who are they? The man or men who wrote this letter?"

"I don't know," I reply. "It's possible they're part of the network, a member of one of the Catholic families we already know about. But it's also possible they just knew of the network's existence and opted to take advantage of it."

"If they don't know the network has been compromised, then you can continue to watch it," one of the ministers says to me. "Follow the trail of communication and it will lead us straight to them." I lift my brows but don't reply. There's a problem with this strategy, one I don't have to voice because the queen does.

"But what of the other letters?" she says. "There were others preceding this one, letters not intercepted by any other watcher. How were those sent?"

The minister doesn't venture a response to that, but I do. "Another network," I hazard. "One we don't know about. Or they were passed from hand to hand. Or there weren't letters at all, but face-to-face conversations. Either way, I don't think we can rely on the network alone to track these men down."

"Then what would you have us do?" another minister snipes at me. "Since you seem to have so many opinions about what's already been done?"

"Essex," I reply, ignoring the slight. "I would start there. He and four of his co-conspirators were executed for their part in his plot, yet three hundred of them were set free."

The minister scowls. "I suppose you would have had us execute each one—"

"Enough," the queen commands. "Tobias, continue."

"The night of Essex's rebellion, you sent out a public warning denouncing him as a traitor," I say. "Most of his men disappeared after that, to say nothing of the supporters who never even showed up. But just because his rebellion failed doesn't mean the insurrection went away." I tip my head to the letter I intercepted last night, now in the queen's pale hand. "I don't think it did."

"We have their names," one minister starts. "We could round them up for questioning—"

"Alerting them to our plan yet again," the queen says. "You may as well issue a written invitation for them to flee the country. No, I think this time we do this quietly. Carefully. We do not even put our men on it, except for Tobias. We need someone new to this. Someone young. Unknown. Someone who can slip in and out of this tangle with ease and without detection."

Were I not prepared for this—I knew it would not be an ordinary summons the moment I discovered the queen was present—I would be surprised. Still, I have a part to play.

"Me, Your Majesty?"

"You," she replies. "Will you find my assassin, Tobias? Spring this trap on them before they spring it on me?"

"As well as a hunter in the blinds," I reply.

Her black smile is benevolent. "You have demonstrated your

loyalty to me, and your skill. Find me the men involved in this plot and you will be rewarded. Handsomely. You will receive tenfold your stipend, and a further bonus at the execution of the traitors. If you succeed, you will be a rich man, Tobias. You may do what you like," she adds with a flutter of her hand and the smile of a practiced coquette, "even if it means I lose you from my service."

I think of what I could do with that money. I think of all I wish I could do, were I not enmeshed in this endless web of treason and conspiracy. I have been in the queen's service for six years, the last four looking for a way out. A way free from the lies I tell others and myself, keeping anyone and everyone at arm's length to ensure they'll never know the truth of who I am and what I do. And now she's offering me that freedom, as if she knows it's what I've wanted all along.

But as with everything, I trust nothing and so I reply, "Your service is my only reward."

Chapter 5

KATHERINE

GUNNISLAKE, CORNWALL
26 OCTOBER 1601

Jory and I find a shabby lodging house in Gunnislake, the first stop in what will be a seven-day journey to London. The trip was fraught but uneventful—fraught because of the cold and the rain and the dark, because I have never been this far from St Mawgan in my life, because we rode fast and hard as if the devil were on our tails. Uneventful because we made the four-hour ride without being robbed, lost, or followed. Maybe Trelawney's men caught up to the horse Jory had set loose, maybe they didn't. Maybe they figured out we left them a false trail and that we intended on traveling somewhere other than Plymouth. Either way, I doubt they imagined we'd set out for London.

After a few hours of broken sleep and a small breakfast, it's now afternoon and I'm at the table in our room, Jory sitting across from me, wearing an expectant expression. Between us is the bundle of Father's letters I took from Lanherne.

"This is why I decided to go to London." I begin untying the black ribbon still holding them together. "What I'm about to tell you about them, were it to get out, would mean your life. It would mean mine. I need you to know this before you agree to hear it."

I half expect the scraping of the spindly chair across the floor, a Hail Mary, and a goodbye. Instead, Jory leans forward, dark eyes gleaming in the dull light. "You can tell me."

"Father didn't know I knew about them," I start. "I wouldn't have, if I hadn't noticed the messengers arrive. Two one month, four the next. That was strange enough in itself. No one comes to Lanherne that often." I remember watching them ride up, boys my age or a little older, climbing off lathered horses and wearing clothes that looked both grand and travel-worn: from someplace far off. At first I thought it was business, a missive from the queen that sometimes comes with great ceremony. Only Father never received his own correspondence; his valet did that. Father meeting these messengers at the door, as if he expected them, was my first clue something was different.

The second was that he never offered for any of them to stay, which is often the custom as Cornwall and St Mawgan are so far removed from the rest of England. And then there was the way the correspondence was read. Not quickly, while standing, with a nod or a murmur of assent. These letters required candlelight, a desk, a quill and an inkpot, several sheets of parchment and at least an hour; it looked as if he was puzzling over a particularly difficult passage in Latin. I hid in the shadows of his library and watched him while pretending to read a book, wondering what the letters could mean. I watched him wander through the house, the bundle in his hand, looking for a place to hide them, finally deciding on the niche in his library. The moment he retired to his chamber, I retrieved them and I spent the whole night reading them by shaky candlelight.

"Father was involved with something," I continue. "A plot. Involving seven other Catholic men in London. And the queen." I say this all in a whisper—there is no telling who can hear us and secrets carry like shouts. I unfold the first piece of parchment and lay it flat on the table.

Jory's face never changes expression. But something in his eyes shifts and I recognize it right away: understanding. "What does it say?" he asks.

I pull out the second and third letters and place them beside the first. The second contains the key to the cipher in the first, showing which symbols correspond to which letters, words, and spaces. Even with this key I can see how it took Father so long to decipher it.

a	b	c	d	e	f	g	h	i	k	l	m	n	o	p

q	r	s	t	u	v	x	y	z

and	for	with	that	put	have	all	of

from	your	in	noble	when

spiritual	is	what	low	then	send	restoring	we

I	pray	you	catholic	will	ready

state	realm	its	cause	work	troops	the	must

gentlemen	who	they	to	await
≈	ξ	ω	5	ƒ

Nulls: ff. ◡. ◡. d.   Doubles: σ

The third sheaf contains the translation.

we will undertake the delivery of your royal persons from
the hands of your enemies for the dispatch of the ~~queen~~...
usurper... eight noble gentlemen who for the zeal they
have to the catholic cause will undertake that tragical...
execution... and put in her place the noble archduchess
isabella... restoring the state to its rightful realm...
when all is ready... the ~~vix~~... *eight gentlemen must be set to*
work and when it is accomplished spiritual assistance
from rome troops from france and the low countries
then we will await foreign assistance from spain

There's a protracted silence as Jory takes it all in. "They want to kill the queen." A pause. "If you were caught...if Trelawney's men do manage to catch up to us...you should burn this. Right away—" Jory reaches for the candle on the table, fumbling with a match.

"I can't get rid of them." I hold out a hand to stop him. "Not until I reach the man who wrote them. That's who I'm going to find in London. I can't exactly show up at his door, going on about an assassination plot and asking him to take me in. I need proof that I am who I say I am, and these letters are the only thing I've got."

"How do you know who wrote them?" Jory picks up the pages

from the table and begins leafing through them. "There was no name here, not that I could see."

"A man called Robert Catesby," I say. "And it's not on the letter. It was in Father's journal, along with the names of the six others. Don't worry. That I did burn." Every last leather-bound page went into the dying fire in his library, the next-to-final act of Lady Katherine Arundell of Lanherne.

Jory lowers the papers. "And you mean to go to this man's—Catesby's—house to ask him . . . what?"

"The queen killed my father, Jory," I say. "She might not have stabbed him herself, but she killed him all the same. Her laws sent those men to our house. If he hadn't been killed then, he would have been killed eventually. They would have brought him to London, put him on trial, only to hang him the way they're going to do Ryol. . . ."

I start to cry again. Once I would have been embarrassed to do this in front of Jory, someone I hoped to impress. Now that couldn't matter less. And he lets me do it, too; he doesn't try to stop me or tell me it will all be fine. Not because he's indifferent but because he knows it isn't fine, for either of us.

Eventually I am calm enough to speak. "I'm going to find Catesby because I want to take my father's place in this plan." I decided this the moment we left St Mawgan. No, I decided this the moment my father fell onto the varnished hallway at Lanherne and never got back up. "I want to help them kill the queen."

I finally accept that Trelawney and his men aren't following us. I still find myself looking over my shoulder, something Jory says makes me look guilty so I vow to stop. By the middle of the seventh day, I can tell we are close to London, even if I didn't have Jory calling out the distance as if we were in a footrace. I would know by the way the trees and the grass begin to thin, the way the air goes from crisp and clean and green to something dense and smoky and feral. Everything is moving, none of it in the direction you want it to. All the streets look the same, thin and dark and twisted, and we clop our way down the slimy cobblestones, people staring and pointing, filthy children rushing up to paw the horses and making them nervy. I've wanted to come to London as long as I can remember, asking Father to take me with him every time he came. But now that I'm here I hate it, and I can see why he did, too.

"We'll have to find a place to stable the horses," Jory tells me.

I nod, but already I'm worried. The bag of coins I took from Father's library is dwindling faster than I thought it would. It was only a few pounds to begin with, and we've spent nearly half a pound already. Between stabling and feeding, the horses cost as much as we do.

We keep moving, Jory now and then asking around, and eventually we're directed to a stable in an area of the city called Dowgate Ward, just north of the Thames River. We have to dismount and walk the horses to get there, across the enormous thoroughfare of London Bridge, noisy and dirty and crowded, buildings piled on top of one another and the smell of terrible things everywhere. The horses buck and rear the whole way across, and by the time we reach the other side, we're all four sweaty from exertion. A few more twists and turns—the streets look the same on this side of the river, too—and we land in a shadowed courtyard, the air rank with manure. A hand-painted sign above me reads WICKER STABLRY, which I don't think is a word but it gets the point across anyway.

"I'll go find someone." Jory hands me Pallas's reins and disappears through one of the arches. A handful of stableboys scurry in and out of them, hauling hay and tack.

By the time Jory returns it's almost dark, and he doesn't look happy. "To board and feed them both is a shilling a week," he says. "Tack another shilling, shoeing a further crown—that's for each—grooming a farthing, also each—"

"That's robbery," I gasp. "We can't afford that."

"I know," Jory says. He looks stricken. "They offered to buy them."

"Buy them?" My voice goes screechy. "What you mean to say is, they ran up the prices of boarding so high we'd have no choice but to sell them. I assume they offered nothing."

"Three pounds," he confirms. "That's up from the two they originally offered."

I close my eyes. Samson alone cost eight pounds; Pallas is worth at least ten.

"Forget it," I say. "We're leaving." I start to lead Samson through the courtyard, away from here, but Jory stops me.

"Where will we take them?" he says. "We can't wander all over the city with them, especially not at night." I'm shaking my head, even though I know he's right. "I know you don't want to. I don't, either. But I think we should sell them."

I am crying, again, as we lead Father's horses into the stable.

These horses were his pride, and they're just one more thing that's been taken away from me. Jory manages the transaction with a foul-faced man I presume is the stable owner. I glare at him through blurry eyes, but he doesn't seem to notice. It's over and done with quickly, the way I'm coming to learn all bad things are, and soon we're back out in the streets.

Jory leads us back toward the river. The sky tells me it's coming up on five, and soon the sun will disappear completely. I don't want to be outside in all this when it does. Not to mention that I'm filthy and I smell like horse and mud and rain; my clothes are itchy and damp and Jory isn't looking too well, either. I want to find a room and I don't really care where, just as long as it's cheap and we don't have to cross the bridge again to get there.

We turn off a street named Candlewick, onto a smaller lane called St. Laurence Poultney Hill, for no other reason than it's a ridiculous name for a street. It's lined with rows of buildings, white plaster and brick and alarmingly unsturdy, leaning this way and that, the roofs of some nearly touching the others.

I spot a sign hanging over a nearby door, one of a dolphin that I presume was once entirely blue but is now bare wood speckled with flecks of fading blue paint. Above it are the words DOLPHIN SQUARE LODGING HOUSE. In the yellowed window is a handwritten sign that says ONE WEEK=ONE PENNY, WITH LAUNDRY. It's shoddy, just as every other place we've stayed since leaving Lanherne. But for a penny a week we can live here for several months, and by then I figure either the queen will be dead or I will.

Chapter 6

TOBY

ST. ANNE'S LANE,
ALDERSGATE WARD, LONDON
2 NOVEMBER 1601

Aknock on the door sends me to my feet and my fingers underneath the mattress for my dagger. I rarely get visitors and when I do, it's only the laundress to collect my clothes or the landlady coming round to take my rent, though neither comes this early in the morning. Anyone else, no matter what time, can only be trouble. I reach the door just as there's another knock and a familiar cracking voice from behind the battered wood.

"Do I need a secret knock to gain entrance?" There's a brief minuet of knocking-scratching-pounding. "Dammit, Toby, open up. I know you're in there."

I unbolt the latches on the door, swinging it open to find George Carey on the threshold, sharp and polished in a blue doublet, black breeches, and a black cape held in place with a jeweled clasp that is probably worth more than the building I live in.

"What's with all the locks? Hiding from your many suitors?" He looks over my shoulder hopefully, as if he expects to find a harem.

"Hate to disappoint you," I reply. "How'd you know I was here?"

"Your landlady, speaking of your many suitors." Carey's mouth quirks, making his yellow pointed beard twitch. The widow who owns my building is pretty, and young, and more than once she's invited me to her room for supper and a few things more than supper. I've since broken things off, which she didn't take kindly to, but I couldn't exactly tell her I was more interested in her brother than in her. To do so would be to break a law that not even I, high as I am in the queen's favor, can afford. "Are you going to let me in, or do I have to stand on the threshold all day?"

I hold open the door and Carey walks in, navigating piles of clothing and books. He looks around at the rumpled bed and the clump of coal that sits unlit in the brazier.

"Dismal," he says. "Surely we pay you more than this." Carey signs the promissory note for my salary and does know—down to the farthing—what I make. But the way I see it, the less I spend the more value it has.

He pulls out the stool from under the table and eases into it somewhat gingerly, as if he's afraid it will splinter to pieces beneath him. "How goes the search?" Carey asks. "I assume you were out half the night, if not all of it, trailing one of your men?"

I lower myself back onto the mattress and nod. "I have a list of forty men fined for their parts in the Essex rebellion and then released. I thought to start with those who have had prior arrests or were placed under watch before, then work my way from there."

"Sounds exhausting."

It takes seven men to effectively trail a single suspect for a single day. For me to follow each man on this list is not a viable solution, but as of now, it's my only option.

"Is that what brought you?" I say. "Inquiring into my well-being? I'm touched."

"In a way, yes." Carey tugs out a slip of paper from his doublet and sets it on the table. I recognize it immediately as a promissory note. "I can see by your face you're pleased. Actually, no, I can't. But you're welcome anyway." Carey rises from the stool, picks it up, and pointedly tucks it in. "Come. I've got to pay a visit to one of my clients and I could use the company. I need someone who can recognize a lie at a hundred paces."

It's a sign of prestige to patron the arts, and as a titled noble-man and favored courtier, Carey has his pick of potential pro-tégés. He shares the queen's love of the theater and sponsors a half-dozen writers, along with a company of players that bears his title, the Lord Chamberlain's Men. It's a profitable troupe and a favorite of Her Majesty's, the only company that's been asked to perform for her at one of her many palaces. I hear they're very good, but I wouldn't know. I don't go to the theater anymore, not after Marlowe died.

We squeeze through shadowed alleys and past nearby St. Paul's Cathedral, making our way to the pier at Poles Wharf. Carey would never take London Bridge to cross the river and I appreciate not having to, crammed as it is with merchants and cutpurses and drunks. A whistle later we're seated in a shallow wooden wherry helmed by a single rower, drifting toward the south bank of the Thames.

"What's the occasion for the visit?" I say. "A writer who needs money or a player who needs money?"

"Nothing so pleasant as extortion, I assure you." He glances at the ferryman, the spymaster in him always alert. "Damage control."

To aid in his rebellion, the Earl of Essex had commissioned the Lord Chamberlain's Men to stage a special performance of *Richard II*. It was an odd request: *Richard II* was several years old and had fallen out of favor. But Essex claimed it was his favorite and paid the company an extra forty shillings for their trouble. At his trial, Essex confessed that the play was instrumental to his plan: The scene where Richard is deposed, imprisoned, and murdered was a signal to Essex's followers to pour into the city, rousing Londoners to depose their own queen.

The wherry approaches the shore, the hull scraping silt and the bow knocking against three others as we all angle toward the same pier. The Globe Theater is right off the bank, so we don't have far to go to reach the entrance. It's a gaudy thing, twice as round as it is tall, all plaster and timber and open thatched roof. Above the wooden door is a plaque that reads THE GLOBE. On it is a painted image of Atlas, holding up the world.

We push through the door and press down a narrow, dimly

lit hallway that leads inside. It is all the sounds and sights of another world in here. I have been to the neighboring Rose Theatre, many times and many years ago, and though the Globe resembles the Rose in structure, it is grander and more theatrical, outfitted with three tiers of seats, painted ceilings, columns frescoed to look like marble, and a stage curtain made of rich velvet.

Carey and I funnel through players standing in groups and muttering their lines. Musicians hover in the cobbled yard, strumming lutes and blowing fifes, drummers tapping out beats with their fingers. Still more men flutter onstage, disappearing and reappearing behind the dark blue curtain, giving wide berth to another group of players rehearsing there.

Finally, we find the man we're looking for: William Shakespeare, playwright and part owner of the Globe. He's standing beside the stage, a quill in one hand though there's no inkpot to be seen, a sheaf of parchment in the other. White shirt unlaced at the top, wrinkled cloak, one leg of his breeches unbuttoned, both of his boots untied. He's the most famous playwright in London and he looks as if he's just come from mucking stalls.

Maybe he's seen Carey, or maybe he's only sensed his presence by the way the conversation in the theater lulls as we pass. Either way, the moment before we reach him, Shakespeare turns from us to hop onto the stage. Carey lets out a grunt of annoyance and clambers onto the platform, me close behind.

"Will."

"You." Shakespeare doesn't stop walking, pressing into the narrow backstage hall past yet more players and stagehands who part for him but not for us.

Carey is undeterred. "Is that any way to greet your benefactor?"

"It is when he is also my antagonist," Shakespeare replies over his shoulder. "What brings you?"

"The queen, of course."

"The queen!" Shakespeare marches up to a wall, empty but for three sheets of paper hung there by small nails. He rips them down and replaces them with three other sheets from the stack in his hand. "If you're here to interrogate me about the content of the play, rest assured. There's nothing of politics in this one. Nothing but lovers and monkeys and Ganymedes; clowns and melancholy and mistaken identity. Nothing you can possibly object to. It's just as you like it."

"I see." Carey looks doubtful. "Does it have a title?"

Shakespeare turns around, ripping the discarded papers into shreds. "*The Forest of Arden? Rosalind's Golden Legacy? A History of Orlando de Boys?* What think you? Never mind, I can see by your face you hate them all, damn you. Well, you're the *fliondoso*; you know what the people like. You figure it out." He thrusts the shredded paper into Carey's hand, hops offstage, and wanders back into the yard.

Fliondoso? I look to Carey.

"He invents words," Carey tells me. "You get used to it." We climb offstage and Carey hurries after him. "Actually, you don't. Will, hold up. Did you say monkeys? You don't mean real ones, do you?"

"Oh, certainly." Shakespeare dodges two men fencing with wooden swords. Carey is nearly struck in the head by one, but I pull him out of the way before it lands. "It's difficult to get men to play them, you know, so we're stuck with the real thing. Underfoot, somewhere. Haven't you seen?"

Carey looks around him, his yellow hair puffed in alarm. "No."

"Well, they're somewhere." Shakespeare waves his hand around as if he's warding off flies. "I'd watch your step if I were you. They do tend to shit everywhere." As if on cue, a monkey scampers by wearing something tied to his head.

"What is it wearing?" Carey asks.

"Antlers," Shakespeare replies. "It's meant to be a deer. The story is set in a forest, Carey. A *forest*. I tried to get real deer, but as you know—or perhaps you don't—they're terribly difficult to capture and they tend not to take kindly to direction. We all do what we can."

Carey throws me a helpless glance. "So you brought in monkeys instead? Why not, say, goats? They at least resemble deer."

"Fantastic idea." Shakespeare taps his temple with a black-stained finger. "Procure me some goats, will you? Now, I really must be going."

Before Shakespeare can walk away from us again, Carey reaches out and snatches his sleeve. Shakespeare looks to the sky and sighs, a great, drawn-out thing.

"Will, never mind this play," Carey pleads. "I need to know about the play you promised Her Majesty for her Yuletide celebration. The one *I* promised Her Majesty. What of it?"

"It's coming."

"Coming? It's not even breathing hard. You plan to give her monkeys, too?"

"Why not? It's court. There's shit everywhere anyway."

Carey drops his hand. "You dance dangerously close to treason, Will."

"I'm a playwright. I tell the truth. What is truth these days if not treason?"

Carey's beard twitches with affront. Maybe it's unwise, but I smile.

"Who's this, then?" Shakespeare's keen eyes pass over me as if he's just noticed me. "Lean cheek, beard neglected, unquestionable spirit. And those eyes. So blue! Blue as the heavens. Blue as…"

"Larkspurs in May?" I offer.

Shakespeare snaps his fingers. "Very good. You one of the queen's, too?"

"Not at all," Carey lies smoothly. "He's a man of the arts. I'm thinking of giving him patronage. He studied under Kit Marlowe, you know."

I go quiet, but Shakespeare's dark eyes light up. "Marlowe! He's a good man. Was. Good playwright." He looks me over again. "You a writer, too, then? Player?"

"A bit of both," I reply, and this at least is the truth. Carey, sensing yet another digression, interjects.

"What of the play, Will?"

Shakespeare twirls his hands in the air. "Twins, mistaken identity, lovers, a fool. It's wonderful."

"That's *this* play."

"No, it's different. I'm calling it *Shipwrecked Twins of Grupela*."

"*Shipwrecked Twins of Grupela*?" Carey's mustache wilts. "What's it about?"

"Shipwrecked twins."

There's a pause and Shakespeare, finally acknowledging Carey's distress, claps his shoulder. "You'll have your play, Carey. That I can promise you. In the meantime, try not to worry, eh? It leaves lines." Shakespeare is off again and this time, we don't follow.

Carey places a hand protectively over his forehead. "He's got to deliver me a play—a new one, not one the whole of London has already seen—in less than two months," he mutters. "Sooner, because I've got to see it to make sure he's not buried some blasphemy that might amuse him but put my head on the block." His blond curls stand so high on his head they look as if they've already given up and begun their way out the door without him.

"Marlowe was never like this, you know," he goes on. "I'm sure you do. He was an artist, yes, but a consummate professional. Never these damned verbal acrobatics and monkeys and—*shit*." Carey lifts his foot and shakes off a clump of whatever clings to it.

When I don't respond, Carey turns his attention from his shoe to me.

"I'm sorry," he says. "I know what Marlowe meant to you."

It's been eight years and I'm still working out what he meant to me.

Carey and I climb aboard another wherry. He's in a fine piss of a mood, muttering obscenities and denouncing everything from derelicts who call themselves authors to the perniciousness of the written word. His beard is mutinous.

"You've not said a word the whole way back," Carey snaps when we finally disembark at Poles Wharf. "You think I'm over-reacting, that I should have more respect for the art I patron and all this folly-fallen nonsense."

"I don't think that," I say, although I do.

Carey throws me a look. "Always cautious, aren't you? Well. It's not your concern, at any rate. This play will get written, this wretched thing about shipwrecked twins from wherever it was, it will be performed and it will be a disaster and the queen will have my head—figuratively if not literally—and she'll cut my funding and I'll be the one orchestrating a rebellion. See how history repeats itself? Maybe that will give Shakespeare something new to write about."

It's an incredibly careless thing to say even for Carey—especially for Carey. There's nothing and no one around but waves and wheeling gulls, but I don't trust even them not to fly their way to Whitehall to parrot each and every treasonous word into the queen's ear, the way a good watcher should.

The way *I* should.

"Sir Carey—"

"For God's sake, Toby, drop the *sir*, would you? You make me sound a hundred years old. Call me George, or Carey if you must."

"Can we speak?" I continue. "Freely?"

"Can we? I don't think I've ever heard you speak more than ten words in a row before, much less freely."

I let this go. "I'd like to talk about the play. About the twins from wherever. And about *Richard II*."

"Of course you would. The very two things I'd prefer never to talk about again," Carey says. But his curiosity must get the better of him, because then he says, "Go on, let's hear it. Before I change my mind and toss you into the river."

"Essex used *Richard II* as a call to his followers," I say. "The scene with Richard's assassination was meant to rouse the audience, for them to take to the streets and to persuade others to his cause, to gain enough Londoners to effectively storm the palace and stage a coup."

"I am all too aware of what Essex did."

"What if we used this new play to the same end?" I say. "Not to incite an insurrection, but to attract those who would? The men who would bring danger to the queen, and are of Catholic leanings—what if Shakespeare wrote a play to attract them the way *Richard II* was meant to attract Essex's supporters?"

"Can't be done," Carey says. "It can't be done because it's already *been* done. Were we to try that again, they'll know it's a trap. We may as well hang a sign from Whitehall announcing our intention."

I shrug. "To a mouse, cheese is cheese. It's why traps work. And they do: time and time again. If I've learned anything in my position, it's that there's nothing more deceptive than the obvious."

Carey gives me a shrewd look. It's as if everything I know of him is an act, the bright eyes and bouncing curls and cracking laugh a mask to hide the calculating man beneath. He looks out at the busy river, at the boats with their pennants fluttering against the steel-gray sky. A long moment passes, in which I imagine any number of responses he might be considering, ranging from a cry of genius to a cry of treason.

Finally, he speaks. "How might such a play go?"

Two hours later I find myself genuflecting before Queen Elizabeth in her privy chamber at Whitehall, surrounded by her ladies-in-waiting. They titter behind fans held before their faces, a dozen girls in all shades of skin and hair color and squeezed into gowns made of a fortune's worth of fabric, whispering as they bustle about, never taking their eyes off me. I feel as if I'm being hunted.

"Tobias, you've returned so soon," the queen says. She, too, holds a fluttering fan that doesn't hide her smile.

"And yet, it was far too long," I reply. "Time travels at different speeds for different people. I can tell you who time strolls for, who it trots for, who it gallops for, and who it stops cold for." I pull from memory lines Shakespeare's men were rehearsing earlier. Considering what I'm about to propose to her, I think the flattery can't hurt. "While it gallops in your presence, it turns to ice in the in-between."

Carey's beard quivers. The ladies and their gowns sigh.

"Very pretty," the queen says. "You are a poet yet." She turns to her ladies and with a single wave of her hand dismisses them. They flock through the heavy curtains and disappear, all of them silent and obedient as hens, only one or two daring to look back over her shoulder at me. "Despite your flattery, I know this is not a courtesy call. By all means, relieve me of the suspense."

"We just came from the Globe," Carey begins. "Paid a visit to your favorite playwright to see how his Yuletide gift to you was coming along."

"Yes. And how is it coming?"

It's not even breathing hard.

"Splendid," Carey lies. "It's unlike anything he's done before. There are twins, a shipwreck, mistaken identity, and love, of course. It's all very amusing."

"Delightful." The queen claps her hands. "Carey, you do spoil me."

Carey's mustache is triumphant.

"But I don't think you came here to speak to me about Shakespeare's play, either."

"Actually, Your Majesty, I did. Rather, Tobias did." Carey's hand is on my shoulder and then I am on one knee, bowing for permission to speak.

"Oh, do rise," the queen tells me. "The back of you is not nearly as pleasant as the front. Well then? Tell me something good."

I don't know if it's good, but I tell her anyway. Everything I told Carey, every last word about Essex and treason, all the things Carey said he wished to never hear about again and, judging by the look that passes over the queen's face, turning it dark and hard, she doesn't, either. She clips her fan shut and drops it into her lap.

"What makes you think Catholics would be fool enough to be drawn from the woodwork by such a plan?" the queen says.

"Whatever I think of them, Tobias, they are men. Not vermin, not children to be baited by insults to their faith."

"The play would not be an insult to their faith, but a celebration of it." I glance behind me to Carey; he looks as if he's holding his breath. "The play Shakespeare is writing for you, it's meant to be written and performed as a Yuletide gift. Instead, I propose it's written for and about Twelfth Night."

"Twelfth Night?"

"The night before Epiphany," I reply. "A festivity marking the conclusion of the twelve days of Christmas—"

"You presume too much, and that I presume too little," the queen snaps. "I know what Twelfth Night is. I know what it celebrates. I know it is revelry to some but religion to others."

"That's the idea," I say. "Catholics love their celebrations, do they not?"

"What you call celebration, I call idolatry," the queen says. "Saint worship."

"Which we will play to full effect," I say. "We name some of the characters after Catholic saints. Andrew, Anthony, Madonna—"

"Madonna is too obvious," she interjects. "Call her Maria instead. Who would be the main player? Is he to fall in love?"

"Yes, there is always that," I reply. "I thought Burbage could play him."

The queen *tsks*. "I have no wish to see Burbage fall in love. Not when I could watch you."

"Me?" I look again to Carey. His mouth is working mightily beneath his mustache as if he wishes to say something, but instead says nothing. "I am no player."

"But you are a watcher and that is halfway to it," the queen replies. "Besides, how else will you steer the ship if not behind the wheel?"

It is a command and I do not dare refuse it. "Yes, Your Majesty."

"So you mean to write a vaguely heretical play, give it to Shakespeare to perform—assuming, of course, he will agree to this—and then what? Hold an audition for every would-be murderer in the whole of London, dangling the promise of performing before me, in a darkened room in my very own palace, a perfect place to attempt an assassination?"

"Yes," I reply.

From behind me, Carey utters a strangled noise. I half expect his hand to land on the scruff of my neck, hauling me from the queen's presence chamber like a recalcitrant hound.

"I cannot allow Your Majesty to willingly step into harm's way," he says instead.

"Nonsense." She is intractable, and I see again the iron will she exerts over her men and her subjects, one I suspect she wields out of necessity for her gender. Were the queen a king, Carey would not have intervened.

"Let's set it at Middle Temple Hall—that will give them a false sense of security," the queen continues. "With direct access to the river, it will be easier to escape, or so they think." Her eyes grow bright, black against her white skin. "How do you propose we find these men? We can't exactly issue a bulletin inviting traitors to participate in a heretical play that will call them out as such, or expect them to come willingly."

"No," I say. "The play and its location will be kept a closely guarded secret. One that will accidentally and inadvertently get out, to be whispered about and passed around like gossip. I give it two weeks before it's known throughout every tavern and inn and market in London."

The queen smiles. "It seems you have thought of everything."

"I think of nothing but your safety."

Chapter 7

KATHERINE

NORTH HOUSE, LAMBETH, LONDON
2 NOVEMBER 1601

It took us an hour to walk from our lodging house to Catesby's home in Lambeth, the address helpfully noted in Father's journal and memorized by me before committing it to fire. North House, as it's called, is dark-bricked and stately, four stories tall with stone sills and thick mullioned windows. It's set in a row alongside others but still very much its own, ringed by a high brick wall, an iron-gated door the only entrance from the street. I push it open, and Jory and I make our way down the cobbled path to the black-painted front door. I lift the knocker—heavy and brass and shaped like a fox—and tap it three times.

Eventually the door is opened by a stiff-looking woman in

gray who does not smile to see us. I spent a few shillings on new clothes for us both—a decent dress for me and a better cloak for Jory, all of it wet after an hour's walk in the rain—and we are bathed and clean. Even so, neither of us look like the kind of people you want turning up on the doorstep, not when it belongs to a house like this.

"I'm here to see Mr. Robert Catesby. Sir Robert." I am unsure if he is a man of title—the letters didn't say, but it doesn't hurt to add it. "I'm the daughter of a friend."

"Sir Robert is not home at present." This is a lie. I know by how quickly she says so, how her eyes shift into the hall and back; I know it by the fresh horse tracks in the mud out front, leading straight to this house. "Perhaps you could come back at a later time."

She starts to close the door. But I won't be turned away so easily, not after everything I did to get here, so I jam the toe of my boot against the door and force it back open. I've only been in London a day, but I already know what it takes to get by here and it isn't kindness.

"Tell him Lady Katherine Arundell is here," I say. "I am Sir Richard Arundell's daughter and this is his groom, Jory. We've come all the way from Cornwall to see him."

I don't know if it's my title, Father's title, or my foot in the doorjamb but she does what I ask her to, waving us inside before disappearing down the hall, shoes tapping against the lacquered wood. I hear another door opening somewhere, murmured voices, and after a moment she reappears with a man I assume is Robert Catesby.

He's very tall and very handsome, sandy-brown hair to his shoulders, a pointed beard and a pointed smile, dressed in starched linen and fine velvet, jeweled buttons and polished boots. He doesn't look like someone who would be interested in religion or a political coup so much as an afternoon at the hunt or a glass of brandy by the fire, but then again, neither did Father.

He looks me over.

"You're Arundell's daughter?" His dark eyes take in my face and hair, freckled and red and so close to Father's own, then he gives a short nod to show me he believes it. "What brings you here?"

I pull the letters from my cloak and Catesby's handsome face goes still. It didn't occur to me until now that we may be killed for this, Jory and me, struck down in this pretty parquet hallway by the sword strapped to Catesby's side, leaving that stone-faced maid of his to clean it up.

"Where did you get those?"

"From my home," I reply. "Lanherne in Cornwall. I took them after the sheriff and his men came for us. After they killed Father and took Ryol away."

Catesby turns to the maid in gray. "Bolt the door. Turn down the shutters and send for the others. Discreetly." The woman nods and vanishes once more down the hall.

"They took the priest?" he says. "Where?"

"Yes," I reply. "And I don't know where. I presume here, to London. They'll torture him, won't they? He'll tell them everything he knows, and then they'll kill him, too, just like they did Father." I am in danger of crying—yet again—but I can't. Not here and not in front of Catesby. So I fix my eyes on a point across the room, a gilded portrait of a pretty, dark-haired woman and the matching face of a dark-haired boy I assume are his wife and son, until I regain control.

"I'm sorry," Catesby says after a moment. "Your father was a good man, a devout man. We shared much of the same views. He thought, as I do, there's a better way for us than this." He pauses, as if deciding what to say next. "He would be glad to know you escaped unscathed."

I nod, though he's wrong. I am not unscathed, and I never will be again.

Catesby gestures down his long hallway. "Why don't you come in? I think we should talk." He leads us into a library and it reminds me of the one at Lanherne, dark and important with an ever-present fire and decanters of amber-colored liquid. He ushers us into a corner, four chairs around a small table, and offers us a drink which we both decline.

"What can I do for you, Miss Arundell?" he says. "I gather you've come to me for help. Money, I presume? A new identity and safe passage out of England for you and your"—he waves a hand at Jory—"suitor?"

Jory turns purple.

"He's not my suitor; he's a priest. In training," I add. "And no. I don't want your money, and I don't want to leave the country. I don't want anything from you at all. In fact, I've come here to help you."

"I see." Catesby lifts his brows. "How might you do that?"

All the things I rehearsed on the way here, all the ways I devised to help him—maid to messenger to squire to seamstress—none of them seem right now that I'm here. Catesby seems like a straightforward man. He needs a straightforward answer.

"I know of your plan," I tell him. "And I'd like to play a part."

An hour later, Jory and I find ourselves sitting in the drawing room of North House, shutters closed, door locked, surrounded by men I've only read about in letters.

Thomas Winter, whom I call Tom One, is Catesby's cousin. He sits at a table alongside John and Christopher Wright, brothers so near in age and dark looks they could be twins but I'm told are not. Thomas Percy, whom I call Tom Two, is as tall and attractive as Catesby, but is forever scratching himself in a way that quite detracts from those looks. Even now he's rubbing his back against the doorframe, like a dog we once had with mange. This makes five of the eight men involved in the plot. The other two, John Grant and Francis Tresham, live in the country. And then, of course, there was Father.

"Katherine and Jory arrived from Cornwall last night," Catesby says. "They bring news that Richard's been killed, Mendoza captured."

"Mendoza?" I say.

"That was Ryol's real name. Antonio Mendoza. 'Ryol' was an alias." Catesby turns back to his men. "Katherine thinks he's been brought to London, and that would be my guess as well. Even so, we need to find out if he's arrived, what prison they've put him in, and what he's confessed, if anything."

"Aren't you going to try to get him out?" I say. "Surely you're not going to just leave him there?"

"Too dangerous," Tom One says. "And he won't expect it. It's something we all agreed to when we started this thing."

"It was incredibly risky of you to take her in, Robert," Tom Two says. "She could have led pursuivants straight to your door. No recovery, no allegiance. Remember?"

Catesby spreads his hands. "What was I to do? Turn her out in the streets? With all that she knows? To do that seemed far more imprudent."

"We weren't followed," I say.

"Not that you know of." Tom Two peels off his cape, a pretty thing trimmed in sable, and continues scratching. "The queen's watchers are paid to be unseen."

"They were searching all over Lanherne for her," Jory says, the first thing he's said since we arrived. "I released one of the horses as a diversion. Sent it toward Plymouth, and they followed thinking it was her." He shrugs. "The horse was a charger. If they somehow managed to catch up, it would have taken hours before they realized it wasn't Katherine. If they didn't, then they'll be searching the wrong part of the country for her. Either way, I very much doubt they think we'd come here."

This seems to satisfy them, or at least they don't challenge it.

"What do you propose we do with them?" Tom Two asks. "They're too innocent to be couriers, and they don't know London well enough besides. What could they possibly do for us?"

Catesby nods, as if he's given great thought to the matter. "We send the girl out to learn the city," he says. "Into taverns. Inns. The markets and the stews. She's a new face and, as you say, an innocent one. She'll fade into the background. She can be the eyes and ears we've never had."

"What will I be listening for?" I say.

"Anything. Everything. If it has to do with the queen, her court, her men, even her servants, I want to know about it." He smiles at me, his eyes shrewd but kind. "Can you do that, Katherine?"

On the one hand, I got lost four times this morning just leaving the lodging house. On the other, I have a long and practiced history of listening to servants gossip at Lanherne, overhearing things I was not meant to. And I did find those letters, which I was not meant to do, either.

I nod.

"And Jory—" Catesby looks to him. "I never did get your surname."

"Jameson."

"—is a priest. In training, as it were. We could use a holy man to bless our mission."

This announcement causes a bit of uproar, the men turning to Jory as if he were already anointed, crossing themselves and murmuring blessings. Jory turns purple again.

"I—I'm not ordained," he says. "I don't have the authority…."

"These are complicated times," Catesby says. "As such, we all do what we can. Consecration notwithstanding, would you, Jory, be willing to take on this role?"

Jory bows his head as if taking the vows. "I will."

"I suppose it's settled," Catesby says. Then, because I'm beginning to see that nothing escapes his notice, he reaches into his doublet and hands me a small drawstring bag full of coins. By the weight and heft I judge it to be about a pound, another six weeks of lodging and food. "I know you didn't come here asking for money. But your father would want to know you're being looked after."

"Thank you," I say, and tuck it away before he can change his mind about this and everything else, and take it all back.

"I don't see why you think you need to do this." Jory's voice drifts down to me. We're back at the lodging house, where he now stands on top of the table, draping a bedsheet over the ceiling rafters to separate his side of the room from mine. He's already taking his new position as priest to heart, saying it's not proper for us to share so close a space, unmarried as we are.

I'm crouched on top of the mattress, trying to get a glimpse of my reflection in the window because there's no mirror in this room. Beside me on the coverlet is a pair of scissors, borrowed from the downstairs kitchen.

"I already told you," I say. "They need me to listen for gossip. You don't hear gossip in respectable places. I'm supposed to go to taverns. Inns. The *stews*. I can't go there looking like this."

"You shouldn't go there at all," Jory says.

"What would you have me do?" I say. "Refuse? Then where would I be? Catesby gave me an assignment, an important one, and I intend to see it through. I notice you didn't refuse yours, even though you're not qualified for it, either."

Jory ties the last corner of the sheet in place and climbs down from the table. "You don't have to shout."

"I intend to be the best set of eyes they have," I go on. "I can't do that if I'm being stared at, or asked to leave. Girls aren't allowed in these kinds of places, you know that." I pick up my brush, combing my hair this way and that, trying to decide what looks best. "I already disguised myself as a boy when I left

Cornwall. You didn't seem to have a problem then. I'm just taking it a little further, that's all."

"That was an emergency," Jory says. "This isn't. For you to parade around as a boy is illegal, for one—"

"I'm not parading anywhere," I say. "I'm taking on a disguise for my safety. Besides, you heard Catesby. These are complicated times. We all do what we can." I pull some hair over my eyes and fold it back, trying out some fringe. It's no good so I drop it, then try parting my hair on the other side. "Can you come in here?"

There's a pause. "That wouldn't be proper, either."

I hold back a sigh and get up, poking my head from behind the sheet. Take in Jory, now setting up a bed for himself on the floor, and study the way his hair drops across his forehead, skimming his eyebrows, falling over his ears and waving around them. My hair is wavy, too.

"Do you always wear your hair this way?" I say.

"What way?" His hand flies to his head, cupping the back of it. "I . . . yes. I guess? I'm not sure what you mean."

"I mean, is it normally long and unkempt like this for fashion, or is it because of neglect?"

"I don't care for fashion," Jory intones. "It is as the Lord said to Samuel: Man looks at the outward appearance, but the Lord looks at the heart."

I suppress another sigh and say, "Well, I hope you're right. Because God only knows what I'm going to look like after this." I cross to my side of the curtain and climb back onto the mattress, settling before the wavy, cracked glass. Pick up a lock of my long red hair in one hand, the shears in the other. And I begin to cut.

Chapter 8

TOBY

THE GLOBE THEATER, BANKSIDE, LONDON
4 NOVEMBER 1601

Two days later Carey and I pay another visit to Shakespeare at the Globe. It's Sunday afternoon, a time for neither performance nor rehearsal, but that was by design. Carey wanted his words to be heard by Shakespeare's ears only.

Carey outlines the plan: for me to turn Shakespeare's Yuletide gift to the queen into a treasonous play to be performed on Twelfth Night. For me to play the lead role. For Shakespeare to hold auditions and for me to choose the cast in the hopes of singling out potential Catholic assassins. For me to watch them, to learn everything even before they think, say, or do it. Especially before they do it. Then, while the play is being performed, arrest—and possibly kill—the suspect or suspects.

Shakespeare doesn't speak for a long, long time.

"This has Her Majesty's blessing," Carey says soothingly. "She will pay handsomely, of course."

This seems to snap Shakespeare out of his stupor. "*Oh ho.* I've heard that before."

"And you've done it before," Carey reminds him. "It's a favor to Her Majesty, sure to increase her patronage for years to come. You'll be the best-known playhouse in London, and the most famous playwright in England."

"I already am."

"Then I don't need to remind you how valuable that favor is."

"This is madness," Shakespeare says. "My plays are nothing but madness and even I could not comprehend this into words. How do you know this plan of yours will work?"

"Faith," Carey replies. I smile at the joke, but Shakespeare doesn't. "We don't know. Just as we don't know if any of our countermeasures will work. That's the nature of the thing. But look: If it doesn't, the worst that can happen is you've got a new play."

He doesn't mention the possibility of a dead sovereign, a political and religious coup, and a military invasion resulting in England becoming a puppet state for the Spanish, but that's probably for the best.

"And if I refuse?"

Carey holds up his hands in false supplication. "Now, I don't want to threaten you, Will.…"

"I think you just did."

"It was a shame about the Rose closing, was it not?" Carey drops his hands along with the pretense. "Such a lovely theater, though what could we really do after all those complaints from city officials? I suppose, given its proximity to the Globe, it was a boon for you and your shareholders. Two plays, six times a week, three thousand spectators, a thousand pounds in your pocket and those of your men. I'd hate to see that go. For your sake."

Shakespeare points at him. Opens his mouth, but nothing comes out. Points again. And again. His face is nearly purple, suffused with apoplectic rage.

Carey is undeterred. "Her Majesty is prepared to offer you eighty shillings for your cooperation."

"Pass."

"I really don't think this is a negotiation."

"Five pounds or this conversation ends now."

"Two pounds, take it or leave it."

"Are you trying to ruin me?" Shakespeare lowers his voice this time, unnecessary, but the words carry anyway. "Because I can't survive another scandal. Half my men have gone across the river to the Fortune—how's that for irony—and if I give the lead role to that one"—he throws an impatient hand in my direction—"and lose Burbage for it, I'm done. He'll go to the Admiral's Men and take his audience with him. Ten pounds is my price," Shakespeare finishes. "Plus funds for costumes and salary for new players. You can't think you can bait a hook with rotten fish, do you?"

"You said five pounds not five seconds ago," Carey protests. "Ten pounds is robbery."

"You would know," Shakespeare replies, not the least bit perturbed.

Carey pretends to consider it. I know he was prepared to give a lot more if it came down to it. "As you wish."

Shakespeare makes a face; it seems he knows it, too.

Carey extends a hand to him and Shakespeare, reluctantly, shakes it. Then Shakespeare turns to me and snaps his fingers. I'm standing in the slim shadow of the roof, not wanting to draw attention to myself during what I knew would be an unpleasant negotiation. "You. Larkspur. Come here. Let's see what kind of disaster I've just agreed to."

I step forward to where they stand beside the stage, smoothing out the stack of parchment in my hand before passing it to Shakespeare: my ideas on how to turn his play about shipwrecked twins into treason. The pages are only slightly less damp than my palms. It feels the way it did when I would show Marlowe my work, only worse. Where Marlowe was encouraging, I know Shakespeare won't be.

As his dark eyes rake over the pages, he frowns. I think of telling him it's only an outline, that it's just the first pass, that I've not written in a long while, that words were slow in coming. In the end I say nothing at all.

"Toby kept the basic premise, of course," Carey preempts. "It would be suspicious were he to change it altogether, and he assumed at least some of your players knew something of the story."

Shakespeare ignores him and keeps reading. "It takes place in Illyria? Why'd you change that? What's wrong with Grupela?"

"Illyria sounds a bit more romantic," I reply. "Besides, it's Italian."

"*It's Italian*," Shakespeare mimics. "I know it's Italian. Don't you think it's a bit heavy-handed? 'Attract Catholics by setting a play in Italy'? Why not just set it inside the Vatican and be done with it? The main character could murder the pope. That would bring them in droves."

"We can change the setting if you like," I say. I'd rather give on something I don't care about than something I do.

Shakespeare heaves a put-out sigh and continues scanning the pages.

"A boy called Valentine washes up on Illyria, losing his twin brother, Sebastian, whom he believes to be drowned—you kept the shipwrecked twins, I see. Valentine enters the service of a duke called Toby"—Shakespeare throws me a look—"who is in love with a countess called Seraphina, but she does not return his affections. Duke Toby sends his new servant, Valentine, to persuade Seraphina of this love, and in turn Seraphina falls in love with him." He rolls the parchment up. "So much love in this play. You told me the queen wanted laughs, not love." He directs this accusation at Carey.

"Her Majesty's request for this particular play was very specific," Carey says. "She said she wanted to see *him* fall in love." He jerks his chin at me.

Shakespeare tips his head back and laughs. "Oh, I bet she did. Tired of watching old Burbage swan around stage with a man-child young enough to be his grandson? Very well, now we have love. But I don't see anything in this play that would incite

Catholic fervor beyond it being set in Italy, and the characters being named after saints."

He taps the roll of parchment against his open palm, over and over, and begins walking in circles around the pit.

"What we need is misrule. It's the germination of Twelfth Night, is it not? A disturbance of the peace, the normal order of things reversed, all those on high become peasants and vice versa. Chaos is set in motion, only to be set at rights at the end. Just as the way of all great comedies."

"So, then, what makes misrule?" Carey prompts.

"Monkeys?" Shakespeare mutters. "Traitors? Players? Fucking *patrons*—"

"Servants," I cut in. "A countess would have plenty, would she not?"

"A steward, a maid, and a page, for starters," Shakespeare agrees. "This countess seems to be beautiful, as you already have two men falling in love with her, so for the sake of chaos let's add another suitor. A squire, perhaps. A drunken squire, a friend of the family."

"The squire can be introduced to Seraphina by her father," I offer.

"No, not her father." Shakespeare shakes his head. "You see, Seraphina is unable to love. She cannot love as she is in mourning, because her father is dead. While we're at it, let's kill her brother, too. Two dead relatives are always better than one."

"I thought you said this was to be a comedy," Carey says. Shakespeare ignores him.

"Seraphina, she suffers greatly because of all the death. She must do if she is to resist your persistent suit, *Duke Toby*."

Shakespeare stuffs the roll of parchment under his armpit and clambers onto the stage. He disappears behind the curtain, reappearing moments later carrying a pot of ink in one hand, more parchment in the other, and a pen clamped between his teeth. He drops back into the pit, thrusts it all into my hands, and continues.

"The drunken squire, he can be a friend of Seraphina's uncle. They all stay in her home, and despite her unrelenting grief, they *disturb the peace* of the household with their constant revelry— are you writing this down?—only to incite the anger of the uptight steward. We'll call him...Malvolio. He hates revelry, you see, and wears all black—just like a good Puritan should. He can be in love with Seraphina, too. *Seraphina.*" Shakespeare turns to me. "I cannot with this name. So obvious. So clunky."

"Yes, and Lavinia Andronicus just rolls off the tongue."

He swats me aside the head with my own play. "Are you mocking me, boy?"

Yes. "No."

"What else might you suggest?" he demands. "Let me guess. Perpetua? Febronia? Aquilina?"

Carey peers over his shoulder, as if the mere mention of Catholic saints is enough to cause an executioner to appear.

"Olivia?" I say. "The least clunky saint."

"Fine," Shakespeare says. "Olivia, then. The men all love her, it is all unrequited, *la-di-da*, but Olivia, the saucy wench, she falls in love with the servant! Ha! What's his name again? Valentino?"

"Valentine."

"I see." Shakespeare pauses. "For the sake of misrule, let's make Valentine a woman. She's survived the shipwreck, making her way alone in the world, in disguise as a man to ensure her safety. We'll call her Viola."

I say nothing to this, nor do I write it down. Shakespeare folds his arms and gives me an appraising look. "Larkspur, if you expect to write, you'd better prepare to have yourself overwritten, and learn to like it."

Without taking my eyes from his, I uncork the pot of ink, dip in the nib, and scratch out *Valentine* and replace it with *Viola*.

"It seems we have ourselves a play." Carey plucks the parchment off the stage, blowing on it gently to dry the ink before handing it back to Shakespeare. "At least an idea of one. How long do you need to finish it, Will? It will need to be soon, I think."

"Soon?" Shakespeare looks mutinous. "I have not yet finished my current play, the one that is to be performed in less than a month's time, and now you give me this? This life-or-death play, as you say, this disaster of words, and ask how long I need to finish it? What is 'soon' to you? A month?"

"I was thinking a week."

Shakespeare falls silent again.

"Unless, of course, we have Toby here finish it for you."

"You!" Shakespeare rounds on me, his ink-stained finger in my face. "You know that's fraud, don't you? My ideas, put to paper by another person—"

"To be fair, this incarnation of the story is Toby's idea," Carey interjects.

"Not originally, it wasn't!" Shakespeare shouts. "Ideas are the lifeblood of a story. They cannot be simply parceled out for another writer to translate. It is a denigration of the art. No decent writer, no decent *human*, would allow for that."

"Now, now," Carey soothes. "It won't be like that at all. Think of Toby merely as your assistant. He can start it, then once you finish your play about the forest, this will be waiting for you. You can change what you will, of course."

"Where am I to get these players?" Shakespeare changes tack. "This play calls for three women, which means I'll need three boys to play them. I don't have three boys. I did"—he flings a hand at Carey—"only they're gone now. I can't borrow from the Children of the Chapel—they've only got twelve as it is and they're contracted out to Jonson—"

"There's always the Children of Paul's," I suggest. Like the Children of the Chapel, the Children of Paul's is a troupe of choristers who play boys' or women's roles for theaters in London. There was some controversy that got them banned from the stage, but they've recently begun performing again. "They'll be looking for new roles for their players, won't they? I'm sure they'll be happy to assist however possible."

Shakespeare throws me a murderous look.

"Then it's settled." Carey turns from Shakespeare and starts toward the door. He walks swiftly, no doubt to leave before Shakespeare changes his mind. "I'll have the funds sent to you straightaway. Divvied up per usual, of course. One-third now, one-third when the play is complete, one-third when it's performed."

"I want it all now!" Shakespeare calls after us. "None of this parceling business. A man's got to make a—"

His final words are cut off as Carey shoves open the Globe's heavy door and we thread into the muddy street. It is dusk, deep blue skies divided by a pink-and-purple haze, ushering in nighttime and a new crowd, vastly different from the day. Merchants give way to pickpockets, washwomen to harlots, peddlers to pilferers. I keep an eye on them as we walk, but a closer eye on myself.

"That could have been better," Carey says as we make our way to the pier. "But it could also have been worse."

"The man is impossible," I say.

Carey chuckles, though not unkindly. "Now you know what I put up with, perhaps you'll have more sympathy. Writers are insecure, temperamental beings, aren't they? I daresay they're more difficult than queens."

Maybe, but at least writers keep their murders to the page.

Chapter 9

KIT

ELEPHANT INN, SOUTHWARK, LONDON
15 NOVEMBER 1601

So far, I like pretending to be a boy.

I had my regrets at first, especially after I cut my hair. It turned out to be a lot curlier than I remember, and though I meant for it to be shoulder-length like Jory's, the curl pulled the ends up all the way to my chin. Jory said this made me look like a monk—and he didn't mean it as a compliment—so I gave myself a little fringe which might have also been a mistake, as it does nothing but fall in my eyes and bounce across my face and generally go every which way except the direction I want it to.

But it's not all bad. For all that my hair looks absurd, it's done nice things for my face. My gray eyes, already wide, now look huge. My lips seem fuller somehow; my smile bigger and brighter. And the height I had as a girl, one I always saw as a disadvantage, suits me well now, too. I even bought myself some new clothes—new to me, at least: a pair of breeches, a few shirts, boots and a cloak, a hat and some gloves. I even cut up a strip of linen to wrap around my chest to flatten it. All in all, I think I make a very convincing boy. Catesby thinks so, too; when he saw me dressed this way for the first time, he said I looked like Father. And for the first time in nearly a month, I didn't cry to hear his name.

Speaking of names, I took on a different one: Christopher Alban. Christopher after my favorite poet, Christopher Marlowe; Alban after the Catholic saint, the first martyr of Britain, patron of converts, refugees, and torture victims. It's fitting. Catesby suggested I go by Kit for short, to differentiate me from the other Christopher in his house, Chris Wright.

Kit Alban it is.

But the best part of dressing as a boy is all the places I can go. Nowhere is off limits to me in breeches. I spent the first few days wandering the city, learning it as Catesby ordered, seeing things I have never seen before. Men pissing in the streets, women selling their bodies for money, children begging for food. I have seen people arrested and flogged; I have seen heads set upon pikes at London Bridge, crows roosting in their hair and pecking out their eyes. Then I got a little braver and ventured into an inn one day, a tavern the next, a gambling den the day after that.

Living life as a boy is to have a veil removed from my eyes I wasn't aware existed. It's to see, hear, and know things I only imagined; it's to know all those imaginings were wrong. The way men hack and belch and make other terrible noises when a woman isn't around to stop them. The things they say about women in their absence, about their faces and bodies and hair; the things women say but men think they don't mean, the things women do—or more often don't. It's almost enough to turn me off men forever and shut myself away in a convent, if only I were as pious as Jory.

Catesby and his men are pleased with my progress. They're gossipy as maids, no detail too small or insignificant to them. They want to know everywhere I go, everything I see: who said what to whom and when. And it all changes, depending on what part of town I frequent. Around St. Paul's Cathedral, where the print shops are, booksellers complain about limited distribution and the review process determining what is fit to be printed. Closer to the Parliament buildings I hear grumblings about the members of the House of Commons and the Lords, how long until Parliament would be summoned, and whether the queen would refuse to sign their bills. Every now and then a provocative pamphlet will come my way, something much talked about everywhere and by everyone. Sometimes it's about taxes. Other times it's about the war with Ireland. But most frequently it's about the queen's policy against Catholics, the recusancy laws, and the execution of priests.

The latest pamphlet, one I picked up just two days ago, is a little more pointed. It's a series of drawings that depict the queen on a boat in the middle of the ocean, sailing toward the New World. She is blindfolded and smiling, as if awaiting a great surprise. What she doesn't see is the pope, on shore back in England, standing with the statue of the long-dead Catholic Queen Mary

Tudor on one side, a priest on the other. Mary wears the queen's crown; the pope carries a scepter. They're all laughing. It pleased Catesby and his men, and told me what they and Father already knew: There is an undercurrent of anger against the queen, there are others like us who disagree with her laws. It helps me to feel not so isolated, to know we aren't the only ones.

Tonight there are no whispers of the queen, or of pamphlets or Parliament or wars; just ale and dice and conversation among men. It's my third night back at the Elephant Inn in Southwark, and even though this leaves me not much to report to Catesby, it is valuable in other ways. If I'm going to learn how to act like a proper boy, I need someone to teach me, and I'm rapidly learning it won't be Jory.

I'm a good dice player, excellent even. I learned it from the stableboys at Lanherne, and I even used to win money from them, though Father always made me give it back. I've been here for a few hours, at a table with three other boys playing a game called Hazard. I'm ten pennies up, half an ale in, and it's only going on seven in the evening.

"Chance," the boy beside me says. I've just rolled a five, the main is eight, which means I neither win nor lose but get to roll again. "Bet in?" He wants to know if I'll put in more money on the chance I throw the main in my roll.

I don't answer, just reach into the pile of pence on the table before me and throw in three. I'm learning more and more that boys talk by doing, not saying. I roll again and by sheer luck—which is nearly all this game is, luck—I roll an eight and win the pot. The three others at my table groan at the loss. Inside,

I'm shrieking with glee because I've just won nigh on an angel, which will keep me in food and lodging for another three weeks. Because I'm also learning that boys do not show this type of emotion, I simply rake the coins into the same drawstring bag Catesby gave me and shove it in my pocket.

The bell at the door rings then, as it has done over and over as people come and go. But this time, a hush falls over the crowd and that, if nothing else, gets my attention. I look up from my winnings to see a group of ten-odd men and boys enter the tavern. They move to a large table beside ours, one that's already occupied by a dozen men playing cards. The moment they see the newcomers they leap up, careless of the game, shaking hands and slapping shoulders before relocating to a new table.

"Who are they?" I ask the boy sitting beside me.

"They're players. From the Globe. The theater," he clarifies. "See the tall one? With the beard?" They're all tall with beards. "That's Richard Burbage. He's tops, you know. In all the plays. That one there, the ginger, that's Will Kemp; he plays the funny roles, clowns and fools and the like. And the one beside him with the dark hair? That's William Shakespeare."

The names *Burbage* and *Kemp* mean nothing to me, but *Shakespeare* certainly does. When Father would go to London, he would bring home poems from Christopher Marlowe and plays from Shakespeare, fresh from the stationer with the ink practically still drying. *Titus Andronicus*, "Hero and Leander," *Love's Labour's Lost*, *The Jew of Malta*—I loved them all and daydreamed about the men who wrote them, how dashing and romantic they must be. Now, in a twist of fate that would not be out of place in one of Shakespeare's own plays, he is sitting not five feet away from me. He does not look dashing or romantic at all. He is sloppy and strange, boots untied and shirt unlaced and hands and face covered in ink.

Shakespeare and his men settle into the now-vacant chairs. They don't even need to order—not the way I've learned to do by rapping on the table and holding a finger in the air, one for ale, two for something stronger—the man behind the bar has their drinks on the table before they've finished pulling off their cloaks. Immediately they begin drinking and talking and laughing, all of them loud and animated as if they know everyone is watching them and they want to give them a good show, even off the stage.

I start to turn away from them and back to my game, but then I see him. A dark-haired boy, shabbily dressed, sitting at one end of the table. He holds a tankard like everyone else, nodding or smiling in response to things that are said to him. Even as he does, I can tell he's not really paying attention, at least not to them. I can tell by the way his eyes move from one thing to another, slowly and deliberately as if taking inventory. One bearded man, check. Second bearded man, check. One mahogany bar, forty drunken patrons, two racks of antlers on one green-painted wall. Check, check, check.

His eyes land on me. I wait for them to move past—one ordinary boy, check—but they don't. Maybe it's because I'm the only one in the tavern also not minding their own business, maybe it's because my hair is mad and looks as if it's been attacked by hedge pruners. Either way I feel a momentary thrill at his attention, until I remember I'm dressed as a boy. *Then* I think he's somehow been able to see through my disguise, and then I start to panic. So I do the most boyish thing I can think of and raise my drink to him, as if I'm toasting him from afar. It's another small freedom allowed to me dressed as a boy; as a girl, I could never be so forward.

The boy doesn't lift his tankard in reply, he only looks away. But not before I see the smallest of smiles flit across his face. This doesn't exactly resolve my worry, but at least his attention is off me and onto someone else. Namely the ginger, the one called Kemp, who is talking loud enough to be heard throughout the entire room.

"How are we meant to get players on such short notice?" He addresses his question to Shakespeare, who tips lazily back in his chair as he drinks from his cup.

"There is no lack of players in London," Shakespeare replies. "I could put a notice out tomorrow and have them lined up outside the Globe."

"Ordinary players, yes," the one called Burbage says. "But you can't mean to put ordinary players before the queen."

With that word, I all but abandon my game of dice.

"Their ordinariness will only make you shine all the more," Shakespeare intones, to which Burbage puffs out his chest. "And do keep it down, won't you? It's meant to be a secret."

I strain to hear every word that follows, above the noise and the chatter of the players, who begin talking all at once.

"Why is it a secret, again?"

"All the queen's performances are meant to be secret. They're more exclusive that way—"

"Which palace is it to be held in? I hope not Greenwich. The acoustics there are appalling—"

"She'll be front row. We won't need to worry about acoustics—"

"*Shh*," Shakespeare repeats.

The boy next to me elbows me; it's my turn to place a bet. I throw a penny into the pile, then look back to Shakespeare's table, not wanting to miss a word.

"It's about Twelfth Night and it's to be performed on Twelfth Night?" Burbage says. "That's a bit blasphemous in this current climate, is it not? Why the change from Yuletide?"

"Because I am an *artist*," Shakespeare says. "I am meant to push *boundaries*."

"But isn't Twelfth Night rather…heretical?"

"I wouldn't go that far," someone else says. "Else she'd not allow the Twelfth Night revelries—"

"*Shh*," Shakespeare says once more.

I wait until the players begin talking about something else before I excuse myself from the table and walk out the door. Straight to North House, and to Catesby.

"A private play before the queen." Catesby paces before the fire in his library. I sit in a chair next to the window. We're alone, the first time I've been in his house without Jory, his maid, or his other men hovering about. "You're sure about this?"

I nod. "It's about Twelfth Night. To be performed then, too.

That's what one of the players said. And then another player called it heretical."

Catesby gives me a sharp look. "Did you hear where it's to be performed?"

"No," I reply. "They started talking about acoustics, how they wouldn't be ideal but that the queen would be sitting so close to the stage it wouldn't matter. They were also worried about getting players. Apparently there aren't enough to fill all the roles, and they're having to open up auditions."

Catesby turns from me back to the fire. He's silent for so long that I think maybe he's forgotten I'm there, or has gone on to think about other things. But I haven't.

"I want to audition for it," I say. "I want to land a role and perform for the queen. I want to stand before her and look her in the eye. And then I want to kill her."

Catesby whirls around and for a moment, he just stares at me. I expect him to tell me it's too dangerous, that I'm a girl, that I can't do it. Instead he says, "What do you know of the theater?"

"Enough," I reply. "I've read Shakespeare and Jonson, Lyly and Nashe, Peele and Chapman and Heywood and Marlowe. I know every story, every character, every plot. My elocution is excellent, and there's not a line in any one of those plays I couldn't recite." It's not often I get to boast about my education, which is as good as any boy's and I know it. "I can sing, too, and I'm good before an audience. I performed at church every week."

"I don't like it." He holds up a hand to stall my argument. "Not for the reason you think. We just went through this with

Essex not even a year ago, his using one of Shakespeare's plays to incite rebellion and failing. It was disastrous for all of us."

Catesby didn't tell me about the Essex rebellion, but tavern gossip did and he doesn't have to elaborate.

"But we aren't trying to incite a rebellion," I say. "We're trying to get rid of the queen. Once and for all." Catesby narrows his eyes at this, but he doesn't interrupt. "She killed my father. Even if I'd never shown up on your doorstep, that would still be true. I would still want revenge for what she's done. The way I see it, I'm giving you two chances to achieve your end. Because if I fail, you'll still have your plot and your innocence intact."

There's a long, drawn-out pause. I can almost see the struggle going on behind his eyes, measuring risk against reward and opportunity against responsibility. He barely knows me, but he did know my father and maybe he feels he owes it to him to keep me from harm.

Eventually, opportunity wins out. "If they catch you, or if you're otherwise found out, they'll kill you. Do you understand that? And we won't be able to save you."

I think he means to scare me with this, but it doesn't. Because the worst thing that could happen to me already has and there's nothing left to be afraid of.

"I know," I say. "But for now, all I want is to audition for a play."

Chapter 10

TOBY

GLOBE THEATER, BANKSIDE, LONDON
23 NOVEMBER 1601

My play—now formally titled *Twelfth Night*—has been written. We've got the plot, which after much hair rending and parchment tearing and Shakespeare's cursing me into the ground for my pedestrian plotting and ponderous prose and mundane milieu and endless, endless rewrites, now resembles a story.

It has all the things of the Feast of Epiphany: There is revelry, there are servants dressing up as their masters, there are mistaken identities. There is a reversal of social order, there are characters who act as Lords of Misrule, there is a character who opposes it. It's all tremendously fanciful, and as for the matter of using this play to provoke Catholic plotters, well. Title aside, it's less straightforward than I might have liked, but Shakespeare and Carey argued that if it were too sincere we would risk exposure, both to plotters and players, who would surely revolt if they believed themselves to be part of yet another political plot.

The play is also cast, at least partially. We have the usual players: Richard Burbage, Will Kemp, Nick Tooley, Tom Pope, Will Sly. These are Shakespeare's men, his mainstays for every production, the ones he flatly refused to do without. The part I was to play has been changed, too; Duke Toby now recast as Duke Orsino, Shakespeare arguing that Toby is not a proper name for a duke. It is, apparently, the proper name for a drunken squire, now called Sir Toby.

We make up six of eleven principal roles, so the remaining five must still be cast, as well as all the players' alternates, men who will step into the roles if the need arises. Then there are the stagehands and the musicians, who seem to change as rapidly as the queen's favor. This leaves sixteen new players and twenty hired hands: thirty-six chances for the queen's assassin to come forth and audition.

I made sure they would.

I drew up anti-Catholic pamphlets, had them printed and distributed throughout the city to incite anger against the queen. I wrote anonymous letters denouncing the incarceration and torture of yet another priest, captured in a raid last month in Cornwall, circulating them into the very Catholic network I've been watching. Then there were Shakespeare's men. They were romanced by the idea of performing before the queen again, and their nightly forays into taverns gave them a new chance to brag, to whisper every last detail in hushed tones heard by everyone.

For all that, I still wasn't sure it would work. I began to wonder if the queen was right, if the Catholics were not to be baited with a celebration of their faith. I worried I'd wasted Carey's time, Shakespeare's time, my time. That while I was busy with my machinations, the plotters would be closer to enacting their plan, eluding mine altogether.

I worried my plan wouldn't work until I received news that it did. An encoded letter, captured in the same Catholic network as the first. It read simply:

twelfth night

And so begins the difficult part: finding the assassin. It's safe to assume that the eight noblemen, the men referenced in the letter I intercepted, won't be the ones to attempt the assassination. They're too recognizable and have too much to lose— family, money, titles, their *lives*—by doing it themselves. They will have hired someone to do it, and whoever that person is, when I catch him, will lead me right to them.

Shakespeare was right when he said potential players would be lined up around the Globe to audition. For the past week I've watched what seems like every man and boy in every borough in London step out from behind the curtain and take his place onstage. Today I've got thirty-two boys reading for the three women's roles. I have already been here for three hours, watching each one as they read their lines, pages damp and trembling in their hands.

There's a creak and a yawn of wood, and I turn to find Carey sliding onto the bench beside me. He's here because he says he likes to see how I'm coming on, because it's the last day of auditions and he wants my final list. But I also know it's more than that. He's watching those onstage every bit as closely as I am. I expect it: The central tenet of good spy craft is to never let anyone or anything go unwatched.

We sit in silence as boy number seventeen chokes his way through his lines. I watch every expression, every gesture, listen to every inflection and every word. I watch for performances too bad to be believed, for delivery that is too practiced, nerves that are too jangled, nerves that are not jangled enough. For those who regard the stage and the surroundings as if it's everything they've been told it would be.

I watch for players who are playing as players.

I take copious notes in a fat, leather-bound book, my fingers stained with ink, as black as Shakespeare's own. There is the usual: name, description, height, prior experience, what lines from what source material they choose to read. This information is concrete, easy to put into words. What is not always easy is the abstract. The facial tic or stutter; shifting feet or ramrod posture. Lines that are too emphatically pronounced, too mumbled. How desperate they seem to get the role because desperation, at least in my experience, usually precedes guilt.

Although I am the one running this audition from the shadows above, it is Shakespeare who directs it from the pit below. Each boy states their age as they climb onstage. They range between thirteen and seventeen, but they all look the same to me: thin, tousled hair, tremulous voices, and wide, searching eyes. They don't read from *Twelfth Night*, as Shakespeare doesn't want literary thieves or artistic ruffians—his words—hearing his work (my work) and stealing it for their own. Instead they read from his other, well-known plays. *A Midsummer Night's Dream* appears to be a favorite.

"Thus I die. Thus, thus, thus. Now I am dead, now I fly—"

"'Am fled,'" Shakespeare corrects. His tone is boredom. "Rhymes with *dead*."

The boy, so pimpled I can count them from here, tries again.

"My soul is in the sky. Tongue lose thy light, light, light—"

"Just one *light*," Shakespeare corrects.

"Moon take thy flight. Now die, die, die, die, die, die, die—"

"The line calls for five *dies*," Shakespeare calls. "Not seven. I think the moon is well and truly dead by now."

"Good god," Carey whispers. "Are they all like this?"

"Overall, no," I reply. "Today, yes."

Carey watches as I scratch the boy's name off the ledger, another of the many men and boys I've dismissed—and in truth this makes up most of them—before turning back to the stage. The pimpled boy is gone and in his place, yet another. Tall, insect thin, shabby clothes. Ginger hair that looks like it's been caught in a thicket of brambles; eyes like a doe, so large they're almost comical. He holds himself very still, hands clasped behind his back, as if he's willing himself not to run away. I feel a jolt of recognition—I've seen this boy before, I'm sure of it. But I can't place where.

"Name?" Shakespeare intones.

"Christopher," the boy replies. "Alban. You can call me Kit."

"Age?"

"Sixteen. Seventeen," he corrects himself quickly.

"Well, which is it? Sixteen or seventeen?"

"I turned seventeen last month," the boy replies.

"Which means you're probably eighteen," Shakespeare says. He said the boys would all lie about their age, the older boys wanting to seem younger to increase their chances of landing a role. "Stage experience?"

"None as such, sir," the boy says. "Although I sing at church every Sunday and I'm quite good. You may be thinking I'm not much to look at, but I assure you, my voice is a siren."

Several players in the yard titter at this, and I find myself smiling. It's not true: He's pretty and I can tell he knows it.

"Let's hope not," Shakespeare notes wryly. "What will you be reciting? *Merry Wives of Windsor* or *A Midsummer Night's Dream*?"

"With all due respect, Master Shakespeare, neither. I'd like to recite from Christopher Marlowe. 'Hero and Leander,' if it pleases you."

I feel Carey's eyes on me. I keep my eyes on the boy.

"If it pleases me, ha! Kit Alban reciting Kit Marlowe. Very well, then. Let's hear it."

The boy looks to the boards. I can see his chest rising and falling, quick and uneven, nervous as all the rest. But when he lifts his head up, his eyes find the stands in the gallery as if he imagines an audience there, as if he's speaking to them, as if the rest of us, watching and whispering and judging in the yard, don't exist.

"It lies not in our power to love or hate,
For will in us is overruled by fate.
When two are stripped, long ere the
    course begin."

His voice is different from the others, not high-pitched or uneven but mellow and smooth, with a lilt to it that tells me he's from the West Country, Devon or Dorset maybe. There's a characteristic hardness to the consonants he's trying hard to round out but that still linger, particularly his *R*s. Even so, he called his voice a siren and he's not wrong; it's the kind of voice that makes you want to close your eyes.

"We wish that one should lose, the other
    win.
Where both deliberate, the love is slight;
Who ever loved that loved not at first
    sight?"

I find I'm sitting forward in my seat, no longer hearing this Kit's voice but Marlowe's. I remember when he wrote this poem. I was twelve, the playhouses had been closed because of plague, and he'd turned to poems. There was someone who turned his heart inside out; I knew this by his distance and by his absence, by the way he never finished this poem, as if he didn't know the end of it himself. After he died, someone else finished it for him—not me—and when it was printed a few years later it was not by me, either; I couldn't stand seeing words attributed to Marlowe that were not his own. Yet now I've done the same myself, attributing Shakespeare's name to my words, and I start to understand his anger toward me. If something so pure as one's own ideas are degraded, what else is there?

The theater is silent when the boy finishes, then a smattering of clapping among the rest of the would-be players still lined up in the yard.

Shakespeare glances my way and I give him a nod. "I think you'll do nicely," he says. "With that face, you'll make a perfect Viola."

The boy, Kit Alban, looks momentarily dazed, a blank expression falling over his face instead of a smile or a laugh or even a blush, all of which I might have expected. Finally, he backs offstage, pushing through the curtain and disappearing into the tiring-house. I put a tick mark by his name.

"Why him?" Carey asks. I'd almost forgotten he was there, my thoughts still on the boy.

"He fumbled his age," I reply. "Eleven others did that and I chose them, too. Their age may not be the only thing they're lying about. He's poor—did you see his clothes?—yet articulate. The two generally don't go hand in hand and again, it points to a lie. I've got seven more on my list with the same discrepancy. Lastly, he's good. Too good not to have experience somewhere, which he claims he doesn't. That may or may not be true. He's one of a dozen I've flagged for that as well."

I confirm the names of players, musicians, and stagehands on my list, then pull out a fresh page from my book and copy them down before handing it off to Carey.

He skims the page, eyes bright with curiosity. "So this is them."

I nod. "If there's a man using this play as a means to murder the queen, he's here."

"You're sure of it," Carey says with satisfaction.

I am.

"I'll start watching them tonight." I stand up, crick my neck from side to side, stiff from a day of sitting. With this many people to watch, it'll be a long few days, more of them stretched out before me. There won't be much rest in any of them, and I'm feeling it already. "I'll have a more focused list for you by the end of next week. We can present it to the queen then."

Chapter 11

KIT

THE GLOBE THEATER, BANKSIDE, LONDON
30 NOVEMBER 1601

Despite Catesby's initial reluctance to the idea of using Shakespeare's play as a means for me to murder the queen, he came around quick enough. Mainly because both of his proposed ideas on how it should be done—an arrow shot bankside as she sailed along the Thames in her barge, or a pistol fired as she rode through the countryside on a hunt—left too much to chance. The arrow could miss its mark; the pistol could misfire. Neither Catesby nor his men have the ability to shoot at a distance with that kind of accuracy so they'd have to hire someone to do it for them, one who could turn traitor or coward. For me to stand onstage, dagger in hand, with only a few feet between me and the queen, will make it a lot harder to miss. Since I'm already a traitor—and certainly no coward—there were more reasons for them to say yes than to say no.

The rest of Catesby's men were enthusiastic about the idea. Once I landed the role, the Wright brothers, Chris and John, were sent in to apply as stagehands. Catesby reasoned I'd be so occupied with learning my lines that I'd need someone to sort the details and logistics of when and how the job—Catesby's words—would be done.

Of Catesby's men, Chris and John—aged thirty-one and thirty-three, respectively—were the best choice, the others being too old or too recognizable to take on such a disguise. The Wrights are clever, too; Catesby says they're always inventing little contraptions, and he showed me one they gifted him, a tiny gold compass set into a ring. It was easy enough for them to figure out the workings of stage props to bluff their way through an interview with the Globe's lead stagehand. They showed him a firecracker they'd made with gunpowder stuffed inside a roll of paper; they made black, white, and red smoke by mixing alcohol with different kinds of salt; they threw bits of resin into a candle flame to simulate lightning. Chris said they had everyone in the theater watching them, and by the time they were through, the jobs were theirs.

At any rate, here I am, at the Globe. It is no less grand the second time as it was the first, on the day of my audition. Today is clear and blue but cold, the wind whistling through the tunneled alleys and whipping the gray waters of the Thames into little white-capped waves. A day like this would be remarkable in Cornwall, as nearly every day past October is filled with nothing but weeping skies and sodden clouds. Maybe it is here, too, as it seems nearly every person in London is out in it, clustered in markets and streets and bridges. The walk to the theater took me well over an hour when it should have taken twenty minutes, and now I am late on my very first day.

As I approach the door of the Globe, I can hear the voices within, loud as if a performance were already in progress. The nerves I felt at my audition resurface. I stand for a moment, my hand on the brass ring in the center of the door, and give myself a little encouragement.

I am a boy, I tell myself. *I am a player, and I am here to play a part. I am not a girl, and I am not here for revenge. I am not here as part of a plot to kill anyone.*

This does no good, of course, because telling myself the things I shouldn't be thinking makes me think them all the more. My thoughts begin to career in the manner of overexcited dogs, like the hounds Father used to take with him hunting, yipping and snarling and completely out of control.

Finally, I pull the door open, a creak and a whine echoing down the narrow hall that leads to the theater. I step slowly, passing the staircases that lead to the upper galleries, and into the pit. It is as busy as market day in Truro here. There are two men onstage, each holding a crumpled piece of parchment. They call out their lines, measure their steps, speaking words so clear and loud they can be heard all the way to the rafters. In the pit a dozen men cluster together in whatever scene they're rehearsing, murmuring instead of projecting so as not to disturb those onstage. A group of musicians sits in the balcony, fingering lutes and citterns and softly blowing flutes and pipes, ambient sounds, though every now and then a cymbal or a bell is struck and quickly silenced.

In the middle of it all is Master Shakespeare, looking as frazzled as he did the day of my audition. His shirt is untucked, face at least three days unshaven, a nest of black hair pointing in all directions. He stands in the pit, his elbows resting on the edge of the stage as he listens to the scene in progress. He holds a quill in one hand, furiously writing on the parchment before him.

I start toward the stage, keeping to the shadows as much as I can. My heart is a cornered Cornish jackrabbit; sweat begins to collect between my breasts and trickle through the binding. As I grow closer, I can hear more clearly the scene and the lines being spoken. They are between a boy who, with his spotted face and breaking voice, can't be more than thirteen and the ginger-haired man called Kemp I remember from the Elephant.

The boy is speaking, and his lines are as butchered as a spring lamb and without half the grace. I wince at the way he runs the words together, as if he's speaking them without considering their meaning. Master Shakespeare apparently thinks the same and holds up a hand to stop him.

"You. Viola." He points to the boy. *Viola!* That is my part and my scene he's rehearsing and for a moment I panic—I'm late but not *that* late, surely Master Shakespeare hasn't replaced me already?—until I realize the boy is my understudy and not nearly good enough to take my place, so I relax a little. "What's your name again?"

"Wash."

"Wash?" Master Shakespeare blinks and shakes his head, presumably for the same reason I do, that this boy's name is less a name than undoubtedly his mother's profession. "Try to remember, Wash, that you're playing a woman, and you want your voice to be high. Let's hear it again, but this time in falsetto."

The boy nods and tries again. *"By my troth, I'll tell thee, I am almost sick for one; though I would not have it grow on my chin. Is thy lady within?"*

Master Shakespeare groans. "No, no, *no*. You've got to give it some cheek, Wash. Remember that Viola is a girl dressed as a boy. *You* are a boy dressed as a girl dressed as a boy. The clown has jested that you would have a beard, but as you are not capable of growing a beard, that is the actual jest. Do you see?"

"Yes, sir."

"Do you truly, or are you just saying that to please me?"

"Yes, sir."

"Gods!" There is the waving of the quill and of the parchment, there is ink in the air and there is rending of hair. Bless Master Shakespeare for his words, but he is as dramatic as a woman in labor, it must be said. "Break, would you? Break before I pitch myself into the drink. Or begin to drink, either will suffice. Mistress Lovett!"

A dark-skinned woman in a muslin dress steps forward from behind the curtain, her mouth full of pins. She spits them into her palm. "Here, sir."

"Fit this . . . *Wash* for a dress, will you? Maybe if he looked like a girl it would help him remember to act like one."

Mistress Lovett snatches Wash's arm, dragging him behind the curtain. Kemp leaps offstage and into the pit to join the others. They laugh and slap him on the back and congratulate him for doing approximately nothing. I use this opportunity to step forward and present myself.

"Master Shakespeare. My apologies for being late." In my nerves and haste, I forget to bow like a boy but instead curtsy like a girl, like an *idiot*, and the trickle of sweat beneath my binding becomes a flood. But Master Shakespeare seems to delight in it, clapping a hand to his chest and tipping his head back and letting out a throaty laugh.

"Ha! If it isn't Viola. The *real* Viola. Thank the gods you've arrived. The *gods*." He plants himself before me, looking me up and down, stroking his sandpaper beard.

"Not even in costume and already playing the part," he continues. "A boy as a girl, through and through. Did you spot your understudy's trouble in that last scene? How would you have delivered it? Tell me."

I feel a little thrill at this, at one of the greatest playwrights in London wanting to know how I—a nobody—would deliver one of his lines. I almost demure—had I been Katherine in a corset I might have—but my breeches give me a courage she never had. I step back a little, to give myself room and to give him a better look at me.

"*By my troth, I'll tell thee, I am almost sick for one.*" Then I turn from him, as if addressing the audience in an exaggerated stage whisper, "*though I would not have it grow on my chin.*" Without breaking, I turn back to him and finish the line. "*Is thy lady within?*"

Master Shakespeare grins at me, maniacal. "That's it. That. Is. *It*. And that voice. Dulcet! Euphonic! Mell-i-flu-*ous*. I knew the moment you stepped onstage you would be perfect, and here you are. Perfect." I am flush with his praise; it warms me like a summer's day. I smile so hard my cheeks hurt.

"Do you know your lines?" Shakespeare claps his free hand to my shoulder. "I want to hear more. I want to hear them all."

"This is my first rehearsal, sir," I say. "I don't have them as yet."

He turns from me and leaps onstage, waving me up after him. There must be a graceful way to climb onto that four-foot platform, but the way I do it—one hand, then the other, followed by one knee, then the other—is not it.

"Mistress Lovett!" Master Shakespeare bellows. "Bring me the boy." There's a great thump backstage, followed by a high-pitched squeal, then a cross-looking Mistress Lovett pokes her head through the curtain. Shakespeare motions her over with an impatient wave and she obliges, trailing Wash behind her. He's wearing a green dress fitted together with pins.

"Your lines, Wash. Do you have them?"

The boy thinks on this a moment, then plunges his hand into the bodice of his dress, reappearing with what looks to be a sweaty wad of parchment. He passes it to Shakespeare, who receives it as if Wash were handing him an internal organ. Shakespeare motions them both away with the same impatient hand and proceeds to untangle the paper, which turns out to be individual scraps of parchment. On them are words that will take me approximately five years to decipher. They look as if they were written by a child in the dark on the back of a moving horse.

"Your lines." He hands them to me. I suppose the surprise of this shows on my face because he says, "I have only one copy of the play. It would be a judicious waste of my time to copy it in full, thirty times over, for each player to have one. I certainly cannot trust others to do it. Have you heard of literary thieves,

Viola? They exist, and they are *out there*. There is an outline posted in the tiring-house."

I nod in response, but he doesn't see it. He's already turned away from me, squinting into the rows of seats that surround the stage. They're all empty, I already looked, but I am beginning to imagine that one can never be sure what Shakespeare sees that the rest of us don't.

"Orsino!" Again with the bellowing. "Where are you? Orsino!" Shakespeare spins on his heel, still looking. I presume Orsino is another character in the play, as Shakespeare seems to prefer calling us by their names.

Above us, in the second row of the gallery, there's a shift in the shadow, the only place in the bright theater not illuminated by the midday sun. I follow the movement as it disappears, then moments later reappears from the mouth of the hall leading into the pit. It's one of the players. He makes his way toward us, his pace unhurried, Shakespeare's snapping fingers having no effect on him.

I've seen this boy before, first at the Elephant and then on the day I auditioned. He sat in the gallery then, too, high at the top as if he thought himself invisible, as if he thought he was the only one who knew something about hiding. What he doesn't know is that I watched him as he watched me, how he leaned over the wooden railing as I began to recite Marlowe's poem, the way he pulled up a notebook and rested it on the edge of the railing and began to scribble in it. The way he closed it and sat back on the bench, fading into darkness. If I hadn't known him to be a player, this behavior might worry me: I've been in hiding for far too long to feel comfortable with that kind of stealth and scrutiny. But before I got too worried, I remembered how those men tripped all over themselves to impress Master Shakespeare and I figured this boy is no different. He's simply sussing out his competition, making sure I don't replace him in Shakespeare's favor.

He takes a graceful leap onto the stage and comes to stand beside me, and I finally see what he looks like in the light. He is not tall, in fact not much taller than me. He is made of shadows and sharp things, dark hair and dark brows and cut-glass cheekbones. Even his eyes are hard, a shade of ice I've only ever seen on an irritating goat we once had named Tin—which sounds sweet unless you know the Cornish word for *arse*, which is also pronounced "tin." He doesn't look like a player, someone who lives out other people's words. He looks like he lives out his own and none of them pleasant; the kind of person I would run from if I ever met him alone after dark on one of London's many look-alike streets.

"Viola-Cesario, meet Duke Orsino," says Shakespeare. "Orsino, meet Viola-Cesario."

If the boy recognizes me, I can't tell; he just looks me over with his goat eyes and gives me the same barely-there smile he gave me at the tavern. What seemed friendlier in the haze of drinks and dice now seems dismissive, as if he fancies himself too good a player to trouble himself with an upstart like me. I return the barely-there smile, making sure to add a head-to-toe once-over, as if I, too, am taking in what I see and am not impressed. It's not the best way to start off my first day, but I am not here to make friends, not when I have a *job to do*.

Nonetheless, Shakespeare delights in this wordless exchange and lets out another throaty *ha ha ha*. "Very good! Antagonists already. This will come in handy, Viola-Cesario, when Orsino accuses you of marrying Olivia, then kills you in the final act of the play. I can scarcely wait. It's going to be simply *looplab*. Orsino! You know your lines, boy?"

While *boy* seems an inaccurate sobriquet—I don't know if this Orsino was ever a boy; he was probably born a surly nineteen- or twenty-year-old—he nods, once and sharp.

"Let's begin where we left off, in act one, scene four. Viola, those lines will be toward the bottom of your pile—not there, they're not in order so you'll have to sort through them—it's Viola's first day on the job with Orsino, dressed as a boy and disguised as the servant Cesario. Have you got them?"

My fingers fumble through the parchment as I look for the numbers scrawled in the corners, finally landing on the ones that read *1.4.14*, *1.4.15*, *1.4.41*. The lines make no sense out of context, as I don't know what comes before them or after them. But as with everything else, I'll just have to figure it out. I shuffle them in order, quickly commit them to memory, then look to Shakespeare and nod once, sharp. Two can play at this game.

Orsino steps away from us, taking his spot at the front of the stage. He glances around it as if he doesn't see me, and speaks his line. *"Who saw Cesario, ho?"*

I think of Viola, how she is not a servant but merely acting as one, who needs this position in order to further her own, and who wishes to keep it. Shakespeare said it was her first day on the job, so I think she would be nervous and wanting to please. I imagine her mind would be somewhat like my own at this moment, so it is not difficult to think of how to react.

I scurry toward Orsino, subservient yet enthusiastic, full of smiles. *"On your attendance, my lord, here."*

Chapter 12

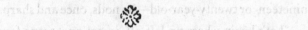

TOBY

THE GLOBE THEATER, BANKSIDE, LONDON
6 DECEMBER 1601

The first week of rehearsal is a disaster.

There is no way it wouldn't be, not with a barrage of new men upsetting the micro-universe that is the Globe, with its own order and its own way of functioning. Burbage and his men, professional players with years of experience onstage, have made no secret of their distaste for the newcomers. They say they were poorly chosen, there were better players who were turned away, their inexperience is hampering the play, that it takes away from their performance. This is all true, of course. Shakespeare bears the brunt of these complaints and manages it as well as he can, which is to say not well at all.

He paces onstage during the new players' scenes, changing lines on them sometimes midsentence, scribbling indecipherable prose on a scrap of parchment and thrusting it their way with ink-stained fingers, shouting if they drop it or, God forbid, can't read what he's written. Burbage and his men offer no help, either; they stand off to the side smirking, rolling their eyes, coughing insults into closed fists: children playing at being grown men.

All this chaos makes my job harder, too. First there is my play, which is being rewritten so rapidly it's becoming increasingly difficult to stay on top of my lines. It takes my attention away from what it should be on, which are my suspects. The five new principals—three boys and two men—are so frightened by Burbage and his camp that they have yet to do anything other than behave deferentially, standing alone and quiet backstage until they are called for. The eleven alternates and twenty stage-hands are even worse: They fade so completely into the background that to seek them out would call undue attention to me.

And so, after one week of observance and inquiries into their backgrounds which are slow in arriving, I have very little on anyone, only what I picked up at the audition. I should have more, enough to whittle down my list of thirty-six suspects to those I can focus my attention on. As it stands now, no one is more suspicious than any other, so I am in the unenviable position of having to watch them all. All I see is that they're uncomfortable. An uncomfortable suspect is a careful one, less likely to make mistakes or to begin to establish regular patterns that, at least if those suspects are not who they say they are, invariably get broken.

It is coming up on three o'clock, the end of the rehearsal day, the long shadows of the short afternoon crawling through the open roof and turning the stage cold and dark, when Shake-speare finally calls for us to quit. I am in the tiring-house along with the other players as they throw on cloaks and scarves and hats, readying to leave. We aren't rehearsing in costume yet—that comes later—but Shakespeare likes us to be nimble onstage and says outerwear is a *ruination of dexterity* even though it's winter and we're all stiff with cold regardless.

I decide now is as good a time as any to try to strike up a friendship with one of my suspects. The better I know someone, the easier it is for me to tell if they're lying.

I take in my options. First there's Thomas Alard, the boy cast in the role of Olivia. He's blond, blue-eyed, and tall, with knobby limbs and an Adam's apple that bobs when he talks. He is quiet—they are all quiet right now—but I recall his audition, with his high falsetto and the dress he wore, even though it was not required. I also recall the way he said his age was eighteen but that his beard read twenty, the way his eyes darted through the gallery at his competition. The way his breeches are too short and his doublet too tight but that he wears new shoes made of leather, shined and mud-free. Too many contradictions always point to lies.

There is also Aaron Barton, who was cast as Maria. Short, stocky, seventeen—this is the age he claims and I believe him. He's freckled and ginger, with a diluted Scottish accent that still drops the Gs. He came from the Children of the Chapel, the boys' choir. He started there three years ago but left after a year, only to return last winter, coincidentally (or not) right after Essex's execution. The master at the Children of the Chapel told Shakespeare that Barton didn't give him a reason for why he left, nor did he tell him where he'd been or why he came back. These kinds of gaps—both in knowledge and in background— are always suspicious.

Next is Gray Hargrove, who plays Sebastian, one of the shipwrecked twins. Dark-haired and lanky, he says he is seventeen but in truth looks closer to fifteen. He is quiet but well spoken when he does talk. He says he was part of a traveling theater group in Nottingham, performing at inns and guildhalls before moving to London last year to try his hand at playing for the Globe or the Fortune. I had no reason to dislike his audition only that I did; he read from Edmund Spenser's *Faerie Queene*— somewhat pretentious for a vagabond—and the nerves he showed by way of shifting eyes and posture unusual for an experienced player.

And then there is Christopher Alban—Kit—the one playing Viola. The boy with the bewitching voice and the moonstruck hair who recited Marlowe at his audition. Who said he had no experience playing at all, who told Shakespeare he is a mere stable hand from Plymouth, whose voice took the fancy of the master of the house he served in and who sent him off with a bit of money and his well wishes to become a player in the great theater of London.

It is all most certainly a lie. Kit is a decent player, a quick study, always prepared, and, since the first day, always on time. Despite all the changes Shakespeare makes to his lines, he appears the next day with them memorized, sometimes delivering them in a new way. He holds his own in the scenes he has with the Lord Chamberlain's Men and even they cannot find fault with his delivery. His behavior is impeccable, and he is rapidly becoming a favorite. And that's just the trouble. No stable hand should be a favorite, not in this theater and not with these men. No stable hand should be able to read his lines, much less know how to interpret and deliver them the way they were meant to be heard. I intend to find out why.

My last four suspects are also present. Simon Sever, in the role of Valentine; Mark Hardy, who plays Antonio; and the Bell brothers, both stagehands. Sever and Hardy are already dressed, and I know from watching them that they'll be the first out the door, heading home without so much as a farewell. The Bells dash in and out of the curtain, still working, scurrying in frantic obedience to the stage master's commands. They'll be here well past dark, so it's doubtful I'll be following them tonight.

The players begin exiting the theater. I fall in with them, keeping an eye on Alard, Barton, Hargrove, and Alban as we make our way down wood-plank stairs to the back door. As I expected, Sever and Hardy are first in line, first to exit the building. Outside, dusk is rapidly falling, the blue sky melting into pink and orange. Despite the beauty of it things will soon turn ugly, when the brothels open up and men with too much money and time come here for gambling and drinking and women.

And that's where half the crowd from the theater goes— Alard and Barton included. The rest turn onto Rose Alley—the street that runs beside the Rose Theatre and the Globe—and move north to Bankside, onto London Bridge and the other side of the Thames toward home. I've just about decided to follow Alard and Barton—it's more efficient for me to watch them both at the same time—when my attention is drawn back to Alban. He loiters in the middle of the street, the only still thing in the jostling crowd, just long enough for distance to grow between himself and the others so they don't notice him breaking away.

Kit begins to move south, toward the Rose. There's nothing in that direction but the theater and beyond that, pastures and farmland. This alone is enough to pique my curiosity, but when he gives a furtive glance over his shoulder, it's decided. I allow him a twenty-foot lead before starting after him, memories of the theater and of Marlowe sneaking in with every step.

The Rose Theatre was pulled from use just over a year ago. Marlowe was the Rose's main playwright, much the way Shakespeare is the Globe's. When he was putting on as many performances as the Globe—upward of six a week—I came here more times than I can count. The lath-and-timber walls are familiar, as are the heavy thatched roof that by now must host more birds than it once did audience and the neighboring rose garden that gave the theater its name. It's now untended, but instead of dying off the roses grew wild, now tangled brambles thick with thorns and deadhead blooms.

Kit picks his way to the Rose's back entrance. He's been here before, I can tell by the way he moves with surety in the shadows, the way he knows the door sticks, that it has to be pulled, then pushed before the latch will open. He enters the theater and shuts the door carefully behind him. From my place in the street I wait a beat, two, before proceeding after him. I'm halfway down the path to the door when I hear it: that voice, rich and high and lilting, wafting through the timbers.

"*Disguise, I see thou art a wickedness, wherein the pregnant enemy does much.* Does *much*? Or *does* much?" Kit breaks off and tries the line again, deciding on the latter. "*As I am a woman now,* alas…" There's a rustle of paper, an irritated grunt, then in a muttered undertone, "*the day.* Alas the day indeed."

He's rehearsing, and now I have an explanation as to why he is such a capable player. I repeat Kit's trick with the door latch and slip into the theater, up the stairs, and into the dilapidated tiring-house. I watch as he paces the stage, back and forth, idly chewing a fingernail as he murmurs his lines, over and over. There is not enough light for him to read the slips of parchment he holds in his hand, but maybe that's the point—the dark forcing him to commit what he does know to memory.

"*O time, thou must untangle this, not me? Not I.*" Kit stops, squints down at his lines, which by now must be unreadable, and sighs. "*Not I…*"

I step forward and give him the line he's looking for: "*It is too hard a knot for me to untie.*"

There's a sharp intake of breath—I've startled him—and he reels backward, into the shadows where I lose sight of him for a moment. "Orsino," he says finally. "What are you doing here?"

As always, I'm prepared for a lie. "As it happens, this is where I rehearse, too."

"It is?" A pause. "I've not seen you here before."

"Then I suppose we were bound to run into each other eventually."

Kit steps forward, into the space onstage not overshadowed by the roof. "I was just finishing up," he says, though I know it's not true. "I'll be out of your way in a moment." He turns back to the shadows, searching the boards for his cloak, a thinning thing which he shrugs over even thinner shoulders.

"I've got a better idea," I say. "Why don't we rehearse together?

We have a lot of the same scenes, and if we're both here, it just makes sense."

Kit stops midshrug, looking at me with a vigilance one might reserve for a dim corner or a dark alley. He doesn't look at all inclined to take me up on this offer, and I need him to. I need this evening to yield me some information about him, as I've already missed an opportunity with Alard and Barton and Hargrove.

"I guess the other option is to draw up a schedule," I say when he doesn't respond. If I can keep him talking, he'll be less apt to leave. "You could have the stage every day from three to six and I could take it six to nine—I'll have to hold you responsible for any injuries I might sustain in the darkness, of course. Or we could alternate days so we each get it three days a week, and roll dice to see who gets the fourth. Or, look: We could just duel over it. I didn't want it to come to violence, but it seems that beneath your calm exterior lies a contentious heart, and I have no doubt you would cut mine out neat just to suit your own nefarious purposes."

Kit's mouth quirks, something just short of a smile. "Why wouldn't you just rehearse with Burbage and his men?"

"Why would I do that?" I reply. "I barely know them."

This makes him frown. "I thought you did. It seemed like you did. I've seen you before, you know."

Six words a good watcher should never hear. I'm surprised by this announcement, and a little concerned, but Kit is looking at me so I try to make light of it.

"You have," I confirm. "Earlier today. Also yesterday, and the day before."

"I meant before the play began," he says. "I saw you at the

Elephant a few weeks ago. You were with Shakespeare and Burbage and the rest."

Now I remember why Kit looks so familiar. He was sitting
nearby playing dice, all insane hair and feigned swagger, throwing coins I now know he can't spare onto the table. He was
looking at me even before I noticed him, but I did notice him.
He was the most interesting thing in the room that night, one
of many spent with Shakespeare's men going from tavern to
tavern, spreading news about the play. I assume that's how Kit
heard about it; it's how all of London was meant to hear about
it. There's nothing to deduce either way. But Kit seeing me that
night puts me in their company before auditions began, something I'm prepared to explain.

"I remember you," I acknowledge. "That was a long night.
I'd been cast for the play that afternoon, and apparently Shakespeare and his men have a ritual: First name in the books buys at
the Elephant. All I really wanted to do was go home."

I watch Kit take that in, make it mean something to him. His
frown deepens. "You didn't have to go through auditions?"

"Not formally," I reply. "I did some acting with a troupe in
Canterbury. Shakespeare was in the audience at one of the
shows last year, and afterward he invited the players to call on
him if we ever came to London. So I did."

For the sake of anonymity, and of safety, Carey and I agreed
on my backstory, which casts me as a graduate of the King's
School, also in Canterbury—which Marlowe attended—where
I lived before striking out to become a player in London. It
explained my sudden and constant appearance at the Globe,

not just to Burbage and his men, but to the rest of the crew, shareholders, partners, and financiers.

"It was good of Shakespeare to vouch for me," I continue. "But his men were a little harder to convince. It doesn't help that the lines keep changing, and I'm having trouble remembering them. If that happens onstage, I'm done." I spread my hands. "That's why I come here. For the extra practice."

Kit folds his arms and lifts his chin. "No, you aren't."

"No, I'm not what?"

"You're not having trouble with your lines," he replies. "Your delivery could use some improvement, I can't argue that. But you remember the words just fine."

Now I'm the one folding my arms. "Excuse me?"

"Don't worry, I won't hold it against you." Kit goes on. "At any rate, you're not the worst one onstage, so at least you can take comfort in that."

"Good to hear," I say. "Are you always such a pisser?"

Kit narrows his eyes at me, his mouth working on either a smile or a response. But I get neither and so I say, "Look, are we going to rehearse together or not? You're a good player, and I suppose I can't get any worse."

"Now look who's the pisser." Kit peers at the sky, now a deep gray. I think he's going to tell me it's too late, that he's got somewhere else to be when he says, "If we're going to rehearse together, don't you think I should know your real name?"

"Toby." I extend my hand and there's a beat before Kit takes it, his grasp cool and firm.

"You can call me Kit."

Chapter 13

KIT

NORTH HOUSE, LAMBETH, LONDON
8 DECEMBER 1601

I t's Saturday, and there is no rehearsal today, as Shakespeare and his men have a performance at the Globe, one of his newest plays called *As You Like It*. I don't know what it's about, but yesterday after rehearsal they began setting up for it and there were goats brought in, and for some unfathomable reason Mistress Lovett began draping brown cloth over them and fitting things on their heads that looked like antlers. Toby whispered to me that this is what would happen to him if I didn't help him with his lines, that he would be replaced by livestock because they cost less and don't argue as much. I think he was joking, but I made sure that we had plans to meet at the Rose next week, just in case.

At first, I was wary about agreeing to rehearse with Toby. The day I met him he was frosty at best, ill-mannered at worst. But then, I wasn't exactly the paragon of politeness, either. At any rate, he's friendlier toward me now, a bit more talkative, so I reason he was simply nervous, just as I was.

I've not told Jory about this arrangement, nor do I intend to tell Catesby. Even though the extra rehearsal will improve my performance, thereby keeping me in the play (and thereby ensuring the job is done), I don't think they would want me spending time with anyone outside Catesby's circle, no matter the reason. The concern that I might give away my cover, or inadvertently slip up and mention the plot against the queen, would be too big a risk for them to feel comfortable with. But I have lived my entire life behind a veil of secrets, so I reason two more won't hurt.

I'm considering all this as I walk through the streets toward North House to see Catesby and his men, Jory alongside. It's bitter cold and gray today, the air swirling with a fine mist of snow that gives even our appalling part of the city a festive feel. I've not seen Catesby in over a week, not since rehearsal for the play began, and I've seen very little of Jory. In his new position as Catesby's priest, he's been there every day from dawn until well after dark, doing I'm not sure what. I feel guilty about this, too, not knowing what's happening in his life and not caring enough to ask.

"How have things been at Catesby's?"

Jory glances up at me beneath his brown wool cap, his face a little expressionless as if maybe he forgot I was there.

"Very well," he replies eventually. "Catesby has been good to me, giving me full run of his library. I spend most of the day there, studying. His collection is impressive. He's got all the lay Catholic texts: the Apocrypha, the martyrologies, manuals of prayer and preparation for taking Holy Sacraments—"

"*Shh.*" I look over my shoulder because even in a frozen alley in the center of nowhere, London, you never know who might be listening. Today it's just a shopkeeper emptying a steaming bucket of something awful into the street; I wait for him to finish and disappear back inside. "You don't have to list them."

"We spend a lot of time discussing theology, ethics, academics, politics." Jory continues undeterred. "Catesby reminds me a lot of your father, Katherine. Kit. He's a very learned man, just like your father was."

My father was fond of Jory, admiring his intelligence and religious conviction so much that he allowed him to sit in on my tutoring sessions. I never minded, and sometimes it even worked to my benefit: Jory would get into such heated discussions with Master Litcott, the theology tutor, that I could slip out unnoticed and spend the rest of the afternoon doing what I pleased.

"He's helped me to see what I'm here to do," Jory says. "He's shown me my purpose. My *true* purpose." He looks to the sky and crosses himself.

"Stop that." I slap at his hands. "And what do you mean? I thought you already knew your purpose. It's to be a priest, isn't it?"

"Of course," he replies. "But it's more than that now. Much more."

We near London Bridge and Jory quiets, either not wanting to be overheard by the jostling crowd or not wanting to tell me what he means. Either way, I'm curious about this new revelation. Is Jory somehow getting involved with the plot against the queen? Beyond *blessing the mission*, as Catesby called it? I can't see it. Jory is fervent and faithful, but someone who lives by the rules isn't going to risk everything in order to break them.

A long hour later we reach the other side of the river, pressing through the still-crowded area of Southwark and into Lambeth. The streets are wider here and the trees thicker, grounds packed with frozen mud and sewage giving way to crisp air and cobblestones blanketed with pristine snow. There's not a soul around and so Jory begins speaking again, just as abruptly as he stopped.

"When you first told me about your father's plan, I didn't understand it," he says. "I knew how he felt, of course, and I even agreed with it. At least in theory. But to kill someone—" He cuts himself off before I have a chance to. "I didn't know how I could involve myself with something like that, or allow it to happen. It went against everything I believe."

If Jory weren't speaking in past tense I would be frightened to hear this, because it sounds like the words a person says before they turn someone in.

"But I'm starting to see that it isn't about belief. She took belief out of the matter the moment she executed her first priest." *She*, of course, means the queen. "She took a spiritual matter and made it a political one. Catesby says if we play by rules that no longer exist, then we are destined to lose. And if we lose, what is left for us?" Jory's voice has gone up, and up, and I'd quiet him if I didn't think it would upset him even more. "It wasn't clear for me, seeing Catesby's plan as retribution for your father. But now I know it isn't about him, or the queen, or even about Catesby. It's about everything."

I nod, though I don't agree. It may not be about Father or the queen, not for Jory. But for me, that's all there is.

Finally, we reach North House. It looks desolate with its shuttered windows, snowdrifts piled by the front door, cold lanterns and branches littering the front walk. But it's meant to look this way, just as Catesby is meant to look the part of the busy gentry doing what men of means do, traveling to one of his many homes in the country or paying a visit to one of his many friends, as opposed to what he's really doing, which is holing up in this dark house and plotting dark deeds.

Jory and I take the side entrance, the one meant for servants, a graveled walk that leads down a flight of stairs to a small windowless door. Catesby's slate-faced maid, whom I now call the Granite Gargoyle, opens the door, bestows a smile on Jory and a frown on me. She motions us to follow her and we're led to the drawing room, the same room we were brought the first day we arrived.

Catesby is seated by the fire, wearing red and looking handsome. Beside him are the Wright brothers, their look-alike heads bent over something mechanical-looking; Tom Two is scratching, and Tom One is leafing through a book. Catesby thanks us for coming, then invites Jory to say Mass.

Jory crosses to the cabinet in the corner where, after a moment of fumbling, he begins pulling items from the drawer and laying them on the table. A Bible, a cup and cloth, a loaf of bread, and a waterskin no doubt full of sacramental wine. He is of course calm and pious as he does this, as are the rest of the men, which infuriates me. That Catesby would keep his relics so open—not in a priest hole or behind a lock but in his cabinet, as if they were dishes or linens and not something to hang for—is as dangerous to me as him placing a life-size statue of St. Peter in his front garden. I suppose he believes that if he were caught, his wealth and his position would save him, except I am living, breathing proof it does not.

I sit here fuming and afraid while this interminable Mass goes on, sitting and standing and kneeling and reciting *Amen* or *Lord have mercy* or *Blessed be* and only half listening to Jory speak of light and darkness and immortal souls because I am too busy watching the door, waiting for the pounding of fists and shouts of accusation. They don't come, but by the last *Alleluia* I am so wound up I'm shaking and gripping the chair arms so hard my fingers ache.

"Is there something the matter, Katherine?" Catesby says. "You look a bit tense."

"Tense!" I repeat. "How can you do it? Say Mass out in the open like this?" I whisper the word *Mass* as if that's going to make a difference. "You know what would happen if we were caught. Or do I need to tell you the story all over again?" I've given up all attempts at being calm, and all the men are looking at me, even Jory turns his attention from purifying the chalice to me. "We could at least go into the cellar! Or lock the door!

Or not say Mass at all, because of laws and punishment and treason and death!"

I am on my feet now. My face is hot and my palms are damp; my pulse is unsteady and it's as if I'm back there again, in the corner in the dark hall at Lanherne. Watching the sword fall, watching Father fall; kneeling over his body and clutching his already cold hand and whispering words he'll never hear.

Grief is as fickle as the Cornish sky and I never know when it will clear or when it will break, but it is pouring now. I count backward from five and try to pack it away; if Catesby sees I can't control myself then he'll take away *my job*, and that job is all I've got left now. I sit back down, pinching my nose shut to stop the flow of tears, but Catesby is on his feet and reaching for me, his hand firm but gentle on my arm and stopping me.

"Don't," he says. "You can't use it if you don't feel it. Don't let them take that from you, too."

The drawing room has gone quiet now, not in beatitude from Jory's lovely and dangerous Mass but because men never know what to do when a girl cries. Maybe it's too much for Catesby to take, maybe he's trying to give me privacy when there is none. But as I sit there, whuffing and sniffing in his plum velvet chair, surrounded by the snap of the fire in the hearth and the silent roar of pity and discomfort, he says this:

"Everything begins with an idea. Ideas are infallible, they are indestructible; the only thing stronger than an army of men is an idea whose time has come. It was with this conviction I conspired the very plot we sit in steward of."

Catesby's voice is the hush of the tide, but behind it, the

power of an entire ocean. I've stopped crying and the men have stopped shifting and Jory has stopped cleaning and we're all listening, not just with our ears, but with every part of us.

"But ideas, as strong as they are, do not write history—men do. Women," he concedes with a smile at me. "We are what give ideas life. Were an idea to die, we could not mourn it. But we can mourn a man. We can speak his name and remember him. What is history, after all, but the biographies of the greatest of us? I hesitated to give this plot a name, as is custom for all great conspiracies. But I think now it is fitting we christen it the Arundell Plot; named after Richard and carried out by Katherine. Man and woman, making history."

Catesby looks at me. There's a smile on his face, an echo of the one now on mine. A smile not of happiness but of determination, and that's the closest thing I can get to feeling happy right now, maybe ever.

After Jory puts away the altar items—now locked in the cellar to appease me—Catesby turns his attention to the Wrights.

"Did you get it?" he asks them.

John lifts a stack of parchment from beside his chair and passes it to Catesby: a copy of *Twelfth Night* in its entirety. Even if I hadn't seen them lurking offstage during rehearsal, copying down each word, I'd know it right away by the pattern of words on the page and because I've seen them a hundred times, tacked up on the wall in the tiring-house at the Globe.

Catesby flips through the pages, his handsome face impassive as he scans the lines. "We'll need to copy this so that everyone has one," he says. "Each of us needs to memorize every line—even as they change—and every cue to every entrance on and off that stage. We must be familiar with every detail if we're to plan around it. And speaking of plans." Catesby reaches under his own chair and pulls out a long roll of parchment, unfurling it and spreading it on the table before him: a hand-drawn map of the interior of Middle Temple Hall, where the play is to be performed for the queen.

"The play, of course, represents the *when* of our plan," Catesby says. "This map represents the *where*, and we will need to know it just as intimately. Every entrance, every window, every corridor to every room and every step to every door. I'm thankful to Winter and Percy, who spent the whole of last week at Middle Temple, posing as students to gather this information and render it into a sketch." He gestures to Tom One and Tom Two. "Fortunately for us, and for our plan, the security was quite lax, and we were able to get what we needed without undue trouble."

The six of us spend a moment hovering over the drawing and all that it means. Four rooms, a single door, two hallways; one play, one plot, one knife, and the end of the queen's life.

"The main Hall is where the play is to be performed, of course." Catesby taps his finger on the parchment. "But what of the Prince's Room, the Queen's Room, and the Parliament Chamber?" He directs his question to the Wrights. "I assume they're to be used as tiring-houses. Do you know who or what will be assigned to each one?"

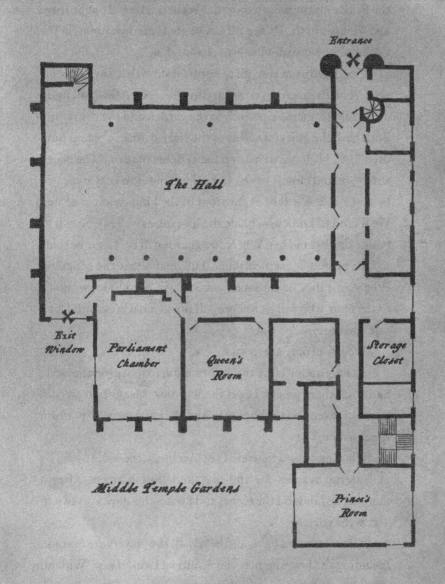

Entrance

The Hall

Exit
Window

Parliament
Chamber

Queen's
Room

Storage
Closet

Prince's
Room

Middle Temple Gardens

"Not as of yet," Chris replies. "Parliament is the largest, but the Prince's is the most removed. My guess is they'll put Burbage and his men in the Prince's. They've got their own rooms at the Globe, and they're not likely to change that."

"Good. Do what you can to ensure it stays that way," Catesby says. "The Parliament room has direct access to the Hall itself, as well as the most exits, both to the garden and the courtyard. Both have the quickest access to the river, a little over four hundred feet." He looks to me and the Wrights in turn. "The queen will be seated closest to the stage. Find out how that stage will be laid out, if it will be at the front of the Hall or in the center. We'll need to know which side she'll be on, as well as who will sit beside her, behind her. Where her guards will be. I assume some will be posted at each entrance, but what about the windows? Where will they be stationed outside? We need to know, down to the man, who will be where at all times. That is essential for a safe and unimpeded exit."

"We'll find out," Chris says.

Catesby nods. "Have this information to us within the week, and from there we can begin the logistics. Meanwhile, we will turn our attention to the play to find the ideal scene to perform the dispatch."

"I thought toward the end," I say. "Act five, scene one."

Catesby reaches for the play and flips it open. After a moment he lands on the scene, and I watch his dark eyes twitch across the page.

"There's a sword fight, and nearly all the players are onstage, including the boy who plays my identical twin," I say. "With all the chaos and confusion in this scene, attention will be divided.

All I need is a moment. To separate from the others, drift toward the queen. Pull the knife from my doublet and slice it across her throat." I remember the way this was done during spring slaughter, Father's men bringing down a two-hundred-pound hog with the single pull of a knife.

Catesby and Tom One exchange a look.

"I know you are well schooled," Catesby begins. "But I imagine that education does not extend to swordsmanship, or the art of combat."

My silence is answer enough.

"I imagine not," he says. "Richard was progressive, but I think even he would not see the value in imparting these skills to a woman." I don't have time to be offended, because then Catesby says, "No matter. Winter is an excellent swordsman." He nods toward Tom One. "He'll teach you everything you need to know."

Chapter 14

TOBY

THE MERMAID TAVERN, LONDON
13 DECEMBER 1601

A s it was the last time I came to this tavern with Burbage's men, they take it over: the space, the table already occupied, the patrons' attention. It's no less crowded tonight than it ever is, this stuffy, unremarkable place with its soot-stained fireplace and yellow plastered walls, mismatched chairs and tables. I wondered at its popularity then, but as the uptick of noise and energy in the room becomes more noticeable I see it's not the place that people come for, it's us. Rather, it's Burbage. He knows it—as do the rest of his men—and they revel in it.

Burbage settles in at the head of the table, per usual, the others taking their places around him. The seats that remain are at the other end, the side farthest from the center of the room, the door, and the attention. The rest of us slide into them in turn: myself and a handful of players and stagehands. We've just come from rehearsal, and while most everyone went home, a few accepted Burbage's offhand invitation to accompany him and his men to their favorite tavern. I was going to decline, until I heard Thomas Alard accept.

"Why are we here again?" Alard drums his fingers on the table. I don't know who he's asking as he's not looking at any of us, his gaze fixed on Burbage.

"Because they invited us?" I jerk my head toward the other end of the table. "Although I'm not sure why, since they've exiled us to Tomis."

Alard makes a noise halfway between a scoff and a laugh, and I know I've accurately pinpointed his agitation. His role as Olivia is a lead—the only new player besides Kit and me to be given one, the rest appropriated by the Lord Chamberlain's Men—and he wants to be treated as such, not relegated to the sidelines. He's afflicted with aspirations, certainly, and there's the possibility that his being in the theater is nothing more than their culmination. But Marlowe said aspirations have a way of corrupting and it's true: I wouldn't be in my position if they didn't. Either way, this tells me a lot about Alard, and how best to proceed.

"I say we order every drink in the tavern, and all the food, then put it on his bill. That will teach him to put us in the gallery. And if it doesn't"—I hold up a hand to hail the serving woman; she's already brought Burbage and his men their drinks but ignored us—"our revenge will be sweet."

This earns an appreciative smile, then a laugh the moment a host of women appear, bringing everything I ordered. Platters of raw oysters, bowls of hazelnuts and peascods, dried fruits and artichokes, and pitcher after pitcher of ale. I watch with satisfaction as Alard reaches for his cup and fills it. We have rehearsal tomorrow, but I won't be the one telling him to pace himself tonight.

A few minutes pass, idle talk and the sound of eating and drinking. Alard is not easy to approach and he's not good company; there's something about him that's slightly feral. He has a head that turns quickly to melancholy and from there worse, especially when he drinks, something I observed both times I followed him. I'm working out the best way to engage him in conversation when Burbage gets to his feet, six feet of peacock, and takes a mighty drink from his cup. He slams it down and spreads his arms wide, pulling a coin from his doublet and holding it high. This must be some sort of signal, because the other players at the table fall silent, as do the patrons and even the men behind the bar.

He climbs onto his chair and then onto the table as if it were a stage, kicking aside cups and dishes and bowls and knocking them to the floor. It's surprising behavior for Burbage, who above anything else is posed and mannered. But maybe that's the appeal, because everyone around us begins to cheer and whistle and stomp their feet, quieting only when he begins to speak:

"*My crown is in my heart, not on my head, not decked with diamonds—*"

He's cut off by Tooley, who climbs on top of *his* chair and blurts, "*Then happy low, lie down! Uneasy lies the head that wears a crown.*" Burbage tips his head back, groans a laugh, conceding what appears to be a defeat. There's more applause, more stomping, a hail of hazelnut shells thrown good-naturedly at him as he steps off the table for Tooley to take his place which he does, launching into yet another line.

I turn to Alard, a less-than-kind observation on my lips. But he's already on his feet, along with a handful of others, abandoning my side of the table to join Burbage's.

Reining in a sigh, I run through my options. Spending the rest of my night watching Alard pimp for inclusion will get me nowhere. I've been here too long to try to catch up to Barton or Hargrove. Kit left the Globe at the same time as the others, and since we didn't have rehearsal at the Rose scheduled for today, he said he was heading home. I doubt this is a lie but even if it were, he's also too long gone for me to find out.

I finally accept this is going to be a dead night and pull on my threadbare replacement cloak, feeling the loss of the one I gave to Carey for the tenth time today. I wonder what he's done with it, if it's somewhere in his undoubtedly massive home or if he's done away with it. The thought of the latter is so unbearable I'm considering showing up on his doorstep and demanding it back, to hell with his suspicions, when I see Kit walk through the door.

It doesn't take him long to spot our table, not with Tom Pope now perched on his knees on top of it, wailing a line about the gates of mercy and fresh-fair virgins and flowering infants. Kit takes in the scene before him, surprise evident in the way he checks his stride and widens his eyes. He takes a step backward, as if he's considering leaving—I don't blame him, but I also can't let him. I whistle once, short and loud through my teeth, and he jerks his head in my direction, allowing the barest smile to cross his lips.

After two weeks of near-daily observation at the Globe I've learned he doesn't give those up easily. What I've also learned: He doesn't give up anything easily. He regards everyone around him with an almost wary hostility, as if the world were divided into friends and enemies and he's known very few friends. He speaks nothing of others in his life, past or present. This is unusual—I would know—and does little to ease my suspicion of him. That said, he's also got a sly, fierce humor I've managed to ease out, and in time I may be able to coax a little more.

Kit makes his way toward me, dodging tables and chairs and elbows. Then he's standing before me, freckled cheeks flushed from cold, gray eyes bright. He's wearing a cap, a green wool thing, and when he pulls it off a curtain of curls tumbles across his face. I watch as he tries to rearrange them, swiping one piece of hair from his eyes while tucking another behind his ear. He takes in my empty side of the table and raises a brow.

"Making friends everywhere you go, I see," he says.

"They cleared out when they heard you were coming."

His smile grows marginally wider.

"What are you doing here?" I say. "I thought you were going home."

"I was, then I changed my mind," Kit replies. "But now I'm not at all sure it was the right choice. What is all this, anyway?" He tips his head toward the other end of the table.

"I gather it's some sort of wager," I reply. "Burbage started it. Someone throws a coin on the table and recites a line from a play. Someone else chooses a word from that line, then starts a new line from a new play containing that word. With every line recited, the stakes go higher. I suppose the last one standing wins the pot."

"So it's both performative *and* pretentious," Kit says. "How delightful."

Now I'm the one smiling.

"You going to sit?" I point to an empty chair. "I would. Else you risk being dragged into it. Unless you're in for a gambol?"

"Not for all the shillings in Saltash," Kit replies. "I'm more of a dice player anyway."

"I remember," I say. "You any good?"

"I'm all right." He says this in a way that tells me he's a lot better than that. He's still standing beside me, hat in hand and one foot all but out the door, and now I know how to get him to stay.

"I'm not too bad myself," I say. "I suppose you wouldn't mind playing a few games? Just for fun."

It works.

"I hope you have deep pockets, Orsino." Kit peels off his cloak before folding himself into the chair beside mine, all lanky limbs and threadbare clothes. "Because I'm going to enjoy emptying them out."

"What's your game?" I say. "Hazard? Barbooth? Pair and

Ace?" Dice isn't my thing—nothing is; my job is enough of a gamble without adding more to it—but I've trailed enough men to enough dice houses to know what's played and how to play it.

"Hazard," Kit replies. "But since it's just the two of us, we'll have to make due with Barbooth. You know the rules?"

I pretend to think on it. "The caster rolls three-three, five-five, six-six, or six-five to win. One-one, two-two, four-four, or one-two loses. The fader bets against the caster."

"That's it," he says. "What are we playing for?"

"Honor?" I say. "Valor? The beautiful, incomparable feeling of victory?"

"A penny a roll," Kit says. He doesn't have this to lose and neither do I, which is entirely the point.

"Show-off," I say. "Just as bad as Burbage."

"Worse, I should think." Kit pops a few hazelnuts into his mouth and tips back in his chair, his careful smile now a cocksure smirk. "You in?"

I feel it then, the thrill of a challenge, not unlike the one I get from tracking a mark or disguising myself or decoding a letter. But there is nothing strategic about this game, nothing I can learn about Kit that I don't already know. This is nothing but friendly competition. Even so, I don't like to lose.

Kit lifts a hand and holds it there. A moment later the serving woman appears and, a moment after that, reappears with the dice he requested. He cradles them in his palm.

"Gentlemen roll first." He makes as if he's handing them to me but then snaps his hand shut. "Which means it's your bet."

I lay a penny on the table. Kit rolls 3-3 to win. Instead of sliding his winnings before him, he adds another penny to the pile, upping the stakes.

Just like onstage, Kit's confidence comes out when he gambles. He tries but can't quite conceal his pleasure when he wins a hand, which he does, twice more. I lay another coin on the table and roll. Kit declines to bet against me, so when I lose the roll I lose my money, too. Then it's his turn.

"Five-five." His lips press back a smile.

"I have eyes," I say, and that's three shillings I've now lost. Kit proceeds to roll 5-5, 3-3, 1-2, and 4-4, half winning and half losing, only I've bet poorly and the unsteady gain I had has now become a steady loss. When Kit pours me a tankard and slides it toward me I take it, even though I rarely drink and never on the job.

My turn again. I win, 6-6, but Kit declined to place a bet so I end up with nothing.

"How did you get to be such a good player?" I ask.

"Of dice or of theater?"

"You know what I mean."

Kit eyes me from behind his tankard, then sets it carefully on the table before replying. "The family I stabled for in Plymouth, they had a son my age, and we became friends. Richard—that was my friend's name—invited me to the house for supper one night. His father knew me, of course, but not well, and not outside my duties. But afterward he said he was impressed with me and asked me back the following week. After a month or so, he allowed me to accompany Richard to his tutoring sessions."

"That's unusual," I remark. "For you to be included that way. I imagine not many in your position can say the same."

"I'm lucky," Kit acknowledges. "Richard's father felt it was his responsibility to nurture intellect, no matter where he found it. I learned my numbers, French, some Latin, philosophy, and geography. But the best part was the books and the plays and the poems we were assigned. Richard's father would pick up printings of them in London and I—we—would spend my off-hours reciting them in the garden, by the fire, anywhere. These stories, the words... they meant a lot to me, you know? They do mean a lot."

I nod, because I do know. I've loved words and I've hated them, but I've never been indifferent to them. I've spent the last few years fearing them, the way they have the power to give life to the things you feel, things that are safer left unnamed.

"At the end of each week, Richard's father liked us to stand up and recite the things we'd learned," Kit continues. "I was good at it, and I got it in my head that I could do it for a living. So here I am." He tries for a smile again but this time it falls short, never quite reaching his eyes.

"Where is Richard now?" I ask.

Kit looks away from me, back toward the raucous end of the table where Burbage is back to being front and center, standing on his chair with arms outstretched. "...*the King, Queen Mother on our side*," Burbage intones, "*to stop the malice of his envious heart...*"

"That's from *The Massacre at Paris*," Kit says, by way of reply. "And he's dead."

I've been parceling Kit's story as he tells it, pulling out what I thought was true and leaving the rest for me to sort through later. I make a note to myself—*Richard*—another piece of his background to verify. I don't think what he's told me is a lie, at least not all of it. There's no faking the look of anguish that's come over his face, and for a moment I feel it too: that dark thing that settled inside me the day Marlowe died, one that has shadowed my every day since.

Either way, it's not what I expected him to say. "I'm sorry to hear that."

Kit doesn't acknowledge my words, only nods at the dice in my hand. "Your turn."

I wait for him to place a bet but once again, he holds up a hand to decline.

"You aren't betting because you think it won't be a winning hand," I say. "How do you know that?"

"Probabilities," Kit replies. "Simple math. Well, it's not *that* simple. But it is math."

I shoot him an unkind look, then roll, 1-2. Another loss, and one more of my pennies goes into the pile. That's coal for a week and laundry for two; at this rate I'll lose the game and if I do, I'll have to subsist on stale bread and hard cheese until I get my next draft from Carey. When I look at Kit again, he's watching me closely.

"I think we should raise the stakes," he says.

My pockets are empty enough without this. But I tip backward in my chair anyway, carefully feigned indifference. "Go on."

"I think the loser should be out something much more than coins on the table," Kit says. "Something that's really going to hurt."

I hedge for a moment. I'm not sure what could be worse than losing money, and I didn't figure Kit to be so devious as to suggest it. But despite myself and everything I can't afford to lose, I'm intrigued.

"Let me guess," I say. "You want to wager a duel? A street fight? A midnight swim across the Thames?"

"I was thinking a kiss."

My chair tips back to the floor, front legs hitting the wood with a thud.

"The winner decides who the loser should kiss," Kit continues, undeterred. "It could be anyone, anytime, anywhere. So if I win, I could decide—in the middle of rehearsal—that you have to kiss Shakespeare and you have to do it. No questions."

"Where?"

"I said no questions."

"I meant, kiss them where?"

Kit grins, and as with everything else that's happening tonight, I'm taken aback. His smile is wide and bright and for a moment, he almost looks happy. "On the lips, of course."

I make a noise of half irritation, half amusement. "I'm going to enjoy making you kiss Burbage."

Which is how I end up losing.

Chapter 15

KIT

SPITALFIELDS, LONDON
16 DECEMBER 1601

I have never killed anything before.

At Lanherne we kept a bit of livestock, chickens and geese and capons. When something needed to be slaughtered, our old cook, Wenna, took to the yard with a beaten leather apron tied over a muslin dress and a resolute look on her face. She would march up to whatever bird was to meet its fate, pick it up, slap it down on the tree stump she used as a chopping block, and in the swing of a cleaver it was all over, before whatever it was could squawk even a single note of distress. It all looked simple enough, at least from my spot by the barn where

I would watch, a good twenty feet away so as not to be too close. There wasn't even that much blood. Simple and clean and quiet.

The chickens before me now are not quiet.

"There are five principles to engaging with an edged weapon," Tom One says. We're standing by a slatted wood fence outside a farm in Spitalfields, a remote area north of Catesby's. Inside the fence is a dirt yard packed with dozens of roving, clucking chickens. It's early yet, before eight, the skies still brittle around the edges. "Don't get cut. Expect to get cut. Everything is a target. Keep your blade moving at all times. And don't be in a hurry to die."

"These chickens aren't going to kill me," I say.

"For today, they're not chickens. They're the queen's guards, and if it comes down to it, you need to learn how to evade and engage them," he says. "Now, in you go." He hands me a knife, what he calls a stiletto, handle first. The blade is about a foot long, the end tapered to a wicked, needle-sharp point. I take it, careful not to violate the second principle—*expect to get cut*—and slide through the boards in the fence. My feet sink into mud and manure and feathers and it smells worse than the Thames in here. Tom One, outfitted in his Sunday best of velvet and lace and leather, doesn't follow.

The chickens squabble and squawk and peck at my feet, and for every one I nudge away with the toe of my boot, two more return. They don't seem the slightest bit afraid of me, but I figure this will make them easier to kill. All around me are fields of cold, crispy grass and the occasional sheep or cow, no one to see or hear what I'm about to do. Besides, the owner of the farm is a friend of Tom's so he wouldn't mind anyway, even if he weren't at church. It's where I should be, too, but Catesby wanted me instructed on the *art of combat* as soon as possible.

"Set your stance," Tom One instructs. "It's the foundation from which you will maneuver and engage. Forward fighting is best. Left foot front, weight distributed evenly between the balls of your feet, front knee slightly bent. Chin tucked in to protect your throat. Your cutting hand—that's the one with the stiletto—should be pulled back; your checking hand—that's the one that deflects your opponent's blows—should be pushed forward." There's a pause. "Not like that."

"Not like what?" I say. "I'm doing what you're telling me."

"You look like a lizard," he says. "Untuck your chin a little—there. Straighten your legs a bit, and get off your toes—yes. This is how you should stand, and remember it. It's your mobile stance. Show me how you can move."

I shuffle back and forth, feeling foolish and not knowing how this is going to help me kill a chicken *or* a queen, but Tom One seems satisfied. "Good. Now. I want you to choose your opponent."

"Choose my opponent?" I look around the pen. Some of the chickens are brown, some white, some black-and-white-speckled, some all-black. I feel as if his instruction might be a trap, that for me to choose one will be to choose them all, and so I say, "Why aren't you in here engaging me?"

Tom One waves off my question with a gold-ringed hand. "You've got to learn to crawl before you can walk. Now, choose an opponent before I choose one for you."

"How would you do that? Never mind. That one." I point the tip of the dagger at a black-and-white chicken, a little patchy and old-looking, and I think it might be her time to go anyway so I reason I'm doing her a favor.

"You're going to close the distance between you and the enemy. This is called entering. You step in to do that, just like you did before."

I do my funny contorted walk toward the chicken. It continues pecking at something on the ground, ignoring me completely.

"Good. Keep your weapon forward and position the blade so it's pointing toward the threat," Tom One calls. "Anything that leads before the blade, including your fingers, becomes a target for your opponent. That's principle number three. As you move, remember principles three and four. Everything is a target and keep your blade moving."

He's right; everything *is* a target. The chickens, including my little speckled enemy, are alerted by my approaching crouching lizard stance and they all start to move. They don't run, exactly; they just start doing everything faster. Pecking, scratching, flapping, squawking.

"It only takes two repetitions for a pattern to be established," comes Tom One's voice. I almost can't hear it through the racket. "Keep that blade moving. Side to side, circles, spirals are all good—the important thing is to switch between your patterns often. Good. Very good, Katherine."

I'm moving closer to the chicken, looking at it and none of the others. I imagine that those black-and-white feathers are a black-and-white dress, that the red comb atop its head is a cloud of murderous red hair, that its beady black eyes are her beady black eyes. It takes a lot of pretending on my part, but fortunately I am a player and I am becoming very good at pretending.

"What are you waiting for?" Tom One calls. "Kill it."

I take a breath. Hold up my knife. Think of Wenna and her apron and her fierce, determined expression. Lunge toward the chicken-queen with my needle-sharp stiletto—

And miss.

I may as well have set a fox loose in here. Immediately the chickens are hopping, pecking, flapping their wings, screeching, and then they all start running away from me. There's nothing else for me to do but run after them while Tom One shouts nonsensical advice.

"Use your cutting hand and your checking hand to attack your opponent's weapon hand."

"My opponent doesn't have a hand!"

"You're going to want to hit the wrist tendons first—"

"Or a wrist!"

"You want to incapacitate the arm and puncture the artery," he calls. "This is referred to as defanging the serpent."

Well, that just puts the lid right on the jar. I'm surrounded by angry fowl, he's crowing about serpents, the air is filled with feathers and clucks and the smell of chicken scratch, and this is not at all how I imagined this going. I reach for the queen, lose my footing, go sprawling in the mud. I want to give up, but because I'm a quick study I am thinking of principle number five—*don't be in a hurry to die*—so I scramble to my hands and knees and start crawling after her. This seems to work, maybe because she doesn't see me or because I look less threatening down low like this, or maybe just because chickens are stupid. But all at once she stops running and I grab her right by her scrawny neck.

The queen is wriggling in my grip, her beady black eyes are wide, and everything inside me is yelling at me to do it do it *do it*, and I throw the thing on the ground. This stuns her and sends the other chickens running again, as if they know what's coming. I raise my knife. The encroaching sun flashes bright off the heavy steel blade, winking at me as I lower it, fast and with no hesitation, just like Wenna used to do. And just like that, it's done. The head in my hand is lighter, weightless, strangely stumpy. The body, now headless, scurries around me in ever-slowing circles. And just like I remember, there is very little blood. Just a slow, pulsing fountain from the body and a trickle from the head. But what holds my attention most is the eyes. They're just…blank. Open, black, staring sightless, and *gone*. Gone like Father's eyes, how they were empty even before he slumped to the ground.

"Follow through." Tom One's voice is closer than it was before, and I turn around to find him standing above me. His pretty leather boots are dulled with mud. "Maintain, control, and escape. Remember that last part, Katherine. Escape. It's not enough just to finish the enemy. It's not even enough to survive. You've got to succeed."

I look down at my hand, still clinging to the chicken head, blood oozing over my fist and down my arm. I feel slanted, disconnected; it feels a little like shock, but it also feels like discovery.

"How old are you?" I hear myself saying. When I look up at

him, he's staring at me with a wary expression, as if he thinks I've gone mad.

"Twenty-nine," Tom One replies. "Why?"

"Have you ever killed anyone?"

He looks to the horizon, where the sun still hangs raw, bleeding orange through the muddied fields. I think this is his way of ignoring me, that I've asked what amounts to a very personal question and he's too polite to tell me I'm rude.

"My uncle was a Catholic priest," he answers finally. "Hanged, drawn, and quartered when I was just fourteen. It's not something you forget. I've caused a bit of trouble in the name of retribution since then. I'd cause more if I could, though I think the greatest trouble is to come. Don't you?"

It's both an answer and a nonanswer, but it's one that satisfies me nonetheless. I nod.

"I want you to keep practicing," Tom One goes on. "What you've learned today about stance, about how to hold a knife, how to engage and disengage. From there we'll move on to basic combat. Just as a precaution," he clarifies. "If you're confronted by a guard or a player who gets a little too close to you that night, you'll need to be able to stop them. If you get a chance, it might do you well to observe a fight in person. You might try the taverns or bear-baiting pits, or possibly the dicing houses on London Bridge."

Tom One extends his hand to me, and I toss the chicken head in the yard and take it. Climb to my feet, sweaty and covered in mud and probably something worse than mud. My hands and face sting with scratches and pecks.

I thought it strange that Catesby wanted me to do this, but now I know why. It was my hand that decided to kill this chicken, my hand that carried it out. Not the hand of God, or of the queen who people say is like God. It was God who said show no pity: eye for eye, life for life. The queen decided she would take my father's life. If I can remember that, I know I'll have no trouble taking hers.

Chapter 16

TOBY

BLACKFRIARS HOUSE, LONDON
17 DECEMBER 1601

Every year Carey holds a patron party, an invitation going to every nobleman and theater group in the city in order for the players to secure patrons for the upcoming season. Most actors, unless they're of Burbage's status, or those of the rest of the Lord Chamberlain's Men, have no way of earning a living unless they're sponsored, usually by a nobleman. For men of means it's a matter of prestige, as well as a competition: They fight to secure the best actor from the best company, which raises their status as well as the player's.

It's not a long walk to Carey's from my room, fifteen minutes around St. Paul's Cathedral to St. Andrews's Hall, then all the way to Blackfriars along the Thames. I have never been to Carey's house before, but it is just as I expected it to be. Bricked and tall and crowded in with the others beside it, typical of city homes in this area but still elegant with its rows of trees and graveled paths and banks of mullioned windows. He's even got his own pier, guests gliding up in wherries or barges to disembark and enter through the private garden. The rest of us, without the benefit of our own boats or pennies to spare for others', enter street side.

Lanterns filled with candles line the front walk leading to the open front door, music and laughter spilling into the cold, clear evening air, mingling with the rich scent of roasted meat and the mellow smell of tobacco. I show the guards my invitation—green writing on parchment thick enough to shave with—and they step aside to grant me entrance.

The shiny foyer bustles with even shinier clothing, feathers and jewels and golden chains and pomade. And that's just the men. The women all wear red lips and white faces and gowns that resemble Yuletide sweet cakes: puffed and frosted and dripping with candied toppings. Then there's me, in my least tatty breeches (dark blue, wool, decidedly unshiny), my cleanest shirt (not really clean at all), and Carey's borrowed and brocaded cloak. I scan the space, counting the rooms that branch from the entrance hall (eight), all of them filled with fireplaces and furniture and musicians and servants, when I hear a familiar voice.

"Ah. Toby." Carey is beside me then, resplendent in black and pearls and fur. I nod in greeting, and he claps a hand to my shoulder in response. "You showed! I was hoping you would."

"I didn't think I had a choice."

"It is only by choice and not by chance that men make their circumstance."

"You're unusually esoteric tonight," I remark.

"Downright Delphian, ha! Oh, don't mind me. It's the sack. Have you tried it? Sweet wine topped with brandy. I'll have a terrible headache come morning, which gives me approximately twelve hours before I have to start worrying about it. Now, look, here comes the lady of the house. Do behave yourself, Tobias. Try not to unleash your charm all at once."

Carey's wife makes her way to us and it takes a while, as she's stopped every few paces by her guests, offering their greetings and well wishes. She's a handsome woman, in her fifties I would guess, same as Carey. Also like Carey, she's got a head of the curliest hair I've ever seen, standing a foot off her head in all directions in a cloud of dark brown. She's wearing a dress that's as wide as the hallway, heavy with gold and pearls and starched white ruffs.

"This is Tobias Ellis." Carey introduces us. "Toby. He's one of the new players in Shakespeare's latest. Used to be a writer, then came to his senses. A face like that belongs on the stage, not behind the page." Her smile is appreciative. "Toby, this is my wife."

She extends her hand and I take it. "Baroness," I say.

She giggles. "Please. Call me Bess. Elizabeth if you must." I smile a little at that, her and Carey's shared refusal to wear their formidable titles. "A fresh player! How wonderful. William could use more of you, I'm sure. Have you a patron? Or are you still on the market?"

"On the market," I reply, though it's not true: Carey and I

already agreed that while I am to engage prospective patrons for appearances' sake, I am to accept no offer but his. "I can only hope to be so lucky as to find someone to be my benefactor."

"Oh, nonsense. It would be we who would be lucky to have you," she continues. "You've got my vote, if a woman's opinion matters."

"I should think your opinion matters most of all," I say, to which Carey laughs and the baroness blushes.

"Tobias is quite right, of course," Carey says graciously, then kisses her lightly on the cheek. She takes this as a sign to leave us which she does, looking over her shoulder at me just once before melting back into the crowd. Carey watches her go, then turns to me and as if by magic, the glassy-eyed look he wore when I greeted him is gone, replaced by the sharp gleam I am more accustomed to.

"Good work," he says. "Now she'll be telling everyone who will listen about you. She'll think she's staking you as her claim, but all she's really doing is marking you the prize the others can't pass up. You'll have to let them romance you, of course, but for God's sake don't run your price up too high."

"Wouldn't dream of it."

"Keep your eyes open," he continues, lowering his voice even though there's no one nearby. "Half the city is here, which means there's half a dozen plots unfolding at this very moment. Damn if I don't hate these things, yet I have them every year. What is the matter with me? Don't answer that." He holds up a hand. "So? You're three weeks into this thing. What of our suspects?"

"I've got my eye on a few," I reply. "Aaron Barton. He's the one from Scotland with the two-year gap in whereabouts, the one playing Maria. He likes his ale, keeps late hours, likes a street brawl. Not your typical boys' chorister. Thomas Alard, the one cast as Olivia. I followed him twice to a dice house, twice to the bear-baiting pits, skint both times. A gambling problem doesn't hold with a typical player's profile, but does a hired hand's."

Carey nods. "They're both here, and they've already got a few suitors. Shrewsbury and Pembroke and Berkeley, last I checked. They always want the leads. Who else?"

"Gray Hargrove. He plays Sebastian, one of the shipwrecked twins," I reply. "Refuses to spend any time with any of the players outside rehearsal, despite repeatedly being asked. He lives alone, dines alone, walks to the theater alone, and walks home alone. Sleeps alone. So far, there's no one else for me to follow to find out more about him. He's too isolated. A profile like that reads a little too familiar."

In other words, a little too much like mine.

"Suspicious indeed," Carey says. "He hasn't shown up here tonight, either, despite being asked, despite the opportunity of securing funds he clearly needs. What about the other newcomer? That boy. The one who recited Marlowe."

I hesitate, just a moment, before replying.

"Kit Alban," I say. "Serious about his role. Doesn't miss a line, much less a rehearsal. He does a bit of gambling, too." There's no real reason to tell him about our meetings at the Rose, at least not yet, so I don't. "He's very good at both."

"Seems unusual," Carey remarks, "for a boy who says his only experience in performing is at church." So he remembered that, too. I forget, at times, that for all his good humor, Carey sees everything, forgets nothing, and is a lifelong player in this game.

Whatever I know of dishonesty and deceit and half-truths hidden behind half-lies, he invented it.

"Well? What do you know?" Carey's voice breaks into my thoughts.

"Nothing as yet," I reply. "I dropped a few inquiries into my network last week, but they've yet to come back. Followed him home a few times. Lives in a dodgy lodging house in Dowgate. And you've seen the way he dresses. Seems his master, who wished him so well on his journey to London, didn't exactly fund him for it."

"Hmm." Carey isn't impressed with this assessment and he shouldn't be: If lack of funds made a murderer then nearly the whole of London would be under suspicion.

"None of this is suspect in and of itself, of course," I say. "But newcomers are always suspicious. I'll keep watching him."

"Good. You can start tonight." Carey jerks his chin in the direction of the front room I passed on my way in. There, standing beside the window and half hidden by drapery, wearing clothes as shoddy as mine, is Kit. I knew he would be here; he told me he would be. But I'm not as indifferent as I should be to see him, and I'm mindful about keeping the smile off my face.

"He's been standing in that corner since he arrived," Carey tells me. "Not spoken a word to anyone. He'll not find a patron that way, though he could have his pick, and as you say, he needs it. See what you can do." Then he's off again, snatching yet another cup of sack off a passing tray.

I consider going over to him. But I have work to do, and there's nothing about Kit I could learn tonight, or that I couldn't find out at the Rose. Barton is the one who keeps eluding me, my efforts to get to know him continually thwarted. Kit hasn't seen me yet, so I stay clear of his line of vision, making my way down the entrance hall to search the house for Barton. I pass room after room, all of them crowded and loud. I finally find him in the garden, being romanced by two noblemen. He's dressed only a little better than me, in dark blue breeches and cape, a feathered cap tipped over one eye. They're standing at the end of the graveled path, close to the river.

There aren't many guests out here, not when it's this cold outside and the food, drink, and warmth are inside. Just eight by my count. They're all smoking pipes or rolled tobacco leaves, the acrid smell of it enough to turn my stomach. If I'm to stay out here it's what I'll have to do, too, or at the very least look interested in it. I approach the group standing nearest to Barton and his suitors, three men dressed in fur-lined cloaks.

My arrival causes a lot of excitement and overawed greetings, handshakes, and inquiries. Am I really a lead in Shakespeare's latest? You don't say. Was I really a writer before? Smashing. Would I like to try tobacco brought over from the New World? It's charming—they say even the queen herself smokes it. I have trouble imagining the queen choking her way through this stench, but when one of the men offers me a fat, tightly rolled tobacco leaf, I take it. The first inhale is almost enough to make me pass out.

The discussion eventually turns to hawking, only slightly more interesting than smoking. Still holding my tobacco leaf, I step a bit outside their circle, not enough to leave it but enough to get close to Barton's to overhear their conversation.

"And then he jumped me, thinking I'd be an easy mark," Barton is saying.

"A Scotsman through and through," one of his companions replies, and I shake my head. No Englishman is going to admire a Scot unless there's something in it for him.

"There's a rumor, you know, that you might be a bit more dangerous than the average player." Another man winks. "What say you to that?"

Barton rocks back on his heels. His hat falls a little lower over his eye. "I may have served a bit of time in the past."

The men exchange a glance and a grin. "For fighting?"

Barton takes a hit from his pipe, letting the smoke wreathe from his nose. "They put me in Bridewell. Two years. That's for something a bit worse than fighting."

There's a chorus of appreciative hoots and shoulder slapping, not directed at Barton but one another. They see players as a novelty, an item to collect, something to add to their cabinet of curiosities: the more unique, the better. A prison record would play well to that, and it's less to do with Barton than it is the daring of the patron who takes him on.

But it gives me something to work with. If Barton did serve time at Bridewell, it's easy enough to confirm. As is his sentence. Two years is a lengthy one, and if it's true, it certainly was for something worse than fighting. But what? And how was he let go? Why wasn't he sent back to Scotland? Or was he let go, then somehow found his way back into the country, possibly alongside a defiant priest? Many a scheme was born and raised within the walls of a prison; why not this one?

I extricate myself from the men I'm with, making polite excuses against their insistence on me staying. But my head is spinning, both from the smoke and this new information on Barton. I start up the path, weaving a bit, keeping my eyes on the ground to stay steady.

"Orsino, there you are." I look up to find Kit standing before me.

"Viola-Cesario," I say by way of greeting.

"I've been looking for you all night," he goes on. "I wondered if you decided not to come, but then—" His gaze falls to the tobacco leaf still in my hand and his eyes go wide. "You *smoke*?" He sounds so scandalized I start to laugh, but this makes me light-headed so I stop.

"No." I take a few steps off the path and drop onto a nearby bench, dropping the smoldering leaf into the grass and grinding it out with my heel. "But when a prospective patron offers it to you, what else are you to say?"

"No?" Kit suggests. "You could also say tobacco smells like burning chicken feathers, and that smoking it is a foul, disgusting occupation."

"We can't all be as smooth as you," I say. "Tell me: How many offers have you received tonight?"

"None as yet," Kit says. He's standing over me, a cup in his hand and a smirk on his lips. "But I have a plan."

"I wager you do." I lean forward, elbows on my knees and my head dropped low. "I wish the ground would stop spinning."

"The things we do for our art!" Kit drops onto the bench beside me. I feel his arm brush against my sleeve. "First smoking, and then there's this cape. You look like my great-aunt Hegelina, all trussed up like a St. Crispin's Day capon. You even have the same beard."

"This is a formal occasion," I say. "It's called dressing."

"*It's called dressing*," Kit mimics me. "So, tell me. Did your foray into debauchery land you a patron? I hope so. You look as if you're going to be sick."

"I think so," I say. "I think Carey."

"Oh." Kit considers this. "It's a good choice. He seems kind. Generous. Like a person who would be receptive to you walking up to him and pressing your lips oh-so-gently against his."

I jerk my head up to look at him. The sudden movement makes me so dizzy I nearly fall off the bench.

"What?"

"You didn't think I'd forgotten, did you?" Kit is grinning and his eyes are bright, as if he's had one or even two of those cups of sack. "The bet. The one you lost."

"Oh no," I say. "Not tonight."

"Clearly you forgot the 'anytime, anywhere' rule," he says. "But look. I can be reasonable. If Carey isn't your preference—I don't know why not, he's got such nice hair—I can choose someone else. His wife, maybe. There's not a finer-looking woman here—"

"No."

"What about Earl Stanley? He's so dashing! Just earlier he was telling a story about his trip to Egypt, how he fought and killed a *tiger*—"

"No."

"Then what about *his* wife? She's bound to be all right. Considering he hasn't fought and killed *her*—"

"*Kit.*" The word comes out strangled, and now I'm laughing and so is he.

"You're lucky I'm so nice, Orsino," he says. "I may not be next time."

"I consider myself duly warned."

Kit smiles and takes another drink from his cup. I close my eyes and take deep, slow breaths, trying to clear my head. The air smells like grass and moon and expectancy.

"There's something I've been meaning to ask you," he says.

I tip my head to his. Ordinarily, a statement like that would put me on edge. It sounds as if a personal question is forthcoming, and I don't like personal questions. But I decide to allow it.

"Go ahead."

"You never told me how you got to be a player," Kit says. "I told you my story at the Mermaid. But what about you?"

"I wanted to be a writer, if you must know," I say. "But I wasn't very good at it, and playing seemed the next-best thing."

"No. Really?" He says this softly, almost disbelievingly, and I'm reminded of what he said that night, about words and what they mean to him. "What did you write?"

"Plays, mostly," I reply. "My first was about Robin Hood; it was called *The Thief and the Potter*. The second was called *The Sword and the Red Rose*. It was about Hereward the Wake. My third—and final—was about the Beast of Bodmin. I titled that one *Bod the Shadow*."

Kit's mouth quirks. "I think I'd like to read those."

"I assure you, you wouldn't," I say. "I wrote a few poems, too, but the less said about those, the better."

"Poems!" Kit presses a hand to his chest. "Orsino! I had no idea you lived such a tragic life."

"I'm not sure I follow."

"I maintain that no one who leads a happy life goes on to become a writer," Kit says. "Especially not of poems. Not when all they're about is unexpected death and unrequited love and unfulfilled lust—"

"Exactly how much sack have you had?"

He waves a hand. "I'm serious. Poets have to suffer a great deal to write the things they do. You have to have experienced at least *one* tragic thing. How else would you know what it was like? You can't make that sort of thing up."

"You can if you're writing about flowers, or trees, or birds, or the ocean."

"I see," Kit says. "What were your poems about?"

Unexpected death, unrequited love, unfulfilled lust; all three. "Forget it."

Kit laughs then, the sound of it as soothing as rain. "I knew it."

"I don't know if it works that way," I say. "Not exactly. I think it's the opposite. I think the more you feel, the fewer words there are to describe it. It's as if the words don't do it justice; you can only write what is already dead in your heart."

Now I've done it: said too much. I've spoken truthfully—to a suspect, no less—about my past and my feelings and I feel exposed and uncomfortable, as if I woke to find someone standing over me, watching me while I slept.

This runs through my mind in an instant. I glance at Kit and he's watching me in that funny way of his, the same way he did during dice at the Mermaid when he decided to stop wagering money and wagered a kiss instead. It's a look I've not seen in a while, not since Marlowe: He looks at me as if he understands me.

And for the first time since Marlowe, I feel like I understand someone in return.

"So you never did tell me," I say to change the subject. "What is your grand plan for finding a patron?"

"Ah yes." Kit waves his glass around. "Firstly, it involves the sack."

"This does not bode well," I say.

Kit mimes pressing a finger to my lips to hush me. "Secondly, it involves my voice. You've heard it."

"Mell-i-flu-*ous*," I say in my best imitation of Shakespeare. "But I don't see how those two things equal a plan."

Kit gives an exaggerated sigh. "What do men do when they've had too much to drink? Especially of sack?"

"Do you really want me to answer that?"

"They sing," he continues. "All I have to do is wait until they're feeling loose and free with their voices *and* their coin. That's when I go in and sing better than all of them, like a big, beautiful black-spotted song thrush"—I start laughing and so does Kit—"and *lo!* They'll be throwing offers at me. I'm telling you, Orsino, they don't stand a chance. This plan is positively *Machiavellian*."

I stop laughing at once. Kit has explained his education to me—the tagalong of a spoiled, likely flighty son of a nobleman who requires constant entertainment, even during lessons—and it holds. But something about the recall and use of that particular word—*Machiavellian*—suggests instruction far beyond the occasional sit in with a tutor. I file it away for later and put the smile back on my face before Kit notices it missing.

I rise from my seat. "Let's go, then. I want to get a good seat for this show you're about to put on."

Chapter 17

KIT

**THE ROSE THEATRE, LONDON
19 DECEMBER 1601**

Viola-Cesario." Toby's voice echoes through the rafters of the Rose. I hear him before I see him, clomping up the back stairs and into the tiring-house. Ever since the patron party, he's started calling me by the same ridiculous nickname Shakespeare calls me, and I reply in turn.

"Here, my lord." I'm sitting cross-legged at the edge of the stage in my hat and gloves and cloak, trying to stay warm and dry. It's going on dusk now, leaden skies spitting out rain as they have done all day, and it's getting colder by the minute. I warm up almost immediately when Toby appears, even though I saw him not thirty minutes ago at the Globe. "Did you get them?"

Them being the lines that Shakespeare changed on us, yet again, during rehearsal. I don't know how he expects us to remember these changes, which is just what Toby told him. There was a lot of shouting, of course, not from Toby but from Master Shakespeare, who said we were all *weepeggle*, which means nothing that I know of but could pretty well guess by his murderous expression. Eventually Shakespeare found someone backstage who could write the changes down for us. Of course, there was only one copy of these changes, because of *literary theft* not to mention *judicious waste of time*, so Toby stayed to write it all down again before coming to meet me. Not because he's generous, but because I threatened to make him kiss Shakespeare if he didn't.

By way of reply, Toby holds up two slips of parchment, then settles onto the stage beside me.

"Sorry I took so long," he says. "Five players, one pen. I had to wait my turn." He rolls his eyes and hands me my copy, and I begin reading. Toby has a nice hand, letters that are loopy and precise and pretty. He writes like a gentleman, or a poet, which makes me think even more highly of him. I think you can tell a lot about someone by the way they write. Jory writes in cramped, tiny letters that make me think he's hiding something, and Shakespeare writes in crooked, indecipherable scrawl like a madman, which he is.

"So he added three new people to this scene," I say. "And he's got you holding not just me but Olivia at sword-point now. So bloodthirsty! You are really mad for this woman, aren't you?" Even though I acted this scene not an hour ago, reading it now is more or less the same as seeing it for the first time because it's hard to tell what's happening when we're told *Stop!* or *Shhh* or *Hush, fools,* interspersed with long periods of silence with us standing around doing nothing while Shakespeare scribbles on parchment. "Part of me is impressed with your tenacity; the other thinks you're a bit mad yourself."

Toby flashes me a crooked smile, all sass and summer-sky eyes. "Without a doubt," he says. "They really should have gotten someone better-looking to play Olivia, though, because it's a stretch to think one man could like her, much less four, much less brandish a sword for her."

"So crass, Orsino. I'm sure she's beautiful on the inside." I turn back to the page. "And look. Shakespeare's written your lines in all capital letters. You're so in love that you're shouting and everything." I clutch the paper to my chest and pretend to swoon. "It's all so romantic!"

"Yes, I'm so in love with Olivia that I go on to marry you in the very next scene. I pity Shakespeare's wife," Toby says, and now we both laugh. "What a mess."

Maybe so, but privately I think it *is* romantic. And just as privately I was thrilled to see Shakespeare make that change, that instead of Orsino killing me at the end he *marries* me, which just about covers the range of human endeavor. At any rate, there is no kissing, not yet, though with Shakespeare's propensity to change things every other minute, that could still happen. This would be wonderful, and were anyone to comment that I appear as if I am enjoying this kissing a little too much, I can simply put it down to me being a good player and not to Toby being a good kisser, which I am certain he is.

"I guess we should start." I get to my feet and Toby does, too. I cross to center stage, where we usually begin, but he ducks back into the tiring-house. "Where are you going?"

"I brought us a surprise," he calls. A moment later he steps out holding a sword. "I borrowed it from the Globe. I thought it would make things a little more exciting." He tosses it at me, which I almost don't catch. It's heavier than it looks, made of some kind of wood but painted to look real, with a gray blade and black grip, the cross guard dotted with blue circles meant to be jewels. Then he tosses me the scabbard, which I fasten around my waist before slipping the sword inside.

"This scene is really confusing," Toby says, coming to stand beside me. He's still looking at his parchment. "It didn't need to be. Why did he put seven players in this scene when you only need three? It was fine just as I—" He stops. "I actually think me going mad with your sword helps. It will keep things from looking like a Parliament hearing."

I giggle, which comes out sounding a little girlish, so I stop. "So, should I play three parts and you four? Or should we just talk past them?" We've done both, depending on how the scene plays out and whether it helps us learn or deliver our lines better.

"Talk past them, I think," Toby says, eyes still on his paper, only now he's scowling. He looks a bit frightening when he does this, like someone you could easily imagine lurking in the streets of Bankside past midnight, waiting to pop out and beat you and take all your belongings. He doesn't look like this often, and not at me, at least not since the day I met him at the Globe, when he looked at me every bit as stone-faced as Catesby's maid. But every now and again he'll take on this expression that hints at something dark inside, maybe not villainous but at the very least wicked. I wonder what it could be. Is he hiding something, the way I am?

"...Olivia?"

"What?" I pull from my thoughts to find Toby watching me. "What about Olivia?"

"I was saying that I changed my mind, that you should play both your part and Olivia's. That way I can practice blocking with the sword."

"Oh." He's caught me off guard, and now I'm a little flummoxed. I can't let my mind wander when I'm rehearsing. I have to stay completely focused on my role in the play, not my role in the plot. There's a saying in Mass: "Never let your left hand know what your right hand is doing." Father said it means that a person should keep their interests separate from each other at all times, and if there was ever a time to listen to the Bible, it's now. "That sounds fine," I say finally. "Where should we start?"

"Let's take it from Olivia and Maria joining the scene," Toby says. I move to my place at the edge of the stage, Toby to the center. "Olivia and Maria walk on while I'm talking to Antonio and his officers. They move off to one side and I bow to Olivia." Toby bends at the waist, pantomiming taking off his hat. "Then she sees you—"

"And I bow," I say, which I do. "You try to charm her again, but she won't have it. You call her cruel, and that's when you begin your caterwauling."

"Right." Toby is still pretending to hold his hat, so I take off my cap and toss it to him so he has something real to hold.

"*Still so constant, lord,*" I prompt him.

"*What, to perverseness? You uncivil lady,*" Toby starts. He walks across the stage toward me as he continues speaking, swinging my cap in his hands, voice rising alongside feigned frustration.

"Good," I say when he's finished his speech. "That was very good. I could really feel your anger. Now Olivia says, '*Even what it please my lord, that shall become him.*'"

Toby flings my cap to the stage and rushes toward me. Grabs the sword from the scabbard at my waist and raises it high, holding it outward as if Olivia were standing before him and he was pointing it at her. "*Why should I not? Had I the heart to do it…*"

I watch as he delivers his lines. He yells through much of them—caterwauling, I called it—but like everything else in this play I secretly find it romantic. I watch his face as he speaks to the pretend Olivia, wielding that battered sword while shouting about love and savage jealousy, those blue eyes pleading with unchecked anguish. I have no trouble feeling what Viola is supposed to feel as she looks at him, which is that I've never seen anyone so beautiful in my life.

Toby grabs me then, just as the scene calls for. I'm caught off guard again, and when he wraps one hand around my shoulder, pressing me against him as the other hand presses the wooden blade to my throat, his words echoing through the empty rafters of the Rose, I forget. That this is just a play and I'm just pretending. I forget everything except for him.

"I…forgot my line." I whisper this, because I also seem to have forgotten my voice, too.

"*After him I love,*" he prompts, whispering right back. "*More than I love these eyes, more than my life…*" He says my lines for me, his lips by my ear and his breath on my cheek, my hand on his arm as he presses against me. I close my eyes as I listen, hoping the dark that's fallen through the roof will hide the unwilling smile on my lips. I think if I just keep standing here, doing and saying nothing, he will spend the rest of the night speaking the play in my ear, and that would be just fine with me.

"Did you forget Olivia's line, too?" For the second time, Toby's words jerk me back into the present. I whirl around and there we are, standing face-to-face, and I do mean *face-to-face*. We can't be more than a few inches apart, yet somehow in the dark it feels a lot closer and surely he's going to step away or I will, but then neither of us does.

"I...yes. I'm not having a very good night," I say finally, which isn't at all true, but I say it just to say something, as it's gotten very quiet in here.

"I see that," Toby says, and there's that smirk again. "I hope this doesn't happen opening night."

"I don't—it won't," I correct. "I'll be fine. I just...I'm thinking about a lot. The play," I clarify quickly. "All these changes. They're just..." I raise both my arms and wave them around like some kind of idiot. "It's all a bit mad."

"I know," Toby says, and then it's quiet again. I'm feeling very breathless and out of control, and it's hard to know who to be right now, Kit or Katherine, which maybe doesn't matter anyway because I don't know how to react in any situation when I'm alone in the dark with a boy standing before me, looking at me. I've read enough to know all the things that can happen in settings just like this one, and it's hard to know if I'm frightened, or thrilled, or both.

"I think I should go," I say eventually.

Toby nods. "We can always try again another time."

"Tomorrow," I say, though I can't help feeling like I let him down somehow.

I reach the tiring-house and glance over my shoulder, banking on the dark to chance one last look at him. And by the moonlight I find him watching me back.

Chapter 18

TOBY

LONDON BRIDGE, LONDON
20 DECEMBER 1601

Watching Thomas Alard is excruciating.

He has no set schedule, no set pattern, no regular contacts, no routine. Outside of rehearsals at the Globe, he seems to flit around London, doing whatever he pleases wherever he pleases, whenever he pleases. Last night, after Kit left the Rose, I went to Alard's flat in Billingsgate Ward, hoping to catch him coming or going, preferably going. All I got was a closed door and a darkened window and after three hours of watching it in the dark and the rain, I concluded he was either asleep or not coming home anytime soon, so I decided to try again tonight. Which is why I'm sitting in a dicing house past midnight, a filthy place in the middle of London Bridge that reeks of coal and sewage and stale ale.

London Bridge is a wide thoroughfare fronted by gatehouses at either end, upward of two hundred shops built directly on top of it, some seven stories high overhanging the river and others the road, the passage through more a tunnel than a roadway. Eight hundred feet of slick cobblestone clogged with carts, wagons, horses, and a thousand people on foot. Crossing it takes hours day or night, leaving many to duck into the taverns and alehouses to wait it out.

I never come here if I can help it, preferring to use what little coin I have to hail a wherry; the stench and the crowd are enough to curdle the air. Rotted food, animal droppings, human waste, and decay; the heads of traitors that sit atop spikes along the southern gatehouse, carrion for the crows. And now I'm buried in a table in the back, Kit's cap pulled down over my eyes in an effort to hide my identity. Not that it matters, not at this point. This place is so crowded and Alard is so drunk I doubt he'd recognize his own mother, much less me.

Here's what I've concluded about him thus far: He doesn't make much money from being a player; none of the men do unless they're patroned, which he now is. The nobleman he picked up at Carey's party will pay him a stipend to cover his living expenses, along with a modest bonus if the play he's in is a success.

But Alard's biggest problem is gambling. He stakes high, which means he wins high or, more often, loses big. It explains his expensive shoes—in my experience, men with gambling problems rarely use their spoils for mundane expenses such as rent or food, preferring to spend lavishly on impractical things like wine or jewelry or clothes. It also explains his odd hours, as card houses and gambling dens and bear-baiting pits keep nothing but odd hours. For as much as it explains about him, it also creates problems, at least for me. Gamblers are ideal targets for spies or underground groups to use as contacts or messengers. A gambler's very nature is one of risk: They thrive on it. They're usually—always—wanting for money. And they congregate in places where it's easy to pass a note or a whispered word or a bag of coins without ever being seen. This makes my job difficult because to catch it I have to be there, and as I cannot be at Alard's side every hour of every day, it leaves a lot of my success down to chance. I don't like leaving anything to chance.

There's a triumphant shout from his table at the other end of the room—not from Alard, but someone else—and by that, plus Alard's grim expression and a rueful shake of his blond head, I see that he's lost his roll. His agitation grows. He places both hands on the corner of the table and gives it a shove, sending dice and coins and men scattering. That's another thing I've learned about Alard: He's an ass. Away from the Globe, when he's not playing at being someone else, or trying to impress someone else, this is who he is. It makes every moment I spend in his presence feel like a punishment. It isn't like watching Kit, who is funny and free and who makes me forget what I'm really doing when I'm with him, which is my job.

My thoughts begin to drift and I don't like where they're going: back to the Rose. I shouldn't have rehearsed that scene with Kit last night. Or I should have at least rehearsed it in a way that didn't end with me touching him. Because if I hadn't done that, wrapping my arm around his neck and pulling him close, I wouldn't have felt the way he went pliant under my grasp. I wouldn't have seen him close his eyes as I spoke his lines into his ear. I wouldn't have felt his hair, soft as hat feathers against my cheek, and I wouldn't know the way he smells, like wood sage and sea salt. I wouldn't know any of this, and I could go back to pretending that I don't see the way he looks at me, or the way he makes me laugh, or that, for the first time since Marlowe died, I feel lighter with someone else around.

I have to go back to pretending that nothing is happening between us because nothing can happen, not ever. Because Kit is a suspect and could be part of a plot to murder the queen. Because to be with another man is illegal and a hanging offense, and I know not even the queen will save me because she saves no one. Because the last time I felt this way about someone, he turned my heart inside out and then he died, and I am still not the same.

I don't have time for it anyway. Involvement with this or any other boy—or girl—is not part of the plan. The plan that sees me out from under the burden of the queen and her men, their labyrinthine plots and interminable lies. That allows me to go on my way, free from the taint of deceit that has followed me ever since Marlowe stepped foot inside my printing shop all those years ago. That allows me to live my own life, instead of watching others live theirs.

I'll have to put an end to the rehearsals at the Rose. I can cite any number of reasons, from the benign to the uncivil: I'm too busy, I'm losing focus, I'm no longer interested. Kit won't question it, I don't think; he'll take the hint and leave me be and stop making me question things I fight every day to deny.

I turn my attention from Kit back to the drudgery of Alard, feeling resolved yet somehow unfinished. Pull out my journal and begin reviewing my notes while half watching Alard stumble back to the bar while the other men at the table scramble to sort dice and coins. I'm a month into my investigation, and my second report to the queen is due tomorrow. Of my thirty-six original suspects, I've been able to dismiss twenty-eight by way of personal observation or inquiries into their backgrounds. Most were men in minor roles, understudies or stagehands, suspicious because I believed them to be lying about something, age or background or experience. As it turns out they all did, but instead of lying about treasonous plots or Catholic grudges, they were simply hiding wives or jobs or, in the case of Joseph Gill—a boy who was chosen as Kemp's understudy—extreme youth: He is only twelve years old.

This leaves me eight to focus my attention on. Barton. Alard. Hargrove. Mark Hardy, in the role of Antonio. He is brown-haired and brown-skinned, quiet and unassuming. He lives alone in Holborn—the very outskirts of London, very nearly farmland and a two-hour trek from the Globe—where he has done for the past six years. He's in his early thirties but has no family to speak of, spends his nights reading and writing, which points to an education that runs counter to such a humble background. There's also Simon Sever, who plays Valentine, one of my (Orsino's) attendants. It's a small part, but he plays it well. The trouble with Sever is that, though he says he's lived his entire life in London, according to my inquiry there's not a boy, man, baby, or elder called Simon Sever in the whole of the city. He's lying about something. The Bell brothers, Jacob and Jude, two new stagehands. They're not twins, though they could be: dark hair, dark eyes; they say they're twenty-five and twenty-seven and I believe this. They're mischievous and clever, quick to come up with solutions to Shakespeare's many prop problems (in the end, they were the two who procured goats to act as stand-ins for deer in the latest play), despite never having any prior experience.

Then, of course, there's Kit.

Despite the promise I made to myself to not think about him, despite the report before me and Alard behind me and the hundred other things that could occupy me besides, I go back to thinking about last night, a staged sword fight and forgotten lines whispered in the dark and a boy.

Chapter 19

KIT

I stand in the tiring-house along the left side of the stage, listening for my cue.

Onstage, and sitting on a bench at a long trestle table, are Thomas Alard and Aaron Barton. Today is the first rehearsal in full costume and so it is a merry one, all of us dressed in gowns and wigs, our faces full of stage paint.

First there is Aaron, who is stocky and short and is wearing crookedly drawn-on lips and a low-cut gown—lower than it should be—that displays half his naked chest. The seamstress who sewed it, Mistress Lucy, is only an apprentice and somehow mixed up Aaron's measurements (confusing his height with his width? I do not know) and Mistress Lovett nearly wept when she saw him in it, the hem trailing the ground a full three feet too long and the bodice practically down to his navel, a nest of ginger chest hair on full display. Aaron laughed and laughed, and Master Shakespeare declared it *ploosnar*, which none of us understood, but it must have meant something good because the chest hair stayed.

Thomas Alard is just as entertaining as Olivia: thick Venetian ceruse covering his face, splashy red lips, and pink-flushed cheeks, dark penciled eyebrows under a pitch-dark and tightly curled wig. His dress is no less severe: black, long-sleeved and high-necked, topped with an elaborate white ruff. He is eighteen, too old to play a woman by at least two years, too tall and too broad, the ruff deemed necessary to hide his bobbing Adam's apple. His voice is an unsteady falsetto, and in this scene he starts out wearing a black veil over his face, all but a shroud. Even so, Thomas is a good player. He plays up his masculinity to great laughs, and he's got this funny walk he does that makes him look as if he is floating underneath all that velvet. The first time Master Shakespeare saw him do it, he laughed so hard I thought he'd rupture something.

It is also our first rehearsal with an audience. The players not onstage, the stagehands, the costumers, the musicians, and Master Shakespeare gather in the yard to give us a sense of what the performance will be like.

"Remember, the stage will be in the center of the Hall, so the audience will be split. Half sitting on one side of the stage, half on the other," Will Kemp says knowledgeably, as he's performed before the queen and her court countless times. "Whichever side the queen is on, she will be sitting at the very front. Her eye-sight isn't what it used to be, nor her hearing, so she needs to be quite close. Her ladies will be with her; they'll take up the whole of the first row. Behind her on one side, her favorite noblemen and their wives. On the other, her favored courtiers. All the way in the back are her ministers and, behind them, her guard. The worst seats in the house, as usual." He exchanges a glance with Burbage; they both snicker. "They've been to two dozen shows, yet I doubt they've seen a single one."

This is more helpful than he realizes.

We make it about halfway through the run-through before ending rehearsal, the sun beginning its early winter descent, shadows looming long and low across the boards. I asked the Wrights why we couldn't simply light some candles or torches so we could continue rehearsing, and they explained that having fire inside the theater is a terrible risk. A single spark falling into one of the rushes would send the whole building up in flames.

All of us crowd into the tiring-house, every player and stagehand and costumer and musician, and I'm now faced with disrobing in front of them. I did this at the start of rehearsal, changing into my costume from my street clothes, but the room was less crowded then. Most of the players had been milling about the yard or were being attended to by costumers and face painters. None of them were watching me then, and probably none of them are watching me now. There's nothing I can do either way, so I decide just to get it over with.

My costumed shoes, hose, and garters come off easy enough, and before the backstage winter breeze can even raise the skin on my bare legs, my breeches are on, up, and laced, my boots pulled up to my calves. But it's the doublet part of my costume that presents the most trouble. Stiff white jacquard sewn with a hundred black felt-covered buttons down the front, hooked at the top, a cape chain-clasped to the shoulders. It took Mistress Lucy twenty minutes to get me into this thing, in that order; and it's got to come off in that order, too. The chain unhooks easily enough, releasing the cape in a puddle on the bench. The hook holding the doublet tight and flat against my collarbones unclasps quickly as well. But the buttons. They're as damnable as they are beautiful, and my fingers shake and sweat with the effort of pushing them through the too-tiny buttonholes, over and over and over.

Finally, it's done. I slip the weighty fabric from my shoulders and now the only thing that separates me from them, the truth from all this falsity, is a thin muslin tunic, wrinkled and now slightly damp. If you looked closely enough you would see the strip of binding wrapped around my chest, the shoulders that aren't quite broad enough, and the collarbones that are just a bit too dainty; you would see skin that is too soft and too smooth to belong to a boy my age. But no one is looking and so I tug on a shirt and then another one over that, then my shabby cloak and gloves. I don't have my hat, not after I gave it to Toby two nights ago at the Rose.

Now that I'm safely dressed, I think about trying to find him. But all I see when I look around are players swanning about shirtless or strutting about in their altogether, slapping asses and shoving shoulders. This is a sign I should leave so I do, averting my eyes the best I can as I make my way to the stairs, to the exit, out the back door, and into the street.

It's freezing tonight, bits of snow drifting from the sky, a powdery swirl to coat your lashes and breathe through your nose that in Cornwall we called *lusow*, which means "ash." I should go home, cold and hatless as I am. But Jory will be at Catesby's until late in the evening, and being alone in my drafty room isn't exactly something I relish. Instead I start down Bankside, looking for a way to pass the time.

When I first started working for Catesby, and before I landed the part in Shakespeare's play, I spent a lot of time wandering through London. I did this to get to know the city, to become comfortable on my own both before and after dark, in situations I've never been in before. I was never able to walk around like this at Lanherne, not as a girl and not as a Catholic, certainly not as the daughter of a nobleman who determined everything I did. I would give it all back if it meant Father were still alive, but I can't deny that I like my newfound independence. I'm careful not to call it freedom, because this isn't a world that gives freedom easily, at least not without taking something in return.

I make my way down one of the many sets of stairs to the Thames, where, on an ordinary day, wherries would be waiting, bobbing in the tide. But now, in the cold, parts of the river have frozen over and the boats have moved elsewhere. People flock here to glide and skate down the ice, enterprising merchants have set up temporary shop along the shore, wooden lean-tos selling mulled wine and roasted chestnuts, sugared canes and apples, baubles set with ribbons to hang on trees. It's more festive than this side of the river usually is, yards of lanterns strung along the docks and set along the bank, glimmering light bouncing off the rough river ice. Sounds of laughter and chatter float on scented air, sugar and spice and roasting fires. I hear someone call it a frost fair, and that sounds pleasant enough to me.

I part with a few coins to buy a cup of wine, mostly to warm my hands, but I find I like the sweetness and it warms me, too. I step along the bank, graveled and slick, dodging shrieking children who dart to and from the river, daring one another to travel farther and farther toward the white flag posted fifty or so feet from shore, marking the end of solid ice.

I stop before a stand selling little cakes shaped like stars, hearts, and flowers. They're fat and dusted with colored sugar, yellow and red and pink, jam spilling out the sides. They're a penny apiece, absolute robbery, which I might consider committing if it weren't a sin, and I am already up to my eyeballs in plans to commit an even bigger one.

"Did you know those are meant to hang on trees?" Toby's voice fills my ear and I'm so startled I whirl around, nearly knocking into him. "Originally, I mean," he continues. "As decoration. But I don't know. Were they meant to be admired? Eaten? Or both? Imagine walking into someone's home, telling them you like their tree, then proceeding to eat from it? It seems a strange custom. There are easier ways to take your supper."

I'm so surprised to see him here, snow-dusted and flush-cheeked and standing close, that I can't find the words to respond.

He reaches inside his tatty cloak and pulls out my hat. "I meant to give this to you earlier, but you left before I could find you."

"How did you find me?" I finally say.

"Luck, I suppose," he replies. "I come here for the mulled wine, stay for children falling through the ice." Only now do I see that he's holding a cup as well, which he taps against mine in a toast before turning to search the river. "Did I miss it?"

"You sound so hopeful," I say. "You shouldn't be. There's a story I heard once, about a bay in Corn—myth. Plymouth. It froze over one winter and some boys fell through the ice and got trapped beneath it. They died, of course, and their bodies were never found."

This gets his attention and he turns to face me. "And?"

"And now the bay is haunted," I reply. "Fish wash up dead on the sand, the water is always freezing, even in summer, and the boats that come too close to shore capsize. They say it's the boys, seeking revenge on those who didn't save them."

"That's a good story," Toby says. "You should write that down."

"You're the writer," I say. "Not me. You could tell it far better than I could." It's not an interesting response, nor is it funny or clever. But since our last rehearsal at the Rose, I'm having trouble talking to him, all the things I want to say getting lost between the time I think them to the time I try to say them.

"Maybe we should move," he says eventually. "The last thing I need is a bunch of children exacting their ghostly revenge on me."

The stretch of shore grows narrower and more rocky as we move away from the market stalls. The ambient noise of haggling merchants and screaming children begins to fade, giving way to restless water sounds, slapping tide and lazy gulls and the hollow clunk of boat hulls, clustered in the middle of the river and bumping against one another.

We come to a point where we can't walk any more so we stop,

looking out over the shimmering stretch of water, quietly sipping our drinks. I wait for Toby to finish his and leave, because surely he has something better to do than stand next to me, quiet and tongue-tied, alongside a frozen and frankly fishy river.

"You said, that night at the Mermaid, that you like words," Toby says.

I flush a little, surprised and pleased that he remembers. "I did," I say. "And I do. I love them. Which is why I'd never dare write them. Something that precious can't be entrusted to me."

Toby glances at me, then just as quick turns back to the water. "What do you think of the words in *Twelfth Night*?"

"I think they're beautiful," I say truthfully. "And I wish Shakespeare would stop changing them. Each time he does, the play seems to lose something. Things seem to go from the poetic to the chaotic. It feels somehow…diluted. Maybe that doesn't make sense."

"It makes perfect sense." Then: "I think the same thing."

"We seem to think a lot of the same things."

A smile touches his lips. "Such as?"

"Well, we both like stories, and we both think Shakespeare is mad. Neither of us want to be haunted by the ghosts of drowned boys, nor do we want to eat decorations off people's Yuletide trees. Oh. And we both like mulled wine." I raise my cup, though it's long been empty.

"The basis of all good friendships."

Friends. I suppose that's what we are; I suppose that's all we can ever be. But even that doesn't ring true. It can't; not when everything about me is a lie. Well, maybe not everything.

I've seen the way Toby looks at me: It's the same way I look at him. The way he glances in my direction when he thinks I don't see; the way he holds that glance just a little longer than is strictly necessary. Then there was the night at the Rose. Something is happening between us, I think; something that shouldn't. Were I wise I'd walk away; were I not the utter fool I am, I'd remember the job I'm here to do, one that's got nothing to do with any boy at all. But the wine is giving me both courage and bad advice so instead I say:

"I said something else, too, the night at the Mermaid. About a wager." This comes out before I can think the better of it, but it's too late to take it back now. "I think it's time you pay up. Today at rehearsal I considered making you kiss Mistress Lovett, and then I thought about Barton. But now I've got a better idea. You can kiss me."

Toby goes still. Not still: rigid.

"I mean, how bad could it be?" I continue. "I'm not as intimidating as Mistress Lovett, or as dangerous as Barton. If I made you kiss him, he'd likely punch you in the face, and—"

Toby takes a few steps toward me until he is standing in front of me. Without taking his eyes from mine, he pulls the empty cup from my hand and sets it on the ground beside his. Then, just as deliberately, he looks one direction down the shore, then the other. He's looking to make sure we're not seen—if we were, it would mean trouble and more. But there's no one around, the market crowd a distant sight and the two of us shrouded in night.

Toby reaches out, his fingers passing over my jaw to rest against my neck, thumb brushing my cheekbone as he leans into me, every muscle still singing with tension. But his eyes, now locked onto mine, tell a different story. They're wild and alive and free, a Cornish sea in summer.

I close my eyes, and he kisses me.

It's barely a suggestion of one, just the barest brush of his lips against mine. His other arm slips around my waist, and I feel myself soften. He pulls away the smallest bit, just enough for me to feel his breath, rapid and warm. Then the first kiss becomes a second one, this one just a little longer, a little stronger.

Abruptly, he stops. My eyes fly open and he's looking at me. I'm holding on to his waist, my fingers clutched in the coarse fabric of his cloak. I let go. Neither of us speak.

"I...maybe I should go," I say finally, just for something to say. But I don't want to go. What I want is for him to pull me back and kiss me again, but instead he just nods and says nothing in return. His expression, warm before, has become closed off, controlled, and hard. And the darkness I've seen directed at me once before, my first day at the Globe, is back.

Feeling foolish—and the tiniest bit afraid—I move away from him. One step, then another, then another. Toby doesn't stop me. He's looking at me but he doesn't seem to see me, his attention drifted onto something or someone else.

I don't say anything more; I just walk away. By the sound of only my footsteps on the gravel, I know he isn't following. When I reach the market, and before the crowd can swallow me up, I look over my shoulder like I did when I left the Rose, hoping to find his eyes trained on me. Instead, they're looking out over the water, as if he's forgotten me already.

Chapter 20

❋

TOBY

ST. PAUL'S CHURCHYARD, LONDON
22 DECEMBER 1601

Marlowe used to say there were two Londons: the one in daylight hours, with its gilded and brightly stitched overcoat, full of handshakes and smiles and promises. Then there is London at night, undercover and cloaked, sidelong looks and furtive glances and guilt for what's done or about to be. He said he preferred the one at night because he knew what he was really getting.

Because at night, that's when the truth comes out.

Truth is what I seek, and after three days of uncovering nothing new, I'm ready to resume my search. I'm dressed appropriately in nondescript breeches and boots and three shirts, layered over one another for warmth. Even with my cheap replacement cloak it will be uncomfortable, when all the warmth has long since leeched from the earth and replaced by sodden skies and numbing gales that skirt across the frozen Thames and into your bones. A single letter, carefully written and encoded and tucked between my shirts, completes my preparation. I step from my room and into the cold December night.

The city is stirred up tonight. This afternoon was the execution of yet another priest, dragged on a hurdle to Tyburn, then hanged, drawn, and quartered, another disposable man who dared to dispute the queen's laws and discovered, too little and too late, that it cannot be done. That's why I'm out in it, the alleys between the main thoroughfares of Cheapside and Fleet Street. They're choked with inns and public houses, Devil's Tavern and the Watling and the Bleeding Heart and the Anchor. More or less they're all the same, brown brick lined with sheets of cracked opaque glass, the insides cramped and dark and vaguely humid, full of men who will drink too much and talk too much, and if there's information to be had, now is the time to get it.

I trespass in and out of them, and in each one men slump over tables and against counters, slugging tankards of ale. I order one, too, leaning against the counter alongside a group of men who unknowingly invited me over simply by uttering the word *priest*.

"Receiver general of the Duchy of Cornwall," the man continues. He's dark-haired with light brown skin, an Arabic lilt to his voice. A merchant, probably. "The priest confessed to being his. If he'd not been killed in the raid, he would have landed on the scaffold right beside him. First Essex—"

"*Shah.*" One of his contemporaries glances around the room to make sure no one is listening. His eyes pass over me and keep going.

"And now Arundell," the merchant continues, this time in a whisper. "If they're not safe, who is?"

"We are," another man replies. "I have no intention of breaking this or any other law. If they tell me the sky is green and the grass is blue, I'll believe it. I'll believe anything they tell me to, as long as it keeps my limbs and organs intact."

After a beat passes, two, I set my half-empty tankard on the counter (the other half already carefully siphoned onto the floor) and push through the tavern, back into the street. None of this information is new. I already knew the name of the condemned, information I got several days ago from Carey. A man called Antonio Mendoza, went by the alias Ryol Campion. I know that he was held for six weeks at the Tower of London in a cell nicknamed "Little Ease," and I don't have to guess at its meaning. I know he was tortured on the rack, that he confessed to being part of a conspiracy against the queen, then retracted the confession. That at his trial, the verdict was decided within an hour, that he was found guilty, and upon his sentence of execution he broke out in the "Te Deum," a Catholic hymn. And I know that his head now resides in an ever-growing crowd atop London Bridge set on spikes and surmounted by guillemots and kites.

I also know he found safe harbor in the house of a man called Arundell from Cornwall, the receiver general the merchants spoke of, who has long been on the queen's list of recusant Catholics. He was fined more than five thousand pounds over the last five years for failure to appear at Anglican services, had been under watch by Cornish pursuivants for the last two years, and was killed in the raid on his home, after which the queen granted him a posthumous pardon in order for him to receive a proper burial.

What the priest did not confess are the names of his co-conspirators, though it's safe to assume that Arundell was one of them. I don't know for certain if Arundell was one of the eight noblemen I'm looking for, or if the conspiracy Mendoza was involved in is the same one I'm looking to stop. The letter I hold between my shirts is an attempt to find out. It's addressed to the sheriff in Cornwall, a man called Sir Jonathan Trelawney, who conducted the raid on Arundell's house. Carey said Trelawney's men took each member of the household into custody, some of whom they're still holding, and I need them to talk. I need information about Arundell: what they've seen, who he talked to, who visited the house, if he has sons or other family who might be missing, who might have come to London to fold themselves into a conspiracy against the queen.

Carey says they've given Trelawney nothing, even under the duress of interrogation and confinement. But Trelawney hasn't offered the right incentive. He doesn't have the authority to sanction more persuasive methods, ranging from freedom in exchange for information to torture in exchange for withhold-ing it. Carey does, and it's his words I forged and encoded under a royal seal to drop into my own private communication net-work. It should reach Cornwall in a matter of days.

It's a risk. While Carey does have the authority to sanc-tion the release of prisoners—or to punish them—he can't do it alone. It has to be put before the queen and her ministers; it has to be voted on. This could take days—weeks—and I don't have the time. There's also the possibility of my letter being intercepted. While I've forged other men's words in the past, and often, that was before the queen grew increasingly suspicious and vengeful, before she began chasing ghosts around every corner and cutting down her own men to find them. The old adage that it's better to ask for forgiveness than permission doesn't hold true anymore. Just ask Essex. Or Arundell.

I reach the corner of Watling and Bow. There is a church here called St. Mary Aldermary, empty on a night where men worship elsewhere. Each corner of the bricked facade is laddered with weathered gray cornerstones, and there is one along the southeast wall that is loose; it slides from the mortar just enough to slip in a sliver of parchment. I carry a piece of chalk in my pocket, which, after placing the parchment firmly within the stone and setting it back into place, I use to place a tick on the stone, indicating there's a letter to be picked up.

At least, this is what I would do if I didn't have company.

"Carey." I address him without looking at him, without even turning around.

He gives up the ghost of hiding and falls into step beside me. "Saw me, did you?" His words are blown into cupped hands along with an outtake of breath, an attempt to warm them through. "Where was it? At the Anchor or the Bleeding Heart or the churchyard?"

All three, if he must know. Carey's a fine spymaster; were I not better, I wouldn't have seen him at all. "It's what you pay me to do," I say by way of reply. "What brings you out on such a fine evening? Business or pleasure?"

"Strictly professional, I assure you." I keep moving, rounding the edge of the church and into the surrounding square and festival gardens, in the direction of the river. Carey keeps pace. "Aren't you going to make your drop?"

I stop. Turn around. Fix him with a look that is neither friendly nor professional. That he's tailed me tonight is unsettling enough. But for him to know the whereabouts of my drops is something I won't tolerate.

"Now, Toby," Carey says. His voice is steady even as he takes a step backward. "I assure you, your secret is safe with me."

"I've no doubt," I lie. "But with all due respect, I've got a job to do. I would appreciate it if you would allow me to do it." Once more I turn from him, once more walking toward the river. I've got a thousand things on my mind and not one of them includes George Carey.

"What of the job, Toby?" Carey calls after me. "What of the plot? What of the suspects? What of the play you conceived and wrote and preside over? What of the assassination?" That he says this aloud, even in the blue shade of nighttime, shocks me. I look around, quickly and with my eyes only, and even though I see no one, it doesn't mean they aren't there.

"I have delivered my report," I reply, my voice deadly calm against a rising tide of emotion. "It was sent to Whitehall into the hands of Her Majesty just yesterday. You would have been there for the reading of it, unless you were otherwise occupied, in which case I will tell you myself. Of the thirty-six original suspects, I have eliminated twenty-eight, through both routine observation and background checks, procured for me by Cecil's own office, by his own men. The list of those men and the accompanying write-up of their histories was included—"

"I read the report."

"—leaving eight suspects who have been further sorted into three categories in descending order of caution, observe, and aware. Thomas Alard and Gray Hargrove top the caution list. Simon Sever and Mark Hardy are still to be observed. Jude and Jacob Bell remain on the aware list. Aaron Barton was eliminated yesterday, my inquiry into his background confirming his two-year prison sentence and his relative innocence, at least as it pertains to this plot."

"What of the other boy? Kit Alban?"

We have reached the Thames now, shimmering and shale and as quiet as it'll ever be; ships docked downriver along the Pool and wherries moored bankside, none wanting to navigate the melting but still present ice. I think immediately of yesterday, when I stood beside Kit by the same river in the same dark, where he dared me to kiss him and instead of walking away, as I should have done, I did.

I think of the courage it took for him to ask, knowing I could have said no, somehow knowing I wouldn't. The way his words were light but his expression serious, as if it meant more to him than just a dare. The way he looked when I stepped away, stopping myself from furthering the kiss before I was no longer able to.

I told myself to stay away from him. I didn't listen, and now things have gotten dangerous. For him and for me. Whatever is happening has to end. I shouldn't have let it get this far to begin with.

"He is on the observe list," I finally reply. "Not a top suspect, but not yet ruled out. As stated in my report."

"That isn't what I asked."

"Then what, exactly, are you asking?" I say. "If there's something on your mind, Carey, speak it. Or if you wish me to decipher your riddle, write it on parchment and in code so I can figure it out at home and in peace."

"I saw the two of you at my patron party. On the bench in the garden, heads together, laughing. You seemed familiar—more than familiar. If I didn't know better, I would say you seemed conspiratorial."

Before me, the river. Behind me, the streets and alleyways of St. Paul's square; above me, the clear dark and the moon. I am surrounded by open water, open streets, and open skies, yet I feel trapped, caged in by Carey's words and all they imply. What does he know? What does he *think* he knows? In this queen's England, one is just as dangerous as the other. It seems impossible that Carey could believe I am somehow conspiring with Kit, but maybe plotting isn't the kind of treachery he means. For the first time in months, years, I feel a spike of real fear. It cannot show.

"Was there a question in there?"

"I'd not be so foolish as to put a question to you," Carey replies. "Not when your greatest gift is prevarication."

"At the risk of repeating myself, it's what you pay me for."

"Case in point," Carey says. "I trust you, Toby, but trust is a debt. Eventually, that will need to be repaid."

"I've worked for you for six years," I say. "Without a single misstep. I should think I've built up enough credit for trust not to be an issue."

"Even so," Carey says. "Don't give me something to hang you for."

"The way you did Marlowe?" It's an accusation I've never made, not until now. It's the first step on a dangerous path that leads from me standing here to standing before the Privy Council, and from there to a seat in a tavern and a disputed bill and a knife in the eye, the same as what happened to him. But it has the effect I wanted, which is to turn the accusations around, from me to Carey, from Kit Alban to Kit Marlowe.

"You still believe he was murdered," Carey says.

"I do."

"The inquest found nothing. Not the first, nor the second."

"I am aware of what the inquests found."

"And your last five requests for it to be opened again were denied," Carey continues. "Why do you persist?"

"Why do you persist asking why?" I say. "What are you afraid I'll find?" I stand on ice as thin as what crosses the center of the Thames, and I know it. To ask this is not just to question his authority and that of the ministers; it's to question the queen herself, who held those inquests and ruled Marlowe's death an accident. But it, too, has the effect I wanted: Carey turns on his heel and walks away from me. And through the slap of the tide and the bells of the church tolling midnight, I hear him reply, "Do your job, Toby."

Chapter 21

KIT

NORTH HOUSE, LAMBETH
23 DECEMBER 1601

Since our disastrous Bankside kiss, I've done my best to keep my distance from Toby.

We haven't met at the Rose for practice, I speak to him only when I'm called on to do so while rehearsing at the Globe, and unless I'm in a scene with him, I avoid looking at him entirely. There's no point in doing so as it would only confirm what I already know, which is that he isn't looking at me, either. Master Shakespeare commends me for looking *dolorous* and *impassioned*, just the way Viola-Cesario is supposed to be toward Orsino. If he only knew.

I keep wondering how I misread things between us. Of

course, I have no one to talk to about this, no friends with experience who might advise me, and the idea of confiding in Jory is laughable. I've been round and round with it all, and I've concluded that I simply saw what I wanted to see. That I liked Toby, as more than a friend. That he liked me, too, but only as a friend. I allowed what I wanted to happen to cloud what actually *did* happen, then on top of it all, I forced him into doing something he had no desire to. Telling myself that none of this matters, that it was a friendship built on lies and destined to end with the swing of a knife isn't much consolation.

Speaking of knives. I adjust my grip on the one in my hand, wipe my sweaty palm on the seat of my trousers, and turn back to my victim. We're in the parlor at North House, rehearsing the play but a different scene altogether, the scene in which I kill the queen. All the furniture in the room has been pushed out of the way, the center left bare to mimic a stage. Chairs were dragged in from the dining room and are lined up along both sides, where Catesby and the rest of his men sit and watch. Tom One, once again my instructor, sits in the middle. He's caped and ruffed and bejeweled, pretending to be the queen. Jory is here, too, sitting at the end and watching carefully. He has taken it upon himself to take notes and so he does, filling page after page of a journal with his cramped hand. John and Chris Wright mill about the edges of the room, lighting the candles that were only just extinguished.

"It'll need to land right between the neck and shoulder, but above the bone here," Tom One tells me, tapping his collarbone with a fingertip. "The angle is important. It can't go in straight, or blunt. It has to be acute—less than ninety degrees. You know your angles, Kit? Katherine?"

"I know them," I reply. "Acute: one-quarter turns, one-half pi radians, ninety degrees, one hundred gradian."

"Good. Your father schooled you well," he says. "Once it's in, you pull down. Quick, like pulling a lever. This will sever her carotid artery and she'll be dead in less than five seconds."

I swallow. "Won't it be ... messy?"

Tom One shakes his head. "No. That's why the angle is so important. If you do it right, it will not only incapacitate her but also ensure that the blood flows inside the chest instead of spurting outward, and all over you. She won't even be able to call out for help."

"How do you know this?" I think of Father, how he fell to the floor and couldn't call out for help, either. Remembering it makes me queasy.

"Haven't I told you I caused trouble before?" He starts to laugh and so do the others. But I don't and neither does Jory, who is still hunched over his paper, still writing. "Just remember the angle and you'll be fine. Now, let's take it from the very beginning."

I walk back to the center of the room, slipping my knife into the sheath. It's one the Wright brothers designed for me, one that straps around my waist and is to be worn under my doublet, small and sleek and undetectable.

"Two hours, thirty-six minutes into the play, you will be onstage alongside six others," Tom One says.

"Act five, scene one," I repeat, as I did the first time we rehearsed this, and the second, and the third. Catesby's men need the details drilled into their heads as much as I do. "The first time I appear alongside the actor who plays my twin brother. We will be dressed identically."

"Correct," he says. "This is important. If there are two of you, it makes it harder for you to be identified. You walk toward each other, until you stand side by side. When you hear the line *this lady and this lord*—"

"That's my cue. I fix my position and reach for my knife," I say, and I do. It pulls out of the sheath with a neat snap.

"At this exact moment—two hours, thirty-seven minutes, fifty-one seconds—the lights will go out." Tom One snaps his fingers, and the Wrights once again extinguish the flames. "Dead reckoning."

By this he means: finding the queen using my fixed position, not hers. The moon will be waning the night of the play, and when the candles are extinguished inside Middle Temple, the Hall will fall into near-total darkness. To compensate for this, I "fix" my position in the room in relation to the queen so that all I have to do is walk a straight line to find her.

By my calculation, Tom One is sitting twelve steps before me.

The point of me practicing this over and over again is just that: practice. As it turns out, stabbing someone isn't as simple as it looks. It seemed easy enough when I watched it done to my own father. A blade, a swipe, a slice and the deed done. John Wright said it was an accident, Tom Two said it was bad luck, and Jory said the lot is cast into the lap and every decision is the Lord's. But Catesby said Father was simply unsuspecting, and that's when things happen to people: when they don't expect them to.

This, I understand.

"When the lights go out, it may be silent at first," Tom One says. "The spectators could think it's part of the play. Or they might call out, and you might be tempted to listen for the queen's voice to guide you. Resist this. You won't have heard the queen speak before. It won't be enough to listen for a female voice, as she will be surrounded by her ladies."

One step, two.

"It takes ten minutes for eyes to become adjusted to total darkness," he continues. "You will instinctively be looking for light in the room, but you are to resist this, too. This will allow you to adjust faster."

Six steps, seven.

"She won't see you, she won't be expecting you," he goes on. "Lift the knife up as you walk—primary hand, fist grip, point down—pull it to the top of the arc and hold it there. By now ten seconds will have elapsed. There may be chatter, there may not be, there might be instructions to the players, or to the guards about the queen's safety. Ignore it all and keep moving."

Twelve steps, stop. I sense Tom One before me.

"Now."

I bring the knife down, hard. There's a leather guard over the blade, so I can't do any damage to him, not beyond a bruise. He grunts a little at the impact and I immediately take three straight steps back.

"Good," he says. "Very good. She's likely to fall out of her chair and onto the floor, but because you've now moved, she won't fall on you. You still won't be able to see, so you'll use your fixed position to navigate your way toward the exit."

The exit, in this demonstration, is to my left. I back up three more steps, turn, and begin walking toward it.

"It's likely to be chaos now," Tom One says. "There will be

screaming, shouting, a lot of running around; there may even be light if someone was enterprising enough to bring their own matches." The Wright brothers, after lighting the candles at the start of the play, are to find and remove all others in the building to give us as much time in the dark as possible. "Someone may have seen you stab the queen. Someone may try to grab you, either because they saw you do it or they're trying to keep you away from it. In your haste or nerves, you may have stabbed in the wrong place and are now covered in blood. But whatever you do, whatever happens, keep moving. *Keep. Moving.*"

I do. I am walking, walking to the end of the parlor, where my exit is designated.

"The window latch will be unlocked. Push it open, slip through, out and over onto the green. And for now, that is that." Tom One snaps a finger, and there's a scratch of a match and a candle is lit, then another. "We're still working on the escape portion of the plan," he continues. "We'll be reviewing that next week. In the meantime, I want you to practice fixing your position, wherever you can, as often as you can. Learn how to move your body in the dark."

I nod.

"Again. From the beginning."

Chapter 22

TOBY

St. Anne's Lane,
Aldersgate Ward, London
23 December 1601

The inquiry I made into Kit's background, the one I sent out just after he was cast in the play, came back to me this morning. It's what I expected, yet not what I wanted to see.

It's damning.

Kit claims he stabled for a noble family in Plymouth, a relatively small town in southwest England. But according to my contacts, there are no noble families in Plymouth, at least not Plymouth proper. There are feasible and fairly benign reasons he could have lied about that: Perhaps his coming to London was not under pleasant circumstances as he claimed; perhaps he was fired, or left before his employment contract expired. Were this the case, I could see why Kit would hedge his story. These are punishable offenses, and he'd want to leave as little trail as possible.

Allowing for that possibility, I expanded my inquiry into all noble families in the whole of Devonshire County, where Plymouth is located. There are nine of them, yet not one had a stableboy by the name or surname of Kit or Christopher or Alban in their employ, now or ever. Not one of them had a stableboy by another name who had gone missing under any circumstance, fortuitous or not. And not one of these families had *any* employee who disappeared in the last six months, much less the last six weeks.

It's troubling. In my mind, Kit was already suspect for the things he is—smart, well spoken, well educated. Now he is more suspect for the things he is not. I try to think of what I know about him, reframing it in the light of what he now may also be: one of my top three suspects in an assassination plot against the queen. It's nearly impossible. All I can see is his smile and all I can hear is his voice; all I can think of is his small, slight body. I cannot reconcile that with someone who intends to take a knife or a pistol—probably a knife, pistols are too hard to conceal— muscle his way past the queen's men and her ministers and her guards, plunge it into her chest or her neck, over and over enough to kill her, and think he can get away with it. Maybe he doesn't intend to get away with it; maybe this is some kind of desperate suicide mission. But I can't see that, either. The Kit I know is too vibrant, too full of humor and spirit to throw himself away on an ideal. He doesn't have the conviction for it, not religious or political. He can't: not if he stood on the banks of the Thames and kissed me, when to do so is to go against the preaching of both.

The only hint of darkness I saw in him was at the Mermaid, when he talked about the boy he called Richard. His friend, the one now dead. There's something there. Maybe Richard wasn't the son of a nobleman. Maybe he wasn't Kit's friend at all. Maybe he was something else: father, brother, uncle, lover? It's even possible that "Richard" is a girl, named something else entirely. Whoever this person was, he (or she) meant something to Kit, and that may be the only truth about his past I have.

Either way, I need to know more. Because to name Kit as one of my final suspects is to put him at risk for the rest of his life. Nothing he does will go unnoticed, unrecorded; nothing will be seen without a measure of suspicion. And that's forever. Even if the queen dies this year, next year, or the year following (God forbid, and God save the queen), this list will pass on to her successor. Any time a treasonous crime is committed without a known suspect, Kit will be rounded up. Any time there is a hint of sedition, Kit will be rounded up. Before I do this to him, I need to be absolutely certain.

I'm thinking all this as I sit at the table in my room in the near dark, a guttering candle before me and a quill in my hand. I pull out a sheet of parchment, addressing it once more to my contact in the West Country. I ask him to look into families with a son around Kit's age—give or take five years—called Richard. It's a common-enough name so the list will be lengthy, but maybe there will be something for me to chase. I also ask him to look into families with a daughter in that same age range, one who has recently died. Finally, I ask him to widen his inquiry about a missing stableboy, or any other servant, from Devonshire into neighboring Cornwall. I didn't check the area before because it is so remote, but after learning about the raid that occurred there in October that led to the execution of the priest Ryol Campion—and that it took place in the home of a man called Richard Arundell—it's worth looking into. I'm still awaiting a response to the letter I sent the sheriff of Cornwall with regards to Arundell's household and family. If someone there matches Kit's description, I'll find out.

It takes some time to encode this letter, but finally I finish, folding and sealing it with a few drops of wax and the press of a sealing ring. Heavy and silver and set with the initial *J*, it once belonged to my father and was sent to me after his death, the only thing I have from my past. Then I run through some dates. If I send the letter tonight, it'll take three days to reach my contact. A further four for him to make his inquiry. It's not enough, but it's all I can give him. Three days for his findings to reach me. That puts me at 2 January. The play is scheduled for 6 January, the night after Twelfth Night, to allow for the queen's spiritual observance of the Epiphany. This gives me two weeks to take whatever findings I have and determine whether my two suspects are in fact three. Two weeks before I deliver my final report to the queen, the one that justifies my every thought, word, and deed over the last two months, that lays out my case and leaves no room for error. It is a matter of state security, a matter of treason, a matter of life and death.

I get to my feet and blow out the candle. Scrape some coins into a bag for my messenger, a few more than usual to ensure his haste. It's going on four, and night begins to descend as I leave my room, rosy twilight clouds giving way to a backdrop of black. I push through the crowds around St. Paul's, busier and more frantic now that Christmas is near. Merchants keep shop later than usual and patrons oblige, even though it's Sunday and the square would normally be filled with churchgoers and the barest handful of stalls. It takes some doing, but eventually I find one of my messengers playing cards in an inn off Watling. I wait as he extricates himself from the game and after giving him careful instruction, hand over both letter and coin and send him on his way. I've still got the whole of the evening ahead of me, so I decide to start it at the Mermaid Tavern. Partially because it's near. Partially because it's where Burbage and his men go, and I might be lucky enough to run into Thomas Alard, who I spent the morning tracking yet came up empty. And partially because I might see Kit.

I know from observing him that Kit spends his Sunday mornings at church, his afternoons taking supper at an inn, his evenings playing dice at taverns or taking slow, aimless strolls around the city that invariably end in him sitting on a bench alongside the Thames, staring at the water as if it speaks to him. If I can watch him, maybe he'll give me something that can put my suspicion to rest and allow me to go back to thinking only about Alard and Hargrove. Something that will finally allow me to disentangle myself from thinking about Kit at all, impossible now when it's part of my job.

But when I get to the Mermaid, Kit isn't there. Neither is Burbage or Alard or any of the players. Only Barton, who I spot at a table by the bar, surrounded by a group of boys I don't know, nor do I want to. All five are around Barton's size, stocky and surly; one has a bruise on his cheek, the other a set of scraped knuckles. Every one of them a brawler. Since Barton's been eliminated as a suspect, I have no reason or desire to stay and talk to him. I turn to go but then he spots me, hailing me over with a wave.

"Ellis. What brings you here?"

"Thought Burbage might be here," I say. "Wouldn't mind another free supper." The story of me ordering food and putting it on Burbage's tab spread like fire among the players. Since then, he's been tailed by at least a half dozen of them at every one of his tavern outings, looking to repeat the performance.

This earns a laugh from Barton. "You're the third from the Globe who's come here tonight. I already sent Sever to the Elephant. Might give that a go."

Sever is still one of my top suspects, not eliminated because he's hard to follow. If he's at the Elephant, that gives me a place to start. I nod and turn to go, then stop.

"Who was the other?" I say.

"Whit?"

"You said I was the third from the Globe who came here tonight," I reply. "Me, Sever, and who else?" It's a too-pointed question, one I have no good reason asking. But Barton's Scottish accent is turned on tonight, something that happens when he drinks. He's not likely to ask why.

"Alban," Barton replies. "But he wasn't looking for handouts. Said he was looking for a fight. Thought I might know where he could find one."

At once I know this isn't right. I know Kit, and street fighting isn't part of his repertoire. I adopt a bored tone and say, "That so? Where'd you send him?"

"Vintry Ward," Barton replies. "You know, the alleys off Cloak? Place is crawling with wasters looking for a fight. But there's money in it, if you're good."

"And if you're not?" I struggle to keep the alarm from showing on my face. The fighting that goes on in Vintry isn't friendly, with rules and boundaries and a few shillings wagered for fun. It's an all-out, no-holds street brawl for real money, a chance some are willing to kill and die for. "You know, he's just a kid." My tone is a little less bored now. "He's not a Scot tosser like you."

Barton's friends bristle at the insult, shifting in their seats as if they think they're going to do something about it. The look I give stops them at once.

Barton shrugs, unfazed. "We all have to start somewhere, don't we?"

I push out of the Mermaid and thread through the streets to Knightrider, the fastest way I know to get to Vintry. It's not far, maybe a few miles. Knightrider turns into Great St. Thomas Apostle, which turns into Cloak Lane. It's aptly named, a dark wayward street furrowed with shaky buildings, cobblestones slick with mud, the air chill and damp. Those huddled in the shadows call out at me as I pass, asking for money, food, anything. I ignore them and keep moving. There are a dozen or so alleys that snake from each side of the street, a shouting, wailing crowd in each one. Everyone here is in a fight, and Kit could be in any one of them.

I pick up speed to the dull sound of punches landing and the sharp crack of bones breaking and the tang of blood now mixed in the air. I see beaten boys lying hunched on the ground, some surrounded by people consoling them, others alone. I see other boys, victorious, holding up their winnings in bruised and battered hands. None of them are Kit, which makes me feel better. And worse.

Finally, I find him. He's in the last alley off Cloak, at the back of a crowd of bystanders watching a fight in progress, leaning against a brick wall. Arms and legs folded, dressed as usual in breeches that are too small and boots that are too big. Moss-green cape that's not warm enough for this frozen December night.

He doesn't see me, his eyes fixated on the fight before him, taking in every punch, counterpunch, move, and countermove as if he's memorizing it. Surely he can't mean to go through with this. The boys who are fighting are on the ground now, beating the piss out of each other. They're both as burly as Barton, if not more. There's nothing to be done about it, short of me taking Kit by the arm and hauling him out of here. But to do so is proprietary, assuming a claim over him I don't have. He would not thank me for it, anyway.

I decide to wait. If he steps forward and volunteers, I can present myself as his opponent. Let him land a few good hits, then rough him up enough so he'll think twice about doing this again. I'll even allow him to beat me, if it's the money he's after.

Satisfied with my plan, I settle back to watch and wait. But as always with Kit, he surprises me and pushes off the wall, leaving the fight before it's finished to head off down the alley, in the opposite direction from where I stand. There's no way of knowing if he's giving up or simply moving on, so I abandon my place in the shadows and start after him, evading shoulders and elbows to keep him in my sight.

I turn onto Dowgate Street, Kit fifty or so paces in front of me. The street runs along the border of Vintry, leading into Dowgate Ward, the one Kit calls home. He appears to have come to his senses, and I'm relieved.

Then I see them.

A trio of men stepping from the mouth of another alley, falling into place behind him. Kit has his head down, lost in his own thoughts the way he always is on his night walks, which is dangerous anywhere but more so here. If he knows they're behind him, he appears not to show it, but my guess is he doesn't. I watch the way they trail him, the way they keep a continuous distance, furtive glances ahead and behind them. They're all midheight, midweight, dressed in drab muslin and woolen caps and shoes that slap the ground as they walk, falling apart at the seams. They aren't boys looking for a fight—that much I can tell. They're thieves, looking for whatever they can get.

I consider what to do. To shout is to break cover. But to stay silent is to risk Kit getting jumped, and I can't allow that. I let out a short, shrill whistle, a signal to the thieves that they're not alone. It gets the attention of two of the boys, who swivel around, peering into the dark. I'm far enough behind them that they either don't see me or don't see me as a threat.

Following Kit was their first mistake. This would be their second.

"Hiya." One of the boys breaks from the group and steps

forward to block Kit's path. Kit jerks his head up, and I can see him hesitate, just for a moment. But then he simply sidesteps the boy and keeps on walking. The boy, of course, doesn't let him. "I'm talking to you."

He reaches out, snatches Kit's shoulder, and whirls him around, harder than necessary. At first I think that Kit will stagger, or try to run. But just as in the other ways I cannot seem to predict what he'll do, he does neither and instead reaches into that tatty cape and pulls out a knife.

I suck in a breath. Even from where I stand, fifty feet away, it's not so much a knife as a goddamn pig sticker, huge and solid and so sharp I can almost hear it pierce the air as Kit holds it before him.

"I didn't ask for company" is all he says.

The boy palms Kit's chest and shoves him, hard, into the brick wall. Kit's head punches the surface, I see the dazed look slide into his eyes and the loosening of his grip on his weapon and then I'm reaching into my left boot and pulling out my own.

Kit is on the ground and the other boys are on top of him, clawing at his pockets and his cape, rending holes into tears, slapping his face and punching his gut, all the while his knife flashes in and out of eyesight. If it gets loose, if those boys somehow manage to turn it on him, it will be done and over before Kit can call for help.

I lunge from the shadows and into the row. Reaching down, I snatch the thief who has now gotten hold of the knife, taking him by his filthy, matted hair and wrenching his head backward, exposing his dirt-streaked throat. I hold my blade against his skin.

"Don't. Move," I say.

All three boys go still, Kit too, as if frozen. The only sound in the street is that of rapid breathing. I keep my eyes on Kit's knife and nowhere else.

"Drop the knife. Slow, onto the ground."

He does. I clamp my foot down on the blade and hold up my own so that it glints in the sliver of moonlight slicing from above. Only then do I release him. Thieves are cowards so they scatter, scrambling to their feet and splitting off from one another, the sound of shoes slapping down the alley, and then we are alone.

Kit rolls from his back to his stomach, curling himself to his hands and knees. His hands are spread out over the cobble-stones, no longer smooth and pale but scraped and bloody, his head dropped low so I cannot see his face. Slowly, I kneel beside him. His shoulders are trembling.

"Kit."

He holds up a hand, as if to tell me he's all right. But when he tries to get up, I know he's not. He staggers first to one foot, then the other, then stumbles, pitching forward toward the wall. I reach for him, taking his shoulders and easing him upright before turning him around to face me. His eyes are wide, pupils pinpricked with fear and pain. Everything I keep strapped down is beginning to unravel, one breath at a time.

"Are you hurt?" I ask. But it's a stupid question, because he is. There's a bruise already blooming on the plane of his cheek, a cut on his bottom lip. He can't quite stand all the way up, and then there are his hands, curled into fractious fists, all the punches he didn't land still held inside.

He doesn't answer, but instead says, "Why?"

"What?" I am still cataloging his injuries, taking in every scrape and tear. I am thinking about his knife. I am looking at his hands.

"Why are you here? Did you follow me? Toby." He says my name because now I've looked up and away from him, back down the alley where the thieves scattered, wondering if I can track them down, wondering if I can make them hurt, wondering if it's too late for me to take whatever it is I'm feeling and turn it into something I recognize.

"I saw Barton at the Mermaid," I say finally. "He said you were out for a fight. It didn't seem like you. I didn't want—" I stop. I don't know what I want and what I don't. "Why did you come here?"

He doesn't answer at first. "I just wanted to see one. A fight, I mean. I never have, you know. I thought if I came here to watch, I'd know what to do if I ever got in one myself." He turns away for a moment before adding, in a voice so quiet and knotted I have to strain to hear it, "That didn't work out so well, either."

It wasn't a question. But there's something uncertain there anyway, in the cautious hitch of his voice and the way he now looks at me, gray eyes wide and wondering. I stand at a precipice. On one side is the truth, where I allow myself to put a name to what is happening and give myself permission to feel it. On the other is safety, where I do what I always do and shut it down and subsume feelings into inconsequence and go on lying.

I am so tired of lying.

I take a step forward, bracing my hand against the wall, palm flat against the brick beside Kit's head, caging him in to me. I tip my head toward his, slowly, giving him time to pull away if he chooses to. He doesn't. I am close enough to share his breath. I wait, and I wait, for his hands to uncurl and his posture to relax and for me to find a place to tuck away my fear, both for him and for me. A beat passes, two, before he reaches up and wraps his fingers firm around my wrist. I slip a hand around the nape of his neck and into his hair, curls soft as feathers, then lower my lips to his, soft around his bruise and his cut. He sighs and closes his eyes. He tastes of apples and of salt.

One kiss turns to two. But like before, when the fear and the tide of things I can't control surges forward, I pull back. I feel the darkness slipping in and taking over and I've already half decided to take myself out of this and walk away, when Kit grabs the folds of my cloak in tight fists.

"Don't leave," he says. "Not again."

I lower my head and kiss him for a third time.

Chapter 23

KIT

DOWGATE STREET, VINTRY WARD, LONDON
23 DECEMBER 1601

om One advised me to learn how to move my body in the dark, but I am certain this is not what he had in mind.

Toby kissing me tonight is the last thing I thought would happen. Tonight I was prepared to watch a few fights, pick up a few pointers, then go home and try to convince Jory to let me demonstrate those moves on him. I didn't think I would get robbed. I didn't think I would have to pull a knife. I didn't think I would be punched and slapped and beaten, only to have the hurt soothed away with a kiss, first one and then another and then another.

My mouth is cut and bruised and sore, but with Toby's lips

on mine and one hand firm against my back and the other restless in my hair, the pain turns into another kind of ache. He kisses like he knows what to do but it's been a long time since he has. The tension I felt from him before, that kind that said he wanted to run away, now says he's holding something back. The way he now presses me against the wall, rough brick digging into my spine, I know what that something is. He whispers my name and then some words that barely register.

"We should go." He says this as he kisses me.

"What?" My voice comes out as dazed as I feel, and he laughs, a little breath of air that warms my neck and sends a shiver through me.

"We can't be seen," he says, and he doesn't have to say anything else, because I know what it would mean if we were. I let out a sigh, of frustration and something else, and I can feel his mouth against my skin, curving into a smile. But I don't want to leave him and I don't want him to go. The only solution is one I'm shocked to hear myself say.

"Can we go someplace where we *won't* be seen?"

Toby pulls back to look at me, eyes roaming my face to see if I'm serious. When I nod, he says, "I think I know of a place."

"What are you waiting for, then?" I press my hand against his chest and push him away from me and into the street. "Show me."

He staggers back, eyes bright and smiling, and then he laughs, a plume of breath I can see in the frozen air. He looks at me and shakes his head, and he's still smiling, as if the thought of me is too much. I would like to be too much to him.

"Stay close." He picks my knife off the ground and presses it into my hand before starting off down the road.

I count to three before following him. My steps are slow, slower than I'd like. I'm a little more bruised and in pain than I first thought, without Toby and his lips and his touch to take the sting from it. We spool through one teeming street and then another, every now and again Toby turning around to see if I'm safe behind him. I watch him walk, the way he takes every twist and turn without considering it. He doesn't walk the way I do, head down, afraid of the world. He holds his head high as if challenging the world to come after him.

We turn down a street where the crowds thin and the noise quiets and a church stands empty on the corner. I give a breathless little laugh, thinking what I'd like to do if only I had the courage. But because this night is all about doing things we don't have courage to, I dart forward the ten steps to where Toby stands, slip my fingers into his, and tug him through the church's open gates and under a tree that hides us from almost everything. He knows what I mean to do; I like that he knows, and all at once he's beside me then in front of me and then he's kissing me, again, his hands on my waist, his chest breathing into me. Before I can wind my arms around his neck and keep him there, he pushes himself away and now he's the one breathless with laughter, backing away into the street again.

He leads me onto London Bridge. As always, the crowds run thick here, and Toby closes the distance between us. He's an arm's length away yet still looking over his shoulder, as if I were something of value to him, something he is determined to protect. When we reach the other side, treading the familiar teeming ground of Bankside and the Globe before me, my heart beats rapid as I understand where he's taking me.

The Rose Theatre is still and sentinel in the moonlight, and as we tumble down the well-worn path to the well-worn door I duck around him, but he snatches my sleeves and pulls me toward him, and he's smiling, stopping only when his lips meet mine and starting up again when I push him away. Then we're through the door and up the stairs and on the stage and we are alone. Just as I wanted us to be.

It was a game before. A back-and-forth, push-and-pull game, one of kisses and fleeting touch and nothing that could reveal to him what I really am. There's a sliver of moonlight and we're standing in it, part of us seen, part of us in shade. But Toby is all light, his expression clear and open, and I know what it took for him to be here. For him to push through his darkness to find acceptance and to come here with me, to be with who he thinks I am. To know it's all a lie is bearing down on me from all sides, crushing me the way it would crush him. Do I tell him who I am? Will he still feel the same about me if I do? Or will he hate me for my lies, even though they were told out of necessity? Toby reads my apprehension but not for what it is, and steps forward to touch a finger to my palm, only a finger.

"Nothing you don't want," he says.

His face is open and unguarded and real, and for the first time since I saw him at a table in a tavern behind shuttered eyes and a hundred locked doors, I know I'm looking at the real Toby. He looks both younger and older than I'm used to seeing him; he looks on the outside the way I feel on the inside. He looks almost happy but in the same way I look almost happy, where I can feel joy in a moment, but once that moment is over, the curtains close and I'm faced with everything that is still behind them.

"Kit," he says, and I realize I haven't said anything. I'm afraid of what I might say.

His fingers slide into mine. When I don't object to that, he lifts his other hand, the palm of it grazing my cheek then coming to rest there, fingertips against the back of my neck, his thumb brushing my jaw, slow and soft. There's a shift in the air and the warmth of nearness and I wait for it, for his lips on mine, but they never come. Instead they move to my cheek, trailing a line up to my ear where they stay, for just a moment, before trailing back down. I close my eyes.

I think if I can have this night with him—and if I can keep things from going too far—I can talk to him tomorrow. There must be a way I can tell him who I really am, one that would not compromise my disguise. A way that would still allow us to know each other, or at the very least for him not to hate me.

For all that I'm thinking, I'm not thinking at all. Not about anything but his mouth, now on mine, and the way he shrugs off his cloak without stopping what he's doing, dropping it to the boards only to lower me on top of it, kneeling over me with one hand wrapped around my neck, possessive as his gaze, the other braced beside my head to bear his weight.

We kiss, and we kiss, and with every touch I forget my resolve. I forget who I am supposed to be, I forget everything but what I'm feeling, and it is the sin of selfishness and I promised Jory I wouldn't sin anymore, but then I don't care about that, either. Not with Toby's hand flat on my belly, reaching for the hem of my tunic and then beneath it. He moves warm across my skin, fingers cupped around my waist, and I feel it the way I feel the sun, warming and welcome after a bleak winter, and I am *not thinking.* But when his hand slides lower, over the bone in my hip and lower still, it slows. And then it stops.

There's a moment when I think that he's just having second thoughts, that he knows to push his hand lower is to go too far for the both of us, that he's reconsidering and that's all it is. But then I feel his muscles bunch, arms and legs, and he pushes himself off me, springing backward as if my body were a hot stove and he's just been scalded. His eyes flick from the bare skin on my stomach to my face, then back again.

"You—" He stops. I can see his chest moving rapidly as he breathes. My hand is clapped over my mouth and my hair all over my face and my shirt pushed aside, the warm hand that was just there replaced by a cold slap of air.

"A girl," he finishes. "You're a girl."

Chapter 24

TOBY

THE ROSE THEATRE, BANKSIDE, LONDON
23 DECEMBER 1601

For a moment it feels like a terrible trick. But like the dispute of a bill in a tavern that put a knife in Marlowe's eye and left him for dead, something too unexpected and savage to be true, I know that this, too, is another reckoning.

The night air drifts in and around me, stale and loud, sawdust and dissonance, a mirror of all the things I'm thinking, none of them possible but all of them real. Everything I know rearranging itself around a small, thin figure, hunched before me on a darkened stage.

Kit is a girl.

She shifts to a sit, hands threading through her hair, pushing it over and over behind her ears. Moonlight crawls over her; it drags over the boards, the stands, the lath and plaster, everything coming into focus: everything. The way she curtsied when she first met Shakespeare. The furtive way she changed in and out of her costume when she thought I wasn't looking. The careful way she watched me, mimicked my posture. The way her bare skin felt under my hands and lips, too soft and too smooth. The lies she told, all of them with seeming ease.

The way she is not a he at all.

"Toby," she says. Even her voice sounds different, that mellow, rich tone now inflected with something fractured and pleading.

"Who are you?" I finally say.

"I...I'm not a stableboy. Of course not. I...I'm a maid, from the country, and—"

"You're lying." I know this from her halting speech and the tone of voice that has all of a sudden risen too high. My voice has changed, too, from soft and intimate to flat and short, and she winces to hear it. "Who are you?" I repeat.

"I'm just a girl." She's on her knees now, one hand clutching the top of her shirt and the other wrapped over her stomach as if she's holding herself together. "I wanted to be a player. I couldn't do so as a girl. So I cut my hair and dressed as a boy and took a different name and—" She stops. "I'm so sorry, Toby."

"What is it."

"What?"

"Your name. What is it."

"I...It's Katherine."

She is watching me, hands held tight, still as a statue. I recognize that look; it's the same one she wore onstage at the Globe as she stood before Shakespeare, about to audition. She looks as frightened now as she did then, and for a savage moment I'm glad. I'm glad she's afraid. I want her to feel fear and more, and worse. I want her to feel what I'm feeling.

I want her to feel abandoned.

"Toby—"

"Stop saying my name."

"I—all right. I only wanted to say I didn't mean for this to happen. It's just that I liked you and I thought—" I look at her, and whatever she sees in my face makes her stop. But then she plucks up enough courage to add, "I hoped you'd like me anyway."

I get to my feet. The movement is abrupt enough to startle her; she rocks back on her heels and scrambles to stand. She's disheveled, her hair in her face and her lips swollen and bruised, part of that from being hit but part of it from kissing. Her clothes wrinkled and untucked for the same reason, and I can't look at it. My cloak lies in a puddle on the boards at her feet and I reach for it, pulling it on and looking anywhere but at her.

"Where are you going?"

"That is none of your concern."

There's a pause. "But...don't you think we should talk?"

"There's nothing to say."

"You won't tell Shakespeare?" she says. "I could get in a lot of trouble, and he'd certainly replace me, and—"

"I won't tell him."

"Thank you for helping me tonight." She tries again. Her words are so quiet that were we not standing on a stage built for resonance, I might have missed them. It wouldn't matter either way. "If you hadn't come, things might have turned out worse."

Her words are meant to provoke. They're meant for me to reframe what happened tonight in light of what I now know, to shift the narrative from a boy looking for a fight in a dodgy part of town to a girl being trapped in it. They're meant for me to find sympathy for her, for me to wonder why she'd put herself in the streets and in danger like that. Maybe even for me to remember that the same audacity that transformed a girl into a boy wasn't an act, it was part of her all along. That her stubbornness in the face of my anger is the same whoever she is. Kit or Katherine, boy or girl, is not stupid, and it almost—almost—works.

As if she can read my thoughts, she adds, "I'm still the same person."

But that's a lie, too. The irreverence is gone. The swagger and the daring are gone. In their place are weakness and deference and manipulation and I hate it. I hate her for lying, I hate her for pretending to be what she's not; I hate her for being everything I wanted then taking it all away. I hate Kit for disappearing.

Again.

"Toby. Please, say something."

I chance a look at her. At the gray eyes and pillowed lips and frail posture and shambled hair. At the girl I thought was a boy, who I would have done anything for just moments ago and who I feel nothing for now.

"Stay away from me, Katherine." I push past her, through the tiring-house and down the stairs, into the now-quiet Bankside. I should never have come back to this theater, with its past that haunts and the present that taunts, where I know I can never return.

Chapter 25

KIT

DOLPHIN SQUARE LODGING HOUSE,
DOWGATE WARD, LONDON
23 DECEMBER 1601

"Forgive me, Father, for I have sinned."

I'm kneeling on the gritty boards of our room at the lodging house, in front of the bedsheet that divides the space in two. On the other side is Jory in his role as priest, wearing another bedsheet around his shoulders to act as a robe, preparing to listen as I confess my sins so he can give me penance and absolve them.

Confessing was Jory's idea, not mine. But I gave him no other choice, not after I finally made my way home from the Rose and promptly broke into tears the moment I was safely inside my room. I cried for a good long time while Jory asked me, over and over, what was wrong. I could have said it was because I was missing Father. I could have said I was robbed. Both aren't a lie, but they're not exactly the truth, either, and these days the line is becoming more and more blurred. In any case, I didn't want to lie about Toby, not again, not when I've lied so much already. So I decided to tell Jory everything.

"I kissed a boy. Twice," I start. "Well, by that I mean two separate times. The first time was a few days ago, and it wasn't for very long. But the second, that was tonight. It lasted a while. Hours—" I stop. "That is not in and of itself a sin, at least I don't think so. But I think him touching my bare skin might be—" I stop again. "But my real sin is that I lied to him. I lied in all the ways you can lie to a person. He knew me as a boy, and I let him think I was one. He thought I was a boy when he kissed me, and I didn't tell him I wasn't. I didn't care that I forced him to show me something about himself he wasn't ready to. I didn't care about compromising my disguise. I did all these things and not once did I care about anyone but myself. I was selfish, which is yet another sin on top of all the others."

Jory is silent for a long, long time. Part of being a priest is to not judge the sinner; that is God's job, after all. Even so, I can practically see his pursed lips, his wringing hands, his dark eyebrows pitched in a frown that grows deeper by the second. I can also hear him breathing, a little too rapidly, as if the flames of hell are coming through the floorboards, after me for all my sins and Jory for being corrupted at the hearing of them, and he's trying to blow them out before they engulf us all.

"I take it he found out," Jory says finally. "That you aren't a boy."

I nod, but of course he can't see me. "Yes. And he was so angry. He looked at me as if he hated me. He probably does. He told me to stay away from him—" I swallow, thinking about the flatness in Toby's voice and the blank look on his face when just seconds before he touched me as if I were a wonder, the way he couldn't look at me and how he couldn't wait to get away from me.

"I tried to tell him I'm still the same person I was before." I pause to pull myself together. "But even that was a lie, because he doesn't know who I am. *I* don't even know who I am."

"You're Katherine Arundell of Cornwall," Jory says.

But that's not true, either. Katherine Arundell was devout, quiet, obedient, and always, *always* afraid. But the moment I became Kit Alban I turned into someone different. Someone who didn't watch what she said or did; someone who said and did exactly what she wanted, not what was expected. Someone who finally felt permission to decide who she really is. The moment Toby found out who I was, I felt myself reverting back to Katherine, a quick unwind to someone I don't want to be. Not anymore.

"Do you wish to confess anything else?" Jory asks.

I shake my head. "No."

"For your penance, I assign you ten Our Fathers and ten Hail Marys."

"Ten!"

"And one Our Lady of Fatima."

"A Fatima!" I gasp. "What for?"

"Sins of the flesh," Jory replies. "And for being an accessory to the sins of another. And one Magnificat for questioning your penance."

I open my mouth. Close it. Open it again, but only to recite the Act of Contrition to conclude my confession before I get myself in any more trouble.

"His mercy endures forever," Jory intones, which is good because it's going to take me approximately that long to finish this penance he's given me. But then I cross myself and it's all over, and I rock back onto my feet and crawl onto my mattress, where I plan to spend the rest of the evening in peace, quietly weeping into my pillow. But there's a scrape of a chair, a busy pause, the whisper of a curtain and then Jory is poking his head around the curtain.

"Who is he?"

"Jory!" I'm shocked he would ask me, because a priest is never supposed to ask someone about their confession once it's over.

"He's someone from the Globe, right?" Jory continues. "Players. They're all depraved, salacious, lewd, profane, *sinners*—"

"Excuse you, I'm a player."

"Exactly. Which is why you find yourself in this position." Jory folds his arms, mouth pursed in disapproval, just as I imagined. "What did he do when he found out?"

I drop my head into my hands. "I already told you."

"That was Jory the priest. Jory the groom didn't hear you." Even though he's no longer wearing his sheet-robe, now dressed in his usual muslin tunic and trousers, I feel as if he's bending the rules to suit him and I don't like it.

"Where did you think it would go?" he continues.

"I don't know," I say. My voice is muffled. "I thought maybe he wouldn't care. That he would like me anyway. But obviously I was wrong."

"It's wrong for a lot of reasons," Jory says. "He *kissed a boy*."

"No, he didn't," I say. "I'm a girl. Remember?"

"Yes, but he didn't know that," Jory replies. "You don't think you're the first boy he's kissed—or thought he kissed—do you?"

Toby kissed me tonight as if I were the only one in the world. I don't care who else came before me.

"This boy, whoever he is, gave you good advice," Jory says. "Stay away from him. There's nothing else you can or should do. Because in fourteen days this will all be over. The queen will be gone. There will be a new rule in place. And those who do not fall in line with it, or who have sinned so grievously that there can be no salvation, earthly or heavenly, such as your sodomite player—"

I jerk my head up. "Don't call him that."

"—will be declared a sinner and a heretic. And there will be penalties."

"Penalties?" I say. "What do you mean by that?"

"The Inquisition, of course."

The word stuns me into silence. I'm too young to remember it, and so is Jory, but Father wasn't and told me the stories, when the queen's own Catholic sister sat on the throne and made being a Protestant illegal, how eight hundred men and women were forced to renounce their religion and when they didn't, they were burned alive in a square that lies not a mile from our very room.

"Catesby wants to bring back the Inquisition?" I say at last. "He's never said that."

"Not in so many words," Jory says. "But Spain has long been an enthusiast. As has France. It would be considered retribution for the condemnable acts that have been committed against our faith. There's not a country in Europe that wouldn't support it. But it's not something for you to worry about, Katherine," he says to my silence. "You have sinned, but you are of the true faith. You will be saved."

"But isn't it the same thing they did to us?" I say. "They persecute us, make our religion illegal, kill our priests, and then we turn around and do the same to them? You can't simply get revenge on someone by doing to them the same thing they did to you."

"It's different," Jory says, then disappears behind his side of the curtain again.

But it isn't really different at all.

Chapter 26

TOBY

ST. ANNE'S LANE,
ALDERSGATE WARD, LONDON
24 DECEMBER 1601

The revelation that the boy called Kit is actually a girl called Katherine is proving to be troublesome, in more ways than I expected.

It changes my investigation, as I've now narrowed three key suspects down to two. Ordinarily I'd consider it a victory to be able to eliminate someone. To do so is the culmination of days and weeks and sometimes months of hard work, watching and writing inquiries and chasing leads, enumerating each and every piece of information I've gathered to officially declare someone innocent. But I've not yet found the words I need to explain how

Kit is now off my list. How, after weeks of watching her, spending time with her, getting to know her, kissing her—

I didn't see it. I should have, and I didn't.

It's not that she's innocent: Not a single person I've ever watched wasn't guilty of something. Kit—Katherine—was guilty of lying about her gender, and all the suspicions I had about her were simply part and parcel of that. From the background inquiry that came up empty to her strange Devonshire accent that sounds stronger than it should, her shabby clothes and her exemplary education. My best guess: She's the daughter of a nobleman. Possibly contracted in marriage, running away to London to escape it and dressing as a boy to evade being caught, fulfilling some long-held fantasy of acting on Shakespeare's stage. Whatever else she's lied about, it no longer matters to me.

With a savage stroke of my pen, I cross the name *Kit Alban* from the list on the parchment before me. As a suspect, he no longer exists. He never existed at all. My focus now is on Gray Hargrove and Thomas Alard, and that is all. The play is in two weeks and by then I need to have these two narrowed down to one.

I push from my desk and shrug on my cloak. Today is another rehearsal, the last before we break for Christmas, and one of just a few before the final performance in January. *The final performance.* I cannot make a mistake. I need to deliver the assassin to the queen, collect my stipend, and then, without notice or warning to anyone, board the first ship to France, ridding myself of this life of lies forever. The only thing standing in my way is my missing cloak. The one I gave to Carey at Whitehall, the one with my entire life savings stitched into the lining: six thousand eight hundred pounds. Carey still has it, and if I can't get him to give it back without alerting his always-suspicious mind, I'll be forced to break into his home to take it back, absolutely a last resort.

I run from my room, past my landlady who is angry with me for turning down her early Christmas gift, offered by way of a late-night knock on my door, and into the perpetually muddied streets. Today is bright, crisp, clear and cold, the sun off the water blinding me as I approach the Thames. The city is seething with preparations for the forthcoming Twelfth Night celebration, so I opt not to take London Bridge, clogged as I know it will be with even more merchant carts and horses and carriages and people. I reach Poles Wharf and hail a wherry to get me to the Globe.

"You a player?" the wherryman asks me when I tell him where I'm going.

I nod my reply.

"Very good," he says. "I just saw Shakespeare's latest. Last week. *As You Like It*. And I did, very much." He laughs at his own joke. "I hear he's got a new one. Very secret, playing for the queen only."

"That so?" I say. I leaked this information six weeks ago; I'm always surprised at how quickly word gets around and to whom. "Can't be much of a secret if you know about it."

"True, ha!" the wherryman says. "Well, you know what they say. Two people can keep a secret as long as one of them is dead. That'll be a penny," he adds as the boat tips and bumps along the shore. I pay him and climb up the stairs to the bank.

Inside the Globe I'm greeted by the sound of lutes and

citterns and drums, musicians onstage practicing their opening song. The tiring-house is in a fervor, costumers fussing over buttons and collars and gowns and wigs, stagehands dashing to and fro, dragging out and setting up props, players trying and aborting lines, nervous chatter and laughter. The Lord Chamberlain's Men are clustered in a corner, running through voice exercises, cricking necks, or staring straight ahead in a trance of preparation. And then there's Kit.

She's standing with Mistress Lucy and if she sees me, she doesn't let on. She too stares straight ahead, not in preparation I think, but in avoidance. Her short hair is pressed beneath a long red wig, cheeks flushed and lips painted on, body buttoned under a doublet and breeches and hose that leave her legs nearly bare. I've seen her in costume before. Dressed as a girl before: a boy dressed as a girl. But now that I know she's a girl disguised as a boy and dressed as a girl, I find myself wondering if that's what she really looks like. Before she cut her hair, strapped herself down, and traded skirts for trousers. In costume she looks the same but also different, eyes still huge, jaw still sharp but with her hair long it's all rounded out somehow, softer and more feminine; her lips—

"Toby Ellis." Mistress Lovett snaps her fingers before my face. "Have you gone shy on me today? Vestments need to come off. Now. You're ten minutes late as it is."

She circles around me, pulling off my shirt with practical hands, gesturing for me to take off my trousers. She thrusts a scrap of lace in my hand that is my shirt, which I pull on, then my brown doublet, then my hose and breeches, voluminous things that make me look...what did Kit call it? Trussed up like a St.

Crispin's Day capon. She said that at Carey's patron party, not about my costume but about Carey's cape I was wearing, which had more or less the same effect. In thinking about it now, it was an odd description. St. Crispin's Day. A feast day for Catholics.

Mistress Lovett reappears in front of my face, wielding a comb for my hair and a puff of powder for my cheeks. I dislike both and I wave her away, but she's not having it so I am forced to endure her ministrations until they're done to her satisfaction. Finally she finishes and crams my hat on my head, snatches my sleeve, and gives me a great shove toward the curtain.

"Orsino! You're late," Shakespeare says by way of greeting. I don't know how he saw me walk on; he hasn't even looked up from his parchment.

"Not very," I say.

"Better three hours too soon than a minute too late," he intones. "*Ah*. I do love that line. Boy! Take your place onstage, for God's sake." We're all boys—well, not all—so we look around at one another, unsure of who he means.

"Orsino. Viola-Cesario." Shakespeare snaps his fingers. "Fabian. Feste. Center stage. *Immédiatement*. We're starting from the top of act five, scene one."

From the corner of my eye, I see Kit look to me and then just as quickly look away. The scene we're rehearsing is the last one we practiced at the Rose, where I took her in my arms and she forgot her lines, and even then I knew why. I knew I had her in that place where a word is strong as a spell and a look as intimate as a kiss, the rush of feeling when you know someone is aware of everything you do, when a touch means everything and sometimes, it is.

"Orsino! Get that yearning look off your face," Shakespeare bellows. "You're meant to be agitated at the start—yes, *that's* the look I'm after. There's plenty of time to be doe-eyed at the end, when you realize you're in love with Viola-Cesario. And speaking of Viola-Cesario, tone it down a bit, lad, eh? You look absolutely *incensed*. Take your places." I look back at Kit then, and Shakespeare is right. She looks furious, glaring at him as she moves to her place onstage. But I don't think he's the one she's angry at.

"From the top," Shakespeare calls, and we begin.

I know this scene well enough. For all that it's changed, Kit and I manage to keep up with it from our rehearsals at the Rose. I'm glad, because with all that I now know about her—the dynamics of this scene where her character professes her love for me, this play where I think I love one person but turn out to love another—everything has changed and I'm distracted.

It progresses the way it should. Kit and me and three other players, giving our lines and blocking our steps. Two more players join in—the Parliament hearing, we called it—then I'm shouting my lines, pulling a sword from the scabbard at Kit's side, and thrusting it at Olivia's face before turning the force of my fury onto Kit.

I come at her from behind, wrapping my arm around her neck the way the scene calls for and the way we practiced at the Rose. But the moment I touch her, Kit clamps both her hands over my arm and shoves me off her, turning to face me with a look so fierce I take a step back.

Shakespeare raises a hand to object to the change in choreography. "Viola-Cesario, Orsino is meant to push *you* away, not the other way round. Let's try it again—"

But Kit ignores his direction and I do, too, finishing my lines, shouting them at her: words about sacrifice and love, spite and a raven's heart within a dove.

"—or not," Shakespeare sighs.

"After him I love," Kit throws back at me, her voice rising and rising. *"More than I love these eyes—"*

"Not how I'd recommend demonstrating love," Shakespeare calls, "not with all that screaming—"

"More than my life—"

"—and glaring—"

"Punish my life for the tainting of my love!" Kit stops. Her speech is meant to end here, to be picked up by a line from Olivia before continuing on. But the whole of the Globe has fallen quiet, looking from Kit to me to Shakespeare to one another. Her eyes are wide and she holds one hand to her mouth while the other is wrapped over her waist, a gesture I've seen once before, only on a different stage. It makes her look vulnerable and afraid and entirely too female, and I want to tell her to stop, that dressed this way and looking this way there's not a soul in England who wouldn't see her for who she is. But then I remember I don't care, that she is none of my concern, that it doesn't matter what happens to her because I told her to stay away from me.

"Well," Shakespeare says. His dark eyes, canny as a goat's, shift from Kit to me and back again. "Well, well, well. Viola-Cesario, take ten. As you're to appear in the remainder of act five, we'll take it from the prior scene, act four, scene two, all the way through scene three. You can rejoin us then, if you're done taking the piss. Gentlemen, *des endroits.*" Shakespeare waves his hands and his men, Burbage and the rest, scamper onto the stage while the rest of us climb down into the pit to watch them. Except for Kit. She marches straight for the tiring-house, disappearing through the curtain. After a moment, a long one in which I make sure no one is watching me—and decide whether this is something I should or want to do—I follow.

She's sitting on the plank bench that runs along the back wall, elbows resting on her knees, head turned and dropped low, black feathered cap off and swinging idly in her hand. It's a boy's pose, the one she affected sitting beside me on the bench at Carey's, mimicking mine. Something in my chest pushes against my rib cage, hard.

Maybe she heard my footsteps creaking on the boards, maybe she felt someone standing before her. But the hat stills and she looks up at me, the anger on her face from only moments ago now gone, in its place a look I've never seen before, not from her: disinterest.

"Has it been ten minutes already?" she says.

"Not quite," I reply.

She nods and turns her head back to the floor.

"The scene," I say eventually. "It was a little different from how we practiced."

"Yes. I suppose so." Then: "I apologize. I was angry, and I took it out on you. I shouldn't have done that."

Angry at me, or at something or someone else? I don't know. I find myself wanting to ask, but I know that I can't.

Instead I say, "I guess I don't have to tell you not to go looking for a fight." I regret the words as soon as they're out. They're too light, too teasing; they're something I could have said before, when we were . . . not what we are now. They're a reminder of a night that started one way and ended up another. That was her doing, yes. But it was also mine.

"No. I won't be doing that, either." Kit gets to her feet. Brushes the sawdust from her breeches and pulls on her hat. Without another word she nods at me, brusque, then slips past me, back through that velvet star-studded curtain and onto the stage.

She's staying away from me, just as I asked her to. But it doesn't feel as satisfying as I thought it would.

Chapter 27

KIT

DOLPHIN SQUARE LODGING HOUSE,
DOWGATE WARD, LONDON
24 DECEMBER 1601

Tonight is Christmas Eve.

I am on my way to Catesby's to celebrate the evening, to hear Mass, and to begin our final preparations for the play, now just thirteen days away.

The evening is sharp and cold, the sky spitting hard rain that every now and again turns to flurries of snow, then back to rain. I am dressed in my best, which isn't all that good anyway, dark blue breeches and white shirt, the same things I wore to Carey's patron party. I also have on my cape—the tears in the fabric from my scuffle with the thieves now mended—along with my lumpy green hat and gloves. These are not my best, either, nor do they match or even look good. But there is no one at Catesby's I need to impress, at least not with my looks.

The walk to North House in Lambeth takes just under an hour. Each time I go I take a different route, sometimes taking the wide village roads, other times trespassing through pastures. This wasn't one of Catesby's instructions, but it is a rule I made for myself after Toby started popping up everywhere I went. But now that I know he's done with me, I take the shortest and most direct way, a wide, cobbled road that grows progressively narrower and dirtier as I get closer to the outskirts of town. Jory left this morning, saying he needed to be there early to prepare for Mass. This is true, I think, but I think it's also true that he's avoiding me, ever since my confession last night. Afterward, I caught him looking at me, shaking his head ever so slightly before looking away again. But I can't think about Jory and his judgment and disappointment right now. He'll have to take his place in the queue, as it seems everyone else is disappointed with me, too: first Toby (even though he is *none of my concern*) and now Master Shakespeare.

My little outburst during rehearsal at the Globe wasn't as bad or as revealing as it could have been, but it was close. I didn't miss the way everyone in the pit looked at us afterward, trading funny little smiles as if we just confirmed something they already suspected. I didn't miss the knowing look on Shakespeare's face, either. Not that he knows I'm a girl—I would have felt his certain and immediate wrath for that—but that I acted like a jilted lover to Toby's real-life role of insensitive heartbreaker.

I didn't realize until today I was angry at Toby. I didn't think

I had the right to be, not really. I lied to him, after all. But when I think about it, he lied to me, too. He made me think he felt something for me, but he couldn't have. Not really. Not when it was so easy for him to pull away, then tell me to stay away, no matter who I am.

I contemplate this and all the other problems I have created for myself, barely a dent in the surface by the time I reach North House. I almost don't recognize it, decorated as it is for Christmas, a stark change to the lifeless facade it was before. The many windows are strewn with branches of holm interwoven with ivy and berries, the doorways wreathed with bay. The lanterns that line the front path are lit with candles, still more candles flickering from the windowsills.

The Granite Gargoyle wordlessly pulls open the servants' door for me, and I'm nearly knocked over by the smells that waft out behind her: a Christmas feast in the making. I'm surprised and touched at the effort, as this is surely all for Jory and me. Catesby and the rest of his men have families, wives, and children in the country they will travel to see and celebrate with tomorrow. There's no need for all this otherwise.

I walk myself into the dining room. Catesby and his men are scattered throughout, holding thick, cut-crystal goblets filled with deep red liquid. They talk and laugh and scratch, Catesby and Tom One and Tom Two by the fire, all of them looking handsome and happy in bright clothing, black velvet and gold brocade and white starched ruffs, fur on collars and feathers in hats. Even Jory manages to look pleased: He's deep in conversation with the Wright brothers, who nod emphatically at whatever he's saying. Behind them, the table is covered and set and the Yule log has already been brought in and burns merrily in the fireplace, where per tradition it will do so until morning.

"Katherine!" Catesby spots me and waves me over. "You've arrived." He reaches for a decanter and a glass to pour me whatever it is he's drinking. "It's wine," he says. "Spanish. From Seville, in fact. It was your father's—"

"Favorite," I say. "I remember. Ryol liked it, too." I always thought if someone were allowed in our cellar, stacked to the rafters with barrels of Spanish wine, they'd know our religion just from that.

"An homage to them both, you could say." Catesby tips his glass to mine. "I hope you've come hungry. Madeline has been cooking all day." It takes me a moment to realize he means the Granite Gargoyle. *Madeline* seems too cheerful a name for her. And why is she here on Christmas Eve? Does she not have family to see? Or is Catesby who she considers family?

"It smells wonderful," I say finally. "Just like Lanherne. We would always have boar's head for Christmas Eve, and roasted pullet, plum porridge, mulled wine and a Christmas pie—" My throat sticks at the memory, of the trumpeters and carolers and mummers Father would bring in, how I would wear my best, prettiest dress and dance the Sellinger's Round and play Shoeing the Mare, Hoodman Blind, and Hot Cockles. It was the best day of every year, and now it's gone and I wonder how it will be going forward, after this year, if there is a next year.

What will happen to me after this is all over? Will I always be looking over my shoulder, fearful of an assassin just like me? An angry, rightly wronged Protestant seeking retribution for the death of their queen, a catalyst for a new rule and a possible

Inquisition, followed by months or years of fear and lies and planning for what I would do if I were caught? Will killing the queen solve anything? Everything will be different, but will I still be the same: angry, lonely, uncertain, now a murderer and a target for revenge to boot? Or will I simply be caught and executed for my part in all of it and not have to worry about anything at all anymore?

There's a warm hand on my shoulder and I look up, at Catesby's knowing gaze.

"I know this night must be difficult," he says. "But use whatever you're feeling to dictate your actions from now until Twelfth Night."

I don't know if this is what he would advise if he knew that what I was feeling was confusion.

When the goose and beef and gilded fruit are cleared from the table, Catesby lays out a map. This one is not of the interior of Middle Temple Hall but of the exterior—a finely drawn sketch of each street, garden, and building that makes up the whole of the Inns of Court, of which Middle Temple is just a small part.

There are Xs drawn in strategic places, there are distances marked, there are time stamps and symbols that denote which man will be where and when, which boat will be leaving which pier when. There are a primary escape route and a secondary escape route, skulls and crossbones lurking in corners and alleys and even the nearby Temple Church to denote expected placement of the queen's guard.

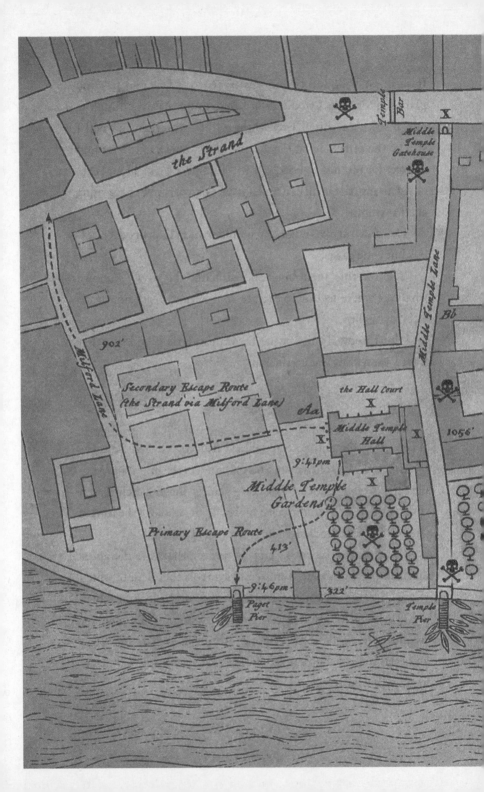

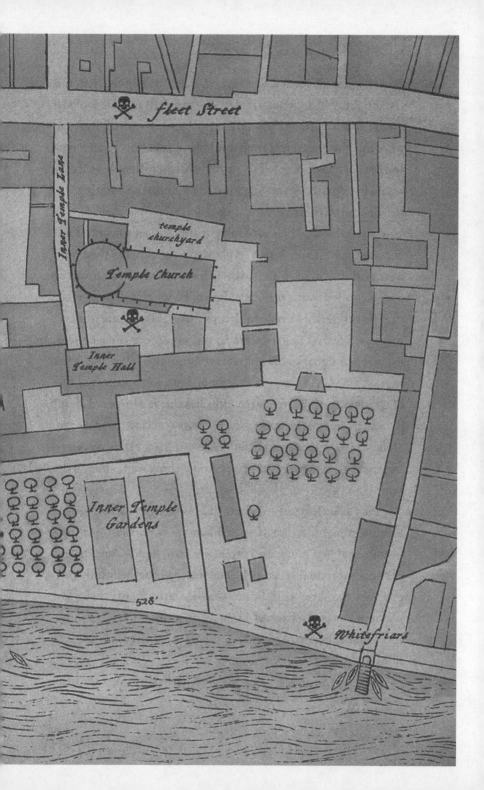

Fleet Street

Inner Temple Lane

temple churchyard

Temple Church

Inner Temple Hall

Inner Temple Gardens

528'

Whitefriars

"The play starts at seven o'clock," Catesby begins. "Kit and the Wrights will arrive at five. The queen at half six." He looks to me for confirmation. I was sure—and careful—to ask Burbage what the queen's arrival time would be. I told him I had a nervous stomach and wanted to ensure whatever illness came of it would have passed before she stepped foot into the building.

"Six thirty, that's correct," I say.

Catesby nods. "Her attending retinue is significant. This, of course, we already knew." A glance to the Wrights then, who were both involved in the last rebellion attempted against the queen, headed by the now-dead Earl of Essex.

The similarities between that plot and this one are unnerving: Essex hiring Shakespeare to put on an out-of-favor play, using it as a signal to his followers to begin their uprising—one that included every man in this room. I pieced together the rest of the details of this rebellion after hearing it whispered about in taverns and on the streets after Ryol's execution two days ago, alongside my father's name. But Catesby feels it's those similarities that will save us, because who would think we would use the same plan twice?

"Fifty Gentlemen Pensioners," Catesby says. "Including captain, lieutenant, and a standard bearer. Now, these men are ornamental, for pomp and ceremony only, and it appears this play does not qualify as such. The seating chart helpfully procured by the Wrights indicates that her duty guards that night will number ten to twelve." He gives an unpleasant smile. "One time, I imagine, we can be thankful for the thrift of the queen's household."

Catesby continues. "The Wrights have confirmed that the

guards will sit along the back, that Her Majesty will be sur-rounded on all sides by her favored courtiers and their wives, as well as her ministers. All but the women will be armed, and while this is of some concern, I think the element of surprise—and of darkness—will be on our side. Even so, the Wrights will be on hand to deflect any potential attacks, and to lead Kather-ine safely outside once the mission is complete.

"The Wrights will exit here"—Catesby points to the window at the southeast end of the Hall—"as will you, Katherine. This will put you in the Middle Temple Gardens. There is only one door into the Hall, which will be guarded. Once the job is com-plete, and once the queen's men understand that the commo-tion inside the building is not due to the play—at least not the intended part of the play—they will give chase. We estimate you will have no more than a five-minute head start. Five minutes from the time the Wrights' candles extinguish, your knife meets the queen's chest, then out the window and into the garden. You have a further five minutes to reach Paget Pier at the river. There will be a wherry waiting for you."

The stretch between that window and that pier is a tenth of a mile. Two hundred and eleven steps at a walk, half that at a run. I know this; I've measured it a hundred times. But on the map, the distance looks miles long, an eternity: the distance between my life and my death.

"Where will you be?" I say. "And Tom One and Tom Two?" The Toms exchange a glance, confused; I've never called them that out loud. "Winter is One. Percy is Two," I clarify.

"Winter will be on the ground, a safe distance away to watch the proceedings," Catesby says. "Once I receive confirmation that all went as planned, Percy and I will continue on to White-hall. Presenting this." From his festive doublet he pulls out a let-ter, creamy and rich and wrapped with a thick black ribbon and stamped with a wax seal nearly the size of my fist. "Letters pat-ent from Pope Clement VIII and Philip III of Spain, promising friendship with the sovereign state of England contingent on the safe transfer of power into the hands of Archduchess Isabella." He waves it once, then slips it back into his doublet. "A gesture the ministers will agree to, if they do not wish this country to be invaded by the collective power of Spain, Portugal, Italy, Aus-tria, and France."

"And what of me?" I say. "Where am I to be, after I row away in the wherry?"

"We are paying you a sum of two thousand pounds," Catesby replies. "You may go where you like. You may stay in London, under our protection, or you may go back to Cornwall, if that pleases you instead. In the new reign, we will reinstate Lanherne to you, along with your title and the rights to the rent from your tenants. You will be a wealthy woman, Katherine. And you will live in peace."

Catesby means this to be comforting, I know, a reward for a job well done. But there is something deeply unsettling about this story ending where it began, as if it never happened at all.

Chapter 28

TOBY

St. Anne's Lane,
Aldersgate Ward, London
5 January 1602

The final rehearsals of the year are complete. I brought in Christmas alone, as well as the new year, an unwilling tradition that started the year Marlowe died and has continued ever since. I turned down an invitation to join the Christmas Eve festivities at Whitehall—another tradition—as well as one from Carey to join him and his wife and family for New Year's supper. It's not that I don't enjoy company. But the idea of spending an evening spinning and perpetuating lies seemed tiresome, not to mention at odds with the occasion. It's safer and easier to be alone.

Melancholy threatens, so I turn back to the unopened letter in front of me.

It arrived four days ago, a day earlier than expected, from my contact in the West Country. Inside is the response to the inquiry I made into Kit's friendship with a boy called Richard, and my request to widen the search for a missing stableboy or any other servant from the area of Devonshire all the way into Cornwall. The response to the letter I wrote when I still thought Kit was a suspect, the same night I followed him to Vintry Ward and kissed him, the same night I discovered Kit was really a girl called Katherine.

I haven't opened it because the response is no longer of interest. Maybe there is a stableboy gone missing, but unless that boy also happens to be a girl, he is irrelevant to me. The same goes for a boy called Richard. Kit told me her friend was the son of a nobleman, and while I thought she was telling me the truth, I could be mistaken about that, too. Maybe he doesn't exist at all, or does but by a different name. But whoever this person is, whether he's Kit's betrothed, jilted and left behind in Plymouth or Cornwall, enraged or thrilled or heartbroken or uncaring, it still wouldn't matter to me.

Except in the cold, damp, disquieting solitude of my room, I find that it does.

I pick up the letter. Folded parchment that's worse for the wear, dirt-stained and rain-cockled, inelegantly sealed with a thumbprint in a patch of black wax. I consider burning it. Tossing it into the low crackling fire now in my fireplace, six pence spent on wood, my one concession to the holidays. Then I would be free of her, free to turn my attention back where it should be:

My suspects. My job. The culmination of a plan two years in the making, one that concludes tomorrow. Free to go and do and think and be anything I want to be, without anyone to watch over at all.

Before I can change my mind, I crack the seal and open it.

Devonshire (Plymouth, Tiverton, Torrington, Salcombe, Ford, and Exeter). No families noble within report member called Richard missing or having died. Records of three boys not noble named Richard (aged twelve, fifteen, twenty-one) died year 1601, February, April, and July. No missing employee, groom, or stableboy. Cornwall (Newquay, Truro, Camborne, St. Ives). One family noble reports member called Richard Arundell having died (aged thirty-seven) year 1601, October. Record of one boy not noble named Richard (aged fourteen) died year 1601, May. One missing employee, groom, 1601, October. Jory Jameson (aged seventeen), employee of Richard Arundell.

Richard Arundell. The recusant Catholic from Cornwall who was killed in a raid on his home in October. The nobleman housing the priest who was executed last month after confessing to conspire against the queen. A missing groom, of the same age Kit says she was at the audition, gone since October.

I set the letter down.

If I still thought Kit was a boy, this would be enough for me to give up on Hargrove and Alard and devote the rest of my time, from now until the play, to watching him. It tracks with everything I knew about him. The story about being a stableboy for a nobleman. The unexplained education, the intimate knowledge of all those books and plays. I think of words she uses, her impeccable manners, the perfect curtsy she dropped to Shakespeare her first day at the Globe. Knowledge you don't get unless you've been around it. All of it holds, even down to the friend called Richard. All of it, except for the fact that Kit is a girl called Katherine.

There's a coincidence here I can't put my finger on, and every sense I have after six years honing them in this job tells me something isn't right. I don't know if I'm hanging on to her because I'm suspicious, or because I don't want to let her go.

It's something I didn't allow myself to think about before: What would happen if Kit *were* the assassin. How it would feel to turn his name over to the ministers. To arrange for the queen's guards to come to somewhere I know he'd be, not the Globe because it's too public, but to his lodging house, or the Rose, or on one of his nighttime walks. To apprehend him, snatch up his fragile wrists in irons, drag him to the Tower because that's where they take the worst kinds of criminals, the ones who threaten the queen and her realm. They might even cram him in that three-foot cell called Little Ease, at least until they took him out to torture him, to find out the names of the conspirators the way they did that priest. To stretch him on the rack until his bones snapped, then toss his broken and bloodied body in the back of a wooden cart to take him to Tyburn, not a private execution at the Tower like Essex but somewhere public, someplace where people could shout and batter him with rocks and sticks and insults before the executioner hanged him then cut him open, before his limbs were hacked off and then his head—

I close my eyes. The world tilts beneath me.

But this can't happen because Kit *is* a girl called Katherine, and this means something different to me now. It's not just that she is no longer of any interest to me in this investigation, or that the queen or the ministers need never to know her name or who she is. It isn't even that she is a liar, even though she isn't lying about being involved in a Catholic plot to kill the queen.

It means that my interest in her—one I can't continue to deny—is no longer dangerous, for either of us. I am angry with her, yes. But that anger is competing with everything else I feel about her—sympathy, curiosity, desire—and it is losing.

I glance to the window, to the noise and activity below. A city in the throes of Twelfth Night, yet another celebration I traditionally avoid. For the crowds, for the drunks, for the revelry I don't feel this night or any other. Because of the last time I went with Marlowe, fragmented memories now, him with twigs in his hair and me with berries in mine, both of us dressed as Holly Men—the winter guise of the Green Man, a character from pagan mythology—his hand in mine and my heart in his. Because it is a night spent pretending to be something you are not, something I do every day.

What would I do were I not Toby: watcher, cryptographer, consummate liar? Were I not living in this room, mean and small as the life I live in it, locked up tight to keep everyone out? If I could finally tell the truth at last. Would it change anything, this reversal of order, one day before everything is to change for good? I don't know. But I know the answer doesn't lie here. I rise from my desk, throw on my cloak, and set out into the noisome streets.

Chapter 29

KIT

DOLPHIN SQUARE LODGING HOUSE,
DOWGATE WARD, LONDON
5 JANUARY 1602

My stomach is a bed of snakes.

Tomorrow is the play, and everything that comes with it. Avenging my father, bidding goodbye to Toby, disappearing forever. It is all the things of poems, unexpected death and unrequited love and unfulfilled lust, a lifetime of events compressed into two hours and fifty-eight minutes.

I'm lying on my mattress, and through the cold, cracked window, I can hear the noise in the streets below. It is Twelfth Night, and the city is alive with it. Preparations have been going on for days, there is music and food and bonfires, parades and mummers and troubadours. There are makeshift wooden stages set up along crossroads, lanterns strung across streets, windows and doors and fence posts hung with ivy and trailing boughs of fir, ribbons tied everywhere in every color of the rainbow. The air is thick and sweet with the smell of Twelfth Night cakes and wassail, and on my way home from the market this morning, I passed a marble fountain in Cheapside being filled with wine, to be piped out through a cherub's mouth for passersby to fill their cups with. I've gone to a smaller version of the festival, in Truro in Cornwall, but it was nothing compared with this.

If I close my eyes and think very hard, I can remember going with Father. Before I said I was too old, before I said it was too childish, before I said—in a fit of anger and despair I now regret—that I spent every day pretending and I didn't need a festival to do it. The last time I went I was twelve, maybe, Father and I both dressed as paupers, a scratchy wool dress for me and breeches for him, an ill-fitting shirt and cape and a flat cap worn low—looking a lot like I do right now, in fact. He loved Twelfth Night and continued going long after I stopped. Maybe he liked the freedom of being someone else for a night, too.

I roll off my mattress and begin pawing through a stack of clothing piled in the corner. I bought them this morning, yet another disguise to put on after the play: stockings and delicate lace-up boots, a shift and a kirtle and a jaunty feather-capped hat, a dress of black and gold and gray. Clothes just like those I wore when I was still Lady Katherine Arundell. It takes a while for me to put them on, fussing with laces and stays and garters and all the things I'm no longer accustomed to wearing. My hair, wild as it is, doesn't fit neatly under the cap the way it once did, so I find some pins and arrange it the best I can. If Twelfth Night is a night for disguise, for being what you are not, this is a good choice.

"Where are you going?" Jory's voice drifts to me from the other side of the curtain. I imagine he heard the rustle and occasional bit of foul language (a habit picked up from my time in the taverns—Father would not be best pleased) as I struggled into the dress.

"I thought I'd go out for a bit," I say. "Get some air. See what Twelfth Night looks like in London."

"What?" I hear a mighty creak as he hauls himself out of his chair, then his voice at the mouth of the curtain. "Are you sure? The play is tomorrow. It's too risky to be out in those crowds. You could get robbed again—what are you wearing?"

I've stepped through the curtain into Jory's side of the room now, and he's looking at me as if he's seen a ghost.

"Why are you dressed that way?"

I pause a moment, try to frame my reply in a way I think Jory will understand. "Tomorrow is the play."

He blinks. "Yes."

"After tomorrow, everything will be different," I continue. "For you, for Catesby and his men, for England, for Catholics. As Catesby says, it will change the world." I don't allow myself to consider failure—I can't; there is no amount of counting backward from five in Cornish that could allay that fear.

Another blink. "Yes."

"Everything has already changed for me, Jory. It changed for me the minute Father was killed. I don't feel like Katherine Arundell anymore. I'm *not* Katherine Arundell anymore."

"Then you aren't Katherine." He sounds unconvinced.

"No matter what happens tomorrow, I will never be her again. Even if everything goes to plan, even if Catesby reinstates Lanherne to me and I am free to live there how I please, titled and moneyed and landed, I still will not be her. After tomorrow, I will be a murderer. A regicide." I mouth these last three words. "Retiring to the country and pretending isn't going to change that."

"If it's sin you're worried about—"

"It's not." I don't say this because I'm not worried; I say this because I've gone far beyond worrying. I have lied and I have dishonored; I have despaired and I have hated. I have chosen malice over benevolence, recklessness over care, and I am up to the silken neckline of my low-cut bodice in impure thoughts. I am steeped in sin and there's nothing to be done about it, not anymore. Because no matter what Jory in his sheet-robe and his prayers and his penance promises, after tomorrow there will be no saving me.

"This is my last chance to be me, whoever that is and whatever there is left, before it all changes for good."

"Are you worried about... Is this about dying?" Jory's dark eyes are wide. "You won't die, Katherine. Kit. Not if you follow everything according to Catesby's plan. They won't let you die."

"Oh, I think they would," I say. "No recovery, no allegiance. Remember?"

"Are you having second thoughts?"

"No," I say, and if I don't know anything else, I know this. "I made promises. To myself and to Father. I promised I would make someone pay for his death. I intend to see that promise through, no matter what."

A nod, then silence. "What are you going to do, then? At the end. If you aren't Katherine and you aren't going back to Corn-wall? Are you going to stay here? In London, as a boy? Or as a girl, with a different name?" Jory takes a step toward me. He looks both tall and diminished by the room's gray candled light. "Who will you be?"

Viola-Cesario, Katherine, or Kit—whoever I am is tied up inside this girl dressed as a boy now dressed as a girl. Whoever I will be rests on the outcome of the final act of a play.

"I don't know."

Chapter 30

TOBY

DOLPHIN SQUARE LODGING HOUSE,
DOWGATE WARD, LONDON
5 JANUARY 1602

onight the world feels upside down.

Every street in the whole of London celebrates this night. The last of the twelve days of Christmas, the eve of the Epiphany, the night that the Lord of Misrule, the Abbot of Unreason, presides over the feast of fools, where the order of things is to be reversed and what is turns into what is not: kings into peasants and beggars into queens, men into fools and boys into girls. It is a night that does not recognize servant or royal, minister or spy, truth or lie, when everyday disguises are shed and truth is told if only for the moment.

Mobs of men and women, boys and girls, babies and the

aged fill the streets. Some march in spontaneous parades; others pour in and out of taverns and churches and inns, dressed in outrageous costumes, feathers and silk and fur, painted faces and masks and hair adorned with flowers. Pennant boats clog the Thames, shuttling shore to shore, dumping revelers onto both banksides to start their celebration or to end it. Poets recite, troubadours dance, and minstrels sing. Mummers draw cheers for their pace-egg plays, combats between heroes and villains in which the hero always wins and jesters laugh at our optimism. Conjurers spin forth in robes and make us believe in magic and in lies, and we do.

I move through the streets slowly, with steady ease, making my way to Kit's. I've come here only once before, after inking her name into my ledger at her audition, when I canvassed the whole of London to find out where every suspect lived. There was no need to return, not after we began rehearsing together at the Rose.

Dowgate is a rough area, rougher than even my own: rubbish-strewn streets and decrepit buildings, three and four stories high and tilting precariously at the top. The light here is more unreliable than it is in Aldersgate, too; lamps burn out and are not relit, narrow streets block out the guiding moon, bonfires are cautious and infrequent: A stray spark in a thatched roof would be enough to send the whole of the ward into a pyre.

A push of men dressed as women pass before me: scraggly horsehair wigs topped with floral crowns; lips and cheeks garnished red; ill-fitting gowns scrapped together with lace and ribbons. They leer at me as they pass, pressing their faces close to mine in turn, each baring teeth or exaggerating smiles or growling or feigning kisses. One of them reaches up to brush the hood of my cloak off my head; another presses a cooling cup of mulled wine into my hand. I wait until they pass before hitching my hood back into place and pouring the drink into the dirt.

I reach her street, the absurdly named St. Laurence Poultney Hill, then finally her boardinghouse, a crooked lath-and-plaster building with an uncheerful, chipped painted blue dolphin above the door. I tuck myself into a doorway opposite it, well hidden by the crowds and the rapidly darkening skies, and wait.

I stand there for a long while, watching the flutter of costumes, the stagger of drunks, and not once do I catch sight of her. I begin to wonder if I've missed her, if she's decided to stay home, if she's chosen tonight to do something else unexpected. Then I wonder if I'm a fool to come here at all, that she would want to hear my confession, even if I managed to pluck up the courage to give it.

That's when I see a girl, stepping through the front door of the Dolphin Square Lodging House in a dress of black and gold and gray, red hair swept under a gray plumed cap, shiny pointed boots on her feet. If I weren't waiting for her, I may not have recognized her. As it is, I almost don't. I've seen Kit in a gown before, in a long wig before. But that was onstage, playing: girl as a boy as a girl. But to see her as herself is another costume altogether, waist cinched tight and head held high and every inch the daughter of a nobleman I suspect her to be.

She pushes past vendors who thrust things at her—sticks topped with ribbons and bells, crowns wreathed with flowers and holly, posies stuffed with herbs—she waves them away and keeps moving, all the way to the square that surrounds

St. Paul's Cathedral, the very heart of the city. I follow her every step, stopping only when she begins the climb up the stairs to the front doors of the church, wide open to parishioners spilling in and out. But she doesn't go in. Instead, she tucks herself behind one of the stone columns, a safe distance from the crowd: a spectator to an ever-growing audience.

I watch her as she watches everything else, mummers and tumblers and jugglers. From where I stand, a hundred feet too far, those cloud-gray eyes are bright and inviting, fixed on troubadours who launch into an off-key, off-color song, her mouth pressed into a smile. When she laughs, I can feel it: It feels as if I'm falling.

I watch her for a beat, two, until one song ends and another begins without a break in key. I watch until it's no longer enough and I take a step toward her, breaking my cover. It is an error of emotion; a discordant note in the chorus. She sees, she is too attuned to others not to. Her eyes shift from the musicians in the street to the gap in the crowd and then to me as I step out of it. Kit freezes, goes as still as a doe in the crosshairs of a bow. We lock eyes for a moment, a beat punctuated by drums and my own thoughts—*She's here* and *She sees me* and *What will she do*—and then she's walking down the steps, navigating them carefully in her dress, until she stands before me. I don't disguise my attention, all of it focused on her face and her freckles and the curl of hair that's escaped her hat to flutter against windswept cheeks.

"Toby," she says. "What are you doing here?"

I open my mouth for the lie that is sitting there, the one that says I live around here, too, that it was luck that I saw her, nothing more than coincidence. But tonight is about the truth, an already harder reveal than I imagined it to be.

"I was looking for you," I say. "I almost didn't recognize you." I hope she doesn't ask how I did, because the truth lies in words like *hope* and *want* and *happiness*, and tonight I would be foolish enough to say any one or all of them.

"Why were you looking for me?" she says. "Is it about the play?"

"No." I take a breath. The air around us pulsates, crowds clapping, drums and pipes and lutes rising and falling. "I wanted to talk to you. If you'll hear it."

Her cheeks, cold-flushed before, grow redder. She nods.

"I was unkind to you, the last time I saw you at the Rose. The night we—" I stop. "I was angry at you, but not for the reason you think. Not entirely." I stop again. "It wasn't that you were a girl—are a girl. It's that you lied to me. I know why you did," I add quickly. "But you knew my secret. That I like"—another breath—"boys. It wasn't something I was ready to share."

Kit nods. Her lovely face is grave. "I didn't know I would come to like you," she says, as straightforward as if she is telling me the weather or the time, impassive as if it doesn't much matter. "Not that way. And when I did, I didn't want you to run. Which is foolish because of course you would have, once you knew the truth. You had every reason to, and you did." She swallows. "I shouldn't have lied to you, and I won't tell anyone. I promise you that. Secrets are jealous things, I know. They don't like to be shared."

Something in her tone makes me think she's not just talking about disguising herself as a boy. "You say that like you know."

Again the nod. "I've kept them all my life. Just as I will keep yours."

I want to ask her what those secrets are. I want to know if she'll tell me. But I don't want to let myself escape sharing an even bigger secret, one I have to tell her if this is to end any way other than her walking away from me. It may end that way regardless.

"I wish you'd told me because I could have told you that I didn't mind," I say. "I don't mind that you're a girl. I *like* girls. That is, I like them, too." It's the first time I've admitted it out loud, this confusion I've felt since I loved Marlowe, then others like him, who turned out to be nothing like him at all, only to go and involve myself the same way with girls. "I don't know why. It doesn't matter, at least not to me, and I don't know how else to explain it. All I do know is that I liked Kit the boy, and I can't stop thinking about Kit the girl. Kit the *person*."

"Oh," she whispers. "I wasn't expecting you to say that."

"Does it trouble you?"

The troubadours begin marching toward us then, heralded by the sound of drums. We are tangled in a press of a hundred others who push and shove around us as they pass. Kit's voice is lost in their shouts and songs, so she steps closer to me to keep from being swept away. She reaches for me and I catch her hand, winding my fingers between hers. She holds my gaze steady as we stand, the only still and quiet thing in the crowd until she leans in to me and whispers, "Nothing about you troubles me."

I wish this could be true. It can't be, not when she still doesn't know my work or my real place in the play, none of which I can tell her until after tomorrow.

I turn from her then, toward the crowd, searching for what I need. I hold up a hand and within moments a vendor appears, a woman dripping in holly, her face painted green, bloodred berries in her hair. She holds up a basket. Inside are dozens of wreaths, strung together with flowers and ribbons and bells. I hand the woman a pinch of coins, turn back to Kit, and hold it up, asking her permission. A spray of tiny white-and-green blossoms woven with deep purple berries, tied together with a pale apple-green ribbon. She nods and unpins her hat, letting loose an avalanche of curls.

"It's tradition, isn't it, to give a gift on Twelfth Night?" I slip the wreath on her head. I don't bother busying myself with untangling the ribbons, or adjusting it where it lists slightly to the right, or doing anything else to hide the rush of thoughts and feelings I know must show on my face. Whatever she sees there makes her cheeks bloom.

"Now it's my turn." She steps away then, reappearing moments later with a cake in her palm. It smells of butter and sugar, iced in white with love knots in green-and-crimson jelly, wrapped in gilded paper thin as tissue. Each piece is baked to contain one of five trinkets, and whichever one you pull is your fortune for the year. She presses it into my hand.

"Twelfth Night cake," I say. "It's been a while since I've had one of these."

"For me, too."

"Do you remember how the saying goes?" I ask. There's a poem you're meant to recite before pulling apart the cake to reveal the fortune inside.

Kit thinks on it a minute before remembering. *"If you get the* clove you're a villain. If you get the twig you're a fool. If you get the rag you are a tarty lad. The king gets the bean and the queen, the pea." She tips her head to my hand. "Well?" she says. "Which one are you?"

I break open the cake. In the very center lies a small, splintered sliver of wood.

"The fool," she says, and the air between us grows silent for a moment. It's only a trinket and it's only a game, but in a night that for me is all about the truth, it's unsettling all the same.

A breeze slips through the street, ribbons from the wreath swaying like grass against her face and against mine. When I brush them from the flush of her cheek and my fingers graze her skin, she closes her eyes.

Chapter 31

KIT

ST. PAUL'S CHURCHYARD, LONDON
5 JANUARY 1602

oby pulled the fool, but the only fool here is me.

The moment I saw him, standing in the square of St. Paul's, all dark and light and watching me, I knew why he had come. I knew from the way he took in my skirt and then my waist, my bodice and then my eyes, my hat and my hair and the stubborn curls that drifted over my cheeks. He said he came to tell me the truth, but the truth was already there, written all over his face.

I should have run. I should have said the words that would have made him run. I should have said I didn't want his secrets or his affection and didn't care for either of them, a lie only a little less painful than the truth. As it stands, here I am closeted in a corner in an alley behind St. Paul's churchyard, amid the shouts and songs and laughter. Cymbals that clang like overwrought nerves, drums that echo like a heartbeat, Toby's lips on mine and his hands in my hair, his whispered promises a breath in my ear. But the promises I whisper in return can be nothing more than wishes, except wishes have hope and mine have none, so they, too, are nothing more than lies.

It seems as if the Twelfth Night cake I bought for Toby wasn't meant for him at all. Because as always, there is no bigger fool than me.

Chapter 32

TOBY

DOLPHIN SQUARE LODGING HOUSE, DOWGATE WARD, LONDON
5 JANUARY 1602

It is near midnight when I finally leave her, after she allowed me to walk her home through the streets of a city still drunk on itself, shielding her from leering eyes and reaching hands and worse comments, all the trouble that surrounds Kit in a dress.

"I wouldn't wear this again," I tell her after wrapping an arm around her too-bare shoulders. "You're safer in breeches. For now, anyway." The watcher in me can't let her live in this boardinghouse and in this ward any longer than necessary, as much for her safety as for my own peace of mind.

"You're good to me, Toby. Looking out for me this way." Her

words are kind, but her eyes and her tone are reproachful and I don't flinch from it. "But I can take care of myself. I've not done so poorly, thus far. You've seen me put up a fight."

"I have," I reply. "Which is exactly why I worry."

Kit raises a mock fist and brushes my chin with it. "Incorrigible."

"Well, I did pull the fool."

This gets a laugh from her, something small and breathless. "I don't forget it."

There's a shout and a scream from somewhere behind us, not of revelry but something more sinister, followed by the unmistakable scuffle of a brawl. I take her by the arm and bundle her to the door of her lodging house, as blue and battered as the sign above it. Kit pulls from my grasp, and there's a fleeting look of panic as she looks not up the street, toward the source of the noise, but in through the window of her own building. As if more danger lies there than what's in front of her. "Is there something wrong?"

Kit smiles, whatever worry there a moment ago now reined in. "It's just...they think they're renting my room to a boy," she explains. "If they knew otherwise, I'm sure I wouldn't be allowed. And if I'm seen standing with you..." She tugs off her wreath and presses it into my hands. "I try to keep to myself. People ask fewer questions that way."

I understand this and so I nod, taking precautionary steps away from her and back into the street. But she holds my gaze even as people begin to cross back and forth between us.

"Happy Twelfth Night," I say by way of farewell.

She nods in acknowledgment, and by the time the next

throng of people pass, she's gone. I tuck the wreath into the crook of my elbow and set back into the street. I have an evening's worth of work before me, determining which of my remaining two suspects is the queen's assassin. Half the walk home is spent thinking about what is to come, the other half about Kit.

I do not see the boy until he is almost on top of me. He's around twelve years old, dressed not in costume but the rough-hewn clothes of a servant. The only nod to the madness around us is a single sprig of holly, trailing from his cape's crooked buttonhole.

"Message for you, sir."

I raise a brow. A message delivered on a holiday costs at least double if not triple the standard courier rate. Whatever the message, it's important enough that the sender thought I wouldn't mind paying it. I hold out my hand, and the boy pulls a folded piece of parchment from his pocket. It bears the yellow wax seal of the Duchy of Cornwall. The query I forged under Carey's name and sent two weeks ago to the sheriff, Sir Jonathan Trelawney, returned at last. I hand the boy two pennies and send him on his way. It's not until I'm inside my room, door safely locked against revelers and landladies alike, that I light the last of my candles and settle into my chair at my desk. I crack open the seal on the letter and read.

Sir, it begins.

At present, six members of Sir Richard Arun-
dell's household are still being held in custody. No
information regarding the priest called Ryol Campion

(or Antonio Mendoza) forthcoming until your
allowance for further persuasion. New informa-
tion as follows: Prior to Mendoza, Arundell held
two other priests in hiding: Michel Allemande from
France and Edmond Arbeau, also from France.
Arundell's personal horse groom, Jory Jameson, aged
seventeen, disappeared the night of the raid. Accord-
ing to the household, he has been in training for the
priesthood, two years since, with Arundell's blessing.
Assumed to be in exile.

    Would be most appreciative if the funds (three
hundred pounds) offered for the capture of Richard
Arundell were put forth to Her Majesty('s men).

I set the letter down. Arundell's groom, the one mentioned
in the previous letter. A priest in training. Assumed to have
fled the country, presumably to a Catholic-friendly region. It's
the right age, the right timing, almost the right motivation—
assuming religion would be sufficient cause for a groom's retribution, rather than familial. But if any of my remaining suspects
were an alias for this groom called Jory, it doesn't hold with what
I know about them. Alard is the right age, but his background
tracks to Suffolk, not Cornwall, not to mention he's as atheistic
as they come. Hargrove is a closer match, quiet and unassuming
enough to be a rogue priest. Yet records show him to be in London as of last March, long before this raid in Cornwall occurred.
I read the letter again and again. Parsing every word to see if
there's anything here that I may have missed, that I could have
read a different way than was intended. But I finally concede

there's nothing new to be learned here. Nothing but a recusant Catholic who was sold to the queen by the sheriff in his own service, whose more loyal household held out as much information as they could about him until the allowance of torture, admitting only a revolving door of priests and a boy with higher aspirations than a horse. Arundell's story ended with his death and that of his priest.

I start to run the edge of the letter through the flame of my candle, burning the evidence of my forgery, when I notice the postscript on the other side.

Further to your query, Richard Arundell had no sons, brothers, father, or uncles (still living) at his time of death. Only other family members include wife, Mary Arundell, deceased 1584, and daughter Katherine Arundell, aged seventeen, both of Catholic leanings. Katherine was captured on night of the raid on Lanherne but escaped shortly afterward, current whereabouts unknown. Assumed to be deceased.

Katherine Arundell. Seventeen. Daughter of a Catholic nobleman from Cornwall. Of Catholic leanings. Current whereabouts unknown. Assumed to be deceased.

The letter is shaking even before it falls from my hand.

The girl who showed up at the Globe, hair cropped and reciting Marlowe. Who rolled dice with me at the Mermaid, bartering a kiss. The girl I went on to kiss: once, twice, then a hundred times more; the girl I thought was a boy, who I thought was free from any charge of conspiracy, turns out to be free of nothing.

Her accent, too pronounced for Plymouth or anywhere else in Devonshire, is because it is Cornish. The friend she called Richard, not a friend at all but her father. The story she gave me of being a groom to a nobleman belongs to the boy called Jory. Her comparing me to a St. Crispin's Day capon the night of Carey's patron party, St. Crispin's being a known Catholic holiday. The surname she chose for herself—Alban—being the Catholic saint of England. The way her eyes lit up when I placed the wreath on her head tonight, a spray of white blackthorn grown along hedges in Cornwall, a coincidence on my part, but I should have paid attention.

I should have paid attention.

I sit with my head in still-shaking hands for a long time, until my candle dies out, then in the dark for even longer. After my heart slows and my breath stills, I pull out a fresh piece of parchment. And in the shadows of Twelfth Night, I write my final report to the queen and her men, telling them exactly what they need to know.

Chapter 33

KIT

MIDDLE TEMPLE HALL, LONDON
6 JANUARY 1602
5:45 PM

It is more terrifying than I thought it would be.

Middle Temple Hall, where the play is to commence in little more than one hour and end in a little under three, is a place I know well. I should do; the Wrights came here on occasions too numerous to count to investigate every door, every window, every shadow and every sound of this place and its surroundings to then be detailed on Catesby's ambitious map. It was easy enough. Middle Temple is one building in a complex made up of roughly a dozen—collectively referred to as the Temple—including a church, a library, dining hall, and offices, all of them dedicated to schooling London's finest lawyers. All

Chris and John had to do was dress in black, carry books, and look terribly busy doing nothing, and they blended right in.

The Hall, where the play is to be performed, is narrow and long with a dark timbered, high-arched ceiling and white plaster walls inset with rows of square stained glass windows interspersed with row after row of coats of arms. The back wall, opposite the entrance, is hung with a series of oil paintings (the largest being, of course, Her Majesty Queen Elizabeth, her portrait and her position soon to be replaced by Her Majesty Queen Isabella). The whole of the place has a stale, musty smell, that of old men and arguments and righteous indignation.

Chairs are arranged on either side of the stage. Four rows of twenty seats on each—one hundred and sixty total. The stage is simply the floor, wood and nearly bare, scattered only lightly with rushes to prevent slipping, just as it is at the Globe. And it is dark, just as the Wrights promised it would be. Dark because it is nearly six o'clock in the evening and the sun has long since set. Dark because the black oak ceiling seems an expanse of vast nothingness, the Cornish coastal sky at midnight. Dark because the Hall is lit only by candles, flickering both solo and in groups, held in shiny brass tapers and coronas fixed to the wall.

Shakespeare is pleased by the mood it sets, naturally, as it was his idea (proposed to him by a couple of stagehands with ideas of their own), feeling that the dimmed light would lend more reality to the identical twins if viewers could not as clearly see our faces. As for the rest of the building, it too is a place I know well despite seeing it in person for the first time. The Queen's Room is set up for costumes and props, as it is closest to the

Hall. The Prince's Room, farthest from the Hall as well as the other rooms, is reserved for Burbage and his men. The largest room, the Parliament Chamber, is for the rest of us.

I would have thought that separating us into different spaces would cut down on the chaos, but I was wrong. If the Globe was hectic, Middle Temple is more so, because it is smaller, divided up, and unknown. There are costumers dragging clothing into the rooms, players and alternates arriving in rushed clusters, others hovering around the wall where Parry, the book holder, has tacked up the sheets that contain the play, all of them murmuring to themselves as if to recommit the story to memory. Mistress Lovett rushes around with pins in her mouth, stitching men into gowns and doublets and ruffs. Mistress Lucy is in charge of wigs and hair and face paint, wielding brushes and sponges and tubs of Venetian ceruse. Stagehands rush up and down, pushing tables and chairs and floor rugs toward the Hall, setting them up for the opening scene.

Then there is Master Shakespeare. He is the only one acting perfectly normal, which is to say completely mad. His shirt is unlaced, his boots are unlaced, he is unlaced. He speaks in half sentences, then stops as if he's forgotten the other half. His sweaty palms clutch parchment, a pen is clamped between his teeth. He sees me idling in the hallway and scoops my elbow into his hand, giving it a little shake.

"Where is Orsino?" he demands. The pen falls out of his mouth; he almost doesn't catch it. "It's coming up on six o'clock. The play starts in one hour, and he is first on. He should have been here already."

"I don't know," I say. I haven't seen Toby since he left me at my door last night, never letting me out of his sight until I was safely inside.

"You don't know! Fat lot of good that does. I thought you and he were"—he gestures at me with the pen, up and down—"*voonex*."

"I am sure Orsino has many *voonex*," I say, hoping to God this means "friends."

"I'm here."

And there's Toby, standing in the doorway. He's a little flushed, as if he's come here on foot and quickly, his cheeks pink and his hair windblown, and even as he shrugs off his cloak, those blue eyes shift from me to Shakespeare and back to me again. My heart gives a disobedient thud and I will myself to look away.

"The guards," he says by way of explanation. "They've set up six watch stations. One at the Temple Pier, one at Whitefriars, one at the south end of the gardens, and three along Temple Bar and Fleet and Middle Temple Lane. Then of course they're posted all around the Hall itself, every door and window. It took ages to get past them."

I take in this information, measure it against what I already know, pleased that it lines up. I know the Wrights, subsumed somewhere in the madness but always close by, heard it too. What I don't know is why Toby looks at me when he says it.

"I know where the guard stations are," Shakespeare says. "Did you not show them your *trealop*? I specifically gave every player one—"

"I showed them," Toby replies. "It's why I stand before you and not outside, facedown on the grass, with a guard's sword in my back."

"Well, don't just stand there. You're in the opening scene, for the love of God. You need to be dressed. Go. Go." Shakespeare grabs the front of Toby's shirt and gives him a mighty shove toward the Parliament Chamber. Toby stumbles and goes, turning around just once to catch my eye before being swallowed by men and clothing and chaos. Shakespeare crams his pen back in his mouth, grunts something unintelligible—more unintelligible than usual—and pushes past me.

I stand there, stiff and uncomfortable in my costume, already beginning to sweat despite the chill in the hallway from the frosted air that blows in through the open door. In my opening scene I am Viola, therefore dressed like a girl. My hair, plastered beneath the wig cap and then the wig itself, ropy and long and scratchy. My face, stiff beneath the paste of alum and tin ash and egg white to make the skin pale, vermilion to my lips and cheeks, kohl to ring my eyes and darken my eyebrows. I wear a smock and stockings, a corset (stuffed with batting to give the illusion of breasts, the irony), a gown and sleeves. My feet are pushed into shoes that are in truth too small for my too-large feet.

But for all this clothing all I really feel is the sheath, the one the Wrights fashioned for me that holds my knife—no guard on the tip today—beneath narrow strips of leather strapped across my waist. It is sleek and flat and well hidden, but it feels like a beacon, alerting everyone to what I'm about to do.

There is a breath of air, not from the window, and I turn my head slightly to find Toby standing beside me, in costume as Duke Orsino. His clothes are silly and foppish, as they're meant to be. But his expression doesn't match them, his blue eyes showing something I've not seen in them before: alarm.

"I need to talk to you."

"I can't," I say, and it's the truth. I can't afford to be distracted by him right now.

Toby snatches me around the elbow anyway, the same way he did in the street last night when he thought I might be in danger, and pushes me down the hall.

"What are you doing?" I try to pull away, but his grip is too tight and his expression too fierce and it frightens me. "You're hurting me. Let go. You have no right—"

"Quiet."

The players in the Hall part for him, as anyone with any sense would do before his murderous expression or his stride that forces others in his wake. There's a closet at the end of the Hall, one the Wrights said is used for furniture and portrait storage, and that's where Toby takes me, releasing me only long enough to snatch a burning candle from a mount on the wall before pushing open the door and thrusting me inside. I am worried by this sudden turn of things, and I don't know what to do, or to say, but then Toby is in front of me and he speaks first.

"I know" is all he says. The candle in his hand is shaking, the flame throwing light in dizzying arcs over the ceiling and the walls, gilded portraits of somber faces haphazardly hung everywhere, all of them watching us. "I know you've come here to kill the queen."

I reel back as if I've been slapped, but he keeps talking.

"I know your name is Katherine Arundell. I know you're the daughter of Richard Arundell. I know he was killed in the raid on your house and that his priest was captured. Captured, interrogated, then executed, just two weeks ago. I know that your father was part of a plot against the queen and that you took his place." Toby stops, as if to catch his breath. "Do you deny it?"

I do nothing and I say nothing. I look around, portraits and desks and chairs stacked along the wall to the door, as if they were somehow the only obstacles that would keep me from running from all his accusations.

"Kit." Toby jams his candle in a crack between two tables. Steps forward and takes my arms, which are now wrapped around my middle, and shakes me, as if I were a sack of flour he could sift information from. "What is happening tonight? Who else is involved? Are they here? You have to tell me what you know."

"I don't—I—" I press my hand against my mouth. I have gone numb all over. It is like the night Lanherne was raided and everything had gone wrong and I didn't know how to right it or even where to begin. "Who are you?" is all I finally manage.

Toby drops his hands. "I'm a watcher. I work for the queen. I intercepted a letter outlining a plot to assassinate her and put Archduchess Isabella in her place. I was hired to find those plotters, and to stop them." Toby's voice is flat, his pupils wide, black and expressionless as a shark's. "I wrote this play as a means to bait them, in the hope they'd be fool enough to bite. You were one of my suspects. It's why I watched you. When I met you at the Rose, and at the frost fair, and in the alleys in Vintry Ward, it wasn't a coincidence. I was following you because ever since you stepped onstage at the Globe to audition, I have been suspicious of you."

I stagger backward, knocking my head against the hard edge of a portrait frame. The pain barely registers. It can't, not alongside everything else.

"But I didn't know you were the assassin until last night," Toby goes on, relentless. "I had written you off my list the moment I found out you were a girl. I thought that was all you were hiding. Then I got a letter back from the sheriff in Cornwall, a man called Sir Jonathan Trelawney. I believe you know him."

I feel my lips go cold.

"I need you to tell me everything," Toby says. "It's the only way I can help you."

"Why would you want to help me?"

His eyes narrow and I would back away from him if I had anywhere to go. "Don't be a fool."

I look toward the door. From behind it, along the narrow cracks of light at the seams, I can see shadows of figures moving to and fro, hear the hum of voices punctuated by shouts. When I look back to Toby, his eyes are trained on me, blue again, no longer bleak with anger but with pleading.

"One or both of us is going to die if you don't tell me what you know."

"Die!" This, if nothing else, shakes the words from my throat. "Why would *you* die?"

"What will happen, do you think, if I promise the queen an assassin and I don't deliver one? Do you know the queen to be a forgiving woman? A generous woman? Is she understanding, merciful, lenient?" He says this in a breath so low I almost don't hear it. "No. She is none of those, which is why you stand here, orphaned and colluded, up to your eyes in a plot that is bigger than anything you imagined."

I almost believe him—almost. I almost believe he wants to

help me. But this closet is too small to contain all the lies within it, and things have gone so far I don't know if I'll ever believe anything again.

"Tell me," he repeats.

"They want to bring the Inquisition to England." It's not what Toby asked. But it's something I haven't been able to stop thinking about since Jory told me Catesby's plans for it. "Against the Protestants. They say there's not a Catholic country in Europe that wouldn't support it. They want to punish them the way Catholics are being punished now."

I expect Toby to grow hard, or fearsome, for him to show me the face he made only moments earlier, one I never like seeing. In the end he only nods, unmoved, and this is his most frightening expression of all.

"They'll start with Protestants," he says. "But when they grow bored with punishing them, do you think they'll stop? Congratulate themselves on a job well done? That's not how persecution works, Kit. I know you want revenge, but this isn't the answer. No one will be safe—"

"I'm not safe now!"

"No," he says. "And after tonight, no matter what happens, you'll not be safe again."

"But...if you work for the queen and her men, and you've been following me and watching me all this time, don't they already know who I am?" I demand. "Why haven't they arrested me? Why would they let me come here and stand before the queen, if they think I'm meant to kill her?"

Toby is shaking his head even before I finish. "I sent them my final report. This very day. It's why I was late. I delivered it to the gates of Whitehall myself. And in it, I named Thomas Alard the assassin."

I clap my hand over my mouth. Toby slumps against the wall, his hand raking through his hair, over and over.

"He's the only other player I couldn't account for, the only one with questions I wasn't able to answer." Toby goes on. "I waited as long as I could to hand off the report. The queen and her ministers won't read it until after the play is over, but they'll still be expecting me to arrest him. It won't matter that he's innocent. He will still be subjected to hours of interrogation. Possibly torture. And if they don't believe his innocence, they may even kill him. But I had to tell them something. I had to give them *something*."

He looks at me and I see it: in his face and his posture and everywhere, the enormity of what he's done. That he's condemned an innocent man to what could be his death. Something he's done for me, because of me, and I'm to blame for it, too.

"Toby—"

Whatever I was to say is cut off by the sound of Shakespeare's voice outside the door, shouting up and down the hall for Viola-Cesario and Orsino and calling time. The play starts in fifteen minutes.

"What should I do?" I say instead. "I don't know what to do. I don't—"

Toby is gripping my arms again, this time to stop me from shaking. "When were you going to do it?"

"Act five, scene one," I say. "The very end." And then, before I lose what's left of my courage, I tell him everything I've done since I left Lanherne, everything I came to London to do, every last detail I know about the plan. To hear it out loud is to feel a fool all over again, to think that it would have worked. But there is a sense of relief, too: To be a fool is better than to be a murderer.

By the candlelight, I can see his eyes go distant, the way he looks when he's thinking and the way I now know he looks when he's plotting. "All right," he says finally. "That gives me two hours to figure out how to get us out of this."

"Two hours and thirty-seven minutes," I correct, and Toby closes his eyes.

"Do everything you were going to do," he says. "Don't change a thing. If you change something, your men will be alerted to it. I don't want them alerted to anything until you're gone and it's too late for them to find you."

He reaches around me to open the closet door. He allows me out first. I've only taken a few steps before I'm once more scooped around the elbow by Shakespeare, hissing in my ear words about *The queen is here* and *Do I want to drive him to madness* and pushing me forward, into the line of players.

Moments later, Toby slides into the line in front of me just as a blast of trumpet comes from down the hall. Everyone's head turns. Toby's posture kicks up an inch; Shakespeare runs a harried hand through his hair. It's the queen and her retinue, entering the building.

I cannot move for fright.

As if sensing this, Toby turns to face me, ignoring the commotion and the genuflecting. He reaches into the pocket of the jerkin of that ornate costume and pulls out something; it's tucked in his fist and I can't see what it is. But when he opens his hand, I know it right away: a sprig of blackthorn from the wreath he placed on my head last night. He reaches forward and tucks the musky, almond-scented blossom behind my ear.

I wonder if he knows, like I do, that South Devon witches carry blackthorn to protect them against evil. That it's known in Cornish folklore as the symbol of both protection and revenge. That in Celtic mythology, blackthorn is known as the keeper and increaser of dark secrets. That yet other mythos hold that Christ's own crown of thorns was made from it.

Or if it is, simply, a flower from a boy to a girl on a night after which they may never see each other again.

"*I hold the Fates bound fast in iron chains,*" he whispers. "*And with my hand turn Fortune's wheel about.*" A favorite line of a favorite play by a favorite playwright, one about luck and daring and taking on the impossible: the very gods themselves.

Only the Toby I know would never leave anything down to luck.

Chapter 34

TOBY

MIDDLE TEMPLE HALL, LONDON
6 JANUARY 1602
7:00 PM

I t is dark.

Dark, despite the hundreds of candles that light the Hall from every corner: tucked into holders and set in intervals along the floor and the ledge that runs atop the paneling, into iron brackets mounted into walls. But it is not enough.

Not enough to hide her face or her splendor, her arrogance or her expectation. The queen. She is waiting to be given a show, waiting for me to give it to her. She sits in the front row in a confection of a gown, red and gold and green and orange, every color of the rainbow adorned with every jewel under the sun, pearls as large as fruit looped obscenely around her neck, draped from her ears, and planted on her fingers. She is the brightest thing in this room, the most dangerous thing in any room.

On her left is Cecil, dressed in black. On her right is Carey, also in black. Beside them and behind them, their wives and the rest of the Privy Council, noblemen and politicians and courtiers. Their excitement fills the air, their privileged inclusion. The queen chats with them all, gracious and lively, her much-lauded Tudor charm on full display.

But if you were watching closely (and I am watching, closely), you would see those sharp black eyes cut through the Hall. Like all predators, they don't need the light to see, taking in every face, every expression, every smile and every frown, assessing and cataloging to be used later, for or against—usually against.

Then, as if I'd somehow said those words out loud, she turns to me. I stand at the mouth of the door, first in the long line of nervous, shifting players as I am first onstage, but she should not be able to see me. I am behind a screen, a trellised wooden thing that acts as a curtain would at the Globe, shielding the audience from our comings and goings and frantic backstage preparations. But if the Spanish Armada cannot stop the queen and the French conspiracies cannot stop the queen, if Essex and his rebellion could not stop the queen and a French Catholic queen could not stop the queen, then a simple wood barrier will not stop the queen.

Her eyes find me and stay there, as if she can see through it and then through me, into my traitorous heart. It beats out of time with the drums the musicians now play onstage, the pipe and tabor and the hurdy-gurdy. The costumers run through the line of players, agitated as wasps, straightening gowns and doublets, hiking up hose and adjusting wigs and hats. I hear Burbage and Tooley behind me, intoning their pretentious vocal exercises ("Theophilous Thistle, the thistle sifter, thrust a thousand thistles...") while the newer boys and men shuffle their feet, Sever and Barton and Hargrove and the others I cast, all of them nervous but eager.

I cannot bring myself to look at Alard.

Standing two players behind me is Kit, tall and reedy in that wig and gown, and she is watching me, too. Wondering if she can trust me to get us out of this. The sprig of blackthorn I tucked in her hair, a sorry token of that trust, is gone. I don't know if that was her doing or Mistress Lucy's, who hovers around her, adjusting her wig and pressing more color to her lips. Either way, Kit would be right to wonder. Because for the first time in my life, I don't know what to do. When I left my room this morning, it was with every penny I still have left after losing my cloak, every item I can't bear to do without: not much, only my father's sealing ring and a letter from Marlowe, the last one he sent me. No matter what happens tonight, I don't plan on returning.

Act 5, scene 1 is when Kit planned to attack the queen. When every one of those three hundred tapers placed carefully in the wall brackets will extinguish simultaneously, a machination courtesy of the Bell brothers—not their real names, but I was right to be suspicious of them, too. Then, when the Hall is sheathed in darkness, Kit is meant to step forward, wielding the knife tucked carefully beneath her bodice.

This gives me two hours, thirty-seven minutes into the play to figure out how to stop her. Something I must do without revealing to her other plotters that she's been caught, before she assassinates the queen, and before the queen realizes I'm now a part of this plot—whether I wanted to be or not. Then I must get us both out of here, unscathed. It's going to take a lot more than a miracle from one of Kit's Catholic saints.

I don't like to think about what might have happened if I hadn't received Trelawney's letter last night. If I hadn't put together who Kit really was. I don't know how she thought she could have gotten away with it. I know her well enough to know she wasn't entrapped into this—no doubt she bloody well volunteered—but what I don't know is how those men convinced her that she had any chance at all of surviving. She didn't seem fearful of dying, only of being found out. My best guess is she was relying on the element of surprise. But what she doesn't know is the queen cannot be surprised, nor her men. Not a situation exists that they haven't planned a hundred scenarios for. A hundred contingency plans. It's what they do. It's what *I* do.

"Orsino." Shakespeare is suddenly beside me. His face is a map of sweat. "Stop mooning around, man. Is your boot"—he lowers his voice and looks around, furtive; he would make a lousy watcher—"laced firmly to your foot?"

I lean in. "Shoe."

"What?"

"Is my shoe laced firmly to my foot," I say. It was the secret phrase Carey gave Shakespeare, his way of asking me if everything was in place. It wasn't necessary and it's not something that's done, but it seemed to please Shakespeare to be part of the stealth. "And the answer is yes."

"Good. Yes. Good." He swipes a hand across his brow.

"Christ. Is it always like this? I'm sweating like some kind of farm animal."

I place my hand on his shoulder. "It's going to be fine. You have my word."

This brings on a rapid scowl. "Oh, I have your word, all right. Nineteen thousand of them to be exact, this smoldering disaster of a play—"

That is when the trumpet blares. The musicians, now off-stage and grouped behind yet another screen at the other end of the Hall, begin to play a mournful tune. That's my cue.

Shakespeare goes pale. "*Merde*," he tells me; it is French for "shit" and ironically it means "good luck."

"*Merde*," I repeat, then step out from behind the screen. In full view now of everyone I know—everyone. If there's recognition in their faces, I don't see it. I see only smiles from the courtiers, from the noblemen, from the ladies-in-waiting who, if they remember me, only know me as the one accompanying Carey to court. They are all watching me.

I walk to center stage clutching a sprig of rosemary, tearing off the spikes in clusters and letting the needles fall to the lightly rushed floor. I am pensive, I am doleful, I am the embodiment of the tune that dirges around me, until abruptly, it stops.

"*If music be the food of love*," I declare, "*play on.*"

Chapter 35

KIT

MIDDLE TEMPLE HALL, LONDON
6 JANUARY 1602
7:17 PM

I am standing behind the wooden trellis while Toby is onstage, finishing the first scene. But it's not him I watch, nor the two other players alongside him. It is the queen, sitting not twenty feet before me.

She is unlike anything or anyone I have seen in my life before. The words once used to describe her, in poetry and in plays—a Cybele of the Heavens, Diana amid Roses, a Venus in Beauty to surpass sovereigns as the oak overtops the tamarisk—are still not enough. Nor are the words used by Catesby and Jory and even my own father—shrewd, cunning, jezebel; cruel and manipulative and a timeserver. The way she sits there in enough silk for three dresses and jewels for three continents, fiery red hair and china-white face, black eyes and black teeth, seems to defy any words at all. In reality she is horrific; half witch and half goddess, her unnerving stare placing proprietary claim over every last thing in this room, from the Hall itself to the gardens and the church outside, the ministers beside her and the guards behind her, the whole of London and then of England, all the way to our very souls. She owns them, and us, and she knows it.

And I hate her.

But in watching her, and watching her watching Toby, the anxiety I already felt now turns to sheer, unrelenting panic. The queen and her men knew all along that this was a trap. They knew all along one of us came here to kill her, that in the next two hours and forty-one minutes there is to be an attempt on her life, and she stepped into the audience anyway. For a moment I understand why: It's the same audacity and madness that brought me here, too.

Now I have failed. I was doomed to fail the moment this all began, the moment I stepped onstage at the Globe to audition for the very role I stand in now. Toby knew, the moment he saw me, that I wasn't what I appeared to be. *I am not that I play*, he wrote, a line that I, Katherine-as-Kit-as-Viola-as-Cesario, will say just four scenes from now. Did he know then how true that would become? Or was he thinking of himself, Toby-as-Orsino, watcher-as-playwright-as-player?

I think of Father, an inveterate plotter pretending to be a nobleman. I think of Ryol, a priest pretending to be a manservant. All of us lonely, all of us hidden by the danger and imprisoned by the necessity of disguise. Father and Ryol's story has come to an end, and Toby is offering me a better one than theirs. Do I trust it? Even if I did, what will it mean for me to take it? One is to avenge my father, the other is to appease myself. One is to honor my past, the other to abandon it on the whim of a future. One is the sin of murder (even though Jory, *de facto* and *de futuro*, expunged me of this sin), the other the sin of selfishness. I planned to leave this place a murderer, in heart if not in deed. I didn't plan to leave a coward.

Then I think of Toby, who is trying to ensure that I leave at all. For him to attempt this is to put his life at risk. It goes against everything he stands for, yet he does it anyway. I do not think I am worth this trouble, but I don't think it's about me anymore.

Catesby told me that man is greater than an idea, but he can't really believe that. Not when he plans on killing men in an Inquisition for nothing more than having ideas that run counter to his own. He tried to sell me his beliefs, but what he really wants is revenge. It's no less than what I wanted, but revenge can't grant indulgences: forgiveness for a sin before it's been committed, a preemptive strike against guilt. Jory already granted me one indulgence; how many did he grant Catesby? How many did Ryol grant Father? Was that part of *blessing the mission*, too?

Toby told me he needs to deliver the queen an assassin. But tonight it won't be me.

He appears at the mouth of the trellised door then, finished with the first scene and last to exit the stage. I feel his eyes on me, questioning, wondering, an attempt to read what I am feeling. I give him a quick nod before I square my shoulders, and in my ridiculous dress and worse wig I walk onstage, to face the woman who killed my father.

Chapter 36

TOBY

MIDDLE TEMPLE HALL, LONDON
6 JANUARY 1602
7:55 PM

I shove through players and understudies and costumers and stagehands, looking for Shakespeare. I try the Prince's Room first, where Burbage and his men are, then the Parliament Chamber, where the rest of us wait between scenes. Eventually I find him stationed before the trellis that stands at the entrance to the Hall. His nose is pressed against the wood and he's tapping his toe furiously on the floor. He doesn't hear me walk up, or pretends not to. But when I touch his shoulder, he jerks away as if I've burned him.

"Orsino." He scowls. "I'm petrified to ask, but what can I do for you?"

There's no time to prevaricate. "I need you to get Alard's understudy ready."

"What?" Shakespeare stops toe-tapping, his face full of surprise and then: fear. "Why? Is he...he's not the raven?" Yet another word Carey came up with; it means "suspect."

I can't tell him this or very much of anything else, and so I say, as gently as I can, "It's part of the plan. He'll need to be ready in fifteen."

"Don't recite me my timetables," Shakespeare snipes. "Why didn't you tell me this before? Cressy isn't ready. He needs hair, he needs face paint, he needs costume—"

"Telling you ages ago isn't part of the plan, is it?" I interrupt. "And that's not all. I'll need the rest of the alternates in costume and face paint, too."

"Christ *alive*." He snaps his fingers in my face. "What in God's name for?"

"It's just a precaution," I say. "In the event I have to pull someone else out. I don't foresee it, but it's best to be prepared." This is one reason, but not the most important one: If all the players are in costume, it will make it harder for Kit's men to know which one is her, therefore easier for me to make my escape with her when the time comes. "Don't worry," I tell him. "I'm sure Mistress Lovett is up to the task."

Shakespeare is looking at me as if I've murdered his cat. "No offense to you personally, Orsino, but after this is over, if I never lay eyes on you again it will be far too soon." He's gone then, peeling off down the hall in search of Mistress Lovett.

I wait a moment before starting after him, looking for Thomas Alard.

He's easier to locate, tucked into an alcove outside the door to the Prince's Room. Too good to be with the rest of us in the Parliament Chamber but not quite good enough to be cloistered with the Lord Chamberlain's Men, he's stationed himself in some kind of separatist purgatory. He stands stiff in his black gown, eyes closed, while Mistress Lucy hovers around him, administering more powder to his face, red paste to his lips.

"Alard." He doesn't open his eyes when I address him. "I need to talk to you."

"I can't talk. I'm on in fifteen, for Christ's sake." He flicks a ringed hand to wave me off, a gesture he picked up from Burbage.

"It's important," I say. Mistress Lucy glances at me. Alard hasn't picked up on the urgency in my tone, but she has. I rearrange my patience and try again. "It's about our scene together in act five. The blocking."

"Can't you see I'm busy, Ellis?" His eyes are open now. He's glaring through kohl and scowling through purposefully crooked lips, which might be funny under different circumstances. "Shove off. And take your questions with you. You should have paid better attention the first hundred times we rehearsed it."

Of all the people in all the world I'd risk myself to save, Alard is the last. But it's my final chance to fix my mistake before I never can again.

I start to speak again when another voice interrupts me.

"Mistress Lucy, I need you to attend to…something." It's Shakespeare. He stands closer to me than is necessary, his wary gaze on Alard. "Follow me, if you would. Please." Mistress Lucy's eyes have gone wide now, Shakespeare's politeness more damning than my urgency. But when Shakespeare turns to walk away she follows, and Alard turns to me, hands on his hips.

"Didn't I tell you to shove off?"

"I work for the queen."

This gets his attention. Then it gets his skepticism—and his ire.

"Fuck off."

"I was hired to track debtors." I go on. "To capture evidence of their offenses before turning them in. You were on the list of men I followed."

Alard's face, like that of all seasoned delinquents, doesn't change expression. But a muscle in his jaw jumps, showing me my words mean something.

"I followed you to Paris Garden. The Mitre. Crossed Keys. Tabard." I go on and on, listing all the tap houses and taverns and bear-baiting pits and dice houses I followed him to. "You lost money to your opponents, then you borrowed from the house and lost to them, too. You owe purse to quite a few establishments."

Alard laughs then, but it isn't convincing. "If you work for the queen, what are you doing here? Don't you have better things to do than be a shit player?"

"If I'm a shit player, it's because I'm not one," I reply. "I'm only here because of you."

Alard is just self-important enough—or guilty enough—to believe it.

"She's clamping down on debtors, Alard," I say. "It's a misdemeanor, and you might get off with just whipping or starvation. But it's a roll of the dice—sorry for the pun. You could be sentenced to branding or hanging." I shrug. "Dismemberment seems to be back in fashion, too."

"Fuck," he repeats. "Why are you telling me this? What's in it for you?"

I step back from him. He's begun to sweat beneath his white face paint, turning it to paste around his nose and mouth. But his accusation is something I hear often: Those who are the most guilty are always the ones who believe they're being put by the hardest.

"I think you're a good player," I tell him. Somewhere in all this I've managed to find the truth. "Very good. If you paid more attention to that than gambling, you might even be great. But you can't if you're walking around with a debtor's brand on your forehead, or swinging from the end of a hangman's rope."

"What do I do? I don't…" Alard has stopped wondering about my motives and is now glancing around him, furtive as Shakespeare. "I don't have any funds. Papers. Even if I managed both I don't know where to go."

I pull out a scant bag of coins, meant for something and someone else, and press it into his hand. It hurts more than I thought it would.

"It's not a lot," I say. "But it'll see you on a ship to Calais. There's an inn in Wapping. The Grapes. Ask for Mariette—she'll sell you papers for a shilling. I'd go now, Alard, and don't be tempted to spend these funds on anything or anywhere else. The queen is expecting me to turn you in after the play is over. There's a ship leaving at four this morning for Dover. From there, France. You'll need to be on it."

I don't expect gratitude and I don't get it. It takes a second for Alard to shove the bag of coins into the front of his dress, another second for him to turn and march down the hall, through the front door, black gown and black wig disappearing into the black night. He doesn't look back, doesn't think to tell Shakespeare he's leaving, or to make sure his role would be covered in his absence. He doesn't even return his costume. Alard is self-serving, yes. But he is no fool.

Unlike me, who has the wrong assassin, no alibi, no funds, no plan, and little over an hour to figure out what to do about it.

Chapter 37

KIT

MIDDLE TEMPLE HALL, LONDON
6 JANUARY 1602
8:25 PM

I t is the midway point of the play.

The pause between act 2 and act 3, where all the players exit the stage and the musicians play a short interlude. This allows the audience a chance to stand up and stretch, for men with trays of sweetmeats and wine to scurry forth and offer them to the queen and her guests on bended knee. The rest of us congregate in the Parliament Chamber, preparing a short singing number to be performed before the play resumes. As the player with the best voice, I am to be first in line. First to walk onstage, first to stand before the queen, singing sweetly. This is where, in just over one hour, I am to fix my position, as Tom One told me to do. Find the queen and calculate my distance from where I stand to where she sits, take out my knife, and thrust it in an acute angle between the queen's neck and shoulder and pull down. Quick, just like a lever.

What will happen when I don't do it?

On the other side of the room, Mistress Lovett and Mistress Lucy are frantically preparing Cressy, Alard's understudy, to step into his abandoned role. Alard was nowhere to be found, and Shakespeare offered no explanation. The other players speculated that he saw someone in the audience he hadn't expected—someone he owed money to, his reputation as a terrible gambler known to everyone—and disappeared before whoever it was came collecting. But I know better. I know Toby is behind this sudden disappearance, that whatever he told Alard was enough to make him walk away from the play and leave London and possibly England, possibly forever.

Cressy, a tall, reedy boy, is now sewn into a gown the exact same as Alard's, tucked under the same wig as Alard's, and with face paint the same as Alard's. The queen and her men won't know it isn't Alard, at least not until it's all over. Then, even when there's no assassination attempt, Toby will storm the stage, apprehend poor Cressy, and turn him over to the guards. This is when, I imagine, Toby will take advantage of the confusion and the chaos to scuttle me out the door and into the street and down to the river, a whistle and a penny to make our escape, together.

It's too easy, and this frightens me. Nothing is ever that easy.

What about the Wrights? What will they do when I don't pull my knife in act 5? Will they, too, make their escape, thinking it's all gone wrong, and let me make mine? Or will they wait for me somewhere between Middle Temple Gardens and Paget Pier, knives tucked in their doublets, to silence the Arundell Plot once and for all? No recovery, no allegiance. I know what they told me it meant. But maybe, like everything else, it means something different, too.

Shakespeare appears then, pointing and grabbing and pushing us into the hallway and into place. After Alard disappeared and Cressy took his place, Shakespeare had the idea to have all the alternates costumed and ready during intermission, in case someone else decided to *abscond the premises* with *careless disregard for consequence*. As he begins lining us up, there's a lot of confusion and mistaken identity—more than usual—as he can no longer easily tell the difference between player and alternate—or in my case, player and player.

"You, Sebastian." Shakespeare's hand clamps down on my shoulder. "I've changed my mind. I want you in the second row, right behind Viola—"

"I *am* Viola, sir," I tell him. "Sebastian is over there." I turn around and point to Gray Hargrove. At least I think it's Hargrove. It really is hard to tell the difference between him and me and Wash: We all look remarkably, unsettlingly, alike.

"I'm not Sebastian," comes a high-pitched voice. "It's me, Wash."

"Merciful *Zeus*," Shakespeare mutters. "Which one of you is Sebastian? The real Sebastian, if you please?"

Hargrove, standing toward the back of the crowd of players, raises his hand.

"Well, don't just stand there. Get up here. Up, up."

Shakespeare snaps his fingers. Hargrove makes his way through the players, dark eyes cutting back and forth. He looks as confused as the rest of us.

"You. Stand here beside Burbage and Kemp. Tooley, you're behind Kemp." There's more pushing and more snapping fingers as we're all lined up in ever-widening rows. Toby, who couldn't hold a tune if it had a handle on it, is placed toward the back. The alternates, all of them now stage-ready, loiter in the hallway, ready to be called forth at a moment's notice. Finally the drums begin their beat, the trumpets their blares, the fife and the flute, and our song begins. The Wrights appear like ghosts, pushing the trellis aside so we can all fit through the door at once.

"And you're on," Shakespeare whispers, and we step, slow and together, into the Hall.

"*Hey, Robin, jolly Robin,*" we sing. "*Tell me how thy lady does. Hey, Robin, jolly Robin, tell me how—*"

That is when, two acts and fifty minutes too early, the lights go out.

Chapter 38

TOBY

MIDDLE TEMPLE HALL, LONDON
6 JANUARY 1602
8:45 PM

It happens so fast.

The lights extinguish and we are plunged into darkness. The musicians stop, flutes and drums and trumpets cease, song lyrics trail away. Then begins murmuring. Shuffling from the players around me, wondering if they should keep their spots; shuffling from the feet in the audience, wondering if they should, too. There's a jerk of movement in front of me, beside me, I cannot see from who. I cannot see Kit. I cannot see anything.

Seconds pass. The murmuring increases. Someone says, "Orsino." It's Shakespeare's high-pitched voice, now raspy with ill-concealed fear.

"I don't know," I say. It wasn't a question, but it's the only reply I've got. I reach for my boot and pull out my dagger, slow, careful. Any sudden movement will incite more, and if I can't see, I need to at least be able to feel what is happening.

"Places," Shakespeare orders, and the shuffling around us stops. He is trying to restore order, trying to save his show. "Stagehands, are you idle men or do you have matches? Musicians, strike a tune if you may, or have you taken somnolence?"

"No, don't—" I call, but it is too late, the sudden tune filling the air and drowning out any hope I had of hearing the sound of errant footsteps and the direction they come from.

Someone, I don't see who, lights a match. It flickers uncertainly, casting long shadows on faces. There is fear and confusion and even some amusement from Burbage and Kemp, thinking this is all in good fun. I look around them, past them, into the darkness. I don't know what's happening, but I know that whatever it is, it's not part of the plan Kit told me about. Maybe she lied to me, but I don't think so; there was too much truth in her face. Even so, there's been a change, and change, as always, heralds danger.

I need to find Kit. Shakespeare put her at the very front of the line, and that's where I move, one slow step after another. I slide past Malvolio, edge in front of Olivia, brush by Feste the Fool. Finally, I see her, moving toward the mouth of the trellised door. Tall, reed thin and red wig, eyes blinking against the sea of darkness before her. I think, wild and desperate and guilty, that if I can reach her, I can use this distraction to get us out of here. In the absence of a better plan, it seems like the only thing to do.

That is, until I see her press her hand against her doublet where she told me her knife was strapped.

In the flickering light of a dying match, I watch her slide it from the sheath, slow, her eyes fixed in the direction of the queen, now nothing but a gilded outline in the dark. For a moment I cannot reconcile what I am seeing. I cannot believe that she means to go through with it, this insane plan, even though I offered her a way out. Somewhere between then and now she must have decided that killing the queen was worth it, even though she'd be caught and it would mean her death.

Even though it would mean mine, too.

I lunge for her. Shove past the players before me, beside me. I don't dare shout because to do so is to cause pandemonium, the very thing that would create a distraction and give her just enough time to do what she means to. I push past players, some who snap at me and some who push back. Finally I reach her, snatching her arm and whirling her around only to be confronted with a face I don't recognize. Not gray eyes but brown, not pale brows but dark ones. No full lips but thin ones, and no hint of recognition at all, only hate.

In the shock of working out it isn't Kit—nor any of the other players or alternates or anyone I recognize at all—the boy wrenches his arm from my grasp and disappears into the dark, in the direction of the queen.

Chapter 39

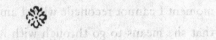

KIT

There is a scuffle, a muffled grunt, a handful of murmured exclamations, and Shakespeare's voice above all of it for us to *hold our places*. I don't know what is happening, the whole of it drowned out by the music echoing through the Hall. I can't see anything, only shadows colliding with shadows, a shaky light from a shaky match but even that goes out and we're in darkness again. I don't know why the lights went out so early, and something tells me this wasn't an accident. Only the Wrights could have managed this.

I don't like being here, at the front of this line, with the queen before me and the rest of the players and the Wrights behind me.

I am in the dark, quite literally, and this is nothing I or Catesby or any of his men rehearsed, at least not with me. Toby won't know what's happening, either; it's not what I told him would and now he'll think I lied to him—again—and that I'm part of it. I need to find him and tell him I'm not.

As Tom One promised, my eyes are beginning to adjust in the dark, bodies that were invisible only seconds ago now emerging as shadowy outlines. I step from my place in line, into the throng behind me. Past Burbage and Kemp—at least I think it's Burbage and Kemp—fixing my position toward the back, the last place I saw Toby. He was a dozen steps from me, give or take; but with everyone shifting around me and their whispered voices overrun by music, I can't tell if the line is still intact, if it's moved, or if Toby has.

I take another step just as someone bumps into me, hard; I can't tell who it is but I'm knocked off balance a bit, and then I bump into someone else. There's a muttered apology and a hiss of annoyance, and by the time I sort myself out, I'm all turned around. I can see nothing but the outline of a figure moving past me, the dark showing me nothing but the sleeve of a white jacquard doublet, exactly like mine. Is it Gray Hargrove? If so, then I'm at the front of the line, back where I started. If it's his alternate, or mine, then there's no telling where I am in this crowd.

Someone lights another match. It allows me just enough light to see this boy, this figure in white, slide a knife—just like mine—from his doublet—just like mine. He lifts it high: primary hand, fist grip, point down. By my calculation, it's been two minutes since the lights went out and I know that the

Sebastian standing before me is not Hargrove, nor is it his alternate or even mine: The Sebastian standing before me is not a player at all.

It's Jory.

I am so stunned at his being here, so shocked, that for a moment all I can do is stare. How is he here? How is he dressed in costume, in a wig and in face paint? How did he get past the guards and past Shakespeare, past Mistress Lovett and Mistress Lucy? How did he get past Toby?

The answer to all this, of course, is the Wrights. Catesby. Tom One. And Jory himself. All that time he was at Catesby's, when he said he was furthering his studies, he was being schooled in the same plot I was, the Arundell Plot, named after me but not to be performed by me. Maybe I am part of this answer, too; I once told Catesby that my volunteering to kill the queen gave him two opportunities to achieve his end with his plot and innocence intact: I suppose he thought to hedge his bet by making Jory his third.

All this passes through my head in a second, but it's enough time for Jory to disappear. Did he see me? Surely he must have. But maybe he doesn't care. Because like Jory during Mass or in his studies or even with Father's horses, his focus is only on what he is doing. Nothing else exists. Not me, standing beside him. Not the stage, empty before him. Not even the musicians, huddled and playing gaily to the left of him. Even the queen's men and her audience, the sea of darkened faces to the right of him, do not exist. There is only her. I imagine Jory counting his steps as we were instructed, tuning out voices and music as he makes his way to the queen in that confection of a dress, ramrod posture and staring straight ahead. She must know this is it, that the play has gone wrong and she is in danger, but she does not move, nor fidget, nor call for her guards to escort her away. She is every bit as determined as Jory.

"Toby!" I shout his name, but it is drowned out by music. Jory has taken three steps, and by the count I made earlier, he has thirteen left to go. I pull open my doublet, feel for the cool iron hilt of the dagger, slide it out, and start after him.

There is a bit of conversation coming from the audience, a few laughs, those not in the know thinking this is all part of the show. A few even begin clapping along to the music. I don't know where Toby is; he must know something's gone wrong. But maybe he can't see in the dark, or has also gotten turned around or waylaid by players. Or maybe—and I don't like to think it—he's decided to save himself after all. It would be easy, now; he could send the queen's guards through that trellised door, and we would be surrounded.

"Jory!" I don't dare speak louder than a whisper. "Don't do it! They know—"

Jory turns around. He takes me in: my face and my stance and my knife raised high, exact copies of each other. I expect something: an acknowledgment, an apology, a surrender, or even a prayer. What I don't expect is for him to take a swipe at me, aiming at my hand to disengage me. If it weren't dark, and if Tom One's instructions—*don't get cut, expect to get cut*—weren't circling through my mind, as they are undoubtedly Jory's, he might have succeeded.

I swipe back, a blind stab in the dark, looking to do the same. The first time I hit nothing; the second time the tip of my dagger snags fabric and pulls away with a rip. I stab once more and this time I hit something; Jory tips toward me and knocks his shoulder into mine, hard and abrupt. I'm nearly knocked off balance, both of us stumbling to stay upright.

Someone slides into sight then. At first I think it's Jory and I ready my knife again, but no, it's someone else and by the surety of his movements, sharp and decisive, I know it's Toby. I hear a hand slapping on skin, a muffled scuffle, a barely audible grunt. Then Toby has Jory by the arm, upright and still and silent and disarmed. It was over so fast, but when I hear Toby's familiar breath in my ear, I know it is not over at all.

"Keep quiet," Toby says. "Follow me and do what I say and don't speak a word."

He takes me by the arm, too, in a grip as tight as he's got Jory's. I don't like it and I want to pull away, but I don't. I let him drag us both to the entrance to the Hall, the one now covered by the wooden trellis that someone (the Wrights?) has slid before it.

Are the rest of the players still out there? Will the play go on? I barely have time to wonder, and then I don't need to. Because on the other side of the door I see that the hallway is cleared of players, bare of stagehands and costumers and empty of Shakespeare; the Wrights are nowhere to be seen. The only thing in the dim candlelit space is a half dozen of the queen's guards, black and red and armed, and Toby holding me and Jory, both poised with daggers in our hands.

Chapter 40

TOBY

MIDDLE TEMPLE HALL, LONDON
6 JANUARY 1602
8:55 PM

I hold Kit firmly beside me, her upper arm in my grasp. She does not speak or move, though I can feel she wants to do both. In my other hand is the boy. I am almost certain he is the one Kit told me she left Cornwall with, the boy also mentioned in the letter I received last night. Her father's groom, Jory Jameson. Both of them still clutching matching, damnable daggers.

I hold him just as tight, though he doesn't feel as if he wants to move or speak at all. He seems dazed and he's stumbling; his knife slips from his hand and clatters to the floor. This could be because he's been caught, but it could also be because when we fought onstage I slapped the heel of my palm against his temple, a move guaranteed to subdue someone if not knock them out entirely.

"You. And you." I address two of the queen's guards. "I need your irons. Now."

One guard, the shorter of the two, does what I say, reaching for the manacles affixed to his belt. The taller one looks from me to Kit to Jory and back to me and does nothing.

"Now," I snap.

"Why d'you have two?" the tall one says. "We were told you'd have one. Not two. That's what Carey said. One."

"I didn't realize the queen's guards were so skilled in spy craft," I say smoothly, though my insides are a storm. "I'm sure her ministers would love to hear your thoughts on the matter after these look-alike players, these would-be assassins"—I emphasize the plural—"are handed over. Perhaps you could also tell one from the other, and determine which is the guilty party?"

The guards look to each other, blank expressions on both their faces.

"That's what I thought," I say. "Now, if you would, do what I say and bind them both." I tip my head to Kit. "Start with him."

I thrust Kit toward the tall guard, who snatches up her dagger before taking her arm and then her wrists, clamping iron around them and locking them tight. The guard pushes Kit back to me, but I don't take her. I can't, because Jory has now begun to slump in my grasp, and he's too heavy to hold with one hand.

"What's wrong with him?" the short guard says.

I don't reply because I don't know; he might be faking it to try to get away, or maybe I hit him harder than I thought. But then Kit lets out a gasp and when I look—really look—I see the blood blooming against the stiff white fabric of his sleeve. She must have tried to stop him with that knife of hers, landing a blow somewhere in his upper arm and slicing open a crucial artery, and it's taken this long for the blood to seep through his doublet's heavy fabric.

Jory slumps to the floor.

Kit lunges for him, and I take my chance and grab her, yanking her to her feet. She cannot fall apart on me now. I turn to the remaining four guards, now standing over Jory's motionless body and doing nothing.

"Pick this one up and take him outside before he bleeds all over the queen's promenade." I press my toe against Jory's outstretched finger. He doesn't flinch and I don't think he's playacting. "When you're done, find the stagehands. They'll be in the Queen's Room. Tell them to light this place up. For Her Majesty to sit in the dark this long is untenable. After you've done that, find Sir George Carey in the Hall and tell him I will meet him at Whitehall after the performance is over."

This gives me one hour.

I shove Kit—more roughly than necessary—toward the open and now-unguarded door, but one of the guards steps in front of me. I don't like when people step in front of me. Whatever he sees on my face shows him this and he takes a step backward.

"You're not leaving," he says. "Not with a dead body here. We don't want responsibility for that. We'll take the boy to the Tower; you deal with him."

"This boy may be an assassin," I reply. "If he is, he managed to get in front of the queen with a knife. Evaded a cavalcade of people to do it. You don't think he can evade you, too?" I give Kit another shake. "Until I determine he's not a threat, I will take him to the Tower and into questioning myself, then I'll be back for the stiff. Unless you'd like to accompany me? If you wish to see the job done for yourself."

Kit struggles in my grip. She may be acting, but her fear feels real. Thankfully my gamble with the guard pays off—I've never met one who doesn't back off at the suggestion of more work—and he sweeps an inviting arm toward the door. Unnecessary. I would have gone through him anyway. Then, before anyone can say anything else, we are through the door, through the courtyard and onto Middle Temple Lane, following it south toward the river, to the wherries, and in the direction of the Tower.

Chapter 41

KIT

FLEET STREET, LONDON
6 JANUARY 1602
9:09 PM

oby's grip on me is relentless. Also relentless: the urge for me to break from it and run. It is not until we reach Milford Lane—a street I know from Catesby's map to be unguarded—that I stop struggling. And even then, not completely.

"Toby—" I start.

"Don't," he says. "Don't say a word."

Toby reaches for my wrist. He palms a tiny key—he must have swiped it from the guard—and in a flash he's got my manacles unlocked, tossing them into a nearby bush. He takes up my arm again, half pushing and half pulling me through endless alleys full of shops and homes and gardens that run parallel to the main thoroughfare of Temple Bar. As always, he moves with surety. I don't know if this is part of his plan; I only know I am free from my bindings and we are no longer moving in the direction of the Tower, and that knowledge keeps me from losing my composure completely.

As it is, I am already weeping at the thought of Jory, slumped in the hall at Middle Temple the way my father slumped in the hall at Lanherne, both killed by an errant stab and both left to die a traitor's death.

"I killed him, didn't I?" I say, disobeying Toby's orders. "I didn't mean to. I was only trying to disarm him. The way Tom One taught me to—" Toby gives me a sharp look and I stop.

"Did you know he was coming?" Toby pushes me down yet another alley—this one called Hanging Sword Court. I doubt it was intentional, but I shiver anyway. "Did you know it was part of the plan?"

"Obviously not." I swipe my hand across my eyes. It comes away in a smear of black and white.

"Nothing is obvious to me right now." Toby throws me another look. "Get rid of that costume and face paint, would you? As much of it as you can."

I yank off my ropy, itchy wig and tuck it between the branches of an evergreen. The bright red will be more than evident in the branches come morning, but we will long be gone by then.

"I don't know how he managed to get in," I say. "Past the guards, past Shakespeare, past everyone. Did he take Hargrove's place? Or Hargrove's alternate's place?"

Toby shrugs. "I couldn't tell. There were four of you, all

looking alike, weren't there? As for how he got inside, my guess is one of your men killed one of the guards on duty. You said they were outside waiting, right?" He glances at me; I nod. "I think the Wrights directed him inside, got him the costume he needed, made him up the best they could to the point that no one else would recognize him. As for what they did to Hargrove or his alternate, he's dead, probably. You would know more than I."

I imagine this is true. The Arundell Plot has managed to kill a lot of people, not one of them on purpose and not one of them the queen.

I wonder if Jory will get a proper burial.

"Who was he?" Toby says. "Jory. Who was he, besides your father's groom?"

"He was studying to be a priest." I scrape off my wig cap and swipe it across my face before grinding it into the mud with the toe of my boot. "After my father was killed, he escorted me to London."

"I know that," he says. "What else?"

"What do you mean?" I say. Then, because I think this is what he's after: "We shared a room, yes. But it wasn't like that. I told you he was a priest—"

"Not that, either." Toby huffs an impatient breath. "He went from mucking stalls to praying the rosary to wielding a knife. I think you're missing something."

"I guess I did," I say. "Jory was always pious, always passionate about his faith. But then I guess he became dangerous and I didn't see it coming." I think of his prayers, his conviction, his determination, and his ambition. I think of all that time spent with Father, with Catesby; his eagerness to be part of Father's plot, one he said meant everything to him. Maybe I did see it coming. Or maybe I simply chose not to.

"Will your men come after you?" Toby says. "Do I need to be on watch for them, too?"

"No. I think they're probably long gone by now." I imagine Catesby is already on his way to the country, Tom One and Tom Two well on their way, the Wrights scattered somewhere throughout the city to hide out until it's safe for them to resurface. *No recovery, no allegiance.* Just as they promised.

Toby steers us onto Water Lane, a street that leads directly from Fleet Street down to the river. We're halfway to the water when we see a fleet of wherries pass, helmed by frantically rowing guards. From our place in the shadows, we watch as they approach the pier at the Temple, a dozen men spilling onto the stairs and onto Middle Temple Lane. Toby watches them closely, as if he can tell something about them by the sound of their shouts and their footsteps.

"It's the queen's men, isn't it?" I say. "How did they know?"

"They know everything" is all he says. One final glance down the street to ensure it's clear and he catches my elbow and pulls me back in it, not toward the water this time but around it, cutting behind houses that grow progressively larger with every block. It's only when we pass Bridewell Palace that I begin to understand where he's taking me.

"Carey's," Toby says, as if I've asked him out loud. "His house at Blackfriars. He's got his own pier, and I can hail a man from Poles Wharf, two houses down. From there, a boat to the shipyard in Wapping." He speaks in a rapid undertone, as if reciting from memory. "There's a ship leaving at four this morning for Dover. Then on to France."

I knew I was in trouble. I knew *we* were in trouble. But it is not until Toby says *France*, the land of refugees and exiles, that I understand just how much.

"Where in France?" My voice comes out weak and small and every bit as frightened as I feel. The answer hardly matters, but it feels as if I should say something to this decision he's made, or to know something about what happens from there. But the only reply I get is Toby's hand clamped on mine as he hauls me in the direction of Blackfriars.

Chapter 42

TOBY

BLACKFRIARS HOUSE, LONDON
6 JANUARY 1602
9:31 PM

arey's.

Getting over the brick wall into his garden was easy enough, shrouded as it is by trees and boughs and luxury, cold grass and pruned roses and sanguine winter ivy dripping from the facade. The house is dark, quiet, and for a moment—no. I nearly thought: For a moment I almost feel safe.

I tuck my hand back into Kit's, leading her onto the graveled path and down to the waterfront. There's no boat, of course; it's waiting downriver at the Temple, waiting for Carey to finish with the play to take him back to Whitehall, where he expects I will be. For me to explain why Alard, the assassin I named in the report, is missing. Why Kit, the assassin I once named as a suspect, is also missing, and why Jory Jameson, someone I never named at all, lies dead in the hallway of Middle Temple Hall. Alard's disappearance is damning, Jameson's death more so. But for me not to deliver Kit in shackles—after promising six guards I would—is treason.

I don't have to ask what would happen if we were caught.

She would be taken to the Tower. Pressed into a chair, her thumb into a screw or her neck into a collar, relentless questioning until she sicks up everything she knows, then tossed into a cell before her inevitable execution. She won't meet the same fate as her father's priest, the drawing and quartering, not once they discover she's a woman. Instead, she'll be taken to Tower Hill, forced to her knees on a hastily built scaffold strewn with rushes like a stage, a blindfold pulled over her eyes, the blade and the damage done. It is the same fate that will be meted out to me, too.

The scene is so vivid in my head I can almost hear the beat of the drums, the smell of the hay, the sound of the ax, the scent of copper. I can almost feel it, the way I could feel the watchers in the shadows as we passed through the alleys to come here, the way I can feel their eyes on me, even now.

"Toby."

I open my eyes to see Kit watching me. Her face is streaked with white, lips still stained with red, eyes smudged with kohl, hair a crazed tumble of curls and she is beautiful.

"Go." I push her to the dock. The pier that serves this row of homes is Baynards, but it is empty for the same reason Blackfriars is: The men and their boats are elsewhere. I step to the end of the dock and press my fingers in my mouth, a short, sharp whistle and a finger held in the air. A single boat breaks free from the knot of loitering wherries and makes its way to us, slow and choppy and *hurry*.

I turn to Kit, who stands beside me now, not watching the wherry's slow progress but beyond it, waves and boats and men. She looks at them the way I do, searching for anomalies in the pattern, aberrations from the norm. She's learning, this girl from Cornwall, what it means to be a boy in London and a man in the world, that you cannot trust anything or believe in anyone. It sickens me, but it also gives me hope that she might just make it. She looks at me.

"The ship at Wapping leaves at four for Dover." I repeat the same instructions I gave her moments ago, the same instructions I gave Alard an hour ago. "Then on to Calais. France." I pull out a small drawstring bag from my costume doublet. Inside is almost everything I have left in the world after I gave half of it to Alard—everything: two pounds, eleven shillings, three pence.

"You said that," she says. "Before."

The shadows in Carey's garden begin to move. Curling toward me like smoke, a casting net coiling around its prey, silent and final. I step close so when I speak it will be just for us, the rest swallowed by river sounds and tide.

"What did you want, when you started all this?" I say. "What did you think to do when it was all over?"

Kit frowns, as if her reply is a memory she's unwillingly forced to recall. "Freedom," she says finally. "To not serve anyone but myself. To do and think and say what I please and not answer to anyone." She shrugs. "Selfish, isn't it? And foolish. We all answer to someone, don't we?"

The wherry is here, knocking its way to the dock. I hold up my hand and the wherryman nods and waits, waves slapping time against the hull.

"I only have enough money for one of us to leave. I had more, but—" I stop. There's no point in telling her what happened, or how close I came to having everything I wanted. "There's an inn called the Grapes. It's on Narrow Street, on the Wapping waterfront, just east of the Tower. Ask for Mariette, and tell her I sent you." I press the small bag of coins into her hand, along with my dagger, since the guards took hers. "She'll give you travel papers, tickets. A new identity if you want it, and I think you do."

My voice catches at the very real possibility that this will be the last time I see Kit Alban—or Katherine Arundell—again.

"No one will come looking for you there." I go on. "But if they do, they won't find you. You'll be safe until it's time for the ship to leave." I push her toward the steps.

"What about you?" Kit says. She's strong and she fights me, first pulling away and then, damnable girl, stomping her foot on mine. "Toby," she says when I don't reply. "What are you going to do?"

"You told me you wanted freedom," I say. "So I am giving you mine."

The shadows begin their murmur; the net begins to knot. She hears it, too, and turns her face to the house, color leaching from her skin, even her lips are white.

"Why?"

"What the queen did to you, and to your father, I was part

of it, too." I think then of words Marlowe wrote so long ago that run through my mind like a whisper.

Birds of the air will tell of murders past—

"I didn't know when I started this what it would turn into," I say. This night, yes, but everything else, too; her and me and everything that meant anything to me, slipping through my fingers. "I didn't know it would end this way."

Might first made kings, and laws were then most sure—

Kit snatches my wrist, the way she did in the alleys in Vintry, her face just as fierce. "Come with me."

But whither am I bound—

My hand on her arm, pushing her down the stairs. Her struggle to break free, her refusal to shout. The last of my coins in the wherryman's hands, a kick to the hull to release it to the tide. A shove of the oars and the crisis of a struggle, her eyes on mine, anger and fear and a thousand unnamed things that slip away as she disappears from me the same way she appeared on the stage at the Globe: slowly and completely.

I turn from the river and the shadow beckons. Up the stairs, slippery and gray to the landing and then the grass, frost-flattened and crisp under my feet, popping and cracking like broken glass. There stand six of the queen's guards, the same six from Middle Temple, all of them armed with both weapons and knowledge of my treachery, as I knew they would be.

Was there ever seen such villainy, so neatly plotted and so well performed?

Chapter 43

KIT

SOMEWHERE ON THE THAMES RIVER
6 JANUARY 1602
10:11 PM

The moment I saw the guards emerge from the shadows I wanted to scream, but I didn't dare. Toby is in enough trouble without me announcing to the world that I'm a girl, not when it's still a secret and possibly the only thing that is keeping them from finding me and dragging me to wherever it is they're taking him.

I am shaking all over, the same way I was when Father was killed. And just like on that night, I have no idea what to do. Toby wants me to go to an inn (without him) to hide out for a few hours, then slip aboard a ship (without him) and sail all the way to Calais (without him). To do so would be to save me, but what about him? Toby, with his bravery and his stupidity and his sacrifice? I don't know what possessed him to do any of it, nor do I know what will happen to him if I don't somehow stop it. How am I going to do *that*? I couldn't manage to stop the queen once. There is nothing I can do to stop her again.

I will try anyway.

"I need you to drop me at Fresh Wharf," I tell the wherryman. It's the pier closest to London Bridge, the only one I know that far east. But from there it's a short walk to the Tower of London, where they took Ryol after he was captured, where they take the worst kinds of traitors, and where I am so afraid they're going to take Toby.

"He told me to take you to Wapping. He paid for Wapping." A frown. "If you're trying to get your coin back—"

"No. I've had a change of mind, that's all," I say. "Keep the pay."

The wherryman shrugs and whistles idly through his teeth as he rows, rows, rows far too slowly alongside a thousand other boats gliding through the piscine waters, not one of those boats Toby's. I reason the guards at Carey's would have hailed a wherry shortly after us. I don't think they would have taken a coach, but truthfully, I don't know how any of this is done at all. I should have paid more attention when Catesby was talking about sending someone into the prisons to find out where Ryol was being held or if he had confessed. But I was more interested in myself.

As we row, I try to arrange myself. Dredge my fingers along the frosty water, run them through my hair to dampen and press down my curls. Peel off my jacquard doublet, turn it inside out. Dip the sleeve in the water and scrub it over my eyes, my lips, my cheeks until it comes away clean. Turn it right side out and slip it back on. I can't do much about the rest: the hose and the breeches, the ribbons and the lace and the shoes. There's no shop open tonight, at least not one that will sell me clothes. The wherryman watches me as he rows, but if he's got something to say, he decides against it.

I don't know what I plan to do even if Toby is brought to the Tower. For a half second I consider breaking him out with the dagger he gave me and my lessons on engagement and defanging the serpent. Then I think I could talk his way out of there. I can be persuasive; after all, I did convince Catesby to let me try to kill the queen (even though it seems he didn't trust me to do it, else he wouldn't have sent in Jory to do it for me). All I know is I can't do what Toby instructed me to, which is to sail away while he pays the price for a crime I tried to commit.

As we near London Bridge, the steady slap of the oars against the tide becomes ambient as other, more erratic sounds take its place. From above: music, shouting, laughing, hooves, and cart wheels hitting stone. Fresh Wharf is a quay for fishermen, hence the name, clogged with men and boats and fish and nets during the day, relatively empty at night. The smell remains.

We reach the pier. Toby has already paid him more than enough, so I scramble from the boat and onto the stairs, slippery with moss and damp, and start the bankside walk to the Tower. I need to get my bearings and understand what I'm up against, maybe charm a guard or two who will take pity on me and maybe, maybe allow me inside.

It's not far, not even a half mile. But with every step the noise from the bridge grows quieter, the sound of my boots on cobblestones louder. It seems to grow colder, too. Or maybe it's my imagination, coming so close to a place I've only read about in stories, those of missing princes, locked and vanished forever somewhere inside: *a thing devised by the enemy, bloody will be thy end, the winter of their discontent.*

It's monstrous. There's almost no light to see by, barely a half-moon, but that's all I want or need to see of it anyway. Miles of stone encircling the buildings within, corners buttressed with circular towers, flags flying facetiously from each. It's a fortress, a castle of horrors, a purgatory of terror. I cross myself and whisper a fast prayer for Ryol's soul and then one for Jory's, the prayer for the forgotten dead.

I am trembling head to toe. I feel sick; I could easily vomit all over these mossy cobblestones if I had anything at all in my stomach. I've learned that the worst things are best gotten over with quickly, so I walk straight to the nearest guard tower, just past a long dark street called Petty Row, and march right up to the single guard standing under the arched doorway.

"I'm here to see a prisoner," I say. Bold as brass.

The guard looks at me, up and down. Hair to face to beribboned hose, back to my face. "Who?"

"Who is calling or who is the prisoner?"

"Both."

"Day Petty to see Toby Ellis." *Day* after a boy I once fancied in Cornwall, *Petty* after the street I just passed. If the guard thinks anything of this, he doesn't say.

"There's no Toby Ellis here." The guard flicks a hand for me to leave, but I pretend not to see.

"Oh," I say. "I thought this is where they take criminals. I know nothing of prisons, you know. I'm only fifteen."

The guard says nothing.

"I've just come from the stews with my brother," I go on. "Well, half brother. My father, he wasn't one for fidelity, so I've got several. Brothers, I mean. Not fathers." The servants at Lanherne were always charmed by my stories, so maybe this flint-faced guard will be, too. "He got into some trouble with girls."

The guard remains silent, but his mouth quirks at this last bit and I know I've got him.

"They had a mind to dress me up like the Dauphin. It's why I look like this. You should see how they dressed my brother! Anyway. There was a fuss over money and he didn't have enough." I pull out the bag of coins Toby gave me. "I went home and got the rest. So maybe if you could let me see him, I could give him the money and then he could pay the girls and we could all go home happy."

"I told you, your brother isn't here," the guard says. "They don't take thieves here. Or common men. That's Bridewell. Or Fleet. They only take traitors here. Murderers. Religious dissenters. Noblemen."

"That's just it, sir," I say. "See, my father is an Irish nobleman."

The guard narrows his past-midnight eyes. "You shouldn't be telling me this." He pauses. "Go sit over there." He motions toward a mess of cannons and pulleys and firing platforms lining the jetty and overlooking the river. "Hide, mind. If your brother is coming, they'll bring him in through Traitors' Gate.

But if they do bring him here, it'll take more than those coins in that bag to get him out."

I do what I'm told, dashing from the guard tower to a spot between cannons, tucking into a ball, my knees to my chest to ensure I can see, but not be seen. The river stretches endless before me, black and quiet and empty.

I pray to every saint I know that they don't bring Toby to this place. That he somehow managed to escape the guards and hail a boat and get away, that even now he is sailing toward Wapping, where he will charm this Mariette with his blue eyes and plaintive voice and she will give him papers and tickets and a place aboard a ship. Even now he could be standing on the riverfront, trawling the quay for me the way I am trawling this one for him, angry with me for not following the steps of his carefully laid-out plan.

Even so, I wait.

Chapter 44

TOBY

ST. PAUL'S CATHEDRAL, LONDON
7 JANUARY 1602
12:02 AM

It is not the usual interrogation.

There are no manacles, no dark chambers, no threats, at least not those that involve chains or whips or whispers of bad things to come. There is, however, Richard Bancroft, bishop of London (BA, MA, DD, all from Cambridge—he would want you to know this), though it could be said he does nothing but whisper of bad things to come.

It takes place in the chapel in the crypt below St. Paul's, with its cold walls and grave lighting, and it takes no great skill to reason why they've chosen this place. It's a reminder of the persecution of years past, heretics brought here to be toyed with words and tricked into confession before being marched into cells, then strung up for treason. It's empty of guards and courtiers and people who come and go, empty of eyes and ears and mouths that would bear witness to what comes next.

There should not be witness to what comes next.

Sir Robert Cecil (secretary of state to Queen Elizabeth I is his official title, spymaster his unofficial. See also: former Chancellor of the Duchy of Lancaster, Privy Councillor, Member of Parliament, and Keeper of the Privy Seal—he would want you to know this, too) makes a big show of laying out his book before him, fat and leather-bound, treachery and lies spilling at the seams. This time, most of them mine.

What we've covered thus far: my name (Tobias Ellis to them; Duke Orsino to *him*); my occupation (watcher and cryptographer to them; player and playwright to *him*); my reputation (tarred and painted; this to everyone).

What remains uncovered: everything else.

"Who is he?"

"That depends," I reply, "on which *he* you're referring to."

Cecil's disdain is a shroud. "There is the one who was stabbed onstage, the one you named as the assassin, and then there is the one who got away. You tell me, Tobias. With which *he* would you like to begin?"

It doesn't matter; any one of them is enough to end me.

"Let's start with the one who got away." Cecil decides for me. "What did you say his name was?"

"I didn't." The ministers exchange glances. This balance I am walking, the line between ignorance and impudence, grows narrow. "He was called Christopher Alban. Went by Kit."

"Kit," Egerton repeats. (Thomas Egerton, Solicitor General. BA Oxford, QC Lincoln's Inn, Master of the Rolls, Lord Keeper of the Great Seal. His eye is sharp as his tongue and he is no fool.) "Interesting coincidence. What else?"

"He came from the country." I bypass the bait and continue the lie carefully, carefully. "Plymouth. He is young. Inexperienced." I want to swallow the words, keep them to myself. But I cannot give them nothing if I do not give them something.

"How did he get so far, then, if he is as young and inexperienced as you say? To the main stage, a principal role with the Lord Chamberlain's Men, to a place before the queen, holding a knife, a goddamned knife?" Such is Cecil's power that his blasphemy does not evoke the ire of the bishop, who has not taken his eyes from me since I walked into the room.

"Letting him get that far was the plan," I reply. "I can hardly ensnare a would-be assassin if the assassination is not attempted."

"Yet this would-be assassin is gone and here you are instead." His stare, a dark and heavy thing, weights me to my chair.

Above me, outside this room, and beyond this cathedral lies London: the whole of the city sprawling and reeling and still recovering from the Twelfth Night revelries. Mummers' plays and music, wassail and Twelfth Night cakes, sticky with butter and sugar and pressed into my hand with a gleam from saturnine eyes and a whisper from a voice sweeter than it all:

> *If you get the clove you're a villain.*
> *If you get the twig you're a fool.*
> *If you get the rag you are a tarty lad.*
> *Which one are you?*

· 345 ·

"What of the other boy with the knife? The one who was killed?" This from Egerton. "He was nowhere on your report. Not the first, not the last. He was never mentioned by you at all. Why?"

"He was unforeseen," I reply.

"It is your job to make sure nothing is unforeseen," Cecil says. "I don't keep you in my ledger and under my protection for anything less." There is a weighty pause, one in which I am expected to understand that the whole of my life rests on that very premise.

"What of the boy you named as the assassin?" Cecil goes on, scanning the page before him. "Thomas Alard? You painted a convincing picture: gambler, debtor, drifter, antagonist. An assassin in profile, perhaps, but not in deed. Yet he, like the other boy, is now gone."

I wait to hear what else they know.

"Was he working with the boy who is now dead? Were they in league with the noblemen who planned this thing? What were their motives? Are they Catholic? Spanish? Supporters of Essex? It's what you said at the start of this, isn't it? Or were these just more of your lies?"

"The queen is safe." It is my lifeline and I cling to it; had Kit not killed Jory or Jory killed the queen I would not have even that. "The assignment was a success—"

"Were it a success," the bishop speaks, a proclamation, "these boys would be sitting before me instead of you."

"I'll ask you again, Tobias." Cecil's book shuts with a snap. "Who is Jory Jameson, and where are Alard and Alban?"

I cannot say it; it will be my death to say it.

"I don't know."

Chapter 45

KIT

THE TOWER OF LONDON
7 JANUARY 1602
1:25 AM

I feel it before I hear it.

A drummer beating time for the rowers. A flicker of torches, growing brighter with every strike. From the count and the space of each flame, six total, I make out that there are three boats. I cannot see who is in them. But it must be Toby. Mustn't it? While it seems like a lot of pomp for one boy, at least one who is not prince nor priest, who else would be coming here at this time of night? I don't want it to be him, not with that ceremony. It lends too much gravity to it. Ceremony is what precedes births and marriage and death. It is for once-in-a-lifetime events, for words that cannot be taken back, actions that cannot be untaken. Bells that cannot be unrung.

And so, it can't be Toby.

I have almost talked myself into this when I see him. Sitting in the wherry, wrists bound and clipped together. Still dressed as Duke Orsino, brown velvet and stupid white ruffs. He faces forward, posture straight, hands unmoving, face unmoving. Only his hair, wild and windblown, shows any feeling at all. Beside him in the boat are two of the queen's guards, the men who were at Carey's. In the boat behind him, a half dozen more; they needed that many to subdue one boy. The other boat, the one to lead the rest, holds the drummer and the torches.

There is a rumble then, something coming up through the ground and into my feet and chest. Then there is the terrible shriek of metal on stone and a violent swish of water. It's the water gate. They slip through it and then they are gone. Disappeared, swallowed, like those long-ago princes. I listen for something: voices, shouting, words. But there is nothing.

I can't think of what to do. Storm this impenetrable fortress with nothing but my dagger and my wits, what little there is left of them? Go back to the guard and demand that he let me in? Even if he did, is that wise with all those other guards from Middle Temple now in attendance? The ones who will remember me and my face and will not be taken in by any tale I could tell them, charming or not?

I decide to take my chances with the guard at the watchtower. He would have heard the gate rumble open. He would know what is to happen next. Maybe whatever he tells me will help me figure out what to do.

I scrabble around the edge of the cannon and start across the cobbled jetty. I'm halfway to the guard tower and the guard staring placidly across the water when I see a man emerge from the shadows. He's coming from the direction of Fresh Wharf, the very pier I came from, walking quickly and purposefully toward the very same guard tower I am. I grind to a halt. Because even though the man's head is down, and the shadows and the brim of his hat are obscuring his face, he is dressed in fur and finery, and I know without a doubt this is one of the queen's men.

If I run, I will be seen. If I stand here, I will be seen. All this man has to do is look up, just once, and he will see me.

Then, as if my thoughts commanded him to, the man looks up.

Sir George Carey.

He, too, stops walking, his eyes wide, as surprised to see me as I am him, probably more. What is he doing here? Is he here for Toby? These are things he is likely asking himself about me. But whereas Carey would know I am not here to harm Toby, I don't know the same about Carey.

By now, he'll know I am one of the suspected assassins. He'll also know Toby let me go. While it is true what I said to Toby that Sir Carey does seem kind and generous, I do not think this extends to would-be murderers. He could very well slap me in irons and drag me into the Tower and a cell alongside Toby.

Or in place of him.

I lift my head high and walk toward him, my stride as quick

and purposeful as his. I don't get more than a few steps before he, too, begins walking, continuing on toward the guard tower as he was before, head down once more against the gale coming off the river. He is acting as if he didn't see me, but there is no chance he did not: It's as silent and still and empty as a cemetery, and I am the only one around.

"Sir Carey!" I hurry my pace to match his. "I'd like to speak to you."

He ignores me, at least until I finally catch up, stepping in front of him to face him. Carey shifts his gaze from the ground to me, taking me in, bright blue eyes oddly pleasant, as if it were market day. He's clutching what looks like a blanket under one arm.

"It was me." I speak before he has a chance to. "Toby had nothing to do with it. Well, not nothing. But not very much. He was trying to protect me, and that's not a crime." I don't know if this is true; in fact I'm almost certain that in this case it is. But it will do no good to remind Carey of this, so I shift tactics. "You wanted an assassin; now you've got one. You can take me in, but Toby should be let go. He shouldn't be in there. It should be me!"

"You?" Sir Carey looks me up and down. I wait for his face to shift from friendly interest to recognition to loathing and then to rage. "Who are you?"

"What do you mean, who am I?" I stamp my frozen foot in frustration. "It's me. Kit Alban. I met you at your patron party. Well, I didn't meet you—I saw you. But you saw me, too! And you saw me at the play tonight. Not looking like this, but with stage paint and a wig and lips and…You know who I am!"

"I do meet a great many people, Mr. Alban—"

"Kit."

"—but alas, I cannot remember them all. I assure you, had I met you, I would remember. You seem quite…charming."

I wave this off. "Are you here to see Toby? You must be. Are you here to get him out? You have to get him out. If you need someone, you can put me in his place. I should be there anyway."

Sir Carey's smile never wavers, even as he backs away from me.

"It was a pleasure to meet you," he says. "But I'm afraid I don't know what you're talking about."

Sir Carey moves past me, toward the guard tower. I open my mouth to stop him, to plead for Toby one more time. I am so distraught I almost miss what he says next.

"Leave here, you silly boy. Leave, and don't ever come back."

I hail another wherry, shaking all the way to Narrow Street.

It is terrible here, this place Toby sent me to: cramped, filthy, stinking of last Sunday's fish and this morning's chamber pot. It must be well past one now, but no one here seems to know it; it may as well be the middle of the day. The muddy streets are filled with half-dressed women and fully armed men, frantic water filled with passenger ships and freight boats, acres of docks filled with sailors and cargo and chaos. I stand in the middle of it all, shouldered and shoved by thousands of stinking passersby, looking for the inn called the Grapes. The wherryman helpfully told me it was on the "left side of the bank," which helps me not at all. I don't dare stop and ask anyone, either, because if I've learned anything, it's that not every person is who they seem to be, and I may as well be walking straight into a trap as a tavern.

Finally I find it: a brown brick building wedged in a row of a half dozen other brown brick buildings. One door, one window, one painted sign hanging above the door of, naturally, a cluster of fat purple grapes. Inside is no less exciting. A length of bar, a smattering of tables, customers the mirror images of the men and women who crawl the dock, heaving bosoms and craggy faces and missing teeth.

I march to the bar, wedge my way in between a pair of over-large men, and set my elbows on the sticky wood.

"I'm looking for Mariette." I direct this to the man behind the bar. He waves over a woman, thin and severe and wearing an apron. She looks at me. "Toby sent me," I add, hoping this means something to her.

Apparently it does. She nods at the man, who reaches beneath the bar and hands me a key.

"Top of the second set of stairs, third door on the right." She looks me over, as if deciding something. "Shall I send up food? Clothes? Something to wash with?"

What I need are tickets and papers, but maybe this is some kind of code. I don't know, but I nod to all of it anyway. A glance at the large clock mounted over the bar reads half two, which means I've got an hour and a half before the ship leaves, less than that to figure out how to be on it.

I make my way up two creaky flights of red-carpeted stairs to the room she directed me to. There is nothing to it, but I am growing used to that. Four dingy walls. One cracked ceiling. One table in front of a soot-stained brick fireplace that is lit and burning low. A pockmarked floor worn smooth as soap, a single narrow bed pressed against a single narrow window. It's made up with a thin blanket and nothing more, but right now it seems like a luxury. I don't take off my doublet or my boots but I climb onto the mattress anyway, pressing my shoulder against the wall and my face against the window.

Unlike the lodging house I shared with Jory, this one has glass that is clean instead of mud-streaked and bubbled instead of cracked, and in its reflection, instead of gray slants of light and mists of rain, I see only me. Me, still with remnants of face paint smeared on my cheeks and vermilion staining my lips and my hair in shambles; me, looking miles away from the girl I've always been. Me, not knowing who that is anymore.

I could blame others: the queen, her men, the country, the laws. I already have done; it is what brought me from Cornwall to London, to the Globe and the stage and all the way before the queen. It is what brought revenge to my mind and murder to my heart; it is what made me think the death of the queen was the only answer to the death of my father and all the troubles that lay before me (though I did nothing but cause myself more).

But not once did I say: I am here because of me.

After Father was killed, there was no one left at Lanherne who told me what to do. No one who told me to take Father's letters to Catesby's doorstep, or to involve myself with his men and his plot. Just as there was no one who told Father to author that plot, or to defy the queen's laws, over and over again. And for all that I was told that Father's death was an accident, bad luck, unexpected, or the hand of God, not once was it said that it was Father's own decisions that led him to it. Just as it was my own decisions that led to me sitting in this lodging house, once again not knowing what to do.

Eventually there's a knock on the door. I almost don't open it for fear that it could be guards, after me once more. But then a voice assures me it is only Mariette, who steps into the room bearing a pitcher of water, some bread, and a stack of clothing—breeches, tunic, cloak—that looks as if it may fit. On top is an envelope stuffed with papers. I hand her the money Toby gave me—the last bit of money either of us had—and she takes it. She does not give instructions or ask questions. She simply drops the things on the table and leaves.

By the time I finish eating, washing, and changing, it is three thirty in the morning. I haul myself from the bed, shrug on my cloak. Ball up my costume and push it into the dregs of the fire, watch as it is lapped up by flames. Then I take a last, final look around. It's the last room in the last lodging house in the last place in England I'll ever step foot inside. Father is dead; Jory is dead. I failed to kill the queen; I failed to save Toby. I am title-less, homeless, penniless. I am so full of grief and fear I could scream. I might, if I thought it would change anything.

Chapter 46

TOBY

THE TOWER OF LONDON
7 JANUARY 1602
1:45 AM

They marched me through the subterranean hallways of the Tower and now here I sit, in a cell all to myself. It is dank and it is dark; it is the end of a path that is only traveled once.

My interrogation at St. Paul's was just the first of many. They will be continued here, not by the ministers but by men who use means other than words to get the truth. I know how it will go. Today's was easy, but that is just to get started. That is the first note of music at one of their parties, the first drink poured, the first tray passed. But then the days begin to stretch. One, to three, to five. The food stops coming, too, then the water. You begin to itch: This from thirst, from filth, from the vermin that begin to accumulate in your clothing. There is no company but the damp air and your own breath and the scratching of things that hide in walls and grow braver and closer, day by day.

Instead of thinking on this, I think on her. It is, by my measure, well past one in the morning. Kit should be at the Grapes, and in less than three hours, she should be on the ship. She should be safely away from London, safely away from this. The word *should*, Marlowe once told me, is as dangerous as hope, as it gives power to things outside and beyond your control.

But inside this cell, hope is the only power I've got left.

"Carey," I say. "What brings you here on such a fine evening? Business or pleasure?"

I sit in the corner, elbows draped across raised knees. He is half in the shadows, half in the light that flickers from a torch somewhere down the hall. I am surprised, yet not, to see him here.

He doesn't reply.

"Let me guess, then," I say. "You're here to give me one last chance to give you the whereabouts of our intrepid lad. 'Sacrifice him to save yourself,' right?" I shake my head. "You can't think I'd fall for that."

"What did you fall for, Toby?"

I fell for him, I fell for her; I fell for the idea that I could somehow have it all.

"Everything," I finally reply. "So what's to become of me?

After all this. What's going to happen? And don't lie. If you lie, I'll know it."

He nods. "Yes. It's what I pay you for."

I manage to huff a laugh.

"I couldn't begin to guess what the queen might do." Carey shrugs. "They might let you go."

"Let go," I say, "but not freed. Let go to give the illusion of freedom, only to find myself at knife's end, dead in yet another accident. Just like Marlowe."

This brings him out of the shadows, as I thought it might.

"Marlowe was a traitor," Carey says flatly. "He was a spy, he was an atheist, he was as overreaching as the protagonists in his plays. He was a ruinous burden and he had to go. Were he not your mentor, your friend, even you would see this."

I turn my head to the floor. In the eyes of Carey and of the court, I, too, am all these things.

"My loyalties lie with Her Majesty, Toby. You know this. I warned you what would happen if you continued along this path. I warned you about the play. I warned you about Kit."

He doesn't specify which Kit; it doesn't matter which one.

"But I cannot involve myself any further," he continues. "I am sorry, Toby. For this and what comes next. I will do my best to ensure that whatever it is—"

"No," I say. For him to make a promise is to give me hope, and I cannot have it. There is no chance Carey can save me; the words are meant for his comfort only.

He approaches the bars, holds up a hand. I see what I didn't see before, hidden in the dark, something equally dark and shabby: my woolen loden cloak. The one he took from me that day at Somerset before my summons with the queen. The cloak with my entire life savings stitched into the lining, the cloak I thought I'd never see again.

"Bess found this in the house," he says. "Couldn't imagine where it came from. Said it looked poor as Job's turkey, so I knew it must be yours." He thrusts the cloak through the thin iron bars. I almost don't want it anymore. But eventually I get to my feet to retrieve it. Once it represented the whole of my life before me. Now all that's left is behind.

When I don't take it immediately he says, "I'll dispose of it if you like. I just thought—"

I reach out and snatch my cloak from his hands.

"Thank you," I manage. "It will..." I search for something to say. "Keep me warm."

"Farewell, Toby." Carey backs away from the bars, into the dark. "I wish that—"

"Don't," I say. I don't want to hear Sir George Carey, Baron Hunsdon, a Knight of the Garter, a member of the Privy Council, and the Lord Chamberlain of the queen's household's wishes.

He bows and walks away. I'm left wondering if he bid Marlowe his wishes, too, just before he signed the promissory note for the assassin he sent to that tavern to kill him.

After he's gone, I rummage through my cloak, finding the torn and carefully resewn lining, where three months ago I placed a bank draft for all the money I earned as a watcher in the queen's service, the money I earned as Barnard's apprentice, the money I earned printing manuscripts after his death. Six thousand eight hundred pounds, enough for me to live comfortably for years, uncomfortably ad infinitum. Now it is useless.

I look at it for several minutes, wondering what I would have done with this money. As a bill of exchange drawn in England, it cannot be redeemed in another country, except for Calais in France, as it was once an English outpost. But there, I could have bought my own house instead of renting from a lecherous landlady; I could have put pen to paper far from a treacherous court, writing the way I promised Marlowe I would. I could have been free.

I pull the cloak on and shove the bank draft in the pocket. It will be more than enough to ensure the executioner takes my head off on the first stroke, unlike Essex.

But there is something else. I almost don't feel it, nestled in the bottom of the right side, my fingers brushing against something cold and hard and not placed there by me.

In the pocket is a key.

Chapter 47

KIT

SOMEWHERE IN THE ENGLISH CHANNEL
8 JANUARY 1602
8:04 AM

As the sun rises, the water of the Channel stretches before me in a hundred shades of blue and black.

I stand at the railing, as I did all night, feeling the ship rock beneath me and listening to the creaking of the timber, the slap of the water against the hull, and the voices around me, men on deck wrapped in blankets and drinking from jugs of wine, playing dice while watching for the horizon to appear. I wasn't surprised to spot Thomas Alard among them: Some things never change and some people never learn.

And I watch for something else.

After I left my room at the Grapes, I waited longer than I

should have before departing for the pier. I lingered all up and down Narrow Street, waiting and hoping. Father always said hope is a terrible strategy, and even though I didn't let that stop me, Toby did not appear. Nor did he show at the shipyard at Wapping, or at the harbor in Dover, where I almost missed my ship because I thought I saw him, black-haired and lanky, idling before a quayside shop. I should have known it was not him: Toby never idles.

I thought that if Sir Carey let me go, then perhaps he'd let Toby go, too. I was nothing to Carey, and I still can't imagine why he allowed me to walk away. Was it because the queen's men already had their story, and I simply muddled the picture? Did they somehow believe Jory was the assassin, caught with a knife and killed in the end, all's well that ends well, as Master Shakespeare is fond of saying?

But Toby didn't show.

I cannot imagine that he will not find a way out of it. Toby, who sees everything and misses nothing. His end cannot be met at the end of a knife blade or a rope's noose or an executioner's ax. I refuse to believe it.

There's a flurry of excitement then, women appearing from below deck in their bright cloaks and men pointing into the distance. I follow their gaze and see it: France. I have never left England before and now here it is, a whole new continent sprawled out before me in the narrowing water, rocky hillside and mossy cliffs and freedom. And as the dock grows closer, I take it in, my first breath of fresh, free air.

It smells like fish.

Quayside in Calais is much like quayside in England, shops

and ships and crowds chattering in French so rapid that I can understand only one in every ten words. I navigate it all with practiced guard, watching for pickpockets and vagabonds, ignoring merchants shouting their wares and looking to rob me in other ways, wanting twice as much for half a reasonable offering. It stretches out before me, this foreign city, but I understand it. It is possibility and promise, penance and predicament. It is everything London once was but will never be for me again. I will have to live the rest of my life in exile, never to be allowed to return.

A heavy price was paid for this freedom, and I will make the most of it.

I turn a corner off the main street, Port de Calais, onto another street and then another, away from the port and into the city, an island surrounded by canals, which a sign tells me is called Calais-Nord. It is all winding cobblestone streets, brick buildings, arched bridges, and carts laid out. I am looking for lodging—which, if memory and tutelage serves, is called *hébergement*—and so I search for signs saying so.

After I secure a room in an inn not much better than Dolphin Square, I turn back out into the streets. I wander the unfamiliar city the way I did London, keeping one eye on myself and the other out for Toby. I pass a pretty village green beneath the shadow of a cathedral spire, glance in the window of a shop selling lace, cross a bridge onto Rue de l'Etoile, for no other reason than I like the name. It empties into a vast market square called Place d'Armes. I like this name, too. It means "parade." And it is a parade here, one of sights and sounds and smells. Green awnings over outdoor stands, giant silver pans roasting chicory, sausages over grill fires; torches over melting cheese and watery vats packed with mussels; stacks of crispy baguettes. I look at it all, but I never stop watching for him.

I pass a stall selling something sickly sweet, the smell of which makes my teeth ache. A crowd hovers, watching the *boulanger* stack pastries into the shape of a pyramid—something someone calls a croquembouche—before dusting it with colored sugars and drizzling it with chocolate and topping it with sugared almonds and edible flowers. No sooner does he assemble the pastries than he takes them apart, wrapping each individual piece to sell to the throng of eager buyers. They're a denier apiece, roughly the same as a penny, which doesn't matter because I can't afford it in this or any other country.

I'm reminded of another stand off another waterfront, a frost fair that feels forever ago, when a breath, soft and familiar, fills my ear.

"You look like a person who would be receptive to someone walking up and pressing their lips oh-so-gently against yours."

I didn't hear him. I didn't see him. But when I turn around, slow, as if I were dreaming and don't want to wake up, there he is. Not dressed like Duke Orsino, nor in shackles the way I last saw him. He is dressed the way I am, trousers and a shirt, a threadbare moss-colored cloak, a smile and his blue eyes trained on mine.

"I'm afraid you've got me confused with someone else." I try hard not to smile, but I don't think I manage. "I think that if you were to try that, you'd find yourself on the receiving end of a fight."

"Oh?" He is also trying not to smile, but isn't managing, either. "I've seen you fight." He leans in, close, and whispers, "You're not very good."

I reel back, laughing, and he does, too; that huff of breath I thought I'd never hear again.

"I wasn't sure you would make it," I tell him. "I thought you didn't."

"I wasn't sure I would, either." Toby falls serious again. "I had some help." He tells me all about Carey then. About the Tower, his cloak, the bank draft, the key. How he charmed his way into papers at Wapping and onto a Dutch cargo ship at Rotherhithe. From there, Calais. It was too close, all of it; if any one of those things had somehow not gone the way they did, he wouldn't be here at all.

Toby reaches for my hand. I almost pull away; he's a boy and I'm still dressed like one, and I don't want to cause trouble, not here and not so soon, not when we just climbed out of it. But Toby seems to understand this and says, "It doesn't matter. We don't have anything to hide anymore. We can do whatever we want now."

This is enough to bring the smile back to my face. "*Journeys end in lovers' meeting*, and all that?" A line from *Twelfth Night*, quoted back to the author himself.

"Only a fool would say that," he says.

"You would know," I say. And he kisses me.

Author's Note

"This book is a work of fiction. Names, characters, places, and incidents are the product of the author's imagination or are used fictitiously."

Now that the fine print is out of the way, let's talk details, starting with the phrase *used fictitiously.*

Queen Elizabeth I is not a fictitious person, of course. Neither are George Carey and the rest of the queen's ministers; William Shakespeare (anti-Stratfordians, hold your fire) and Christopher Marlowe; Robert Catesby, the Wright brothers, Tom One and Tom Two (though I am responsible for their nicknames)—the latter four inveterate plotters who went on to be part of the infamous 1605 Gunpowder Plot (a story fantastically told in Antonia Fraser's *Faith and Treason: The Story of the Gunpowder Plot*). Also not fictitious (though it seems it should be): Essex's Rebellion, the foolhardy and destined-to-fail plot to use Shakespeare's *Richard II* as a means to rouse Londoners against their queen. Whitehall, Middle Temple Hall, the Globe Theater, the Rose Theatre: They all existed, too. These real-life people, places, and events were my stakes in the ground—my tent poles, you could say—the structure and the rules that governed the story. Whatever else happens inside the tent, well. That's where I had my fun.

Twelfth Night is not an easy play to place within Shakespeare's canon. Some refer to it as one of his final plays: the last of his romantic comedies, the last of his cross-dressing comedies, the last of his happy comedies, and the last of the Elizabethan comedies. It was also written at the end of Queen Elizabeth's reign and accurately reflects the anxieties and uncertainties of the time—not just of the Protestant/Catholic conflict but also a dynastic one: Elizabeth was in her seventies, in failing health, and had not yet named a successor to the throne. Still others see *Twelfth Night* as a first: the first of the seventeenth-century comedies and the first of the dark comedies. Regardless, *Twelfth Night* is elusive, and to me served as the perfect inception for my story: a play about illusion, deception, disguise, madness, and the extraordinary things that love will cause us to do, to see, and in some cases, not to see.

Concealment, disguise, gender, and self-identity are features of *Twelfth Night* that are also reflected within *Assassin's Guide* (an excellent discussion of this can be found in *The Arden Shakespeare: Twelfth Night*). It is through Katherine's male disguise that she becomes empowered, discovering herself through the experiences that would have been off-limits to her had she been dressed as female—much like Viola, her counterpart in *Twelfth Night*. Like Kit, Toby is also a character bound by the conventions of the time. Homosexuality, bisexuality, or any homoeroticism in this time period—in England as well as the whole of

Europe—was a crime punishable by death, and would have been an acute concern for anyone identifying as such (although it is worth noting that sexuality during this time was seen in terms of individual acts versus a holistic identity). Toby's reluctance to publicly admit his bisexuality is simply a function of this: a measure of self-protection, not personal repentance.

I came to this book through a long-standing personal interest of the time. The Protestant/Catholic conflict has intrigued me for a while (and in fact served as inspiration in my first novel, *The Witch Hunter*), as has the indomitable Queen Elizabeth I, whom I see as the embodiment of the power of an independent woman: the original feminist queen (though I'm not sure she would see herself that way!).

Knowing this interest, my husband gifted me with a copy of Stephen Alford's *The Watchers*, a depiction of espionage in Elizabethan England. I brought it with me to a beach vacation in Mexico and was introduced to Sir Francis Walsingham (Elizabeth I's secretary of state and arguably the creator of modern espionage), Robert Cecil (Walsingham's successor and the man instrumental in bringing down the aforementioned Earl of Essex), the cryptographer Thomas Phelippes, and the writer/spy Anthony Munday (the latter two on whom Toby was loosely based). The book also showed me one of my favorite poets and playwrights, Christopher Marlowe, in an entirely new light: that of spy craft. *The Watchers* led me to read John Cooper's *The Queen's Agent*, then on to Jessie Childs's *God's Traitors: Terror and Faith in Elizabethan England*. That's when I started thinking. About spies, theater, religious conflict, Queen Elizabeth, Shakespeare...could I somehow combine all my historical interests into a story of my own? A few days (and margaritas, let's be honest) later, I had a very basic proposal for *Assassin's Guide* (originally titled *What You Will*, the alternate title to *Twelfth Night*—which at the time was the only one of Shakespeare's plays to be published with two titles, yet another anomaly).

I have remained faithful to what I know to be true about the play *Twelfth Night*, while simultaneously taking advantage of the things that are not. Dates of authorship of *Twelfth Night* and other noted plays are approximate, as are the dates of performances. Scene divisions within written plays (*act 1, scene 5*, and so forth) were not commonly used in 1601, but I have imposed them within the story, as it's what modern readers are most familiar with. In addition, I took liberties with the closing date of the Rose Theatre (it remained open in 1601, when the novel is set, though declining in popularity; it was permanently closed by 1606) and the casting practices of Elizabethan theater (companies ran notoriously sparse casts, actors doubling or even tripling up on roles; a cast of thirty-six, as described in *Assassin's Guide*, would be almost unheard of). These and other occasional anachronisms (the use of words and phrases coined post-1601, patrilineage and the near-impossibility of women owning their own property, the then-nonexistent concept of fraud and plagiarism in theater and playwriting) were employed in the spirit of poetic license.

I am indebted to historian Rachel Holmes for her in-depth notes on the manuscript. Much of my own research was done at Guildhall Library in London, the British Library in London, and the Globe theater. The Agas map *Civitas Londinum* (a representation of London circa 1561) was invaluable in helping orient me within the serpentine streets of Elizabethan London. I am also grateful to the historians whose works are listed in the bibliography, as this story is heavily built on the information they provide.

To quote the end of *Twelfth Night*: *"But that's all one, our play is done."* I hope you enjoyed the show.

Acknowledgments

This was the hardest book I've ever written.

A cliché, maybe, but the truth nonetheless. It was my first historical fiction, my first full-length novel told from dual points of view, the first time I lost complete control of a story, unsure if I was capable of reining it in. It was also the first time a personal loss interfered with my writing so much that at times, I wondered if I'd have to quit altogether.

It feels nothing short of a miracle that not only did I finish this book, it turned out exactly the way I wanted it to—better, even. There's probably another cliché that says challenges make champions (actually, I think that was it) and while this turned out true in the end, I had a lot of help. I dedicate this book to my brother, who died during the writing of it. But I'd also like to acknowledge everyone who stayed with me along the way.

My editor, Pam Gruber. Thank you for seeing through those insane early drafts, for knowing exactly what I was going for, how to guide me there, and for believing I would make it. I consider this our book, and I am so grateful to you for helping me create it.

My agent, John Cusick. Thank you for saying yes, for jumping in with both feet, and for not running for the hills after reading those aforementioned insane early drafts. But most of all, thank you for having my back through it all.

My agency, Folio Literary Management/Folio Jr., and in particular Jeff Kleinman, for your support.

My foreign rights agent, Melissa Sarver White.

My publisher, Hachette Book Group and Little, Brown Books for Young Readers. Thank you to my talented and dedicated team: Hannah Milton, Elisabeth Ferrari, Katharine McAnarney, Emilie Polster, Jennifer McClelland-Smith, Elena Yip, Victoria Stapleton, and everyone at the NOVL. Marcie Lawrence and Howard Huang for designing my beautiful cover; Dennis Jager and Kelsea Campbell for being on it. Annie McDonnell and Christine Ma for prettying up my words. Special thanks to Anna Dobbin, Rachel Holmes, and Kheryn Callender for your knowledge, time, and in-depth notes. Thank you also to Megan Tingley, Jackie Engel, and Alvina Ling for your support, kindness, and respect.

My fellow author Ride-or-Dies: Alexis Bass, Kara Thomas, Kim Liggett, Stephanie Venema, Melissa Grey, Jenn Marie Thorne, and Lee Kelly.

My lawyer, Scott Jerger.

My readers. Thank you for taking the time to read my words, for writing about them, telling your friends about them, and coming to see me talk about them.

My friends in Oregon and beyond.

Most of all, thank you to my daughter, Holland, son, August, and husband, Scott. Without you, I wouldn't know how to write about love.

Bibliography

Alford, Stephen. *The Watchers: A Secret History of the Reign of Elizabeth I*. New York: Bloomsbury Press, 2012.

Boughey, Lynn, and Peter Earnest. *Harry Potter and the Art of Spying*. Minneapolis: Wise Ink Publishing, 2014.

Bowsher, Julian. *Shakespeare's London Theatreland: Archaelogy, History and Drama*. London: Museum of London Archaelogy, 2012.

Childs, Jessie. *God's Traitors: Terror and Faith in Elizabethan England*. Oxford: Oxford University Press, 2014.

Collins, Denis. *Spying: The Secret History of History*. New York: Black Dog & Leventhal, 2004.

Cooper, John. *The Queen's Agent: Sir Francis Walsingham and the Rise of Espionage in Elizabethan England*. New York: Pegasus Books, 2013.

Crystal, David, and Ben Crystal. *Shakespeare's Words: A Glossary and Language Companion*. New York: Penguin, 2002.

Elam, Keir. *The Arden Shakespeare: Twelfth Night*. New York: Bloomsbury, 2008.

Fraser, Antonia. *Faith and Treason: The Story of the Gunpowder Plot*. New York: Random House, 1996.

Gurr, Andrew. *The Shakespearean Stage: 1574–1642*. New York: Cambridge University Press, 2009.

Hall, Peter. *Shakespeare's Advice to the Players*. New York: Theatre Communications Group, 2003.

Hutchinson, Robert. *Elizabeth's Spymaster: Francis Walsingham and the Secret War that Saved England*. New York: Thomas Dunne Books, 2007.

Kastan, David Scott. *A Companion to Shakespeare*. Hoboken: Wiley-Blackwell, 1999.

MacGregor, Neil. *Shakespeare's Restless World: A Portrait of an Era in Twenty Objects*. New York: Viking, 2013.

Mortimer, Ian. *The Time Traveler's Guide to Elizabethan England*. New York: Viking, 2012.

Nash, Jay Robert. *Look for the Women: A Narrative Encyclopedia of Female Poisoners, Kidnappers, Thieves, Extortionists, Terrorists, Swindlers and Spies from Elizabethan Times to the Present*. Lanham: Rowman and Littlefield, 1986.

Nicholl, Charles. *The Reckoning: The Murder of Christopher Marlowe*. Chicago: University of Chicago Press, 1995.

Sawyer, Ralph D. *The Tao of Spycraft: Intelligence Theory and Practice in Traditional China*. Boulder: Westview Press, 2004.

Twelfth Night, directed by Tim Carroll (2015, Bayview Entertainment), Shakespeare's Globe Theatre On Screen DVD.

Waterson, James. *The Ismaili Assassins: A History of Medieval Murder*. Barnsley: Frontline Books, 2008.

Virginia Boecker

is the author of the Witch Hunter series and *An Assassin's Guide to Love and Treason*. A graduate of the University of Texas, she had a decade-long career in technology before quitting to become a full-time writer. When she isn't writing, Virginia likes running, reading, traveling, and trying new things (most recently: learning to drive a boat). She has lived all over the world but currently resides in beautiful Lake Oswego, Oregon, with her husband, children, a dog called George, and a cat named Thomas.

Find adventure and romance in all of Virginia Boecker's books!

FOR

FANTASY FANS

DIGITAL

NOVELLAS

FOR HISTORICAL

FICTION FANS